Family Laundry

Family Laundry

A Novel

Dorie Friend

A Peter Weed Book

Beaufort Books Publishers
New York

Library of Congress Cataloging-in-Publication Data

Friend, Dorie.
    Family laundry.

    "A Peter Weed book."
    I. Title.
PS3556.R5664F3   1986   813'.54   86–17486
ISBN 0–8253–0388–5

Published in the United States by Beaufort Books Publishers, New York.

Designed by Kenneth R. Hine

Printed in the U.S.A.   First Edition

10   9   8   7   6   5   4   3   2   1

To Elizabeth

I.

Laundry Yards

1942–1959

prologue

DAMNATION and forgiveness; we can't do without them. Best, of course, to take the two together. That way, we've all got a chance to evade eternal flames. Babs said to me once, forget hellfire. Worrying about it just makes you cold.

But Hades interests me anyway, because of the people I imagine might be there—my father, and my first love. And those who might be heading that way—my mother. And myself.

I can't quite escape the ideas of predestination and election to salvation. Drab, old, terrible ideas, but Sunday school wrapped me tight in them. Without, I would feel naked.

I laugh at how deeply these notions grip me, despite the comfort in which I grew up—the luxury, some might say.

I started early to try to shake free. As a teenager I tried to see everything as bounded by time and space, moved by laws of cause and effect. No divine blueprint. No devil's trash basket. Then family crises spurred me to work it all out. How did the sins of earlier generations make for the present mess? What could be said is our own fault? How, just the same, may we rise to freedom?

My friends each reacted in character to my questions. Duffie assumed my effort was necessary—perhaps because he is an orphan and I was behaving like one. Lolly has her own problems, which she doesn't talk about. She listened with care. But Duff told me she wondered about "Randy spending himself in history."

As for Babs, she couldn't understand what I was up to. She began to use my findings anyway, for her own, very

9

different, needs. As the butler's daughter, she responded—
more than any member of my family, perhaps—to immediate clan realities and to possibilities within our tree-walled
reservation and its three large houses. "McCalla," Babs asked
that summer, in her usual way implying that I was crazy
and she quite sane, "Why are you fucking around with the
dead?"

one.

I REMEMBER them all from when I was six. We left our little stucco house on the east side of Panther Hill to move into the family compound, where the elders lived in their three houses. My father had said, "I'm tired of feast or famine in the brokerage business." What he would work at was not clear. But we would move in with Gramma and Grampa. I would have a room on the third floor, a single above the master suites, apart from the servants' quarters. I would be happy there. I would have a good view.

All this my mother and father presented to me with the smoothness of careful rehearsal. I was swept along, but aware of a terrible undertow. Somehow I knew that my father was not a success in business. In fact he never spent another day in an office, except to "consider opportunities" and "manage our investments." For keeping up the front, my mother exacted a price.

The question was trivial—whether we would move in with Grampa and Gramma after breakfast or before supper.

"There's no need to go up there at 9 A.M.," Duncan said.

"There's no point in waiting until 6 P.M.," Adelaide replied.

"Well, I've got a lot to do."

"You can do it after you get there."

"How do you know what I have to do?"

"Well, I don't suppose you're selling the Gulf Oil Company tomorrow."

That wounded him. I bled.

11

He was slow to come back. "Well, what is the big deal you've got going?"

"I want to unpack in a leisurely fashion." She was prim, final, unanswerable. He shrank from her power. She went on.

"I wish not to disturb your mother's household. If we are there early, we can fit in easily and not upset her. And then you'll be fresh, dear"—her tone changed here, into the Virginia brand of solicitude she reserved for moments when his manhood had to be rescued—"and ready for the cocktail hour."

The morning we moved, in July 1942, we took our suitcases and got into the gray Ford V-8 with its red-spoked wheels. I was on the edge of the backseat. My mother sat up front with my father. Stiffly upright, he played with ignition, choke, and throttle; got us rolling ceremoniously up the street. Around the corner to the wealthier, shadier, tree-lined block of the McCalla compound. No one spoke. Cicadas, unseen, sawed away at short lives. Beechbark curled on the trunks and limbs of sentinel trees. Peeling away, it dangled in electric wires overhead, and fell to the street. Our car wheels crunched over little canoes and tee-pees of bark, splintering them into gutter bits and street dust.

I saw the three who would become my friends. A boy on a bicycle pedaled bravely to keep up: Jimmy Duffie, a classmate in first grade who had heard we were coming. He waved as he fell back, and I, behind the window glass, timidly raised a royal hand to acknowledge him.

A girl roller-skating: Lolly Contini. Living, like Jimmy, on Hill and Hollow Road. Her father was an Italian Jew, but her mother's being Catholic somehow made that acceptable, particularly because she was rich. Lolly was a year older than I. She did not wave.

Marble tigers lay in wait for us atop the brick gateposts of the compound. Their eyes bulged, and stylized whiskers rushed like sea foam from their mouths. They were ready to pounce, but let my father's V-8 ease past.

In the wide concrete gutters of the asphalt driveway a

girl was dancing, clickety-clack, with black patent leather shoes, shiny metal taps at their toes. She was looking down for the sparks she struck on cement. At the slosh of our tires on asphalt, she stopped and turned: Barbara Quick, the butler's daughter. She leaned back against the iron rail fence that paralleled the garage. With one shoe hooked over the first rail, both elbows resting on the second, she stared at us imperiously as we passed. A sprig of mint dangled from her mouth.

two.

BETWEEN my entering the compound and my leaving it there were seventeen years. The idea of writing about it came to me with the wrecker's ball.

After smashing repeatedly through my great grandmother's, Big Rachel's, dining room in the Big House, the ball missed a target in one of its downward swoops, rose, snapped loose, and sailed like a medieval cannonade across the backyard. It crashed through the wall around Gramma's adjoining outdoor laundry pit, carried hanging wash to the rear wall, where it hit with a muffled crunch, and expired on the concrete floor, dressed in a tangle of sheets and ropes and broken poles.

We surviving McCallas, dining together punctually the following Sunday evening, considered it a low point in the family history that demolition of the compound should proceed so clumsily. My Great Aunt Martha Desjardins, in whose new apartment we were dining, and who had inherited the Big House from her mother, said she had not felt so awful since Pearl Harbor. The others inquired: was this like a bombing in her mind? Yes, exactly like a bombing. She knew it was coming, so she had fled; but the idea of that ball flying loose still reminded her of bombs. Great Aunt Bekka agreed. She was Martha's older sister, weighed about half as much, and generally followed Martha's lead. She had relied on her younger sister's cheer for forty years, ever since Bekka's husband had died of flu, and Martha had made family history by divorcing hers. Not done, in Presbyterian circles in Pittsburgh, during the First World War.

Bekka referred to the meteorite as "Dinerstein's ball," after the realtor to whom they had finally sold the compound. "It reminds me of a time bomb lying there," she said. My elders had conceded to sell only after much haggling and shrinking from inconvenience. Gramma especially resisted. She was the last to leave, which accounts for her laundry getting bombed. My mother had her own motives for a quick sale and fast clearance, but she was much too astute to betray her impatience.

The old women should have sold the compound because they were short of money, but no one dared tell that to Martha, Bekka, and Gramma. They finally left because after the death of Great Uncle Clellan and my father, Duncan McCalla, there were no more men around.

Still there was Crispin Desjardins—Martha's son, Clellan's nephew, my father's cousin. He was there at dinner to tease Bekka: "Will the ticking bother you, my dear auntie? Shall I go down there after dinner and defuse this bomb for you?" Crispin had moved from the compound years before, and led his own life, as the ladies said: high-pitched and uniquely work devoted, as the rounds of a harelipped bachelor might be.

And there was me. I wished to be thought of as a man but still accepted being considered as someone whose opinions were not yet pivotal in the life of the McCallas.

I had my own life, too, young as I was, and am. I had only just succeeded in getting my mother to respect me, through a moral battle of which I shall tell later.

This innocuous night at Bekka's, my mother, Adelaide, spoke as she usually did, careful of the good opinion of Aunt Martha, Aunt Bekka, and Gramma, whom she had joined in widowhood just a year before. She took a ritual jab at Dinerstein. Then she said, "I don't think I ever felt as low as when Truman got elected. That was eleven years ago, and I'm not over it yet." As a Virginian, my mother might be imagined a Democrat. In such matters, however, she was first of all a daughter-in-law: loyal to Pittsburgh, the Republican party, the Presbyterian church, and the Pirates baseball club. She led cheers for each at appropriate moments, and marked down their critics as enemies.

I could see Crispin Desjardins musing. I had grown old

enough to cease calling him "Uncle." As for "First Cousin Once Removed"—a bit cumbersome. So he was Crispin to me, and my guide in weighty matters. While he listened he exercised his split lip. Crispin knew he could bide his time. Four widows would wait for his opinion and lean on it.

As a boy Crispin had thought his father deserted his mother, Martha McCalla Desjardins, because of his disfiguration. In his maturity he was more disciplined in his logic. Exacting taste and energy had made him director of the art museum before he was forty. He brought to the dinner table his seniority as McCalla male, his wordly success, and the habit of making his words count in proportion to how hard they were to form.

Wifeless because of his lip? Heads shook in matronly sympathy. He was otherwise handsome: aquiline nose and glossy brown hair, worn a little long. He clearly had warmth and flair; it was presumed that his passions were sublimated into aesthetics. I didn't care, so long as I had Crispin's thoughts to reflect on. I waited for him to speak.

The upper lip stopped its preparatory dance across his teeth. He opened with a confident drawl, signifying that there was much to say and time to say it. If the discussion must be of low points in family history, an interesting topic—his brilliant dark brown eyes smiled upon his mother, his two aunts, and upon my mother—surely, he said, there was a lower point than this. In an active and distinguished family, crises were inescapable. Did he not recall discussion, when he was a boy, of something significant in the past? Some turbulence, might he call it, in the otherwise smooth flow of the family fortunes? Something that the women then alluded to only most indirectly? Something for which the men had only euphemisms?

The women around Martha's table looked perplexed. No, they had no such knowledge. What was he referring to?

"Carnegie's cuckoo-bird." Crispin spoke in sentences, not in phrases, so the impact of a fragment from his mouth was palpable, almost eerie. The words seemed to have swooped out of the recesses of his memory and caught him off bal-

16

ance. He opened his eyes in a kind of helpless surprise, as if he were simply mimicking table conversation from his childhood. He took no responsibility for it.

Gramma and Bekka shook their heads emphatically. They were not having anything to do with this discussion. "It must be a contrivance of your memory, dear," said Martha, "or some sort of youthful misimpression."

"I know I am not mistaken," Crispin said cheerfully. "I distinctly remember it had something to do with twenty million dollars."

"Mercy, how would you ever hear about that much money?" Gramma said.

"I really don't know. But little pitchers have big ears, as you used to tell me, my dear aunt. Well, it was long ago, and it doesn't matter now. The only past that I really care to retrieve is that of quattrocento Florence. However," he said with a smile, "my dear ladies, I think we should admit that what goes up must come down. And the grandeur of the McCallas, such as it may have been, one day peaked. Our affairs proceeded in a parabola, like other human events. There was a long rise, then a moment of McCalla might at its crest: a moment that only retrospect can tell us was the acme. Thereafter, slow descent.

"There is no criticism of any of us in what I say. Decline was inevitable. What interests me is the series of factors that one day were making for rise and next day made for fall. How much did the family determine its own fate? How much other figures, outer forces?"

The ladies pretended not to have heard. To be preoccupied with dessert. Spoons toyed with puddings.

"All that rising and falling." Crispin brushed it away. "History is so fatiguing. And quite irretrievable." However genuine his sentiments, his face in amused moments looked derisive, his sounds more like snickers than releases of feeling.

"The wrecker's ball." I spoke for the first time.

"What?" said Gramma, finding the reminder disagreeable.

"What do you mean?" said Adelaide.

17

"I mean that whatever sets the ball in motion, it has a high point, and then a predictable falling back. or it breaks its cable, flies higher and further, but then comes to earth, its free movement ended."

"Precisely." Crispin grinned. "Spengler or Toynbee couldn't have said it better."

"But," I asked, "what broke the cable?"

Martha and Bekka put down their spoons, silver audible on china. Gramma coughed and spoke of the Mount Washington incline. She would never dare ride it up top to the new restaurants looking over the three rivers. The cable was too old.

Crispin shot a friendly conspirator's glance at me and steered the conversation to reminiscence of grand times. Girlish memories of their father's coal-burning yacht on the Allegheny, Monongahela, and Ohio. Travel in the nineteen-twenties to Venice, Luxor, Delhi, and imperial China. Martha, family genealogist, began weaving lineages. Adelaide contributed her conviction that the subject was vital.

"Not McCullough," my mother always says to new acquaintances who get our name wrong. "Ugh, no," she says with a laugh. "McCalla, like calla lilies." Then she would talk about being Presbyterian on both sides: her husband Duncan's family having come over from Northern Ireland in the late eighteenth century right to western Pennsylvania; and hers, forebears of the Randalls, having done so earlier, as part of the group that fanned down into the Valley of Virginia. Not Eastern Virginia, you know, and certainly not West Virginia, but the western part of Virginia, where General Lee came from, who was also a Presbyterian, and had a chapel built on the campus of Washington and Lee. Her own daddy, Theodore Randall, had been a Presbyterian preacher. She and Duncan had named their only child Randall McCalla, so that he had both family influences, don't you see?

In my early teens I heard from Crispin a differently colored view of the family's ethnicity. In the family Bible I had discovered that many of our forebears had come from Belfast. I asked an innocent question at Sunday evening dinner: "So then we're Irish?"

18

Gramma snapped back, "No indeed we're not. The servants are Irish." She named a succession of maids, Agnes and Bridget and Norah, and their present cook, Alice. "We are *Scotch*-Irish. That's different. We *hire* the Irish." There, with customary finality, she would have left it, and others might have dropped the subject, had not Crispin jumped in.

"Yes, most of our servants are Irish." He laughed. "And all of our dogs." In had wandered a silky setter with red-gold hair, latest of a long series, tag jingling on his chain. "But what is so splendid about being Scotch-Irish, Auntie dear? A set of barbarian farmers, Scots, with a strange stripped-down religion, get up and move among another set of barbarian farmers, the Irish, who practice crude Catholicism. The Scotch Presbyterians were too stubborn to intermarry, so they crossed the ocean and claimed the wilderness. Now they look back and claim two old countries as well." Crispin laughed again. "I give them credit for primitive energy; but what have they given the new country in art or science or social distinction?"

Gramma pouted."You know I don't like to argue. And Mother will be frightfully upset if we continue like this." Big Rachel was putting her trumpet to her ear, which was our signal to end any dispute.

Gramma always spoke as if hiring the Irish were the most enlightened and generous thing one could do. I used the unquestioned silence of boyhood to sort out exceptions: German chauffeurs, Italian gardeners, an Austrian maid, Marie, and somehow the most exotic of all—Buddy the butler's wife, Wanda.

She was Polish. I remembered her best through a photograph I took with my first Brownie camera: in her maid's working uniform, black with rounded white collar and white cuffs at the sleeves. I caught her in the garage laundry pit, two thin clothespoles leaning toward her (in an accident of composition beyond my choosing) and framing her with white sheets, making her face an iconographic centerpiece. One hand has just finished fastening a clothespin to a sheet. Awake to my need for her on camera, she has turned, momentarily forgetful that she is presenting to the lens the side which for a week she has been averting from the world's gaze: a bruised left cheekbone with a half moon of fading gray-blue under the eye.

Later, I overheard my elders say that Wanda had gone crazy. One night she picked up a cleaver in Uncle Clellan and Aunt Bekka's kitchen and waved it, ranting at the kitchen staff. Buddy heard the ruckus from the pantry and came running in. She threw it at him. He ducked. The cleaver stuck in the pantry door. The mark remained, filled in with a light-colored putty, a cosmetic error in the highly shellacked golden oak. Buddy subdued her easily: a twist of the wrist and turn of her arm. Wanda they took away, and she never came back. I imagined her in a large building with small windows, still in her black uniform with its rounded collar: an obedient looking costume, suitable to an institution.

All the maids, upstairs and downstairs, wore black. Whoever was on door-answering duty wore the more formal uniform, with a flouncy white apron and white stockings and plain white shoes. She cleaned in it, answered the phone and the bell, took calling cards if the mister or missus was out, and put them on the silver tray by the big blue and white porcelain umbrella stand, stuffed with its malacca walking sticks and gold-headed canes. (Clellan's included a sword-cane, for he had walked streets where married men in the family did not go.) The black uniform stated the dignity of the job and the white apron the fact that although there was much to clean, nothing was dirty. The chauffeurs wore black suits with black bow ties and caps, and white shirts. They wore their white shirts and bow ties even when they were under the cars, greasing them. If the shirts got dripped on, they could be washed.

The whole compound was prodigal about laundry. There were four basement rooms in which to wash it, and four excavated outdoor yards in which to dry it, and Black Rachel, the laundress, on duty five days a week. Queen of our underworld.

Only the chief of Gramma's kitchen, Alice Cook, was allowed to wear "color," her pastels a sign of her culinary art. Her name served well both in uppercase and lowercase: we spoke of her, spoke to her, as "Cook." She was borrowed by all the other houses for their larger dinner parties. She never left the kitchens and the back stairs, and wore a black linen duster when she was outside, so that her colors were one of the compound's better kept secrets.

I realized as a boy that not everybody lived this way. There were several houses on Hill and Hollow Road larger than ours, and some formidably great ones down on Fifth Avenue, right by the trolley tracks. In Sewickeley, lush and countrified grandiosity. On the bus to the Academy, on the trolley to the orthodontist, I could see, however, that most people lived less amply, more simply, or even poorly.

It began to look to me as if nobody lived the way my family did. I began to yearn for a more inclusive definition of what McCallas represented than what I had begun to think was a desolate uniqueness. I looked for occasion to ask my question. When I found one it triggered a rapid and fierce exchange.

The opportunity was a discussion of someone "déclassé." The woman was not referred to by name. She had died a long time ago. I divined that she had involved the family and some others in a controversy. She was therefore cast out. An outcaste? What did these things mean? I asked: "What class are we?"

Gramma: "We don't talk about class."

Grampa: "It doesn't matter in America, all of that business. That's European."

Bekka: "It does, too, matter. Only those that have class don't talk about it."

Randy: "But what is it we have?"

Duncan: "We are middle class, son, like all the people you go to school with."

Martha: "Well, that's not really true. Everybody says they're middle class whatever they are. Whether they carry a lunchpail to work, or take supper at the Lawn Club. Actually, we are upper class. Otherwise, what is the Social Register all about?"

21

Adelaide: "Yes, exactly, I agree. What does the Social Register mean unless it means upper class? You certainly pay enough for a copy. It's a great convenience, especially compared to the phone book. And they drop you if you have a messy divorce. Some prominent people are cut out. The newspapers tell who's dropped every year."

Crispin: "Actually the Social Register is a lame attempt to certify a small class of nobility in a country whose Constitution forbids titles. It's a shame, of course—about the Constitution, I mean—because I would much rather be a duke or an earl than be in the Social Register. Maybe, in fact, I am not in it at all. I have never looked."

Martha: "Of course you are, dear. And I've kept your address up to date since you've moved."

Crispin: "Thank you, Mother, dear. But nobility have no addresses, you realize. Only the mobility do."

Randy: "But I still don't see what class we're in. The mobility?"

Crispin (laughing): "Well might you be puzzled, my dear boy. But, yes, you could say that we are prominent members of the downward mobility."

Big Rachel at this point rang the bell for seconds, very loudly, a simultaneous signal for seemliness and order. Faces around the table recomposed themselves as chastised, vexed, perplexed, or disapproving. Except for Crispin, who was as straight-faced as nature allowed him to be. And Great Uncle Clellan, who was shaking with silent laughter. As the maid entered with a second helping of turkey, he brought his waterglass to his mouth, drank, and gagged trying to stifle his mirth.

The turkey went away and the subject returned.

Martha: "Really, dear," she said to Crispin, "I think you'll confuse the boy unless you explain a little more."

Crispin: "Well, Randall, I think the key thing to get is the idea that ours is a mobile society. Everyone is moving up, down, and around all the time. Like Ping Pong balls in an airshaft. I find it dizzying and distasteful myself. That's why I prefer England, where everyone knows his place and can describe his status to within a fraction of an inch. It helps each person know how to behave. You don't have to bother to be 'sincere,' which is a peculiarly American way of saying 'we are all equal even though we don't believe it.' "

Duncan: "I believe it. *I* certainly do."

Adelaide: "Yes, you're very tolerant, dear, of the lower classes."

Crispin: "Which we will soon join at the rate we are consuming our capital."

Randy: "I still don't quite get it. About us, I mean."

Again restless stirring at the table.

Crispin: "We're haute bourgeoisie, I suppose, if you must have a term. That's French, of course, but it is probably more pertinent to our condition than any American terms. It means the leading members of the property-owning class. At the same time it suggests preoccupation with respectability and material values."

Martha: "Oh, dear, Crispin, you aren't suggesting that we behave like the rich, are you?"

Crispin: "The filthy rich? Certainly not. Nor the nouveau riche. We're above that. As for the Mellons, the Heinzes, the Hunts, and the Hillmans—the decent rich, would you call them?—we can't nearly afford to behave like them. No, at our best moments we might be called bourgeois aristocrats, and in our ordinary moments, just haut bourgeois. But"—turning to me—"watch out for downward mobility. It seeps into everything, if you don't take care."

Randy: "Very soggy-sounding." At which remark, from a boy then twelve, the table laughed appreciatively, glad for a change of mood.

The conversation left everyone restless except Crispin, who had enjoyed his improvisations, and Clellan, who had settled into a beatific smile. He had almost spoken once or twice, but contented himself with bright-eyed nodding. Light from the chandelier bounced off his bald dome. Only he spoke less than Grampa, who was saturnine; and only Grampa spoke less than Duncan, my father, who was taciturn. Sometimes I wondered if my great-grandfather, Rowan Megowan McCalla, had frozen the tongues of successor

23

males with his stern looks. Or perhaps I was hearing not silence, but beguiling clucks and a strange high-pitched frequency from Carnegie's cuckoo. Things that happened thirty years before I was born will go on affecting the McCallas. I can show you.

As for Uncle Clellan, he said nothing at all; but behind his benign and silent smiles, I conjured both ease and imprisonment. Crispin was the only one who seemed to have found a free voice. All in all, being a McCalla in trousers somehow seemed a difficult matter.

three.

I WAS THE only one who used the stone stairway where our family compound verged with the greater world. From the house where Clellan and Bekka lived, it wound down fifty feet or so from our plateau to the trolley tracks laid in the cut between us and the much larger plateau opposite. The iron gate on the avenue was a false front. Our three houses actually faced inward, and oriented their main entrances toward each other. But the shortest way to the trolley, and school, was by scrambling down the stone corridor.

I hear a rushing, gathering noise, and begin to run. The trolley hurtles into the bend, slowing around the corner in a munching, grinding confusion of iron brakes on iron wheels in iron tracks; then forward again in a swift, free roll, thundering like a cannonball on a dance floor. The orange car passes me as I dash, hat in hand, bookbag whacking my shoulder blades. With relief I see the light at the downhill corner turn red. Pebbles and dust shoot up from wheels braking again in their cobblestone-bedded track; gratuitous sparks jump off the trolley wire. I reach the stop, panting, bang on the door. It folds open. I drop a token down the chute, grab a brass pole as the car bucks forward, rotate myself into a wicker seat, draw in air, and sigh. There are chauffeurs to spare, but it does a child good, my elders say, to make his own way to school.

Directly across the tracks from Clellan's iron gate rose Hill and Hollow Road, a reservation of estates with a brass plaque like the sign on a trust company at its entrance. "PRIVATE. NO THOROUGHFARE." Higher on the hill, to the left, at its scalped crest, was the golf course and the Pittsburgh Lawn Tennis and Golf Club. "The Lawn," for short. Lower down the hill was the church, and still lower the Academy, a winding mile away, where Panther Hill flattened out into the commerce and civic bustle of Fox Hollow, and where the world of my childhood merged with the world beyond, its bigger shapes and unknown tests.

As a boy I thought the McCalla compound was forever. As a young man I watched it go, and heard the complaints, retold, of Hill and Hollow folk who said the McCallas "sold out." A synagogue, a parking lot, and how many dinky little houses?

When Dinerstein first approached the family, my father both opposed the sale and justified it in principle. If Hill and Hollow had included the family compound, as they had promised our patriarch, Rowan McCalla, the sale would have been impossible. But they cut us out. So if the McCallas needed the money, then those fifteen families in their hundred acres up the hill had nothing to say about it. From my father's testy voice I sensed a need. I imagined a sucking noise, of money flowing away, to keep our three houses going, their ancestral tone unperturbed.

Big Rachel set the family style, although her Big House was unique in opulent detail. Unlike the rough red brick of Gramma's and Bekka-Clellan's, hers was made of a small, tightly morticed orange brick, glazed and neat as stacked bullion. The first "completely fireproof" mansion in Pittsburgh, erected with steel beams in homage to the matriarch's pyrophobia. There were no carpets within, and as little as possible that might ignite easily. Footsteps cracked sharply across the hard parquet floors. B-Ray could not hear them, but felt the drum tremor and raised her bright, watery eyes to any approaching creature. She did allow lush velvet curtains, dangerous as they might be, to protect her eyes from the sun.

B-Ray was deaf. Her conversation fell in a gentle monotone, uttered in the confidence that others were listening and would attend. She assumed telepathic authority—that her thoughts were consequential and obvious, therefore easily available to those toward whom she directed them. She signalled regally—to the servants a raise of a finger, a turn of the head; to her family, a slight raising of her chin, throwing into greater prominence the black velvet choker about her neck, with its single brilliant diamond. The tilt meant hearken; and she was heeded. The routines of the house reflected a turn-of-the-century male deference to the frail and fair. This patrician doting had, with her collusion, fashioned her into a woman who conceded all decisions made outside the house, commanded every one taken within it.

Widowed for decades, lordless and soundless, she lived out her matriarchate. With an acquaintance not seen for some time she would ask, "What news?" then bend to the answer as if to the result of Caesar's contest with Vercingetorix. After she examined the countenance of the speaker and ceased to attend his lips, a sweet glaze would come over her eyes. Only those practiced with her ear trumpet could prevent it.

With the very young, she had another two-word inquiry: "How's tricks?" The charm of this antique slang captured me. I always summoned a full reply. Speaking into the trumpet, I focused upon the diamond on B-Ray's choker, trying to borrow from it a brilliance with which to penetrate the stone ear, reach the living mind, light up the guarded eyes behind the pince-nez.

Sometimes the eyes would flare with understanding. Always she nodded, approvingly, without comment until the end. Then she would smile. "That's good. Keep it up."

A major rule of our three houses was to avoid embarrassment. It would have mortified the McCallas for anyone to have seen our laundry. Each house, therefore, had an outdoor laundry pit dug next to the servants' wing. These cement-lined excavations were a proud Victorian innovation. No McCalla underwear flew above ground. It hung decorously, rippled by downdrafts floating over the three little above-ground walls of brick that matched the house brick on the fourth side of the pit. These laundry yards could be entered from above by iron-runged stairways, and at base-

27

ment level directly from the laundries in the cellars. The laundries also had large drying rooms. They were cold and damp, but less so than a winter's day or a summer's rain.

The garage had its own laundry pit, a little smaller than the other three, with bushes about it to make sure that the servants' wash, so dangerously near the street and passers-by, could not be veiwed any more than master laundry could. It had only one entrance, through the cellar door. Black Rachel washed there, but it belonged to the garage folk, too. The other three yards were her exclusive domain. Years after automatic washer-dryers were common, we McCallas refused to buy them. We retained Black Rachel. "She preserves the clothes," Aunt Martha said. Which was probably true. She did all the clothes, sheets, and table linen for the three houses plus special items. She arrived and departed by trolley five days a week, and kept score on our lives.

Luther, with his wife, Elise, the seamstress, was the only one of the three chauffeurs who lived in the garage. The other constant family there was the Quicks. Buddy the butler and Barbara, his daughter, came closer to some of us than servants ordinarily come. There are sweet trust and sharp envies in being more than help, less than blood. A dangerous mixture.

The Big House had the largest share of labor, as of everything. In addition to the usual complement of cook, upstairs maid, and downstairs maid, occasional butler-handymen passed through, and Marie abided there: Big Rachel's personal servant, discovered as a girl in Vienna before the First World War. In the compound altogether, excluding the outside gardening crew of Italians, there were twenty servants performing for nine members of the family. Grampa's death, and Clellan's, thinned the family out, but not the employees. When my father and Big Rachel died, only five members of the family remained in the compound, but eighteen servants still waited in attendance. Then Dinerstein's ball began to smash the masonry, and I to compose my memory.

As a child I looked for the secret of family power in my great-grandfather's books. Dark red leather sets behind glass-doored cabinets in the Big House. Dickens, Trollope, Thackeray, Scott; James Fenimore Cooper and Washington Irving. More arcane Presbyterian items I ignored until I was more grown up: Robert Louis Stevenson on *John Knox and His Relations with Women*, pamphlets by Knox himself in Victorian editions, and a huge volume with a gilt lock on it like a chastity belt—the Geneva Bible.

Next to the reverent biography of Andrew Carnegie, in a volume of brief résumés with steel-plate etchings of Pittsburgh business leaders, I found my great-grandfather himself. Rowan Megowan McCalla: slim, bald, with a bushy moustache, glaring so that his features, ascetic reflection of his self-discipline, might be recorded for history. As a little boy I stared at his picture. Two years ago, following the call of Carnegie's cuckoo, I began looking at the etching again.

Had the McCallas been the kind of family that framed men's sayings as we did women's samplers, the words of my great-grandfather would have been on our walls: "Man's three greatest inventions are fire, the wheel, and compound interest." Rowan Megowan McCalla made his fortune from all three.

He inherited McCalla Wheelwright and Bearings from his own father, and transformed it into one of the premier companies making wheels for locomotives, pullman cars, and trolleys. He founded McCalla Iron and Steel, which contributed to the nightly glow on the horizon visible from the porch of the Lawn Club. He created McCalla Capital Shares from the profits of his two manufacturing firms, to supply venture capital and industrial loans at appropriately steep rates of interest. People needed money. The obverse of Rowan's principle of self-reliance was to cultivate the dependence of others on him.

Applying his own ferocity to the three great inventions of man, Rowan intended to establish a dynasty. He moved the McCallas from the North Side to Panther Hill, in four large lots compounded as one—half a city block. He inculcated business principles in his four children so they would rise among regnant fortunes such as Carnegie, Mellon, Frick, and Phipps, and pass their augmented wealth, lore, and discipline to still another generation. But assets and mastery did not grow. They declined in ways affording Crispin mordant amusement. Why that happened was a mystery I wished to solve.

Three houses rose up in the compound: that of Rowan and Rachel and those of their older son, my grandfather, "A. C.," named after Andrew Carnegie, and their older daughter, Rebekka. The younger daughter, Martha, left the compound to marry Desjardins. When she divorced him, stunning social Pittsburgh and the presbytery, she moved back into the Big House. The younger son, Clellan, never married. He moved in with Bekka when she was widowed, before I was born. No one ever built on the fourth lot.

The fortune that sustained all the houses ebbed with Rowan's death. "Overwork," Martha said. "All the McCalla men worked like dogs." In fact, Clellan hardly worked at all. He put in far more hours at the Lawn and other clubs than at the office. "A. C." showed some of Rowan's independence but not enough of his sagacity. He started a little bank on the North Side, with a red velvet curtain hanging from a brass rail over the lower half of the front window. Long after banks gave up such decor to saloons, Grampa sat behind the drape and made loans to immigrants.

"A. C." and Clellan gambled unwisely with McCalla Capital Shares, suffered heavy reverses, dissolved it. They sold the steel company and the wheel company, invested in the stock market of the mid- and late nineteen-twenties, took terrible losses for the next ten years. But they continued to support their womenfolk in damask draperies, handstitched silk lingerie, extensive foreign travel, and teams of retainers trained to impeccable service.

The breath of decay is best recognized by those who inhale sweet air. Crispin set a career for himself in art and chose to live fifteen miles from the compound. He dared speak of "the moribund fortunes of the McCallas." He usually covered against his possible excesses by speaking reverently about Rowan and providing grand compliments to the elder women of the family.

The Sunday dinner explanation for the family financial problems was Franklin Delano Roosevelt. Two other problems with heavy scar tissue were occasionally mentioned by allusion: why the family compound was not included in the protected status of Hill and Hollow, which was a private road; and why Duncan and Adelaide were blackballed the first time they applied for membership in the Lawn Club. Something acrid hung in the air about the second. I picked up the name of Shep Cardigan as presumably the one who had blackballed them. But now they were in, so what did it matter? As for the exclusion from Hill and Hollow, disappointment survived only as a musty odor, suggesting ancient atmospheres.

To such dwindling wealth and lurking problems I was heir. My great-grandfather begat four children, but his progeny produced only two, Duncan and Crispin. In my generation, I was the only begotten. My elders looked to me for continuity; even for restoration of the family fortunes. Their expectations weighed on me the more for their not voicing them. You may say that I lived with the echoes of the past and the dissonances of the present much as other children of a largely comfortable nation. But I felt a difference. I lived among eighteen to twenty servants instructed to call me "Master Randy." I responded naturally except in the hearing of an occasional stranger, when the word "Master" gave me a sharp twang of democratic discomfort. Buddy employed it publicly, but in private dropped it. Babs was two years older than I, and didn't use the honorific. She was my superior. That was obvious to her, and to me.

Porcelain, ivory, marble: I follow the historical sociology of my family in toilet fixtures and Mah-Jongg tiles, in gatepost statuary of tigers couchant. The bathrooms in the master wing had porcelain tubs with a faucet in the center of the wall side and polished brass fixtures attached to polished copper piping. Along the wall side of each tub ran a

31

slab of marble, floor to ceiling, to prevent splashes from cracking plaster. It also prevented conversion to overhead showers. Except for those at the Lawn Club, I never had a shower until sent away to St. Luke's School, to prepare for Yale. Attended by a nursely maid, I soaked in large bathtubs until old enough to wash myself without drowning.

The tubs in the servants' quarters were of cast iron, with a ceramic coating that chipped off to leave dark-hued bruises beneath. The toilet seats were wooden, painted white, worn away at the rims by tens of thousands of maid-sittings into a homely bluish-brown. Old toilet seats in the master wing were replaced, even though the shiny white plastics were discordant with the surrounding fixtures.

We McCallas had a pale vocabulary for excretions of the body. To urinate and to defecate were both the same— "going to the bathroom." Madison the setter also "went to the bathroom." In the servants' wing one day, Babs told me about "turd" and "shit." Dogs made one, people the other. Each word, I learned, could be used about people, too. A "turd" was someone to despise, and a "shit" was someone to hate.

Somewhere in the tottering Hapsburg empire, Big Rachel had captured the shy Marie. For personal service. In a like way, the next generation of McCallas brought back from their travels Mediterranean and Asian objects; they dotted our houses in a curiously effective amalgam with Victorian walnut furniture and heavy maroon curtains. During the nineteen-twenties Clellan, Bekka, Gramma, and Grampa went abroad every other year, leaving Big Rachel home, plush with help. Photographs: Piazza San Marco, 1924, eyes closed against the beat of pigeon wings on their shoulders and atop their hats; Pyramids and Sphinx, 1926, on camels casually controlled by dragomen, traveller's eyes squinting against the sun; Taj Mahal, 1928, before the reflecting pool, still wearing Pittsburgh's dark clothing, men in high collars, women in long skirts, scowling with cultural difficulty or wincing with stomach cramps. China, 1930, no photographs. Could they find no picture-vendors? Back came the goods, nonetheless: large blue and white early Ming ginger jars, brocaded tapestries to use as bell pulls, and several sets of wormwood chairs, hand-carved in gargoyles and dragons incongruous to our Presbyterian aesthetic. They served as occasional chairs in living rooms meant to be overfurnished.

As a boy I fancied the Mah-Jongg sets. Each of the three houses had one: golden ivory with antique grain; willow, bamboo, dragon, and the points of the compass in red, green, blue, and black; ideograms etched in the corners— pieces of an arcane, accumulative game that crazed capitalist America. The Great Depression brought the nation to its senses and to the native game of Monopoly. But my elders continued with Mah-Jongg as a solution for Big Rachel's increasing deafness. Also bridge, with sign language for bidding: hearts—tap left breast; spades—shoveling motion of hand; diamonds—touch one's throat, where B-Ray wore the gem on her choker; clubs—make a fist; no trump—point to one's ear. B-Ray clung to her ear trumpet while others turned to electronic devices. Her antique hearing aid and her famous aversion to argument dominated family speech and mood. I see the long curved ear trumpet still, a kind of inverse cornucopia of loss in a world of affluent din.

China was the last big trip of the elders together. Perhaps they sensed it. They bought far more than they could use, and brought it home to resonant closets, awaiting a day of discovered need. Including the pair of tigers couchant. Despite their lack of mane, my elders thought them lions. A decade later Aunt Martha decided to put the big Shanghai cats atop the brick gateposts facing the street by the garage, replacing frosted electric globes. "We don't need the light," she said, "as much as we need the lions."

Of all the objects in the compound, the one that meant the most to me was Mercury. He stood atop a pedestal on the first floor landing of the Big House, dark bronze, in mid-stride, staff raised high, with winged sandals and winged hat. Lithe and sure, he became my model of grace in a family where the elder men still wore stiff collars and high-button shoes. In a family that shunned nakedness and hated bodily waste, his stripped physique was a unique marvel, his godly superiority above ordinary functions of the body.

Much later I learned that he was the god of commerce, cunning, and thievery; and this, too, given our entanglement with Carnegie and his cuckoo, seemed appropriate to McCalla history. The Romans often portrayed Mercury carrying a purse: in that pose, the perfect god of our household.

four.

BABS was early addicted to mint. Before my father and mother moved into the compound, we were at Clellan and Bekka's house for dinner. I was studying the black and gold Chinese folding screen that hid the door to the pantry. Lost to the conversation of my elders, I was sporting with the Confucian poets and servants who lolled and gamboled on the lacquered panels. Between a sage and a serving maid, sticking out, I discovered a sprig of green. Perpendicular to the screen? I peered closer into the dark joint and saw the round, insolent eye of a young girl.

Babs got full spy of us, I suppose. She vanished. But she and her father made that screen magical to me. Another time I was seated so that I could see behind it. I looked up from my mashed potatoes with the autistic curiosity of the very young. There was Buddy the butler, out of sight to all but myself, feet wide apart, hand towel in his arm, head tilted so far back I couldn't see his eyes. Nothing was visible but his shuttling Adam's apple, his outthrust wiggling jaw, and the heavy-bladed ebony-handled carving knife he was balancing between lower lip and chin. Suddenly he lurched forward and back, tossing off the knife, which he grabbed by the handle in midair. He licked the flat of the blade as if it were a popsicle, grinned at me, and winked.

Buddy meant strength to me, and dexterity. He climbed ladders and painted, and cleaned gutters bare-chested. His biceps were huge; he flexed and relaxed them slowly as if he were exercising a pet. On his right forearm was a tattoo of an anchor and an inscription: AD HOC INVICTA. What did it mean? He grinned: "It means 'I ain't beat yet.' " The translation, I later learned at the Academy, was colloquially correct. And even now it could be said of Buddy, after all his scrapes and struggles and losses, that he is "thus far unconquered."

When I was about sixteen, Babs told us there would be a birthday party for Buddy. Duff and Lolly and I eagerly helped her plan it. Aunt Martha commissioned the party. A celebration was fitting, she said, when a family retainer has a fiftieth birthday after many years of service. Why? I thought, and could remember no other instance. Aunt Martha had a Pygmalion fancy for Barbara Quick. She wanted to transform her, perhaps, into a creature of culture. Or maybe she was trying to design a personal maid and companion such as her mother, Big Rachel, had long ago captured in Marie, or a new style of domestic deputy, to free herself for her club life and the major tasks of running the Big House. Whichever the case, Aunt Martha asked Babs to arrange the party.

Controversy arose. Gramma challenged Buddy's length of service compared to Cook's, whose fiftieth birthday had not been celebrated. Aunt Bekka questioned Buddy's reliability and good repute; and my mother intimated that too much fuss over servants would spoil them, as it did children. Aunt Martha herself later admitted that she had overdone the delegation and underdone the guidance. But it was too late. Babs, aided by Lolly, Duff, and me, had invitations out, and entertainers coming in.

Martha went to Big Rachel on the matter, who was infirm and complaisant, and pleased as dowager empress to affirm all that was done by her daughter and prime minister. Thus armed, Martha calmed the elders: everything was OK with B-Ray, Buddy was the sunniest personality in the compound, and this was a good opportunity for Barbara to help out. She liked to call Babs her "house sparrow," a literal translation of the term Mah-Jongg and a sign of the depth of her affectionate fancy.

Given the complications that later arose, my mother always maintained that such a party should not have been held on Hallowe'en. Buddy, however, had been born on Hallowe'en. Babs, with only one father to honor, no mother in sight, and ascending status in the compound, made the most of it. She invited everyone she could think of. My mother complained that we had only intended to show family appreciation of Buddy Quick as butler and handyman, but Babs produced an extravaganza.

The McCallas who came were heavily outnumbered. Aunt Martha; Uncle Clellan, whose general servitor Buddy was; my parents, Duncan and Adelaide; Crispin, who dined out on the tale for months, telling it with guffaws and the aggressive imitations of others that were one of his defenses against imitation of himself; and me. Gramma and Grampa chose to have guests to dinner that evening, in order to cover their disapproval. They said that if Clellan wished to keep an acrobat as his butler and make a do about him, that was his affair. Bekka took a similar view, even though Mr. Quick (she grew stiffly formal when she was annoyed with Buddy) buttled in the very house she shared with her brother. Clellan had hired the man, fired him, and rehired him; and this was another of Clellan's ideas, she said, for she did not wish to attribute it to Martha, the sister she admired. She stayed away, without excuse. It was not Bekka's wont to give excuses.

As for the servants: we invited them all. They responded as denizens of their different houses. Big Rachel's staff stayed home with the grand matriarch in her decline, but Marie sent a fancifully sewn decoration, a Legion of Honor medal for Buddy to pin on his great chest. Gramma's staff served at her dinner, but Cook, who was senior to Buddy, and second only to Marie, prepared fruits, nuts, and cookies and sent them over arranged around a pink conch shell she had bought on the boardwalk at Cape May. Bekka's staff came because Clellan came; she uttered no objection. The garage was led by Luther Tollhaus, the chief chauffeur, proud that the honoree was one of them. Black Rachel, the laundress, was there and in high spirits. She surprised everyone with her dancing. Crispin said that we, who had only thought about her from shoulder to fingertips, must change our minds about her range. Two or three members of the Pittsburgh Lawn Tennis and Golf Club came, whom Buddy had served in stints there, most notably Kidder Towne. He attached himself as usual to my mother and father. His mode of approval was not applause, but loud laughter and sideline comment, which annoyed me with its partrician nasality.

In addition to six McCallas and ten servants, including Buddy and Babs themselves, there were present a ventriloquist, a magician, a juggler, a clown, several tumblers from the Turnverein, and a fat chanteuse; dwarfs of each sex, several sailors living on pensions, and a few maids and locker room men from the Lawn Club; a barker, a steeplejack, an accordian player, and a female weight lifter. Of course, with Babs and me, Jimmy Duffie and Lolly Contini were there; we four were inseparable.

At her throat Babs wore a cameo that Uncle Clellan had given her when she was twelve years old. "Showy," my mother had called it. A big, eye-catching piece: against a background of rich bluish-brown shell, a pale, translucent white carving of a handsome woman in semi-profile. Five diamonds studded her eyes, her hair, her throat, and the ear that was turned to the viewer. Finely wrought gold frame. "Too expensive a gift for a little girl," Gramma had said at the time of the giving. "Why is Clellan giving away an heirloom?" Bekka had asked. Martha queried whether it actually was. Big Rachel, to whom the question was brought, said it was certainly not an heirloom. Now that the cameo reappeared, after several years, my mother was the only one to comment. "Showy," she said, once again.

If her choice of jewelry was presumptuous, Babs showed a fine sense of territory in selecting a place for Buddy's birthday party. The laundry pit next to the garage. She did not ask for any of the other three laundry yards, but presumed to do as she chose with the one where she lived and where she hung out wash of her own.

The barker took care of all the announcements. The professionals went through their acts to bawdy criticism. My mother and father muttered about going home early. Martha urged them to stick it out. Clellan drank silently and steadily and smiled benignly on all. Crispin grinned and soaked up details for retelling. We McCallas, as he said later, were outnumbered five to one by others, and two to one even if you included servants as McCallas, so we could not be a damper on the party, thank God. He laughed.

Martha later thanked Babs for taking the event off her mind. She did not convey the elders' judgment that matters got altogether out of hand. Had there been only one birthday cake, perhaps there would have been less gossip.

The first cake, with fifty-one candles on it, was a test of Buddy's lung power. He marched around the laundry pit inhaling in mock military posture, shoulders hunched, eyes bugging, and delivered a couple of practice whooshes at trembling houseplants. He addressed the cake with massive insuckings of air that let his pants slide. Then he drew breath, blew, got all but five, and with a gasping reserve puff smothered them, too. Applause and cheers.

Babs announced, "We got *another* cake for you, Buddy." The dwarfs brought in a draped shape from the adjoining laundry room. They revealed a huge ice cream cake; two enormous orange mounds with carefully molded raspberry discs and nodes on top. Buddy laughed; made motions as if slipping out of a bra. "No candles?" he giggled, and then, as if suddenly remembering, he did a bump and grind: "I brung my own."

"How do you like it, Buddy?"

"I always wanted an obscene cake," he said, laughing.

"That's not obscene," I said. "It's just ribald."

"I don't see no ribs at all." Buddy grinned and licked his finger as if getting some icing off.

"Real good," one of the sailors said. "Who done it?"

Babs pointed to the weight lifter. She could clean and jerk three hundred pounds and conceive erotic confections. We babbled with admiration. She blushed. Much jostling and jesting followed about who would cut the cake and who would get the first piece, and what piece, and how it would be eaten. The senior McCallas slipped away at this point, and thus missed what Babs intended as the climax of the party.

The tumblers built a pyramid to Babs' window: two sprang

39

to the shoulders of the three at the base; one scrambled atop the shoulders of the two and tossed a rose to Babs when she appeared at the frame. Applause. The tumblers dissolved. Babs put the rose between her teeth, climbed out on the sill, reached behind her for something, and, illuminated only by jack-o-lanterns below, stepped out into the dark night air. Gasps in the crowd. Followed by knowing murmurs. She slid across a wire strung tightly above us, using a clothespole for balance, while the tumblers followed her below. Across the laundry pit and safe on the opposite wall, she dropped the pole to the lead tumbler and tossed the rose, with a kiss, to her father. The crowd applauded. Buddy smiled, tears in his eyes, and waved to her. She vanished around the north side of the garage, descended into the laundry room, and reappeared at the door of the yard. She took a hug from Buddy and another round of applause.

The accordian player heaved into action. A thin-fingered man, he played with his eyes closed and with a great deal of body motion, as if dancing with his instrument. Black Rachel, a cluster of grapes in her hand from the Cook's cornucopia, dropped one into the accordionist's mouth. Rolling his eyes and munching, he struck up "Dark Town Strutter's Ball." Rachel cut in on Buddy, who was dancing with the fat chanteuse. With a friendly glance at the woman she had just displaced, she picked up the beat with the butler, a fast-paced two-step. They peeled away from each other and back, their hands talking. Buddy's feet glided on the rough cement floor as if it were smooth with soap, and Rachel's, as she danced, flashed pink heel and arch. Goldfish leaping from dark water. Her short black skirt exposed fine calf; the straps on her gown showed off marvelous shoulders, firm arms. Her long hair was straight black, shot with gray.

"Hey Rachel!" Kidder Towne was calling. He knew the compound, and his style was familiar. "Glad to see you out of the laundry tubs, honey. You can *dance!*"

She tossed her head back at him, leaning away from Buddy. "Yeah, Mister Towne, I ain't just hands and I ain't just feet."

Babs, watching, went over and murmured to the steeplejack, who smiled and nodded. Then she spoke to the
accordionist. The steeplejack sashayed out on the floor and
cut in on Buddy. When he swung away with Black Rachel,
Babs moved in on her father. The accordionist whipped
into "The Pennsylvania Polka." Father and daughter swung
out and around. The dancing crowd galloped to the Polish
beat, bumped each other in avoiding the concrete sidewalls,
laughing as they collided. I watched, leaning in the doorway
of the laundry room, ignorant of the polka.

After half an hour of dancing, a racket arose in the driveway above the pit. A clatter back and forth. Uncertain vocal
sounds, of lost animals asking questions of the night. Buddy,
Jimmy Duffie, and I exchanged looks. We headed for the
lanudry room, ran up the stairs, out onto the asphalt. "My
Granny's cows," Duffie yelled. "Get them into the garage
so we can tether 'em."

Two beasts clattered away from us. Out of reach, one
mooed and shat on the asphalt. As the crowd came up from
the laundry pit, Duffie formed Buddy and me into a moving
triangle with himself. We cornered the cows near the center
of the compound. They were sniffling rhododendrons near
the sundial, under the October moon. We worked them
back toward the garage, dodging at them when they threat-
ened to bolt, whacking them when they balked, calling to
the crowd to clear back. Ten minutes of maneuvering, to
the chatter and giggles of the party, brought them to the
garage. "Don't let 'em shit on the Pierce-Arrow," Luther
yelled. Nobody challenged his logic. One cow backed into
the fender of Gramma's Oldsmobile and, in copious calm,
streamed manure upon it.

"Give them some hay," said Elise, Luther's wife. She
was natively Scotch, severe, and saw no way to save the
world but by feeding or starving it. She repeated her suggestion.

"There *ain't* no hay," Luther roared, his West Virginia
twang across her burr. He averted his face from her narrowed eyes and shook his head.

"Let 'em eat cake," said Kidder Towne. He laughed at

his own joke and was joined by a throng ready to laugh at anything.

Duff, Buddy and I conferred. Who had loosed them as a Hallowe'en prank? Answer later. We could tie them here, ferry them, or drive them home. Buddy got a length of rope from Luther, who shook his head and muttered, "This is a *garage*." Buddy looped the rope around each cow's neck, with a few feet of play between them. Duffie uttered monosyllables correcting their movements.

"He'll make them behave," said Elise.

Luther glared at her. To nobody in particular, but loud enough for several to hear, he said, "This is *Pitts*burgh, PEE-AY." He shook his head slowly, not believing this could happen in the world's greatest industrial city.

Lolly Contini explained to a crowd of Babs' invitees about Duffie's grandmother, who belived in fresh milk and kept cows on her estate. Yes, it was odd, in a city in the middle of the twentieth century. No, it was not against the law in this instance; the ordinance for Panther Hill was written to allow pre-existing exceptions to continue. No, Granny Duffie did not believe in pasteurizing the milk. "And Jimmy was raised on it," she said. "His parents died when he was very young," she added. The crowd looked at the boy as upon a miracle of nutrition.

Jimmy got our team organized: himself leading on a joint halter rope, Buddy and I as flanking herdsmen. Luther rolled back the doors on the street side of the garage. Our caravan moved out under the Hallowe'en moon, down the block and across the trolley tracks, up Hill and Hollow Road. We restored Granny Duffie's Jerseys to their high-hedged corner in the backyard of her mansion in the choicest real estate within the city limits of Pittsburgh, Pa. So ended Buddy's fiftieth birthday party. Luther, who had left a West Virginia farm to avoid such chores, got up early the next morning to shovel cow dung.

Babs, Duff, Lolly, and I met after school the next day to plan our responses in case of inquiry from the elders. As we gobbled down the last pieces of cake, we agreed it was a lucky thing that all the McCallas had left early. Maybe they wouldn't hear about the cows and wouldn't ask. Granny Duffie had been told at breakfast, but was so nervous about the ordinance being rewritten that she would not spread the story. Kidder Towne might be the only leak.

"I think he knows how to keep a secert," Duffie observed, "but if he can get a laugh out of it, he will."

"Everybody knows everything eventually," Lolly said: a bit of presumptive wisdom that nobody directly challenged. I said rather sharply, however, that her family was not affected.

The story did circulate freely, from whatever source. Granny Duffie got rid of the cows out of deference to respected neighbors, who suddenly voiced their years of pent-up unhappiness over mooing at odd hours. They pointed out that commercially sold dairy products had improved since her childhood, and Granny had the grace to agree.

I never heard about the matter from my parents or the older McCallas. Perhaps the tale floated by their island and never touched shore. More likely they preferred to concentrate on the peculiar orange and raspberry colored birthday cake. Excruciatingly bad taste. But what could you expect from friends of Buddy Quick? I did not say that the cake had been Babs' idea.

II.

Rules and Games

1936–1954

five.

"*I* AM THEIR inheritance," Dr. McCracken roared. "And ye shall give them no possessions in Israel; *I* am their possession." He was a model of manhood, and obviously a surrogate for the Lord. His insistence on tithing, however, drove the young social set from the First Presbyterian Church of Panther Hill toward Episcopalianism, which they could manage comfortably with their country club, their city club, and their bourgeois hedonism. McCracken held on to an older, more credulous kind of churchgoer, who appreciated his mode of relating the Bible and patriotism. As vivid as Jesus, more mighty than Old Testament judges and kings, was Abraham—the Great Emancipator and the Master General, who had entrusted to Grant the crushing of the wayward South. My mother was offended that a great Presbyterian gentleman, Robert E. Lee, should go without mention before the melancholy, agnostic Lincoln. But such was our brand of militant Calvinism.

Our congregation sang the "Battle Hymn of the Republic" on the Sundays before Armistice Day, Memorial Day, Independence Day, and Labor Day. One hushed stanza gripped me:

> *In the beauty of the lilies*
> *Christ was born across the sea*
> *With a glory in his bosom*
> *That transfigures you and me.*

I kept the tender notion of that verse in mind while rising

47

to the boot-clumping, saber-brandishing repetition of "Glory, Glory, Hallelujah." I conceived myself capable of great deeds in noble causes. Not knowing what songs were sung in other nations, other temples, I believed myself unique.

My Sunday school teacher was Mrs. McCracken. She betrayed me. She didn't mean to. But open love is sometimes betrayal.

She distributed four-color pictures and large print texts every Sunday to demonstrate what Biblical syntax may have left obscure. The stories of David and Jonathan, David and Goliath, David and Saul, David and Bathsheba, occupied us for four weeks. Loyal friend, valiant volunteer, endangered apprentice, sinful king: all of life that I could imagine seemed contained in this sequence.

The leaflets showed a young David of slim, muscular arms and thighs, dressed in a rough tunic, with leather straps around his strong calves, brown curls falling to his shoulders, blazing blue eyes, and an innocent smile. He carried a slingshot and a harp. The text said that David had a "ruddy countenance," but the four colors didn't do justice to flesh-tones.

"What does 'ruddy' mean?" Mrs. McCracken asked.

No one knew.

"One of you is ruddy," she said, trembling on the verge of a disclosure.

We looked around at each other in confusion, dismay, and potential loathing. Which one was ruddy, and how had anybody got that way?

Mrs. McCracken, eyes glistening behind her spectacles, smiled fondly at the boy with the best tied and most conservative necktie. "There is a truly ruddy countenance," she said, with a sensual appreciation that made me gulp and duck. I felt my cheeks and ears grow hot. A babble of relief went around the table among those not singled out. Then the hate began to gather.

Ned Ruark led the gang following me home. "Ruddy!" they called, hilarious and despising. "Randy is ruddy."

"Ru-ud-dee Ra-an-dee."

They threw pebbles at my back. I forced myself not to

48

walk faster up the hill. As I drew nearer the iron gate at the bottom of the steps leading up to Uncle Clellan's, they minced closer. Bigger things clattered on the walk behind, beside, ahead of me; caught my blue serge suit. As I swung open the door, a rock hit me in the middle of my spinal column, and I heard Ned's laugh of triumph. I kicked the door shut and ran halfway up the winding channel of stairs, where I could cry, less in pain than in humiliation. Stones continued to rattle through the gate below, and jeering laughter.

Oppression made me identify with Israel, and Daniel taught me how to prevail against the odds. When the satraps portrayed his praying to "the Living God" as treason, Darius put him in a den of lions and rolled a stone against the door, then went to his palace and fasted without music or sleep.

I reenacted the story. I led Madison, the Irish setter, to the laundry pit of the garage, where no questions were asked of playing children. I rolled a garbage can against the door from the laundry room side. I went up the stairs, lowered myself over the wall from the outside, and let myself drop down, in with Madison, incidentally straining my ankle. Finding the animal's mouth stayed by the angels, and its disposition friendly, even supplicant, I examined its paws for thorns and coat for burrs. Having tamed the king of beasts, I called to the King of the Medes to come out of his chamber and see how the Lord delivereth.

I prevailed upon Buddy to serve as Darius. And the King came, and rolled back the garbage can, and in the great relief of his heart praised the Living God, and set the youth above all satraps, and installed him in his palace. I threw a hambone coaxed from the regal Cook down into the pit and watched as the beast Madison tore into it, consuming wives and concubines and succulent offspring. The red dog dragged the tooth-clean bone around his den, rattling and scraping it against the floor, then settled down with it between his paws to grind and muse and gnaw some more.

Being the sole heir of my generation made me listen for lessons in all that was said by my elders. Grampa, "A. C.," enjoyed taking a starchy one-dollar bill out of his morroccan wallet and pointing to the all-seeing eye on its green back. "That," he said to me, "is like the eye of God. It sees everything. You can't fool it. You can steal a dollar, deflate it or debase it, but always the eye of the dollar is undeceived." I didn't understand what my grandfather meant by some of the words, but I remember the omniscient eye on the back of the buck. It never closed. It never even blinked. It saw all; it knew everything. When I said the Lord's Prayer at night, it flashed into my mind with "the kingdom and the power and the glory." I knew what a kingdom was. As for the powerntheglory, there stayed in my mind the image of the heavy-lidded green orb at the apex of the pyramid, which stood for something before ancient Egypt and after modern America, forevernever, amen.

Crispin, much later, gave me cause to wonder about my inherited values. When I was headed for college, he began tendering me occasional monologues. "Montesquieu said that the English were in advance of everybody in piety, commerce, and freedom. But two centuries have gone by since. English energies are played out, I regret to say, except for the Anglo-American amalgam over here. And as for us: our piety dried up in the nineteenth century, our commerce is beginning to lag, and I am not sure about our freedom. How can we truckle to Joseph McCarthy this way?

"I cherish my hours in Florence, where the spirit of the Renaissance is intact. A greater spirit than the English ever dreamed of."

I could borrow an uncle and older forebears, but like every boy I sought a hero in my father. To him I looked for words and gestures defining male reality. As a child, I watched Duncan barbering himself, fingers of the left hand drawing skin tight, the razored right skimming a path neatly through the lather. I thought I saw masculinity: deft, sure, clean-shaven. But Duncan in the bathtub gave different signals. If I came in, my father floated his washcloth over his genitals. It never hovered perfectly above, but would drift or sag, requiring him minutely to adjust his body beneath it to preserve the privacy—the anonymity?—of his parts. I stayed, waiting for a rogue wave to carry the cloth away, or for my father to wash and dry himself. But Duncan McCalla in my presence soaked on, the large washcloth like a collapsing parachute dragging across his crotch.

My father explained to me how to pour him a beer. A pilsener he would call it, or a bit of ale, or *"ein prosit."* With any of those code words, I knew I was asked to get a bottle of Rolling Rock or Iron City and open it gently, so that fumes might pass, but no beer spill. Then take the tall cylindrical Germanic glass narrowing toward the heavy blob at its base and tilt it *so*, about forty-five degrees, and with the right hand tip in a thin, silent stream of amber; then, as its volume built, right the glass slowly toward the vertical until at an angle where silence was impossible, because beer was now pouring onto beer instead of sliding silently into it; but because you were nearly done, there would be a minimum of froth, and no spillage over the side.

"A short snort, Randy, my boy; a short snort, and *no head* if you please."

I aimed to please. I would serve my father as many beers as he asked, but usually after the third, he helped himself. With bourbon, he never asked help. When the whiskey was flowing at a party, Duncan might come reeling into the pantry to refresh his drink and, if I was there, would catch me in a net of awkward benignity. Smiling, with eyes peering through his silver-rimmed spectacles, he would say, "We love your mother, don't we, Randy boy?" To which I would nod, incapable of speech on sacred subjects in the pantry with a man who was fumbling for a jigger. "Yes, we love your mother, and we'd do anything for her," he would say, raising his own glass in a toast to the woman in the living room. I nodded and blushed, and trembled lest a butler reenter, or a guest in pursuit of drink.

"Why do you always look embarrassed?" Lolly once asked—one of the few unkind questions she ever put to me. I felt my ears flame, my cheeks grow taut. My tongue hid behind my teeth, and an unbidden image came to mind: my left hand tilting a crystal stein while my right silently poured a headless beer. I kept the picture before me until her question went away, unanswered.

At the cocktail parties he and my mother gave, Duncan

hailed male guests with his own nicknames for them. A leading lawyer was "Shyster" and a prominent surgeon was "Slasher." They appeared to tolerate the jest smilingly, indifferent to a flippant accuser who had acquitted no one and saved no one, and who held no position.

In self-accusation, my father had a special style. To persons newly introduced he would explain, "Maybe I look Jewish, but really I'm not." A percipient stranger once remarked that his nose was distinctly un-Semitic: it was not downward hooked, but slightly uptilting in an English way. "Thank you," Duncan replied, "but it's not my nose people confuse, it's my lips and my hair. My hair is black and kind of kinky, as you can see." "Maybe so," the visitor replied, silencing my father with patient tact and apparent sincerity, "but you have beautiful and modest lips." The only feature Duncan ever bragged about was his small feet, inherited from his mother. He said that in school they had made him a fleet center fielder and stealer of bases.

In more aggressively playful moods with strangers, my father would say this: "McCalla's the name. Strange-sounding, I know. Actually it was Mickelberg in the old country. We changed it at Welfare Island, so we could pass as Protestant." Then hastening to undo any misimpression: "No, actually we're not Jewish,"—a little laugh—"although Panther Hill, here, some people call Kike's Peak. Still, you don't find many Jews on our side of the trolley tracks." I squirmed with this slurry stuff. It was cold in my father's shadow. I began to yearn for sunlight beyond him.

Still, he was gentle with me, and proud of me. Was it too much to expect more? I yearned to see him as a guiding star, giving off a steady light. When I was old enough I sorted out his values. "Success" was praised but never defined or achieved; "congeniality" was expressed constantly but diluted by resentment and belittlement of the successful; "tolerance" was much spoken of with regard to Jews, Catholics, and Negroes, but its selective nature and condescending tone tipped it more nearly toward vice than virtue.

The value that Duncan McCalla believed in and practiced beyond his peers was chastity.

52

His exposition of belief was usually indirect, but once I heard him put it forcefully. In my freshman year in New Haven, my father and mother came to see the Harvard–Yale football game. Duncan snorted at undergraduate antics, the loud bonhomie of the men, the giggling, tress-shaking, bracelet-jangling of the women. "Not a virgin in the lot," he said. I, then chaste, went hot in the face with embarrassment at the sweep of the statement and the possibility that I was included in it. But it was not a moment to protest my purity. I had begun to doubt that Christian virginity was a necessary virtue, let alone the supreme value, but I clung to it long afterward.

That night, I took my parents about the town, wishing they had never come, hoping they never would again. Duncan, with three bourbons in him on High Street, sang out at a passing string of student revellers, "Have they no care for chastity?" His voice was thin and liturgical, its register conveying that it was a fanciful question. Yet there was something over-whetted in its tone, aimed at my mother and me.

The three syllables of "chastity" carried me back to a "Family Party" at the Lawn, on a Sunday afternoon during a school vacation period. My father and mother and I were driving home to a clan dinner. Duncan was drunk, handling the wheel with solemn deliberation. Now that Martha had relieved Big Rachel as hostess, we no longer put on tuxedoes and long dresses for Sunday dinner, but she asked us especially to do so five times a year: on Communion Sundays plus Christmas. This, Adelaide reminded Duncan, was such an occasion. Or couldn't he remember as far back as Communion this morning? And was he going to be able to get his shirt studs in by himself, in his condition?

My father did not answer, but began singing to himself, "Oh, Sheppie Cardigan, ol' Sheppie Cardigan, good ol' Sheppie Cardigan."

"It *was* nice to see Shep, again," said Adelaide, firmly, as if to end the subject.

Duncan hummed awhile, went silent, and then spoke, "Sardis, I know thy works and thou art dead."

53

Adelaide was slow to take him up, as she contemplated how to put him down. "Whatever do you mean by that?"

" 'Sardis, I know thy works and thou art dead'? You mean what do I mean by that?"

"Yes. What do you mean by that?"

"Didn't you listen to the Gospel this morning? Revelations of John? It goes like this: 'Few in Sardis have not defiled their garments, and they shall walk with me in white.' "

"What's that got to do with the price of eggs and laying hens?"

"For they are worthy."

"Who? Worth what?"

"They. The ones in the white garments. Their names shall be writ in the book of the Lord."

"Are you going to recite 'Abou Ben Adam' again?"

"It's about Pittsburgh."

" 'Abou Ben Adam' is *not* about Pittsburgh."

"No? Maybe not, maybe so." Duncan sounded sober now. "But Revelations is about Pittsburgh. For sure. *Foah shoah.*" He did a broad Virginia accent when he wished to irritate Adelaide. Her diction was generally Middle Atlantic, with only a thin curl of Virginia sugar in it. "Listen again: 'Few in Sardis have not defiled their garments, and they shall walk with me in white.' "

"I don't know what you're getting at." My mother reverted to the tired voice she used when my father was senseless drunk.

Duncan began humming again. I inhaled something sweet and sickening. It reminded me of the time that I had heard the calling from upstairs in the Big House. I couldn't believe no one was responding. If my great-grandmother had rung the bell, maids would be hopping. I just happened to be there, delivering some cut flowers. But the cry continued and no one answered. I went upstairs. The cry was nearer, like a croak. After knocking, I tried the door of the master bedroom. The croak continued, oblivious to the knock, to my entering. It came from the bathroom. I peered in. Big Rachel had slipped getting into the bathtub. She lay there weakly moaning. She had befouled herself.

The first naked woman I ever saw was my great-grand-mother, with a broken hip, lying in her own feces. She reached out a hand to me. I covered her helpless tremble of old flesh with two towels. I fled her stench and my embarrassment to spread the alarm. Marie came. She gently bathed her mistress on the floor, and slipped a nightgown on her. Dr. Hunnewell came. The ambulance came. Thus began Big Rachel's several weeks in the hospital and, after that, the upstairs years.

No, my father could not have drunk enough to shit in his pants.

My mother then? I wasn't quite sure what the smell of menses was, or if she still had them, or whatever made some women smell meaty and rich. No, anyway, this was different.

Was it coming from *me*? Right there in the back seat? I thought in sudden fright that I had trod in dog poop outside the Lawn. I had slipped away to watch the fires of the open hearth furnaces glowing over the hill of the golf course at dusk. Had I stepped in something?

I tried surreptitiously to raise my shoe soles close enough for a sniffing.

Yes, ugh, it was my shoes. But too sweet for dog-do, I realized. *Gingko*! All the droppings from the gingko trees near the practice putting green. I had probably squashed fresh pods into asphalt and scuffed them into my soles.

"Sardis, Sardis," my father sang, turning into the drive, past the marble tigers. He headed around the circle to drop us at the walk to Gramma's house before returning the car to the garage. "Sardis!" He flicked the lights high against the sundial: "Thy worthies are few and they walk with him in white."

six.

IN A FAMILY embarrassed about physique, the most acceptably sensuous part of my body was my ears. They were generally flushed. With activity, I like to think. They were my seismograph, my lie detector, my best trained organ. And a part of my still young erogenous system.

My elders told me that children should be seen and not heard. So my obedient boyself was slow learning to speak, and quick to listen. My ears were always cocked to attend what others said.

Once, during a feverish head cold, my right ear began to ache, then throb. My mother called Dr. Hunnewell, who looked at it through his gleaming eye tool—his inspectoscope, he called it. He said the ear had to be lanced. He would stick a silver arrow in the eardrum to let the pus out. That would hurt a lot, for a moment, but afterward the ear would get well. Was that a deal? That was OK, I said. All right, then, I must lie *absolutely* still and not move, even a sixteenth of an inch, when the arrow went into the eardrum. But I was allowed to yell, which was only natural, because it would hurt. OK?

OK.

I lay still, head on pillow, right ear to the doctor, who pulled it to open the canal. He put in his cold funnel to guide the lance, and calmly asked me if I was ready. I said yes. My mother was holding my hand. Hunnewell plunged the silver arrow down the shaft and my brain went red with pain and I opened my mouth to a scream I don't remember because of the arrow inside my ear. I dug fingers into my

56

mother's palm, and she gripped me, and the pain slowly leveled back. The doctor said I'd been brave and hadn't moved a millimeter. My mother wiped away two tears and said I'd been good.

It was 1944 and I was eight years old. I wondered if the punctured eardrum would keep me out of the Army. My mother, who was in charge of giving me ear drops, said she hoped the war would be over soon and the Army wouldn't even have to look at my ear.

Pink eye came next, and with it a step to maturity graver, more subtle, than withstanding a lanced eardrum. I was kept home from school and put to bed lest my runny eyes and wandering fingers spread conjunctivitis. My mother was aflight with her large autumn cocktail party. I leaned over the banister and called down that four hours had passed. Time for more eye drops. She finally came up from the social noise, ordered me to lie down, reached into the medicine cabinet, took out a dropper, and squeezed it into my eyes. I couldn't see. I told her so, in some alarm. Even as the blur diminished, my eyes began to sting. She walked back to the cabinet and gasped, "My God, it was *ear* drops. I'm sorry, honey."

She rushed me to the basin and dashed glass after glass of water in my face while cursing Gramma. Why wouldn't she put in just one shower, *just one, now see?* After several minutes of flushing, my eyes felt better. My mother towelled off my head and said she was sorry and went back downstairs, high heels clacking on the shallow stairs. She called over her shoulder, "I'll send up a surprise for you."

In came a man I thought I knew but had never seen. "Hello, kid, I hear you got some dust in your eye." He sat down on my bed as if it were his own. "I'm Lang Delavane," he said. Rugged cigarette-ad face, crinkles at the corners of his eyes, cleft in the jutting chin. What sports page pictures didn't show were the hypnotic irises of pastel blue.

"Where's your baseballs?"

I pointed to the shelf. The man picked one up in his left hand, reared back and uncoiled forward, his pitcher's hand sweeping from bed to window in one sure languid dazzling

57

arc. The glass of my imagination shattered. The smiling man filled the room. The ball lay on the bed. Devalane's lips parted from his white teeth in a slow, shy grin, like a movie cowboy. His face was brown as a baseball glove.

"Here's how you hold it." He sat down on the bed again and clamped his forefinger and middle finger on the stitched seams of the white sphere. "Fastball," he said. Shifted his fingers across the seams and with his wrist revolved the ball under my gaze. "Curve." Placed the ball in my palm and watched me try the grips, correcting me with a few words, his eyes dreaming on my hand and the ball.

"OK," he said. "Nice to know you." He rose and seemed to touch the ceiling. "Practice, kid," said Lang Delavane. Two hundred and ten wins. He smiled his slow smile and left, with a casual backhand wave of his big left paw.

I got out of bed, fixed the ball in my fingers, and assumed the mound. Wearing the ancient white pajamas of the turn-of-the-century Pirates, I mowed down row after row of enemy batters with long-striding back-whipping fastballs and curves, splitting the centerpane of my garret window.

I told my father at breakfast next morning that Mr. Delavane had showed me how he gripped his fastball and curve. "Old Sidewinder, I call him," Duncan said. "Wouldn't be pitching but for the war. Used to throw a great overhand fastball. Now he's creaky—throws three-quarters; sidearm, even. Good he showed you something before he loses *all* his stuff." A little laugh. "I call him Old Sidewinder." My father returned to finishing his fried egg, leaving, as usual, one bite-sized piece on his plate. My mother had her breakfasts in bed.

For several years after the lancing, I looked forward to annual checkups on my ear. I thought of being a doctor myself, if physicians could elicit such courage as Hunnewell had in me. In addition, they could give comfort. Ear-cleaning was deliriously nice. Down the little funnel, swivel sound of long, tickly wire, until it touched an inner place at the heart of the mind. It twisted slowly there, delicate little Roto-Rooter, spinning loose the wax and dirt. My mind swam in happy submission. Out slid the wire; in rushed clean air. The tool came tingling back down the tube a second, third, fourth time. First and second times were always best, but even after the fourth I would have asked for more, were such a request not ridiculous. I was glad I had two ears for Hunnewell to work on. My dazzled brain streaked with secrets, memory of my lancing pain supplanted by measureless licit pleasure.

To ears unhindered came sounds of an unhurried world: bees nearby in azaleas, bumbling; snoring of riverboats afar; mailplane buzzing and smacking air currents overhead. I heard: creak of my father's chair at the dining room table, crinkle of suit-jacket against his vest as he cut his meat, and gristly sound his jaw made as he ate. If there was ever a man who tried to chew silently, it was Duncan McCalla; but he was audible to me.

I needed someone to tell about my ears—about their lancing and their cleaning—and perhaps about the shaft in my heart from my mother's error of haste? But mothers make mistakes, too, don't they? I decided not to mention the oil in my eyes to my father or anyone, and no one ever mentioned it to me. My own silence was from loyalty. My mother's? I could not tell whether she was moved by mysterious embarrassment or by indifference to an error she thought trivial.

But I did not need to know, then. I loved her, and she was beautiful. My father loved her, and she was decisive. Sometimes she appeared protectively haughty, other times innocent and bewildered; always I sensed an underlying resolve. She looked like Ingrid Bergman: strong features, clear eyes. When she spoke there was an initial hesitation, as if she sought the best way to render a thought peculiarly Virginian in a manner acceptable to Pittsburghers. I think of her in such moments as "Bergman, translating from the Swedish." In my teens Pia Lindstrom moved to town with her father the doctor, Bergman's first husband. After the Rosselini affair. She was a dark-eyed awkward thing, full of fugitive meanings. I never talked to Pia. I have my mother, I thought. A peculiar way of comforting myself for my social cowardice. I had yet to learn the ways in which I didn't have her, and my father didn't either.

My confidante was Babs. We were the only two children in the compound's two dozen: McCalla matriarchs, gerontocrats, clubwomen, rentiers, and presbyters; and those who cooked, buttled, dusted, chauffeured, gardened, and laundered for them, accepting the pay and the pleasant, formal thank-yous of the masters, retiring to the *chambres de bonnes* or the garrets in the garage, to sleep; or to wonder, as the moon streamed in under the eaves through narrow windows, whether there were mysteries as great as moonlight; or to plan better employment; or to make sullen resignation into McCalla servitude for life; or to accept, within the compound, the rule observed by aristocrats the world over—that life is stern, and duty lights the clearest path—and thereby to become a McCalla tribalist, a lower form of bourgeois patrician, even if one wore the white apron of the downstairs maid or the black leather apron, white shirt, and black bow tie of the chauffeur under a Pierce-Arrow, lubricating its marvelous works.

I told Babs about the lancing of my ear, how painful; and the cleaning of my ear, how pleasureful. She suggested that she would heat up some ear drops and give them to me. Maybe I would do the same for her. She had never had ear drops, and she wondered what it was like. I thought the idea adventurous to the point of sin. I knew that one didn't make toys of medicines. Yet my ears were a weakness.

Being doubted was also a weakness. "Well, maybe I don't really believe in ear drops anyway," Babs said.

That forced me to say: "But they feel good, not bad."

"I still don't believe you."

"I'll show you. Just let me put some in you. It won't feel bad. It'll feel good. It's sort of like, well, a lollipop in your ear."

"I don't want a lollipop in my ear."

"I mean if your ear had a tongue it would taste good."

"I still don't. But if you want some, I'll give you some."

"Look, here's a deal, OK? I'll go first, if you let me put some drops in your ear."

"OK, just once."

So, against my best judgment, I argued for and received a warm occlusion of my ear canal, and after describing its pleasures to Babs, was giving her the same in her bedroom on the second floor of the garage, when in walked Elise, the seamstress. She knew evil when she saw it. She reported the matter to Buddy Quick, who nodded seriously while trying to suppress a smile. Elise reserved her eloquence for my mother, and by insinuation made such a case that Babs and I trembled for days over possible sanctions.

Would we be expelled from the compound? Each knew, without saying it, that no McCalla by blood would be exiled, but we took comfort from Babs' connections. We would run away and join the circus. She had already learned enough of tumbling and other arts to latch on. "I'll practice for the high wire," she said, "and you can shovel elephant shit." Though affronted, I accepted the role.

The matter, however, was deftly resolved by edict from my mother to me, after a family Sunday supper from which I was excluded. Babs and I were henceforth to play out of doors. It was much healthier, and the sun was good for our bones. I received this simple, and apparently lenient, decision with overwhelming relief. So did Babs.

Crispin joked to Adelaide about the children and the ear drops: "You needn't worry, I think, until they play rectal thermometer." But we observed the rule she laid down for years after she had forgotten she had dispensed it.

One day Babs suggested that we shoot the iceman. The McCallas, slow to adopt the refrigerator, maintained great ice-chests at the rear of each house, reached by a platform outside. As the iceman climbed the iron stairs with a fifty-pound cube in his tongs, he presented a perfect figure for ambush. Wait until the moment he opened the latch to the chests and was hoisting a cube into the zinc-lined interior, then shoot. Man crumples, cube crashes.

I suggested kidnapping instead. Grab the man, tie and blindfold him, seize his truck, store it in the garage. When the prisoner was docile, feed him, and bring him in on the scheme: diverting contraband ice to the laundry room of the garage, and there, using the hand-crank and barrel filched from the Big House pantry, manufacture ice cream. Of course we would need the excess milk produced by Grannie Duffie's cows. That would involve bringing Jimmy into the plot. When our secret ice cream formula proved a magnificent success, his Granny could be persuaded to add more cows to the herd.

Babs agreed. We pictured the marketing of our product, with what families to begin, and where to expand, until our chain of ice cream parlors displaced Isaly's as the major local retailer. We even imagined how Lolly Contini's father, an international businessman, might help us with the foreign market; and we spied on him during his annual one-week visit home to assess his character. We found him aloof and decided we didn't need him.

We then drew up a list of flavors surpassing Isaly's and the new Howard Johnson's on the Pennsylvania Turnpike. Success would be ours. We could taste it. We went to Isaly's one hot afternoon to try our competitor's product. It was inferior to the mind's taste of our own manufacture. But still it was summer, and we wolfed down their cherry vanilla.

Sometimes I thought Babs strange. Luther brought us each an Easter chick from his family's farm in West Virginia, dyed green for sale. We kept them in little hutches with straw on the bottom, and let them out to play on the garage floor. The setter, Madison, got into the play one day. We shrieked, the dog barked, and my chick scuttled and flapped its way under a Pierce-Arrow. Babs' got stepped on and broke a leg.

The next day I came upon Babs at Luther's workbench, putting a large Diamond matchbox into his wooden vise, where we often snapped sticks for fun.

"What you got?"

"Wait and see."

She spun the vise handle until it slowed, then yanked it hard. The box splintered and cheeped. Inside the debris I saw green fluff.

"Why did you do that?"

"It was going to die anyway. It couldn't live on one leg, could it?"

"How do you know?"

"What good is a one-legged chicken?"

Buddy taught me how to ride a bicycle: first, round and round the flagpole circle with him holding my seat and one handlebar of the balloon-tired Schwinn. Then we moved out from "*ass*-fault to real *see*-ment." Buddy let me go, running alongside on the street as I careened, wind blowing in my ears, until we approached the trolley tracks on the Avenue. I braked to a lurching, foot-dragging halt, and he gave me a big grin: "You did it, you rascal, all by yourself!"

I was too concerned about money to ask for a Raleigh with "English tyres." So my second bike, like my first, was a balloon-tired Schwinn. I showed it to Babs. We were Royal Canadian Mounted Police, exploring parts of Panther Hill that needed to be brought the benefits of law and order: the Northwest Territory. But she had a flat.

"You go explore the Territory," she said.

"Won't be any fun alone."

"Won't be for me, staying here, but you go ahead."

"Why didn't you get your tire fixed?"

"Are you going to go, or are you just going to yak at me?"

"I'm going to go, I guess."

"Well, do me a favor first. Ride over my foot."

"What do you mean, ride over your foot?"

"I mean like I said. Just ride over my foot." She gave me a look of sweet passivity, an occasional face she had, which Crispin said was Raphaelite.

"Why should I?"

"You don't have to. I didn't say have to. I just asked would you."

Exasperated to action, I agreed. She extended her right shoe and braced herself while the balloon tires, plump, plump, coasted over it, leaving a faint mark.

When I turned around and cycled back to her, she looked impassive, but a little less smiling.

"Look," I said, braking to a stop, "now you ride over my foot and that will make us even."

I dismounted. Wordlessly she climbed on my new blue Schwinn. I extended my right foot. She circled around and came at me, faster than I had at her, still pumping as the front tire, then the rear, thumped over my shoe, lashing at its leather. She did not look back, but continued gathering speed past the garage, onto and out the driveway, up the street toward the Northwest Territory. I ran after her as far as the marble tigers, then stopped: gulled, crestfallen, determined to learn the workings of a woman's mind.

With Duff and Lolly, Babs and I made a peculiar quartet. I had a jobless father; Lolly an absent one; Babs, no mother. Duff had Granny: his mother died of pneumonia when he was two, his father from driving too fast on a West Virginia mountain road when he was four. Everyone else who lived on or near Hill and Hollow had resident parents and an employed father. These did not guarantee happiness, but defined normality. What brought us four together, despite the fact that the girls were older than Duff and I, Babs by two years, Lolly by one? Eccentric imagination, perhaps, or the mystique of orphanage.

We were all good at inventing games. Jimmy Duffie displayed his flair one day as we considered our waterguns.

"We stand," he said, "between sensuous Syrian and cruel Goth."

"*Who* stands *where*?"

"Lolly and I. Against you two."

"Between *what*?"

"Between Syrians and Goths. They surround us Romans, which is Lolly and me. Babs and Randy get your choice what kind of invader you want to be. To the east are the insidious and decadent but powerful Syrians. To the west are the powerful but vile and barbaric Goths. Which do you want to be? Syrians or Goths?"

Babs wanted Syrians, but I wanted Goths, and she went along. "Now how does it work?"

"If you were Syrians," said Duff, "you would come from

your place because that's east of here. But since you're Goths, you come from across the Aqueduct." He pointed westward from the middle of Hill and Hollow Road, in a grand gesture. "That's Gothic. You don't really have to come from way over there because that's not allowed."

"You mean the old trolley trestle? Is that what you call the Aqueduct?"

"Right. The Aqueduct brings water to Rome. But that's not the point. The point is: Lolly and I are Rome and you are vying against us for the Sacred Vessel of the Senate. That's this." He held up a large empty Maxwell House Coffee tin.

"I'll put it down here. Each side goes back a hundred paces, you to the west, because you're Goths. The point is for a team to get the can to the end of the road, west for you Goths, east for us Romans. You can do it on bicycle or on foot, but if you're shot you have to drop it. Three times wet and you're dead. You can't pretend you're not wet if you are."

We agreed. A half hour of stalking, feinting, and shooting ensued, until, sprayed from two angles at once, I flung the can over Lolly's head to Babs, cruising by on her bike. She caught it one-handed, stuffed it into the basket on her handlebars, and pedalled westward, Duffie pursuing. Lolly and I followed.

When I reached the end of the road, two bikes were already on the ground. Duff was scrambling laterally down the hillside toward the abandoned trolley trestle, yelling after Babs. She was poised at the point where the trestle reached the precipice, at the northernmost boundary of the Hill and Hollow private area.

"Come back, Babs," Duffie called. She had started across the trestle. He yelled and pointed, "You don't need to, you won anyway. Hey, stop, that's not allowed."

She kept on walking, placing her feet carefully on one tie after another, the can held in both hands before her.

"That's against the rules!" Duffie cried. "You *forfeit*! You *lose*!"

Lolly and I reached the precipice. Duffie stared and muttered at the girl with the empty blue can, two hundred feet above the Hollow. None of us dared follow her. She vanished in the woods at the top of the hill on the other side. We babbled in consternation and guilt. What if our families found out?

In a few minutes Babs reappeared. Despite a strong crosswind, she began to recross the span with her deliberate tread and a queenly arch to her back.

"I'm gonna tell," Duffie said quietly. He was plump in those days and quivered when he was angry.

"No, you're not," I said.

"No," said Lolly, "just pray she gets back all right."

"She'll get back OK," I said.

"It's my game," Duffie said. "I invented it, and we agreed, and she broke the rules."

"Then declare a forfeit. You get the can. But don't tell," I said.

"How can I get the Sacred Vessel back? She's not carrying it! Look!"

She drew closer, concentrating on each tie before her, arms wide for balance.

"You forfeit!" Duffie yelled.

Babs did not look up until she was ten ties away.

"Where is the Sacred Vessel of the Senate?" Duffie's voice was cracking.

"Safe on the other side," Babs said, letting her eyes rise to the three of us.

"Whaddya mean *safe*? It's not safe till it's *here*."

"It's a Goth vessel now."

"Right," I said. "Gothic vessel. The Goths win."

Duffie's glasses had come down to his nose. He tucked them back up with his left thumb and forefinger, but he was sweating and they slid down again. "Where exactly did you put it?"

Babs, fully now on Hill and Hollow territory, looked at Duff with sweet command.

"I buried it. So's I can trade it to some Syrians for treasure. When I want to, I'm going to dig it up and get rich."

seven.

"When you're ready to lose a tooth," Babs said, "you've got a whole bunch of blood stored up, ready to bleed." She was sucking a place in her mouth and thinking hard.

I readied myself, boy that I was, for a lesson. Education from Babs usually had a sting in it somewhere.

"Remember the time when we were small?" she said. "We were playing in the hall of the Big House with Madison, and we went skidding on our knees down the hall in our snow pants, and I went too fast and the chair hit my mouth?"

"Sure I remember. You cried."

"It *hurt*. I cupped my hand to catch the blood, and there was this tooth in the puddle in my hand."

"Madison wanted to lick your hand."

"I wouldn't let him because I didn't want to lose the tooth."

"Then B-Ray came in the side door and Marie came downstairs."

"Madison jumped up and tore Big Rachel's stockings."

"And I tried to explain while you were crying and holding your bloody tooth and Madison was barking and Marie was talking German. Big Rachel got her ear trumpet and waved it at us and smacked Madison on the bottom."

We enjoyed conjuring the scene in memory.

Babs poked her tongue in a place in her mouth. "I just lost one yesterday. My last tooth." She was silent for a while. "I'm losing a whole bunch of blood—all over."

"So what's new?" I wanted to read baseball statistics in my *Sporting News*.

"What's so new?" she said sharply. "So, I'm bleeding, that's what." Her face had whitened, and a pair of short vertical lines appeared in her brow just above her nose.

"Same as anybody," I said.

"Not from the tooth, idiot. Not in the mouth."

Her ferocity woke me up. "What do you mean? Where are you bleeding?"

She stared at me until I blinked.

"Dumb," she said, and sauntered down the hall through the door to the pantry and kitchen.

My father arranged for me to learn the facts of life from Dr. Hunnewell. When I entered his office, he asked me what was the matter.

My ears went hot. "Didn't my father say why he sent me?"

"Oh, yes." Hunnewell focused on me his kind, unsurprisable eyes. "I thought he ought to send you to Reverend McCracken instead, for this. But I agreed to do it, as an old friend of the family." He gave a formal, benign smile. "You're reaching an age, you know, when young men begin to grow in their manly parts. Your father, as I recall, wanted me to be sure that you understood the dangers of venereal disease. Do you know what it is?"

I had come across the term in the evening *Sun-Telegraph* and had innocently asked, whereupon my father had barked, "Never you mind!" Now apparently I was going to learn. I said I wasn't exactly sure.

"Well, do you know what a prostitute is?"

"Mmm, I guess not, really."

"Well, lets start with that. Prostitutes are women who sell their favors to men. That's where venereal disease starts. And here's where it finishes." He took down a medical textbook bound in pimply green leather, and opened to "paresis." It was illustrated, in colors far more subtle and drawings far more detailed than Sunday school. "You rot,"

68

said Dr. Hunnewell. "Not only in your private parts, but your brain, too."

"Fornication?" I asked. I was anxious to show knowledge, and to please by submission. Dr. McCracken had just recently given a youth sermon on "the plague," in which he condemned all "lewd, lascivious, licentious and reprobate behavior." The commandment against adultery, he had said, was a commandment against *all*, repeat *all* sins of the flesh. "*Any* sex outside of marraige is *fornication*." And now I was staring at pictures of fornication itself, prissy, ulcerous, sclerotic, discolored private parts.

"Fornication is damnation," I said.

"Right," said Dr. Hunnewell kindly. "I guess you didn't need to come here after all." The whole visit in the office had taken barely five minutes. I felt old, sad, alone, more ignorant then before.

Babs rarely talked about her mother. We were bicycling late one afternoon and stopped at a rest point, when Babs suddenly said, "My mother just had both her breasts cut off."

I imagined Wanda somewhere in her institution's sick ward. I groped to express sympathy, while trying not to appear stupid. "That's too bad. . . . So now she can't have any more babies?"

Babs was puzzled and testy. "If somebody gave her one, she could stick a bottle in its mouth."

I pondered this, afraid that stating any of my assumptions would reveal my ignorance. "But how?"

"How *what*?"

"I mean how could she have babies at all?"

Babs replied evenly, her countenance as smooth as a Fra Filippo Lippi. "Fucking, same as ever. Only she doesn't have anybody to fuck with."

I had heard the word in the Academy locker room but had never understood its use. My next utterance exposed me. "Sucking?" I said.

Babs looked at me with disgust.

From Duffie I had learned some evolution, but this apparently was a different subject. Now I had to put myself at her mercy. "But babies come from up here, don't they?" I asked the question desperately, on the point of tears, covering my shirt with my two hands roughly over my nipples. "From women's breasts? Don't they?"

Babs adopted a tone of dealing with a primitive child. "No, they don't."

I pushed myself to ask the next question, which fluted out in a thin voice: "Well, where do they come from then?"

"They come out of the cunt."

My eyebrows went up, and I felt tears drop simultaneously from each of my lower lashes. So what was that? I still didn't know.

Babs may have pitied me, but she had seniority to preserve and knowledge to convey. "Out of here," she said, putting her hand like a cleaver in her skirt, between her legs. "First they grow in the belly, and when they're ready they come out of the cunt." She paused a moment. "Haven't you ever seen a pregnant woman?"

"No," I said, "I guess maybe not."

"I guess you wouldn't," she said with tolerance. "Not around here, for sure. And not at a *boy's* school." She looked at me with a teacherly affection and expectation of thanks. But I could find nothing to say. Babs hooked up her kickstand, slid onto the saddle of her bike, and pedalled around the circle toward the garage.

The three houses and the empty lot were my cloister. Babs was custodian of its underlore, priestess of its mysteries. She was speaking one day of her father, how quick he was to anger and to laughter. She said: "Once I interrupted Buddy right in the middle of coming."

Coming? Where? Was he angry? Was she shifting the subject? I said nothing.

"I didn't know whether he was laughing or crying."

I decided to play it safe. "Which do you think? Which was it most like?"

"It wasn't like anything. It was like yowling maybe."

I tried to encourage more description. "Sometimes when Buddy laughs, he really goes to pieces."

"Well, he really was gone, and he wasn't laughing."

I grew quiet, trying to avoid mortal embarrassment. She sensed the problem, reasoned backward, laid out a path. "Sometimes when my father has an orgasm, he laughs, yet you wouldn't call it laughing."

"You mean," I said slowly, "he literally . . .? And you were actually right there . . .?" I gulped and added, "Somehow?"

"Sure, that's what I was saying." She saw that I knew a little more than I used to, and wasn't totally stupid, but needed a lot of help. "Look, you know Buddy, he's a carnival man. Living with him, it's a circus in your own house. I mean, how could I have a father like that all these years and not come across him tomcatting?"

I thought: Well, it's my house, too, or my family's garage anyway.

She grinned. "He was yowling like a fool. It must have been really good."

I smiled gamely, to indicate I was catching up. "Yeah, it must have been."

"So you want to know, who was it? Right?"

I hadn't wondered, but I nodded.

"Rachel," she said, as if that were self-explanatory.

Obviously, from the alarm on my face, it was not.

"*Black* Rachel," she said, disgusted with my need for her to be so explicit.

I nodded with smiling dignity, like Uncle Clellan, taking in matters that were my right to know but upon which I would not comment.

In a moment, however, a question did occur to me, and I put it suddenly and aggressively: "*Where?*"

Babs flushed. "None of your goddam business," she said.

Of course I wondered why the place of fornication was more sensitive than the names of the sinners. But when Babs didn't want to speak, that ended that.

We did not always talk, Babs and Duff and Lolly and I,

71

about games and the facts of life. By our early and mid-teens we were discussing something that might be called metaphysics, if you will allow that term for trying to rise above facts, confront categories, grapple with values.

I for a while was chief moralist. Dr. McCracken and his wife were pressing me to bear special witness to Presbyterian revelation, to prove John Knox right for the twentieth century. Weird? I was the only son of McCalla compound, surrounded by elders but feeling alone. I loved my father in a diffuse way, a love as absentminded as his attention to me. He showed me no path, taught me no weapons. I loved my mother from afar. I looked for parents everywhere.

I tried hard to engrave the holy law in my own mind. I wrote Biblical passages from Sunday school down on slips of paper, studied them, put them in my shirt pocket. Until one day, playing with Babs and Duff and Lolly, some blew out.

"You know what he's got in his pocket?" Babs said to Duff and Lolly. "*Scriptures.*" Her voice was scathing. Duff picked up her derision. Only Lolly seemed to understand.

We played golf. Duff and I attacked the nearby course with Lolly and Babs caddying and offering commentary. Occasionally Lolly would play, too. Never Babs; but she would carry a bag. Panther Hill Public Golf Links was short, with little sand and no water. The Lawn Club had sold it to the city decades before, and it belonged now to the Hollow upon which it verged, and to the truck drivers, barkeeps, garter salesmen, pastry chefs who played it for a dollar a round.

Duffie was in his sporting element. His Granny bought him regular lessons. He practiced putting in the rough grass of his own back yard, sending one ball to hit another, and became that adolescent rarity: one whose short game surpassed his long. He broke eighty with some regularity, ceded me nine strokes a round, and usually won. Just before the reopening of school, we determined that the championship of the season would be decided between us, on a handicap basis, match play. When we got to the seventeenth hole, I needed a ten-foot putt to stay in the match. As my fingers tightened on the shaft, I briefly shut my eyes and muttered a request: "Please, God, let this go in."

I underputted by two feet. Duffie stepped up to his six footer and sank it. Victory. As he put down the scores at the final tee, he shot me a shrewd look.

"Were you praying back there?"

"A little, maybe," I admitted.

Duff gave a little smile for the girls and regarded me over his glasses, which had slipped down his nose. With his right hand he absently drew his driver out of the bag. "Golf is not God's game," he said.

But what *is* God's game? Duffie quoted Einstein: "God is subtle, but not malicious." That sounded reassuring but didn't reveal His design to us. Lack of a clear plan raised a question of whether God existed at all, Duffie said. Lolly then demonstrated with syllogisms the existence of God, and none of us could refute her. We assumed that Somesuch existed. Somesuch was Babs' term. She had less appetite for these talks than the rest of us, but a willingness to express views.

Assuming God exists, then He wants things to happen His way, if possible, Duffie reasoned. So the big question is, how should we behave? Duffie made the question concrete enough even for Babs by demanding: "OK, everybody has got to say what's your idea of the greatest saint and the greatest sinner."

For starters we took sinners; it was easier. Lolly named Hitler. Easy and general agreement. Jimmy argued that Warren G. Harding was the greatest American sinner of the twentieth century. He had surrounded himself with bumblers and crooks, and had made love to his mistress in a White House broom closet. How did he know that? we asked; to which Duffie answered it was well known in certain circles. In addition to a mistress in his closet, I teased, didn't Harding have a Mellon in his cabinet? The exception proves the rule, Duffie said, and he pressed me for my greatest sinner.

"Diamond Jim Brady," I answered. The group looked

73

doubtful. I filled in reasons from scraps of Sunday dinner conversation. My family had had unavoidable business dealings with him. He was loose with money and with women. A polysyllabic clincher occurred to me, in the spirit of McCracken's gospel: "Brady was profligate and ostentatious." In my mind's eye, however, I saw Crispin smiling and moving to a defense of Brady as an amusing fellow, no worse than his times, and a great deal better company than a roomful of Presbyterians.

Next came Babs. She shot out her answer with defiance: "Salem the Sword Swallower." Before we could even question her, she said that his name on the billboards was really Salim, but everybody in the circus called him Salem. He was real handsome and real mean, and never did anybody a good turn, and didn't love anybody, and when anybody was nice to him, he used it as a way of getting something more out of them. And he was that way all the time. There wasn't anything nice about him, but he was so charming that people kept forgiving him and doing things for him, which just made him worse really.

Duffie challenged. "Is that as bad as Hitler? I mean, can anybody compare with Hitler killing and torturing everybody? This sword-swallower guy, how many people can he be mean to?"

Babs was ready, eyes blazing. "You don't know anything about Hitler except what you read. Well, I read that he was nice to his mistress, Eva What's-her-name. So at least he was nice to somebody. But *not* Salem. *Never.* He's mean as hell, he's really evil, and he travels all over the country."

That we non-circus people had to accept. We admitted him to the list of great sinners, somewhere above Diamond Jim Brady and below Warren Harding, all of whom trailed Adolf Hitler.

Great saints were tougher, and a thunderstorm was gathering. Duff and I took the golf bags so that we would be struck by lightning instead of the girls. We scattered home before a dark rain, promising to give special thought to saints. When we reassembled next day, competition was high in the air, nurtured by Duffie. "I dibs second," he said quickly. Lolly moved first.

Teresa of Ávila was unquestionably a saint, and a great one, she said. She not only wrote beautifully out of a mystical solitude, but she organized women into a marvelous nunnery, where they did for the world what needed doing so badly—praising God and praying for others. I groaned. "That's too good. Disgustingly good."

Duffie was ready, however, with his extraordinary candidate. Alexis de Tocqueville? There was someone to think about. Saints were Catholic property, he argued, and largely the result of superstition and exaggeration. What the modern world needed was people who could understand state and society, predict what might happen, and help the best come about instead of the worst. Tocqueville had sized up America better than anybody, ever; and he'd been a good politician back in France.

I asked wasn't Lincoln a better politician and more of a saint, for really helping people, not just writing about things? Duffie went on the offensive: "OK, who's *your* greatest saint?"

I put forward my man: Andrew Carnegie. Who else in history had given away three hundred and fifty million dollars? Who else even had *made* that much money, let alone given it away? Think of all the employment he created, and new industry he started. On top of that, he gave his whole fortune to charity. Three hundred and fifty million before the First World War was real money. Here was a saint with some *size* to him.

The more I stressed the figure, however, the tackier my case sounded. So I veered to another conclusion. Ever since the Protestant age we've needed men of action to bring about a better life on earth. John Knox founded the Presbyterian Church, and Andrew Carnegie had brought it new life— individualism and good works. Here my knowledge failed me, so I finished with a maxim. "Neither bishop nor king!" I cried, using the motto my father was fond of blurting in drink. Loudly repeating it, I rested my case for Carnegie.

75

Lolly and Duffie had listened with interest, while Babs looked bored. She had dibbed last. We turned to her. She began uncertainly, as if she had sought end position simply to gain time to think. There was this saint, but she didn't know her name. One of the sisters at the place her mother lived had told about her. She was Japanese, lived a long time ago, and after the first priests had been there awhile, Francis Xavier and that gang, the head of Japan, whatever he was called, not the king, something else, had got fed up with Christians. He said they all had to recant or get killed. If you were a Christian, you had to stomp on a picture of Jesus and say you didn't believe in him.

Well, this saint wouldn't recant, so they gave her the real treatment. They hung her upside down in a pit of awful something.

"In a pit of offal?" Duffie interrupted.

"What?" Babs was annoyed.

"Offal," said Duff. "O-F-F-A-L. It means bodily waste, et cetera."

Babs stared at him, then resumed. "In this pit, they hung her anyway, right over the mess I suppose, with her nose in the shit, and her left hand tied to her body and her right hand loose so she could raise it, which meant she was re-canting. But she didn't, *ever*. She just hung there, fourteen days, which was a record, and never recanted, so I think she must have been a saint."

"How could she, fourteen days?" I asked. "Her brain would bust long before that."

"They cut lines in her scalp so the blood would drip out steady, slow, and not bust anything or black her out."

"Still, I don't see how she could of lasted fourteen days. Two *weeks*, upside down?"

"Maybe," Duffie said, "they took them out at night and strung them up again the next morning. That way you could run up more time."

"Maybe," said Babs. "Anyway the chief Jesuit in Japan, some Portuguese guy, he gave up in hours. Just *hours*, sister said, and he was yammering to get out of the pit. He re-canted and they told everybody about it, and that was prac-

76

tically the end of Christianity in Japan. Except a lot of people never *said* they were Christians, they just *believed*, and pretended they were something else, and that went on for centuries."

"Yes, crypto-Christians," said Lolly. "I like your saint. She kept everything going somehow."

Duff and I were impressed, too. Babs had some saint there, whatever her name was; and if it was true.

"Of course it's true and I can prove it," she said hotly. "Anyway, I can ask sister."

Never mind, we said, it's a good story.

More than a good story, Lolly said.

Babs smiled at Lolly for her help, but she didn't want to surpass us boys too badly. "Saint What's-her-name," she said, deriding her own victory, "of blessed memory."

"I wonder what she was really like," Lolly said. "I mean, what she thought, what she felt."

"Somesuch knows," said Babs. "But who cares?"

We were too thick, somehow; so a decision was made, somewhere. Either my mother, Adelaide, had gone to Granny Duffie, or vice versa, and said, we've been thinking about a good prep school for Randy (or Jimmy), and has that perchance been on your mind; and if so, what about St. Luke's?

Looking back I imagine concern on the part of my mother and father, and Granny Duffie, about two boys, reaching sixteen years of age, whose constant company was two girls, seventeen and eighteen, one of them a Catholic Jew and, as would be shortly proved by her actions, seriously daft; and the other a pagan Catholic of the servant class.

Time magazine spoke of "haughty, hockey-playing St. Luke's" and its "cloistered tyrannies." The description captured far-off parents who wanted athletic competition for their sons along with social distinction and Latin declension. Never mind an arcane and slightly sadistic discipline in the manner of English boarding schools. Duffie and I entered that aura of wealth and achievement. We endured the murmurs and mumbles of the Episcopalian church. A tart old faculty member called us "the Presbyterian subversives." His acolytes from Boston and New York referred to us as "the Pittsburgh hicks." Condescending terms not without fondness. We excelled academically, got elected to student council, chosen to captain golf and squash. I hated the school, thrived there, grew loyal to it. Duff loved it, thrived still more, and wrote elegant criticisms of it for the school literary magazine.

The thought of St. Luke's brings back to me foreign things: Anglican liturgy, Gallic sarcasm, Spartan sodomy, Athenian grace. We were sent, Duffie and I, to separate us from Lolly and Babs, "unsuitable friends." But that action eventually bound us closer, in a strange diagonal to what our elders planned.

eight.

WHEN I came home from St. Luke's for the first time, some things were the same. The dial by the flagpole told suntime; the cowboy's horse reared back from Remington's rattlesnake in Gramma's hall; and by the giant windowsill on Big Rachel's stairway, Mercury with his winged hat and winged feet still coursed upon a mission of the gods, his upright speed privileging him to be the only nude in the McCalla compound.

But I was different. I couldn't seem to get my elders to hear me, for one thing. Aunt Martha suggested that I place my tongue against the back of my teeth as I spoke consonants, and that I *project*. My mother said yes, remember how Crispin despite his handicap has wonderful diction. I writhed at the comparison to Crispin, and when my father said that Crispin's speech was effete, I was secretly glad. I had not yet given up my father as a model of manhood. I stressed my Pittsburgh accent, like my father's, with its gargled "r's," uvular "l's," and flat vowels, so unlike my Bostonian and New York schoolmates. I wanted my speech to contrast with Crispin's, with its pause words, Harvard tones, and lordly speech tics borrowed from English aristocrats. But even as my voice contradicted him, my spirit secretly leaned toward Crispin as the most eminent McCalla since my great-grandfather Rowan.

A new item in the Big House was an electric seat that travelled between first floor and second, following the course of the banister, carefully matched for its wood. B-Ray, leaving the second floor infrequently, now pressed a button for ascents and descents. Waiting for her to come down for tea, I studied myself in the mirror of the hall.

"You've got an Irish face, Master Randy," the maids said, shaking heads in proud commiseration. I saw glossy dark curly hair, not so tightly waved as my father's. My cheeks were highly colored. Would they in age break out like Duncan's; or were those microscopic estuaries on his cheeks and nose simply a faint etching of a drinking habit, the fine vermilion and lavender map of dissipation?

My eyes were cobalt blue, inquiring, diffident, clear, protected by long, dark lashes. I opened them wide at myself as I did to others in conversation, showing my willingness to listen, power to absorb. In their gleam, a latent quickness to anger and a willingness to forgive. My look was steady in query and peril, unlike my father's. His blue-green irises bobbed up and down behind bifocals, unable to determine whether the quandary presented him required nearsight or far.

Big Rachel slid downstairs with a decorous hum of electricity, and we seated ourselves in the library for tea. She had little to ask, some to offer about the party I was attending that night. "The Contini girl, Laura Carney's granddaughter, is she nice?"

"Yes, she is."

"I should hope so. She has a nice grandmother. But what's the sense, I ask you, of a coming out party for a Catholic? What's more, a girl whose father is a Jew. It's all very nice, and the Carneys give good parties. But they shouldn't expect that those who go to the party will marry their daughter."

I flared. But in weighing whether to reply to oddity or to unfairness, I lost my chance to speak at all.

"Catholics ought to marry Catholics and Jews ought to marry Jews," she continued. "That's the way it's always been. When they marry Protestants it's too complicated. And when they marry each other I'm sure it's very complicated indeed. I hope you have a good time anyway."

I said I expected to have a good time, and I was about to venture a remark on the difference between a deb party and a wedding, but I held back. Big Rachel had put down her trumpet and was not watching my lips. She offered more tea. I shook my head.

"Well, you'll have to tell me what kind of party it is," she said. I promised to do that, and munched my English muffin.

I never fulfilled the promise. Two hours before the announced time of dinner that night, Lolly Contini climbed onto the windowsill of her bedroom window and jumped into the courtyard below, breaking both legs. She landed with the greatest force on the left, smashing it badly. Several screws were required to hold the bones together, and damage to the hip socket complicated her recovery for months. Immediately after calling for an ambulance, Mrs. Contini phoned three mothers of girls expected to attend and asked each to take two pages of the invitation list, calling as many people as possible to say that Lolly had fallen and was injured and that the party was postponed. The word went out.

Lolly's mother left word at the Lawn to serve dinner to any who should arrive. I was there after a squash lesson with Jack Costelloe. The buzz of speculation contained two rumors: Lolly had fallen on the ice and had broken a leg, but it wasn't serious. And: Lolly, having attempted suicide, was critically injured. How the second rumor began was not clear, but it may have fed upon the apparently well-known fact that she had not wished to have a debutante party given for her.

Duffie, a late arrival, asked me what I knew.

"I don't know anything. Jumping doesn't seem like Lolly, though."

"But she said she would only go through with the party because her father wanted it as well as her mother. And then at the last minute, her father didn't come."

I was annoyed that Duffie knew more than I. Duffie had soft shoes and big ears.

"Why didn't he come?" I asked.

"Sudden international business complications," Duffie said, ripping it off by rote.

"Jesus. I hope she's OK."

81

We stood there hoping for her, feeling guilty that something had gone amiss with Lolly while we were away at St. Luke's.

After a year Lolly was back in circulation. Her left leg, its ankle bones partly fused, was shorter than the right. To my relief, her eyes were merry. When I dared ask what happened, she laughed and said, "Oh, a temporary loss to Satan. Allowing myself to get dashed on the stone. Good thing there was a big snowfall out there." And she changed the subject with the light confidence of a socially practiced woman.

I imagined that Lolly's fall had not been accidental. But her present mood was buoyant. She had not mentioned her father.

I reported the conversation to Babs. She had her own memorable angle.

"If I wanted to throw myself out a window, I'd go head-first."

I was surprised at her testiness. "Maybe she didn't want to die," I answered. "Maybe she just didn't want to dance."

"Maybe so. But what good is a one-legged chicken?"

I found it harder to talk to Babs. Perhaps St. Luke's, as our elders intended, was putting distance between us. I took the bothersome feeling secretly to Crispin, the only McCalla ever to have graduated from college. His response dismayed me.

"What you seem to wish for, my dear boy, is somehow pumping culture into Buddy Quick's daughter. An admirable thought in itself, and she's a dear girl. My mother and grandmother could scarcely do without her as a maid-of-all-duties. But how much could Crusoe teach Friday besides dignity in his servility, and a bit of trade?

"I remember a fellow at Harvard, a young Negro janitor named Copsey, who picked up a good deal talking with us. I encouraged him with Wordsworth. He could read it to us with feeling, and even talk about it with conviction. Then he grew ambitious to write. A disaster. It ended our friendship, I fear. We had spoiled him for a janitor, and made him neither poet nor critic. I wonder what became of him?

"One of those colored leaders said—was it Garvey? No, DuBois"—Crispin's lips began to twitch—"he was talking about students, of course, 'Harvard has ruined more good Negroes than bad whiskey has.' " He shook with delicious laughter.

Crispin rolled on in my silence. "Our culture is determined in our childhoods, really. We remain primitive or we become educated. To be in between, like poor Copsey, is a terrible plight.

"Remember John Kane? His wife used to cook for your great-grandmother. There was a successful primitive. He couldn't learn painting at the age he began, not properly. And nobody could teach him, either. But he saw the world through the eyes of a child and painted Pittsburgh with a simple hand. And an iron stomach, I might add. Goodness, that man could drink. He painted drunk better than sober, I suspect. McCalla Iron and Steel—he even painted that—the smokestacks wobble. I bought it in my youth and still have it in my office at the Museum. When I was at Harvard several of us gave him a little exhibition. Captivating. I asked him what he thought of Picasso. 'Mixed-up,' was all he said. Brilliantly so, we might say, but Kane was wise to stay clear of him."

I shifted in the chair, saying nothing.

"Has Barbara Quick a talent? If so, I don't know what. Does she need better schooling? Surely that high school of hers is not much use. Private tutoring? Perhaps it would help, but who is going to finance that, and why?"

As I turned these thoughts over, Crispin switched onto me. "And what are you doing with your culture, my boy? Are you aware that you are already formed, and of fleeting materials at that? Are you preparing yourself for life as a bourgeois aristocrat? Are you readying to engage in seemly competition for wealth in a country that has substituted scramble for nobility? Ha!" He laughed at himself.

"Only art endures, my lad. That is salvation for me, and I hope it might at least be consolation to you. All the patricians and plunderers of the late nineteenth century are gone, but you can still read Edith Wharton; you can still look at Mary Cassatt. That is, if you are not up to reflecting on Pascal and studying Raphael." He paused to let these words sink in and then dismissed himself with a little whinny.

There the matter might have ended. But Martha took a Pygmalion step, for reasons of her own. Did she hope to educate Babs, her "house sparrow," as her servant, companion, even confidante? Whatever the motive, Crispin was persuaded, despite his convictions, to try to help. I heard only the end of it. Overheard it rather, a conversation behind heavy drapes, which I parted only when, burning in shame, I heard the turn of a doorknob behind me from the servants' wing.

"What could you expect, Mother? I imagine she never willingly reads anything over there in the garage but comic strips. What she's reading now is not so much because you wish it as because Randy and Jimmy Duffie are back from St. Luke's with talk of T. S. this and W. H. that. Who are Auden and Eliot to Barbara Quick? I can get her to remember that one was an Englishman who came over here and the other was an American who went over there, but she has no clue to the poetry. How could she? A child is formed in these matters by age six, don't you think? You read Jane Austen to me, and Thackeray, and Trollope, and I'm eternally grateful, Mother. I'll pass on the favor to my children, should I marry.

"But for Barbara, dear thing, it's almost too late even for images. I gave her Berenson, but she didn't understand my point. I suggested that she see *The Italian Painters of the Renaissance* as a picture book, not as an encyclopedia. I meant it sincerely enough, but she thought I was talking down to her. She took it grimly and resentfully. We couldn't talk about the book. She says she doesn't believe in the Virgin Mary. Hah! I said that faith has nothing to do with enjoying Giotto, but it was no go.

"She's a *kinetic* person, I'm sure, and very dear to the

family. But it won't do to think of her as an intellect. And as a companion for you, Mother, I wonder. Is she made for waiting, for service? Too restless and ambitious, I fear. You would rather think of her as aspiring? Yes, she is, in her way. She responded passionately to Moira Shearer in *The Red Shoes*. You need only mention the movie and her calves knot and she rises on tiptoe. But she's built for the trapeze, I think, and not the dancer's barre. Ambition isn't enough. You have to have background. And it's too late, I fear, for dear Barbara.

"Oh, hello, Randy." Here I had parted the drapes. "I say, barbarian that you are, you nonetheless have a massive advantage over poor Barbara Quick. Mother wants to culture her like a pearl. But really"—turning back to Martha— "the dear thing is the daughter of her parents, you know. You can put sand as carefully as you please in that clamshell and it won't produce nacre.

"I don't mean to be unkind," he said to me. I was flaming with guilt and scowling with embarrassment. "And Mother, I trust, doesn't think I am wholly cruel. We simply must be honest in such things. Our Barbara is not likely to develop Eliot's Unified Sensibility. She may be worth cultivating as a maid-companion, but even that I fear might frustrate her, and Mother as well.

"It's simply years too late. Either too late," he laughed in his helpless charming way, "or I am a terrible teacher. Very likely so! A terrible teacher!"

Lolly limped. Rising out of a chair she put the weight on her right leg first and twisted up, gracefully and swiftly, before her first step on the other foot. Even with her left shoe built up, she lurched a little. When she spoke, standing opposite one, she canted a little to her left unless she gave a slight tiptoe push. Since she preferred to look at people squarely, with her left heel raised, toe poised, her body expressed an on-the-mark look that was less a distraction (I am poised for flight) than a compliment (I am alert to you). She played golf more than before: walking, the doctor said, strengthened the leg muscles, and the swinging of clubs wouldn't hurt. So she practiced her way into competition with me. I gave her only a stroke every other hole.

The hardest thing, I thought, must be dancing. Was it forced healing, or masochism, that took her to all the deb parties, after her own season? The younger boys didn't know her. Of those slightly older who did, many were afraid to dance with her. Who would cut in, bail you out? Who wants to get stuck with a cripple on a dance floor?

She was my friend, so I danced with her. If not me, and Duffie, then who? To strike a rhythm was at first difficult. The backward dip of her left leg caused a timing and turning problem. "Don't think about my leg," she said. "I can say this to you. Just think about your lead." So I did. She followed in synch, compensating for the bob of her shoulders and head by keeping a little more distance from me than most partners would, and resting her eyes intently on my face. All the embarrassment I felt, of dancing with a self-maimed woman, at first increased with this rapt attention. But it waned in an evening. Others danced with her out of gallantry or curiosity, and they returned. She was incomparably more solicitous of one's mood and ease than the glowing horse girls, the blazing tennis players, the self-idolizing madonnas of the season, who, polished and perfumed, bouncing to Lester Lanin, chattered through ritual inquiries with each partner until another cut in.

A year after Lolly's accident one might have thought she had been in a car crash as a child, so complete was her apparent adjustment, so humorous and outward the light in her eyes. I danced with her often that Christmas season, and in our conversations we found our way back into old times: the foursome of Hill and Hollow Road, Buddy's birthday party and the night Granny Duffie's cows got out; Babs' escapade on the aqueduct; defining sinners and saints. When school resumed in January, I wrote her at Bryn Mawr. Across the weeks during which I waited for a reply, I wondered: did she think it was beneath a college girl to write a boy in prep school? Hadn't she had me as a dancing partner to count on, when she might have been a wallflower? I heard Babs' sharp tongue in my mind disparaging Lolly.

Now there was a rough, straight, vigorous girl: no-nonsense: Babs herself. Why not write *her*, and take on, ever so subtly, the adventure in uplift abandoned by Crispin and Martha? I would write plainly and simply, and see what came back. From Babs, compared with Lolly, I might hope for guts rather than nerves, carnival tones instead of cathedral.

Just then a letter came from Lolly. Light blue stationery, dark blue pen; a slanted and fluid hand with strong capitals, unlike the received envelopes lying on the desks of my friends, with their up-and-down hugely rounded writing, and lowercase letters nearly as large as upper.

Her attunement to my thoughts, and to my application to Yale, thrilled me, and I wrote back to her instead of to Babs. Lolly's deliberate pace of reply kept the exchange limited to four letters each by the end of the academic year. They were, however, epochal letters to me, opening into discussions of what I read, felt, wished to become—matters which, in the McCalla compound, interested only Crispin, who was seldom there.

I came home in June with one intention, but many things happened. Tucked in a case along with collar pins, cuff links and old coins, I carried a small heart-shaped gold-plated pin with the initials "S. L. S." on it, which seniors were privileged to buy at the St. Luke's school store. I intended it for Lolly. A rash of giving and receiving pins had broken out among my peers in prep school. I felt I should be above shallow commitment and brash display, but I yearned to give Lolly something of mine.

The occasion was difficult to arrange. I contrived to take her to two deb parties. Through the first, her conversation was so earnestly of Yale and the opportunities ahead of me that I was content to treat it as a warm-up. Through the second she talked about herself and the trip she was taking through cities undergoing urban redevelopment. Her mother was on the Pittsburgh Bicentennial Committee, which event was only five years away. As part of a diffuse charge to accomplish great things and then celebrate in 1959, committee members were travelling to cities where things were happening: Atlanta, Houston, Denver.

"But none of those places has major league baseball teams," I mused. I thought of them as Southern Association, Texas League, and Pacific Coast.

"Does Pittsburgh?" Lolly shot back. "With the Pirates in the cellar three years straight?" She cocked an eyebrow at me: "What is the test of a city?" She proceeded to a passionate discourse on symphonies, art galleries, slum clearance, and core renewal. Having aroused her in the wrong way, I cursed myself, fell back, listened, waited.

Just before her trip I arranged a handicap match at the Public Golf Links, followed by a drink on the porch of the Lawn. She played well, beat me, one up. I would have preferred to win by the same margin. We sat with gin and tonic in the waning afternoon light on an empty porch. The descending sun smote us through the smogless air. A light breeze caressed me with the clarity of hope. The gin drew to my skin blood not yet summoned there by the sun; my tongue loosened, and I talked of the city's renaissance and the beauty of its hills. She, whose themes these usually were, listened and nodded, chiming in a thought now and then above the light sounds of traffic that rose from the Hollow and the tangle of railways and factories further beyond.

The only way to do it, I thought, was to get the pin out in the sunlight. I extended my leg from the chair, reached in my pocket, and after a swig of tonic with my left hand, opened my right like a prospector with a nugget. "I got this as a senior. Only graduating seniors can have these."

Lolly looked at it as at a baby kitten.

"Now that I'm going to Yale, I want you to have it," I said. I felt a pumping at my temples, a pulsing in my ears. Hearing no immediate answer I followed one *non sequitur* with another. "I don't wear jewelry, and I don't mean you have to wear it, but I mean I would like you to have it. To keep as long as you want."

Lolly raised clear gray eyes to me. "That's a lovely

thought, Randy, and I do appreciate it. But I'm sorry, I can't accept it." She said it so pleasantly and evenly that I did not collapse or drop the pin as I thought I might. She asked to see the pin. I was amazed at how casually I passed it to her, as if it were an oddity and meant nothing. She turned it round in the light and exclaimed on its design before returning it to me, with compliments on my graduation.

"Well," I said, "that's the end of that. . . . St. Luke's School, I mean, for me."

"Ends are also beginnings," she said in a voice neither prim nor metaphysical, as if simply describing a dogleg hole to a golfer who had not played it. We talked of Yale and Bryn Mawr as the sun, paling, slanted across the porch, until the first chauffeur arrived with the first pair of widows to drink and sup together.

nine.

As LOLLY prepared for her transcontinental tour, I teased her: she was an urban industrial pilgrim with no Holy City on her itinerary. She smiled: "Pittsburgh is Jerusalem for me."

When she left, I turned my imagination to the First International Invitational Laundry Yard Squash Racquets Tournament. As St. Luke's top player and captain, I wanted to whet myself for competition at Yale. Ivy Leaguers didn't play squash in the summer. But Hashim Khan did. Khan had learned the game as a boy, under the Pakistan sun, playing all year round in an outdoor court, four walls and no roof, hitting against English officers. He had beaten the best while still in his teens, and had prevailed in England ever since. Now Khan was threatening to come to America and, despite the faster ball, the narrower court, to win at the accelerated American version of things. Jack Costelloe, our old Lawn Club pro, had seen him play in Ireland. Khan's name was the only one in the world that made Costelloe lift an eyebrow.

I imagined tweedy galleries of Ivy League males, paunch-controlling investment bankers, tautly conditioned corporate lawyers, watching a brown-skinned man with broken syntax destroying their best. And I was aroused two contrary ways at once—with nationalistic antagonism against the Pakistani and with underdog fervor for him. The latter, on self-inspection, more.

A new energy in me poured forth with the discovery that I could look upon the tattersall-vested, martini-shaking syndics of the establishment as my adversaries. I, forever searching for heroes—or was it fathers?—would plan my attack on Yale and its afterworld like Khan coming to America. Like the once young Hashim I would play by the hour under the broiling sun, mastering the four walls and their angles. I would command muscle, bone, and nerve; smashing, slicing, dropping the little black hardrubber ball where no opponent could reach it. I would master space and time through body and ball. I would win at this four-dimensional contest of territory and ricochet, this quick, calculating, gladiatorial game. What I learned under the summer sun would decide contests in the clubs where squash was played, fall and winter, in cool white wooden cubes.

But first, a practical matter. Which of the four McCalla laundry yards was closest to the measurements of a squash court? The pit by the garage, I discovered: just a foot wider and six inches longer than the courts I was used to. Furthermore, it was the only yard with no outside steps descending into it, and was reached through the laundry room, which had its own outside stairs. Gratified with the approximation of court dimensions, I inspected the walls with Luther's level. They bowed slightly outward, except for the one identical with the building wall, which was nearly true. All the surfaces were rough and grainy; would supply spin beyond that imparted by the racquet; would chew microscopically at the hardrubber ball; would sandpaper one's skin in careless collisions. So much the better.

The floor bevelled slightly toward the center, where an iron drain with small round holes was set to catch drippings from laundry. Most balls would play fractionally toward the middle, but none would be seriously bent in its plane. The doorway into the court was not flush, and presented the largest deviation from the norm. I chose the service area so that the door would be forward of any reception of service on the left wall. A simple iron-rung ladder as a fire escape dropped down from an iron bar platform outside Babs' bedroom on the second story, stopping seven feet above the cement floor of the yard. I conferred with Duffie, and we decided that anything hitting the fire escape would be called "let" and replayed. All other balls, even those caroming off the laundry room door, were to be played through. What if the ball hit the doorknob? It was so recessed, and close to the front wall, as to be almost impossible. The knob was more a hazard to a striker's racquet than to a running receiver's physique. Play the ball as it bounced, we decided.

"The only thing we've got to be careful of," Duffie said, "is that." He pointed to a hook for laundry line on the right wall—a three-inch protrusion near eye level. "Thank God they use mostly poles in here instead of hooks."

We set up galvanized tin at the front wall to signal low shots. Now all we needed were red lines on the walls and floor to define serving and receiving areas, and what was out of play. I explained to Black Rachel. "Is it OK if we chalk the lines on the court?"

"Court?" Black Rachel said. "You want to make my laundry yard a court?"

"It is already," I said, "and you're the queen. We just want to chalk some royal red lines on it."

Black Rachel shimmied, a brief mixture of true delight and mock ecstasy. "How you talk, Master Randy. So good talker I let you be chalker. You go ahead. But if my sheets gets red, it's got to come off."

The problem was not with the sheets, but the lines. Play swiftly smeared them. I went back to Black Rachel. "We have to paint the lines," I explained. She said she understood, "but for that, you got to see the Big Lady," by which she meant B-Ray, the matriarch, even though she knew as well as we that Martha decided such things now. Martha decided as we hoped.

Roofless, jerry-trimmed, non-orthogonal, and slightly dangerous, the laundry yard took on our steady play. The cement walls streaked with the black scudding of the ball. The balls themselves grew idiosyncratic with chewing by the walls. We loved the uniqueness of it: the only such court in the world.

Worthy, indeed, of an international tournament. The key invitation, of course, would go to Jack Costelloe, an immortal. Nearly sixty but strong and canny, he spoke with a brogue that suggested links with the source of the game. His teaching instructions were simple: "Square off to the ball" and "Use the strings like your hand." When a student couldn't master the idea of one's striking arm becoming two and a half feet longer than normal, and of rapid, skipping realignments of one's feet in shifting perpendiculars to the side walls, he would say, "Hit it as I do." Then smartly illustrate—crouched, clean snap of the wrist whistling the ball down the alley along the wall.

"Devil's Ping-Pong, I calls it." Costelloe's only irony: he would hold up the ball before the eyes of a beginner and say: "It's black, it's hard, and it hurts." Then he would demonstrate wordlessly how to whip the ball cross court, drop it, volley it, so as to gain central position; how to get maximum tactical vantage for striking, yet avoid being struck by ball or racquet; how to move one's opponent into running forward and back, side to side, until an opening could be won, a point seized. "See?" he would ask, his heavy white eyebrows quizzical, his thick white hair glossed into place, untossed by the action.

Duffie and I had learned the game from Costelloe. Now we formally approached him to represent the international element in our tournament: a four-person invitational— Costelloe, Duffie, and I, and, to round out the draw, Buddy Quick. A natural athlete, he had picked up the game with members during a period of employment as masseur and locker room man at the Lawn. Giving away a forty-year age handicap, Costelloe could still beat me on the courts at the Lawn Club. But I secretly felt I had a chance to win in the laundry yard, especially if it were a drawn-out match, favoring young legs.

Costelloe asked, "What's the prize?"

"Fame," answered Duffie.

"I've already got it," he replied, straightfaced.

"We want a chance at it."

"OK," said Costelloe, still sober, but with a glint in his eye. "Have a try."

I prepared: long hours under the sun alone, working on

93

crisper, harder shots, building up stamina and accuracy for
the occasion, striking again and again for minimal targets,
seeking new and tougher angles in rapt absorption with the
ball, my target, my quarry. My own student, my own opponent, I sweated in sweet oblivion to all about me.

"What are you trying to prove?" Babs was leaning out
her windowsill.

I looked up. "I'm practicing to be the American Hashim
Khan." I grinned at her.

"Herschel Kahn?" she asked. It was the name of the
neighborhood tailor and dry cleaner. "We already got him.
Anyway Herschel *is* American. He *thinks* so, anyhow."

"No, not Herschel." My grin, I knew, was wide and
foolish. The game made me happy. "Hashim Khan. Hashim," I repeated. "Watch." I put myself through three
forehand rail shots, a cross court, three backhand rails, a
cross court; I repeated the forehand rails, hit a three-wall
forehand boast; repeated the backhand rails, and went for
a shot I was working on, backhand three-wall boast. I
missed, and hit the tin.

"Does that noise mean you finally won?"

"No. It's not like pinball. It means I lose."

"You know you're making black marks all over the walls.
And you're sweating," she said. She disappeared. I went
back to my routine.

Her voice from the window interrupted. "There's something on the fire escape when you want it." Outside her
window, on the narrow grilled landing, was a small glass
pitcher of iced tea and a paper cup. "Just heave yourself up
when you're thirsty." Her head disappeared inside the room.

I went on to running exercises, corner to corner, zig-zag-
ging, bending to touch each floor-wall joint with thumb
and forefinger, forcing my knees down further into a simian
crouch, springing up and racing to the next corner. When
I had finished a hundred cycles and felt worthy of Hashim
Khan, I eyed the tea. I reached for the lowest rung, just
overhead, and the next above it. Rust bit off, rolled in my
hands and crackled into my face. I shut my eyes, arched
my bottom backward, brought up my knees, sought leverage

94

against the wall with my feet. Steady; open eyes: then, walk the wall, pulling hand over hand up the rungs until a first foothold on the rungs, my toes just fitting in against the wall. When I reached the top, I turned butt inward, slid sideways, and sat on the narrow grill outside the window, parallel the pitcher.

I brushed the rust flakes from my hair. On my forehead they clung to the sweat. A hell of a climb for iced tea. Poured and drank three cups, emptying the pitcher. During the last I looked into the court below, imagining the final, facing Costelloe. How could I use the strangeness of the court to best advantage? Hit deep and wide and close to the wall: the extra width would cost Jack time to adjust, and on the rough surface he might be reluctant to scrape his racquet. On dropshots, hit extra tight and short: they would fall off fast toward the center because of the drainage angle. Satisfied, I turned my head idly and looked into the room behind me.

There was nothing there. I was accustomed to crucifixes in servants' rooms, and polychrome pictures of the saints, and curling family photos stuck in spotted mirrors. This cell startled me. Small bed with brass rail headboard and footboard; bureau; warped white pine chair, liver-spotted as an aged woman. Who lived here? Wasn't this Babs' room? Wasn't it here we had played as children? All I could remember was that Elise had found us here in a forbidden game. I remembered no details, only the scare of being discovered.

I curbed an impulse to swivel myself into the room; instead, let myself down the iron rungs, back into the court. A ringing and cluttering of rust flakes followed me. I found Babs in the laundry room, hanging up a private wash.

"Thanks a lot for the tea."

"You're welcome. You looked hot."

My eyes fell on white lingerie and I was moved to another question.

"That's your room up there, isn't it?"

She looked at me. "Sure it's my room. What do you think it is, the Mellon National Bank?"

Our draw put Costelloe against Duffie in the first round and me against Buddy. The pro arrived as usual in cream-colored long trousers and brown and white saddle shoes. He walked the perimeter of the court, counting paces and wriggling his eyebrows. Humming, he measured the height of the tin on the front wall against his racquet. As he warmed up with Duffie, his hair kept its tonic set, while Jimmy's glasses, as usual, slipped down his nose. Costelloe won three straight games, but Duff got a few more points in each than he normally did at the Lawn.

Buddy entered the court against me bare-chested. Wearing the loose shorts he used when giving massage, he gripped and swished the racquet like a Samurai sword. Sharpness of eye and sheer physique kept him in the match. Babs watched from the ledge at the top of the fire escape, barefoot, heels kicking lightly against the wall. Down two games, Buddy towelled off his face and chest, looked up at her, and jerked his thumb at me.

"Wave your legs a little and see if you can get this guy's mind off his game."

She laughed, extended a leg, and pointed her toe. "Kill him, Buddy."

But I took him swiftly in three games, wanting to waste no points in getting at Costelloe. Buddy shook his head, smiling, towelling off at the end, his huge lungs heaving. "Now let's wrestle," he said to me and flexed his bicep, muscleman style. "I concede," I said. We looked up at Babs, who applauded us again, her wet, bare-chested father, and me in my St. Luke's whites.

The final was early the next afternoon. Duffie beat Buddy, three games to one, for third place, and then climbed the rusty ladder to sit as referee on the fire escape landing, Babs beside him. The sun was beaming directly into the court, but Costelloe still wore long linen trousers. I stretched my hamstrings in a ballet exercise Babs had shown me, then sizzled some rail shots in warmup.

"Don't wear yourself out, laddy."

"Ready for some sport, Jack?"

I won the spin of the racquet and served. I attacked Costelloe with all that I knew of squash, and all the force I had. I took the first game 15–9 and kept the pressure on. Costelloe, eyebrows knit, white hair unruffled, did not change pace in the second game but lofted the ball again and again to the rear of the court, stretching out the points, returning safely most of what I hit, anticipating my cross courts and drops, patiently forcing me into back court position and eventual errors. He won the second game 15–13. I sipped from a cup of water and checked an abraded knee where I had slipped going for a surprise three-wall nick. Duffie, who kept an eye on his watch for length of break, called us back to play.

I tried to adjust to Costelloe's defenses and wear him out. I set myself for long rallies, played the percentages, waited for openings. But whatever home court advantage I'd had was evaporating. Costelloe, controlling the center, snapped out his shots and nipped off my returns. I fought for position, used my power and speed, waited for chances to pass or drop him. I ran a lead to 13–11. Then, looking for winners, I hurried two points and lost on errors instead. Deuced at thirteen-all, I called for a five-point set to determine the game. I took the first point on a backhand volley that nicked the left back wall at the floor. Next my hard overhand serve squirted out dead from the rear wall for an ace. Two-love in a set of five.

I turned on my hard serve again. This time Jack lightly volleyed it and took us into a long exchange, one that Duffie later said was at least fifty shots. I tried to break it open with a drop to the right front. Jack reached it late; lunging, hit it hard to the right side wall, to front wall, to left side, where on the building wall the ball struck the doorknob to the laundry room and caromed over my racquet. The first time it ever happened. Jack looked to Duffie for a ruling. "Point, Mr. Costelloe. Mr. McCalla leads two-one, set five, Mr. Costelloe serving."

Costelloe whacked his first overhand serve of the match. I scraped it off the left wall in a weak volley. Then he rifled a deep right rail, which I just reached and returned. He laid down a drop to the right front. I dived, saved it with a drop left. He sent up a high floating lob, deep to the right rear corner, whiffling in a cross breeze like a shuttlecock. As I scrambled backward, instinct told me of its dying trajectory, and half-turning, I leaped along the wall, right arm high, to cut it off with a blind volley. I missed. As I fell, chest toward the wall, an unseen opponent hit me in the right temple, raked open my face, and knocked me down on the cement.

When my eyes opened, Duffie and Jack were bending over me. Babs' voice let me understand it was her lap in which my head lay, her hands applying the towel to the right side of my face. She was telling Duffie where to get ice to wrap in the towel. I felt pain from temple to cheekbone and the beginning of a throb.

"So you wanted to hang yourself like laundry?" she said. There was no edge in her voice, but a nursing tenderness I had not heard before. Her left hand rubbed my left shoulder in idle, soothing patterns. Her right pressed the ice cubes in the towel against the wound.

I tried to scan the wall for the hook, which I now remembered, but Babs' left hand restrained me. "Settle down. You're done for the day," she said.

"No, I'm not. I've got time by the rules."

"Don't worry, boy," said Jack. "We'll play another time." His voice came through as dreamy and avuncular; concerned, but not definitive.

"No, it's a tournament," I said. "What are the rules, Duffie? You're the referee."

"If you think you can play, Randy, you've got one hour to recover from injury. The score is fifteen-all in the third game, with eighteen points deciding, and games are one-all. By the rules you default in an hour if you can't play. I'm telling you that as referee. But as your friend, I'd say default right now and go see Dr. Hunnewell and get that thing stitched up."

"I'll play," I said. "We'll cool it off and tape a bandage on, and I'll play."

Duffie looked fretful. Jack walked the court, tapping his racquet lightly against the cement as if admonishing it. I couldn't see Babs as she spoke: "We don't need a doctor. Let's just clean it out and get some iodine on it."

The men guided me to a chair in the laundry room while she went for gauze, tape, and iodine. When she came back, Duffie and Jack were talking of famous tournament precedents of suspension of play for injury. I tilted back in the chair, my eyes closed. I opened them when Babs cleansed the wound, and when she put on the iodine. She said nothing as she folded gauze, tore the adhesive tape, fitted it on the gauze, ran it from temple to cheekbone. She had wrapped a clean towel around more ice, and gave it to me to hold to my head.

"There," she said.

While she leaned over me, working at the wound, I watched her bare arm, the pulse in her neck, the bloom of her breasts under her peasant blouse. I grew conscious of her scent: like a garden in the sun. Without raising my head I could just see her chin and mouth as she worked over me. Her lips were parted. On a white incisor I saw a flake of green. Babs, the mint-chewer.

Now she stood back, looking at her handiwork. Her gaze shifted slightly from my temple to my eyes. We looked at each other. Her eyes were soft brown, with flecks of gold. There in the cool of the laundry room, I inhaled and beheld her. Beyond her on a shelf stood six boxes of Mrs. Stewart's Bluing, and around them rose the astringent smell of old detergent, the suggestion of years of unseen mold. My forehead stung and throbbed. Mint. I drew a breath, closed my eyes, and said nothing.

"You couldn't have won and shouldn't have played," Duffie said afterward.

"I wanted to," I said. "I thought I could win in five games. What were the scores?"

"Costelloe," Duffie intoned, "9–15, 15–13, 18–16, 15–7."

We were sitting now in a shady corner of the court in the late afternoon sun, sipping iced tea.

"You're getting better, boy," Jack said. "But you couldn't

have beaten me, even if you kept your head off that nail. Still, you're getting better at keeping the point going. Patience is everything, this game. The devil's Ping-Pong, I say. You have to keep returning the ball. Ping it up, pong it back, move your man around. Hit it where he ain't. Don't be in a hurry to win. Help the other fellow find out how to lose." He finished his tea with a sigh. "Well, have to go." He rose, the faint sweat stains in his long-sleeved shirt already dry. Speech was rare for him, but now, in the flush of it, he would tell a secret. "I knew I could win when I measured the court. One pace wider than the American, and your tin is a little finger higher. So you gave me a British court to play in. I liked it—longer points, harder to put the ball away, harder for your power to kill it."

Duffie and I thanked Costelloe on behalf of the Tournament Committee and waved him out the laundry room door and upstairs. When we went back to gather towels and racquets, Babs was sitting in the court on one of the laundry room chairs.

"I didn't realize that, what he said about the British court," I said to Duffie.

"I knew it," he said. "But it didn't help me against *him*."

"How did you forget about the hook?" Babs said.

"In the middle of a point? How could I remember it?" I said. "Jesus Jerusalem! I can't be aware of everything at once."

"Right. Naturally," she said. "There's a lot you're not aware of. And there's plenty you don't know," she added. Quite pleasantly, I thought.

ten.

WHAT MOVED Aunt Martha, who ordinarily intuited disaster well enough to avoid it, to organize a family party on the Fourth of July 1954? Perhaps Crispin was right—she was still uncomfortable with the party Babs had organized for Buddy's birthday, when the cows came down from Granny Duffie's. Whether or not Martha's July 4th was meant to wipe out memory of the previous Hallowe'en, it certainly overshadowed Babs' party, but not in ways anyone could have intended.

Fireworks were illegal in Pennsylvania, "so the people will have to be the fireworks," Martha said. She invited all to perform acts or present arts. Big Rachel would watch in her wheelchair from the roof of the porte cochere, which served as a porch outside her bedroom window.

We gathered by the flagpole before dusk, family and servants, and Adelaide led a singing of "The Star-Spangled Banner." A caterer provided baskets full of fried chicken, cole slaw in confettied heaps, and liveried men as waiters, so that McCalla servants might be free to mingle with McCalla family, and eat and drink as they pleased. The servants sat together anyway, except for Buddy, who mixed easily by pouring wine. He served the ladies first; then made his way to Clellan, in his starched high collar, cheeks more flushed than customary; and to Duncan, distracted but resolutely patriotic, who swigged while others sipped.

Martha talked to me while we kept our balance on folding chairs, eating chicken with our fingers. Paper napkins blew down, dappled the dark grass in the early evening. Madison romped through the party, getting patted, tangling underfoot. Would he choke on a chicken bone?

"We've *always* had an Irish setter," Martha said. "Four of them now since we moved into the Big House. It wasn't a well-known breed back then, but it suited us McCallas. Now that it's growing more popular, they will probably spoil it by breeding for apartment dwellers, and show people. Look at the Dobermans, all skitter, twitch, and fang. But the Irish setter is so *reliable*. . . . Madison, stop that, someone get him out of the trash. . . . There . . . I remember Jefferson, the one we had in the Depression, how he used to roam. I got a call one night from someone in Homestead, saying I have your dog here. That's five miles away. I said just let him go, he'll come home. And he did. But we can't let them run like that anymore. Too many autos now.

"Luther is showing his whittling, did you know? It's on the display table over there, next to Elise's preserves. Buddy and Barbara will do their acts. This egg salad is atrocious. I remember Washington, our first setter, came home with a dozen eggs once. All wrapped up in a scarf. He just picked it up from a doorstep somewhere and carried it away, gentle as you please. Brought it home, not one egg broken, and laid it down for Cook. I wanted quiche lorraine, but Mother didn't like the idea of us eating stolen eggs, so she gave them to the garage. Irish setters can be a little spooky, you know.

"Adams was even more that way. He brought home a baby's quilt once. He fancied something about the aroma, I suppose. I'll wager he simply nosed his way to a carriage and lifted it off the baby without disturbing its sleep.

"We often said the men in our family worked like dogs. Father did till the day he died. But such *graceful* dogs, I must say. Father could lift companies away from men just like Adams and the baby quilt. Such a silky setter, my father! Steal up on a man, take his blanket away, and he wouldn't know it was gone.

"What's the matter with Clellan tonight? He hasn't said a word. Not that he ever does, dear fellow. When we have the fireworks and the circus acts, I'll send him up to Mother on her porch so she'll understand what's going on. Clellan, will you do that? Oh, mercy, he's not listening.

"Adelaide, my dear, is the investment news not good? It does seem to me that Duncan is rather avid in his thirst tonight. Where did that bourbon come from? Forgive me for speaking about it, darling, but if you need courage to curb his intake you know that I'll support you.

"Oh, it's time to begin. Buddy has lit the spotlights. Duncan, dear, wouldn't you like to touch off the roman candle? It's prohibited, you know, and you always hated Prohibition. Yes? . . . Just a long fireplace match, that's all you need. Otherwise you'll have no part in the action. Go on, dear, it will be fun."

My father, muttering, tried to stoop to touch off the candle, and everyone drew back. He tottered when he bent over, so Buddy put a chair beneath him. He sat, concentrated, leaned forward, and scratched a long match against the box. It snapped. He took another. It broke, too. He fumbled patiently for a third, held it close to the phosphorous tip, scratched it aflame, and dropped it with a curse, shaking his fingers. With his other hand he gestured for his glass, which Buddy provided.

In the silence my mother spoke in a clear, objective voice, as if continuing conversation with Martha. "Duncan is afraid of fire, and terrorized by little explosions. I prefer to think that he is trying to overcome his fear, rather than believe that he is just mechanically inept."

He struck again, ferociously, and this time the flame lit. He leaned over from his chair to set it to the fuse of the candle. He drew back twice, thinking it had caught, but it sputtered out each time. He leaned a third time but shook his hand with a cry, match flame reaching his fingers again.

"It's the same thing when we go skeet shooting," my mother said. Her voice was light, controlled. "Duncan will aim well enough, but when he pulls the trigger he closes his eyes and jerks away and misses. Overanticipation, don't you think? The recoil isn't anything at all, really, if you just relax and let it take you in the shoulder."

Buddy offered to fill Duncan's glass, and Duncan, gratefully accepting, squinted at the ice as he swirled it about. Buddy lit the fuse. It burnt through. The candle fired an orange trail up into the purple velvet sky, and we murmured, "Ooh!" At the top of its arc the rocket guffawed into pink, green, and white spinning sparkles. We sighed "Ah!" It spun down, burned out.

Next, Buddy announced, a high wire walk over the laundry yard of the garage. See Babs cross the great empty pit, defying danger, with *no net below*. Buzzing appreciation, the two dozen of us strolled out of the green circle down the garage driveway to stand around the laundry yard wall. Babs mounted the wall, wearing a light blue circus tutu. Bareshouldered, slight, compact, she held a long balance pole across her hips. My stomach revolved in a slow flip of love and fear. "Miss *Bar*bara *Quick!*" Buddy declaimed from the pit below, and we applauded.

Elise appeared at Babs' bedroom window and turned on her gramophone: "The Daring Young Man on the Flying Trapeze." To the incongruous swing, the undulating song, Babs slid out on the wire. Brightly smiling, staring into the light at the far end, she began her traverse. A series of sliding steps brought her to the middle. She paused, wavered, slipped. Martha shrieked above our gasp. Babs' left foot went down as through a hole in the ceiling. Her right knee bent double. The flounce of her tutu nearly touched the wire. Pole steady, she rose slowly off her right haunch and withdrew her left leg from the void. Eyes unwavering, smile fixed, she resumed her slide across the wire. When she stepped onto the wall, we gave a small roar and applauded. Buddy, who had followed along in the yard below, again cried, "*Bar*bara *Quick!*" Threw up his hand to show her off, starting a new burst of applause to which Babs curtsied.

Babs took over: "Thank you, ladies and gentlemen. Now here's your chance to see the world-famous Strong Man, the rock-ribbed Buddy Quick. Have you ever watched a human being break an automobile chain around his chest? Just by deep breathing and muscular strength? Then proceed to the flagpole for a display of pectoral power by your own favorite strong man, *Buddy Quick!*"

104

"You were good," I said to her. We walked together, trailing the crowd. "Were you afraid?"

"That dip? I practice that. The pole is long enough so I could jam one end on top of the wall, or even in my window, and let the other fall on the wire to hold me. Anyway, Buddy was down there to break a fall."

I didn't want to say I was afraid, because she always treated fear with scorn. Safer, with Babs, to be factual. "How does Buddy break a chain around his chest?"

"It's sawed through in one link and reconnected with putty. All he's got to do is take a deep breath and crack the stuff. But it isn't easy. It hurts your ribs."

We were back in the circle now. "Are you ready for our trick after this?" she asked.

"Yes," I said.

While Babs palavered, Buddy stripped to the waist and got himself into a harness of chain. Babs pulled it tight, binding his arms to his sides, while he winced and groaned and shook his head. She waved a padlock in the air, attached it, turned a key in its lock, and gave the key to Clellan, who accepted it with a limp hand. More palaver. Buddy inhaled three times, then another time as fully as possible. Moaned, shook his head. Four more deep breaths. Flexed his bound arms, clenched his fists. Pop. A link broke. We clapped. Smiling, Buddy wriggled out of the chain, waved it around his head three times to sustained applause, and gave a salute to Big Rachel, up on her porch. Clellan was coughing rapidly. When Martha asked if he was all right, his coughs slowed down, and he wheezed between them.

The climax, Buddy announced, was a joint performance of the Quick and McCalla families, dedicated to Mrs. McCalla, Senior, whom everybody called Big Rachel and everybody loved, sitting up there on the roof. And he hoped Marie up there beside Mrs. McCalla, Senior, was telling her all about this. In mid-circle on a tumblers' mat, Buddy took a standing position with legs apart and hands cupped at his hip. My turn. I ran forward, slipped a foot in the palm stirrup at Buddy's hip, was hoisted up, lit my other foot on Buddy's shoulder, and pivoted with the aid of Bud-

dy's now upraised hands, which were steadying my own.
I raised myself slowly erect on his shoulders. On top, I
heard the proud murmurs of my family, and Clellan going
into another coughing fit, and gagging. Babs ran out. Using
Buddy's hip and hand, then mine, she monkey-swung her
way up onto my shoulders. Using my hands upraised to
hers for balance, she slowly straightened herself while Buddy strained and shifted beneath us to keep the human column erect. When his footing was secure, I felt Babs throw
out her arms in a display of triumph. Loud applause. Cries
of bravo! Anguished coughing from Clellan. As we three
stood high in the glaring railroad lanterns, Babs, as we'd
planned, drew out of her bosom a large American flag
handkerchief, which she waved right and left to renewed
applause. Clellan made a loud gasp. I saw him topple
sideways from his chair, hit an adjacent table, knock over
two wine bottles, and fell a small maid whose eyes had been
on the flag.

My feet on Buddy's shoulders, Babs' on mine. I couldn't
move. Several in the crowd rushed to see the trouble, while
others continued applauding our act, the flag, Babs' dazzling
smile. I saw Clellan roll over on his back. Red wine, rolling
off the table from toppled bottles, poured onto his upturned
face and stiff collar and white shirt. The little maid on her
knees beside him screamed.

Our tower finally threw itself forward—Babs first down,
leaping and dancing for further applause. As I hit the mat,
Buddy threw his arms wide as if to catch the last clapping
in a great basket. I ran straight into the babble around Clellan. Luther had his head up and Elise was wiping it off.
His neck was lolling. Martha cried an order to no one in
particular: "Call a doctor, call an ambulance!"

Buddy burst through the group and went for Clellan. He
took a look at him, put his ear to his mouth, his hand inside
his vest. He slapped Clellan's face, forehand and backhand,
two loud cracks. No response. He picked Clellan up, carried
him to our mat, laid him down, climbed on top of him, put
his mouth on his boss's mouth, began heaving breath

rhythmically into him. Above the miserable cackle of the crowd rose another faint cry, this time from the porte cochere.

Buddy sat back, wiped the sweat from his eyebrows, looked at Clellan. His fingers shot to the wine-stained starched collar, loosened the tie, pried at the gold collar button. He snapped a fingernail, cursed, yanked, ripped the collar open. With one hand he pulled Clellan upward toward him, head dangling, and with the other tried to remove his suit jacket. Babs and I each took an arm, worked the sleeves down, the jacket off. Again Buddy set his mouth on Clellan's and bellowed great breaths into the sunken breast. Babs and I looked at each other across her laboring father, my inert great-uncle. I saw tears on her lower lashes, the first tears in her I could remember. She turned her head away.

From Big Rachel's porch floated down another unintelligible cry. I thought it sounded like an owl hooting, but Crispin, who had just arrived, later said it was *"Mutter"* and *"Mutter Gottes."* He looked at Buddy, humping and pumping at the man on the ground in the burgundied shirt and paper-white face. We milled about for minutes before Marie with her cane reached the flagpole circle, the lantern light, and the jabbering crowd. She didn't even look at Clellan and Buddy, but cried in German to Crispin and pointed to the porte cochere, her jaw wobbling with effort to be heard above the crowd and the distant whine of the ambulance siren.

Crispin spoke rapidly to Martha and Babs and began striding toward the Big House, Marie hobbling after. The siren arrived, dwindling to a low growl. Flashing red rooflight poured among us, and the white-bodied metal can coasted off the asphalt up onto the grass. Servants scattered. Crispin turned, called my name, pointed to the stretcher bearers coming from the ambulance.

Buddy, on hands and knees, looked into the vacant face of his boss as the bearers took him away. Still on all fours, he padded off the mat onto the grass like a sleepy bear.

When he reached a pink hydrangea bush, he heaved and gagged, his white hair bobbing under the blossomheads. He sobbed between spasms.

At the sound of Buddy's retching, Duncan rose from his folding chair, trotted on small feet to a taller white hydrangea several feet away, and vomited quietly into it.

Two days later, Babs invited me to the garage for tea. I entered her room for the first time since grade school. A pot of chives sat on the inner sill of the window. She came in with a tray of kitchenware, put it down on her bed, and drew up two chairs facing each other. She took nail scissors from the top of her bureau, selected a tuft of chives between her left thumb and forefinger, bent them backward, and snipped them off. Then she stood over the slices of bread on the tray, slid her thumb up so that the chive ends splayed out, snipped again, and scattered cuttings on the buttered bread.

I munched a slice. "Good," I said. "Did you learn that from your mother?"

"No, I made it up myself." She munched, too, and poured us tea. "Did you hear Marie?"

"Night before last? I remember thinking, why is an owl hooting in the middle of this?"

"When Marie's messed up she speaks German."

"Anyway, Crispin understands her."

"Big Rachel couldn't talk. Her eyes were open but she couldn't make a sound. Then her head sort of toppled a little, and I thought, 'There she goes, just like Clellan.' Marie kept saying, 'Mooter, Mooter,' and I ran back. One of the ambulance guys had Clellan with a mask over his face. 'His mother is sick.' I said. 'She can't talk.' 'His mother!' the guy said like I was crazy, and how could anybody so old and probably dead have a mother. 'She can't talk!' I yelled at him. 'Something's the matter!' 'Try some hot coffee on her,' he said. I looked for Buddy, but he was sitting with his back against a tree, and there was your dad with his face in the bushes, and I thought, Where the hell is Randy?"

"I was talking with the stretcher bearer. I wanted to ride

with Uncle Clellan, but rules were rules, he said. I said, 'Wait, I've got to get a car,' and he said, very nice and soft, 'That's OK. Don't rush.' That's when I knew. But I got Uncle Clellan's car anyway, and drove out to follow the ambulance, and there was Crispin again."

"Yeah. He was telling the whitecoats, 'My grandmother has had a stroke.' He said, 'She's on the roof of the porte-cochere.' And the driver said, 'Your grandmother is on the roof?' like they got a call about a guy who couldn't breathe, and they were ready to drive him away, and who's this other nut raving about his grandmother on the roof."

"Yes, but Crispin started giving orders. 'Drive my uncle under the porte cochere and wait. We will bring my grandmother down. You will drive them both immediately to the hospital.' "

"Funny word, porte cochere."

We sat there, she and I, on the wall of the laundry yard in the late afternoon sun, remembering.

"You were pretty good," she said.

I wasn't sure what she meant.

"In our act. The three of us. I said to Buddy I didn't think you'd like it, but he said sure, and you'd be good at it. And you were. For a beginner."

"You can't stand three people on top of each other without someone in the middle."

"You were pretty steady. I felt OK up there."

"Buddy was like Gibraltar."

"He's a rock. But after that he puked and cried all night long."

"He tried to save Uncle Clellan's life."

"Nobody could. Massive heart attack, they said."

"We didn't know then. Buddy tried to bring him back." If I'd kept my next thought to myself, maybe my voice would not have faltered. "Clellan never talked about himself. I wish I'd known him better."

Babs was quiet, staring at the rhododendrons around the laundry yard. When she answered, it was only to part of what I'd said. "Yeah. He gave it a good try."

I didn't want to ask what she was thinking. She gave the

lash to those who crossed her line of privacy. So I asked, "What's Buddy going to do now?"

"I don't know." She spoke mildly. "He's not most people's idea of a butler. And he's much too old for the Navy. The guys he was in with are retired now. *Retired,*" she repeated, with scorn.

"What about the circus?"

"He loves it. But he was never that good—a third-string catcher. Can you see him on a trapeze at his age? What could he do in a circus? Clown? They want them young, to train them. You can't train an old clown."

"Around here then?"

"Around Pittsburgh? Too bad he's not a physical therapist, or a masseur even. Big Rachel is going to need someone like that. Maybe the Lawn Club needs a locker room man. With tips, that's better than lots of things."

"Yes," I said, wondering what lots-of-things included; wondering what was in store for her. I knew that once Bekka let Buddy go, the council of elders would not see a place for Babs. Aunt Martha would pine a bit for her, but Bekka and Grandma and Adelaide would tell her that she had Marie as a personal servant, and that was enough.

Finally I asked, "Where will you go?"

"I don't know. Maybe with Buddy. Maybe by myself. It depends."

I saw in my mind's eye my family again and our retinue of servants, around the porte cochere and on the stairs, in formal dress, the drunk and the sober, the tearful and the stoic, staring at the small peaks of blanket at the ends of stretchers where two pairs of the famous McCalla small feet lay toes upward, side by side, discreetly separate; devoted son and doting mother, he dead, she paralyzed. Still I felt a greater loss impending; and guilt at feeling it greater.

"What will you do?" I asked.

"I don't know."

Our conversations in the days that followed seemed like one long talk, extended, suspended, resumed, repeated. We met when Babs took time off from light duties for Martha, as I returned from squash lessons with Costelloe. We sat on the wall of the laundry yard, dangling our feet as if over the ocean. And we talked.

The last day before I headed off for Yale, my pocket was heavy with meaning, my heart strange with hope. I walked back from the Lawn with racquet stuffed in a knapsack, its handle projecting over my head, fancying that from a distance I looked like a biped unicorn. I came up through Clellan's gate, the weedy, unkempt part of the estate, its outer stones hot with sun retained, inner stairs cool from hours of shadow. At the top I turned toward the empty lot, entered the field and its stillness of bordering willows. She would be sitting on a low limb of the biggest tree, hidden by the yellow-green leaf-vines drooping around her. Faint breeze rippled willow fronds, random as sunlight on water. A buzzing: along the ragged edge of the lot, goldenrod toppling with blossom. On each flower a swarm of bumblebees clambered in abandon, swivelling bellies over yellow budlets, grappling for concupiscent footholds, pumping in clusters of saffron dust. From my ankles to my knees, as I walked the outer rim, stems bobbed with bees, stamens hummed with them, in slow pulses of submission.

"Hi."

"Hi." I spread the willow fronds and entered her tent. She parted her hair and straightened it right and left on her shoulders. I unbuckled my knapsack and laid it by the tree.

I sat beside her on the low limb. There we stayed a long time looking at the undersides of leaves, and sweet stutters of sunlight within our chamber.

"I have a present for you." I managed to say it. I could feel her surprise.

"It's a very little thing. It doesn't mean much. But I've never given a present like this, and I don't know anyone who has one."

She turned her head to me, still silent.

"It's from my great-grandfather. From the coins he collected when he was a boy. Minted the year he was born. It's like new. You've never seen one before." I drew it out of the white handkerchief in which I had carried it in my pocket. "You could put a string through it to wear around your neck," I explained, "if you wanted to."

111

She turned it over in her fingers: she placed it on the nail of her middle finger, which it barely covered. She held it up in a pencil of sun to block out the light; she turned it between thumb and forefinger.

"It's a three-cent piece," I went on. "Dated 1854. It's a hundred years old, and like new, except for the little hole drilled above the head of Seated Liberty. That's so it could be used as jewelry. That's the way it came to me through my grandfather."

"What's this?" She pointed to the obverse side.

"That's a Roman numeral three inside a large 'C.' It means three cents, that's all. They only made them for a few years, and then they stopped. It's rare."

She looked at it over and over, one side, the other.

Then she spoke, her eyes away from me, looking outward, as if through the willow fronds upon the compound. "Are you sure," she said, "you wanna give this to somebody who's half-Mick, half-Polack?"

I felt a small buzz of alarm and irritation. We didn't discuss that stuff. "Sure, I meant it. I wouldn't offer it otherwise."

"I mean," she said, "it's your great-granddaddy's three-cent piece, same year as he was born and all that. It's probably *valuable*." Her eyes widened at the last word.

"Well, it isn't terribly valuable numismatically . . . as a coin for collectors, I mean . . . even though it looks new. That little hole drilled there, that kills it for collectors. Maybe you don't want it, even. Because it's not valuable. I mean, if you don't, just say so. It's nothing like the cameo that Uncle Clellan gave you. I won't be hurt if you say no. I just wanted you to have it, that's all." She wasn't speaking, and I felt that more had to be said about the coin. "When it's perfectly new, like that, except for the hole, of course, it's called mint."

Seated there on the low willow limb, feet just off the ground, Babs looked at me with eyes wide and lips just parted, in an attitude of insouciant innocence from which, I knew well, she could move swiftly to enthusiasm or to sarcasm, or retreat to silence.

"I want it," she said.

"Good, I'm glad." I must have smiled a vapid smile. I was enormously relieved. "I have some fishing line if you want to wear it."

She nodded.

I slipped the fine silk line through the hole in the coin. She made no effort to take it, so I gestured as if to put it around her neck. She nodded again and bowed and pulled her long hair forward over her head. I drew the string together in a simple knot at her topmost visible vertebra, noting the faint golden hairs that swam like minnows up her spine. I ached to touch her.

"There," I said. "It's silver."

"Thanks."

I didn't know what else to say, so I blurted the next thought that came to mind.

"It's still legal tender."

She turned her face toward me, her mouth slightly open. I saw her tongue move between her teeth as if she were rehearsing and savoring her thought before she spoke: "Legal, I don't care about."

I laughed, a little louder than I meant to, and turned my face up to the willow ceiling above us. I let my eyes rove the leaves, as if they were a sacred rotunda patterned with meaning. After a long time I uttered one more thought, my heart pounding, my throat tight, so that it came out almost a whisper.

"I'll miss you."

Her voice was level, unhesitant.

"I'll miss you, too."

We sat a while longer on the big willow branch.

"It's near suppertime," she said. "I've gotta go in."

"OK, me, too."

We slipped off the branch. She lifted my necklace over her head and gathered the coin in her fist. I picked up my knapsack. We parted the willow-bead door of our room and stepped out into the pale sun. "Good luck," I said; and she answered, "Good luck." We walked different ways, she for Bekka's kitchen, I for Gramma's dining room.

We did not see each other for four years.

III.

Death and Love

1958

eleven.

IN MY senior year at Yale, while my father was dying, I was writing about John Knox. I couldn't save my father. Nobody even told me he was dying. But I might have drawn my own conclusions from the rate of his drinking at Christmas, and his taking to his bedroom in January. They say after that he didn't leave the compound once.

Meanwhile I plugged away in New Haven, in the scholar-of-the-house program, with a senior thesis on "The First Presbyterian Revolutionary." When I was done, I knew more than anyone else I knew knew about Knox. The reason was that nobody else cared, except Crispin, to a degree.

Why did I care? What need had I for the founder of my sect of Christianity? I accuse myself: why wasn't I home caring for my father? I answer: I couldn't have done anything for my father, even had he wanted anything done, which he did not. He and I implicitly agreed that getting an education was the most important thing for me, and I secretly felt that my graduating from Yale in a timely way would somehow atone for Duncan's failing in days when almost no one flunked out of Yale.

When I face it, I admit that I did not love my father as much as I should have. How much was that? More than I did anyway. How much could I have loved him? Infinitely more. Oh, sure, I answer myself, but you are not a saint, and your capacities are strictly finite, and maybe your ability to love is meagre, whatever the reasons. *Meagre*. There's a self-judgment that freezes me in my footprints.

In defense, let me say that my father did not encourage

117

expressions of love. He was not, my mother once said, "the demonstrative sort." When my grandfather died, we all tip-toed around the house for weeks, less out of concern for my grandmother than for her son, my father, who wept a lot in his bedroom. That's what pulled the remark out of my mother: he was ordinarily not that sort, but now he was crying his eyeballs out for my grandfather and I must be respectful of his grief and not disturb him.

Mysterious, but convincing. I respected his grief. I think I respected all my father's feelings that he ever declared, or I could guess at. But that is not loving, to come back to the problem.

My complaint—I have criticized myself enough to earn the right to one complaint—is that he did not father me. Oh, I am from his seed, surely. But I looked for the principles of maleness in him, and found opacity, angularity, mannered reserve instead. What is it to be a man? I began asking that early, and continue asking it.

If I didn't know what a father was, I had a good idea from Crispin of what an uncle could be. Yet he was a hare-lipped bachelor aesthete, to be stereotypic about it. I know that's like calling FDR a paraplegic politician: it misses the being, to say the least. But I could not model myself on Crispin, not in manliness anyway, any more than I could on Duncan.

I realize that John Knox was a strange person to turn to. In him I was seeking what I called "the male principle," somewhere, somehow revealed. All those books in my great-grandfather's library suggested that our family patriarchal tradition traced itself to him. As I pursued that path, I gave it a scholarly cover—"looking for the sources and effects of Scottish Calvinism." That sounded OK at Yale cocktail parties.

What did I find? A kiltish brutal country, mud-poor, shit-rude. Clan marauders invade homes of enemies, kick to death babes in the bellies of their mothers. Protopresbyters slay the British cardinal in Scotland, in revenge for one of their own, then piss in the dead man's mouth. How did we

118

McCallas dare scorn Sicily, as we did at the family dinner table?

In this darkness, I found Knox. From Exodus and the Book of Kings he taught a duty to fight for the right against papal and royal authority. It cheered me to know the source of my father's slogan: "Neither bishop nor king, Randy boy!" Through those breached doors have rushed the Jacobins and Bolsheviks, later imams, assorted seers. The Grand Acquisitors of industry and trade drew their own conclusions. Grow rich. Save all you can, and lay up a treasure in heaven. Onstage comes Andrew Carnegie, defying Calvin, denying predestination, and offering the world a gospel of his own: work and philanthropy.

My faculty readers were not impressed. Nor did they impress me in turn with their criticisms. Back home, Dr. McCracken was too busy contending with declining membership to read the paper as he had promised. I, raised in the texts, was forgotten by my lector. Presbyterianism, in its final illness, will copulate with television.

Crispin, however, gave me the gift of appreciation. He asked to read the thesis and sent it back without marginal cavil. This letter accompanied it:

My dear Randy,

I think this is a most engaging piece of writing and you are certainly the most promising lad in this clan since my mother produced me by Père Desjardins. No matter that there are no others to compare you with in your generation; I mean what I say as an absolute statement, and an encouragement. Given the mind and style you show here, I think that you have probably selected well in choosing to go on to law school (though Yale may be a bit too sociological, from what I hear, in its approach to the law).

I have no useful comment on what you have written, but I am certainly moved to some remarks on your subject, Johannes Cnoxus.

His deeds and words leave me with a terrible sense of Scottish parsimony. Such a pedantic imagination! I have rarely read anything sillier than your quotations from his "First Blast of the Trumpet Against the Monstrous Regiment of Women." I find myself sympathizing both with Elizabeth I and Mary Queen of Scots, against Knox.

Other than politics, whatever he touches seems to shrivel. Poetry and art are absent. Even his theology is small. I am tempted to comment on the Semitic ferocity of his idea of God. Maybe it comes from all that clan warfare in Scotland, and the raiding parties by and against the English. Rather like Old Testament life.

You have a strong point, of course, when you say that his brand of thinking inspired both political and economic visionaries. His became the political religion of an intellectual vanguard and the social religion of the industrial adventurers. Pittsburgh, of course, has none of the former, but plenty of the latter. I suspect further study would reveal more connections between Knox and the gospel of our own Scots, the great Andrews, Carnegie and Mellon, with their stewardship of wealth. Despite their distance from the church, I think of them as crypto-Presbyters. I believe they gave to charity as a sign of being the elect, touched by grace. They bought and issued their own tickets to heaven, so to speak. But don't quote me! I have given my trustees enough to think about as it is.

I once knew an art historian who suffered a sad thing in our trade: an area of pathologically diminished vision. The medical term for it is scotoma, *and the pun overcomes me. The term is from Medieval Latin, meaning "dim sight," derived from the Greek* skotoma, *"dizziness, vertigo," from* skotos, *"darkness." So much for the vision of our Scot leader, Mr. Knox. I fear such blindness as his is transmissible. I hope and trust that anyone whose vision is afflicted may cure himself by ceasing to be (at least altogether) a Scottish Presbyterian.*

Thank you for the privilege of reading your work, my boy, and for the critical distance you supply on your big fellow. It has been a great stimulus to my weary brain. I leave for Italy tomorrow and a delicate series of purchases.

Sincerely,
Crispin

What the diagnosis of my father was by April and May, I don't know. "Terminal ennui," perhaps, or "creeping morbidity of the secular passions." No one told me. When my mother phoned in June she was at last specific. They were not coming to my graduation because "your father has pneumonia and I must stay with him."

When I arrived home in the compound my mother kissed me lightly on the forehead as if taking my temperature. "Your father is sicker than he realizes." I promised not to disturb him, which pledge seemed to strike the right note from her point of view.

Duffie then produced the first reunion of the Aqueduct Quartet, which gave me something else to think about. Trying to size up life after Harvard, he sent written invitations to us, promising a drink out of "the chalice of the Senate." Lolly, working full-time for the Pittsburgh Bicentennial Commission, wrote that it was "a lovely idea." Barbara, located at a part-time job, phoned him back nonplussed: "Jeez, how many years has it been?" But she promised to come.

Convening in Jimmy's living room, we looked at each other with covert appreciation and calculating wonder. Duff carried himself with Cantabrigian urbanity, while continuing to wear the social equivalent of golf shoes—spikes for traction, and if necessary for his enemy's instep. Lolly looked on the world with cool, amused gray eyes, her eyebrows tilting this way and that like French punctuation, keeping the reader precisely tuned to her accents, aigu, grave, circumflex.

Babs dressed for the occasion—peau de soie, it seemed, which rippled and glistened in the sunlight, beige, neutral, unbecoming. She was overdressed: antithesis to the underdressing of which Adelaide complained—tutus and leotards, bra and halter outfits, as if the McCalla compound were a circus or a sunbath. Her face was unchanged; unmarked by the logic that was beginning to wrinkle Duffie's brow, untaught by the philosophy through which Lolly looked upon the world, with her wise controlling smile. Barbara Quick at twenty-three still looked like Vermeer's girl with the yellow turban: wide, limpid eyes, lustrous whites with soft brown irises; full lips parted for an unspoken question, moist with anticipation for a taste of the cosmos.

"Jeez, Randy, you look successful," she said.

"Successful, you think?" Duffie said. "To me he looks like most Yalies, innocent aspirants to a diminished inheritance."

"Jimmy, you're hardly objective." Lolly smiled. "Or hardly fair. The only thing I see different in you two, demeanor being roughly the same in Cambridge and New Haven, is in complexion. You, the golfer, should be more tanned, but Randy, the squash player, has more color in his cheeks."

"Ruddy right," I agreed. "Still there's something becoming about your pallor, Duff. It lies between Sherwood Anderson on Saturday night and Oscar Wilde on Sunday morning. Yes—don't interrupt my flow of compliment— you clearly have suffered for us all, a special kind of metaphysical debauch, relieved by magnums of cheap Chablis."

Duffie, not ready for frontal combat, veered into abrupt disquisition on his senior honors work on Tocqueville. Babs blinked and looked out the window. Feeling that he would rather attack than defend, Duff asked me about my thesis.

"Mother Yale came through on her promise of educational attention. Both of my readers hold endowed chairs. But one was a constitutional pedant who said I was indecently free with the texts, and the other was a symbological theologian who said my imagination didn't soar enough. I wonder who's right, or if they're both wrong, or if I'm nuts."

"It's you." Duffie smirked.

"No, it's not you," Lolly said.

"You're not nuts, really," Babs smiled. "Just a little loony, is all."

She asked if anyone wanted a beer. No one objected, so she punched open four Iron Cities and we drank them: Babs swiftly, Duffie surely, Lolly ritually, and I superficially, disliking the taste. We talked about Duffie's plans for graduate work in political science, and mine for law school.

Someone remembered the night that Granny Duffie's cows were set loose, the night of Buddy's fiftieth birthday party. We laughed and talked of characters, civic renaissance and smogless skies, changes in Hill and Hollow (very few), the disrepair of the aqueduct.

A silence fell. Babs spoke:

"Did you know that the sky is full of diamonds?"

"What a poetic thought, Babs," said Lolly. Her voice was even, but Babs shot her the look of one who feels patronized.

"I don't mean twinkle, twinkle, little star. I mean there's a lot of stuff out there which might be diamonds. In the interstellar dust."

"That's great news, but so what?" I said.

"So what good is your college education unless you can rig up a space exploration and bring back diamonds?"

"I see what you mean."

Duffie asked, "Where did you learn about all this, Babs?"

"Astronomy, in night school," she said.

The conversation lapsed. Babs picked up the beer cans. We promised to get together again next year. Lolly and Babs left. I stayed to talk with Duffie.

"Well," he asked me, "have you got laid yet?"

"No, not yet. I suppose you have, and that's why you're asking."

"No, me neither. Here I am, twenty-one, a healthy American male in the last half of the twentieth century, and I haven't had any cunt." He ducked his head and pushed his glasses back on his nose with his left thumb.

"Well, think of it as retaining your virginity."

Duffie looked at me. "So you think of yourself as a virgin, do you? Well, good for you. But it's not for me. Because *conceptually*," he stressed the word, "I think of it as being cock-retentive. I don't think there's anything *to* virginity, and I don't aspire to it. It's either a non-condition, or a negative one. I want to learn how to fuck."

"They don't teach that in the Harvard Graduate School? And you can't find a tutor?"

Duffie looked flustered. I changed my tone. "Actually,

I think there is something to say for virginity and chastity. It isn't highly valued in fraternity bull sessions, but I can find guys, when you talk, just the two of you, who think that a man offering his virginity to a woman in marriage is just as important as the reverse. It's mutually sacred that way."

"Sure," said Duffie, not looking at me. "That's the theory. You're going to practice that? That's going to be your way?"

"Oh, yes and no." I wanted to get away from the charge of prudery. "Yin and yang, you know. If I find someone who seems just right for me, all our characteristics complementary like yang and yin, then love might be its own sanction and virginity could be sacrificed."

"Aha," Duffie leered, "so *there* it is. You're really on the lookout to do the old yin-and-yang with somebody."

I smiled and shrugged him off. I suggested a game of squash to determine who would succeed Hashim Khan as international champion.

After the match we sat and drank ginger ale in the locker bar of the Lawn, empty but for us in the mid-afternoon, serene as a choir boys' dressing room.

"I've got to go back and see my father. He's got pneumonia. It doesn't seem to get better."

"I heard that. I'm sorry he's not feeling well." Duffie was his most formal, though the solicitude came through as genuine.

"Shouldn't they be able to cure pneumonia faster, with sulfa drugs or something?"

"It takes time, even with sulfa, to fight bacteria."

"My mother is with him all the time."

Duffie looked up over the rims of his glasses. He was sweating even after the shower, and his spectacles slid easily. "All the time?" Duffie asked.

Whatever the question was, I tried to answer it. "I guess it isn't bad enough for a nurse, but he needs company, so she stays home with him."

Duffie just nodded. His eyes roamed over the names of club tournament winners in tennis and squash, rows of darkwood medallions with stately gold-painted names. "Who do you suppose won the men's squash most consecutive years?"

"I don't know. I was thinking about my father," I said. I was conscious of waiting Duffie out, squinting at my empty glass, my voice narrow, as if I had sand in my throat.

Duffie let the silence build.

Finally I asked, "Do you know something about pneumonia? Are you trying to tell me something with that rare Harvard silence of yours?"

Duffie fiddled with his glasses, pulled them down nearly to his nostrils, and looked over them wide-eyed at me. Churchill as a pup, I thought. "Don't you know what's going on?" he asked.

"What do you mean 'what's going on'? What don't I know?"

Duffie hesitated, his eyes still wide on me, and I had the awful sense of knowledge as power, and an imperial possession in his grasp, which I was unhappily going to share. "About your mother, I mean."

I wanted to kick over the table and flee. "What *about* my mother?"

"Jesus, you don't know. I'm sorry I brought it up."

"What the hell is it? She's not sick. Don't tell me she's sick, too."

"No," Duffie said quietly. "I didn't mean that. We're friends, aren't we? If you don't want to hear, I'll shut up." He paused again. I saw my hand lift to recognize and beckon him on. I felt like a child by the train tracks, waving to an engineer roaring past. "I meant," Duffie resumed, "about Kidder Towne. About her and him. I thought you knew. Everybody knows. Then I figured you didn't know, and I had better tell you. I'm sorry. I didn't mean to surprise you or hurt you."

Duffie's tenderness of tone made me gulp and blush. All I could say was "No." That sounded like a denial, which I didn't mean. The phrase "everybody knows" reverberated in my brain. So I said, "I didn't know." A huge question was heaving up, and I almost let it lunge out. "What about

125

her and Kidder Towne? What do you mean anyway?" But I didn't ask, because I somehow knew. I slowly spun my empty glass on its bottom edge and wondered what I could ask, should ask. Nothing came to me.

Costelloe entered the locker room with a boy who had finished a tennis lesson. I was grateful to exchange greetings.

"Guess I'll finish dressing," I said to Duffie. As he knotted his necktie, my eye roved over the medallions. The longest successive string of wins came, 1934–1939, when the men's squash champion repeated. I read the name down and up and down again:

> KIDDER P. TOWNE, JR.
> KIDDER P. TOWNE, JR.
> KIDDER P. TOWNE, JR.
> KIDDER P. TOWNE, JR.
> KIDDER P. TOWNE, JR.
> KIDDER P. TOWNE, JR.

I turned away and tried to think of something else. The German scholar Harnack came to me through a quotation I had cut out of my thesis: "Virginity was the specifically Christian virtue, and the essence of all virtues; in this conviction, the meaning of the evangelical law was summed up." Some things you cut come back at you, asking to be better understood.

The most terrible thing my father said to me in the weeks that followed, I have tied to a stake like a vicious dog; it still barks at me, but I keep it leashed at some distance from the ordinary mind and the day's routine.

There I was: home, observing my father's complexion, disposition, growth of stubble; his ability to sit up in a chair, or his preference for lying in bed; the dullness, or occasional brightness of his eyes, the fetor of his breath. With that, noting my mother's attentiveness or abstractedness; her bringing of meals on a tray or her leaving that to a maid; her conversation at table with Gramma about Duncan; her brightness or occasional dullness of eye; her choice of perfume.

I thought too much about such little things, perhaps, but I was, after all, an only child. My parents were my center, the compound was my circle, and all else rolling about those fixed points outlined the cusps of my imagination: a trivial design, but certainly my own.

Something made my father talk to me about his grandfather. Rowan had had a plan for Duncan's life. Its motto was, "Add a zero." For the boy Duncan, grandfather Rowan had poured pennies on the lip of his little leather change purse. When he was feeling good, on a holiday or birthday, he'd say, "Take a penny and use it wisely." When Duncan was bigger, he said, "I'm adding a zero. Now you have an allowance of a dime a week, to spend wisely or to save." He jumped it to a dollar when Duncan was twelve; ten dollars at sixteen. When Duncan went off to Yale, Rowan made it a hundred and expounded his theory in full: a penny at six, a dime at nine, a dollar at twelve, ten dollars at fifteen, a hundred at eighteen. At twenty-one, initiation to a new plane: capital management instead of income management. A thousand at twenty-one; ten thousand to come, then a hundred thousand, then a million by the time his grandson was thirty. By the time Duncan was forty he should be able easily to handle tens of millions as his grandfather did. "He wanted me to be a hundred million dollar man. But I flunked out of Yale playing roulette."

I was wondering why his grandfather gave him his allowance, rather than his father.

" 'Take a penny,' " Duncan repeated. " 'Use it wisely.' Now I never did that to you, did I, Rand? I didn't put temptation in your way, did I? No. I learned my lesson, that's what. I became a gambler, but at least I admit it. Gambling ruined my life. My grandfather staggered me with zeros and flunked me out of Yale. He didn't mean to, but he made me a gambler, really."

Adelaide had heard him. "But who made you a drinker, dear?" She came in carrying soup and a sandwich on a tray,

127

with a bright smile on her face that said joking-is-good-for-his-health. "Who made you love Old Grand-Dad, eighty-six proof?" She fussed with my father's laprobe, laid the tray across his lap, and left. He wrinkled his nose at the soup, nibbled the sandwich.

"Pour me some medicine, Rand," he said, his voice defiant and trembling. "Over there, in the jacket pocket, on the clothes tree." I searched where he said and found a silver flask. "A little pour of the old medicine, Randy boy," he repeated. My father took his waterglass, poured the water into the soup, and extended the glass while looking out the window. I tilted the flask gently into the glass, two ounces of amber by my measuring eye, while my father extended his arm and averted his gaze like a patient receiving a hypodermic needle.

He drank half of the glass and sighed. "A snort of bourbon neat. Good for what ails you." He nodded to me to put the bottle down nearby, a gesture of benign dismissal. I obeyed and departed.

"No, he won't go to a hospital. He won't stop what he's doing. And we can't keep it from him." The meaning of my mother's answers was clear to me, even if the language was evasive.

"But the drinking won't help his pneumonia. It'll make things worse, won't it?"

She pursed her lips and replied levelly: "I hope not too much worse."

My father seemed to welcome my company. I took to visiting him after lunch. With the morning behind and his late afternoon "nap" ahead, he talked readily. Bits of family history brewed up, musings of the Calvinistic elect popped out, all of which I cherished.

"Did you know I had an older brother, stillborn? You are an only child, Randy boy, but I was not. I had a stillborn elder brother. 'Jacob have I loved but Esau have I hated.' How else can you explain why I lived and he died? God hated him in my mother's womb. He was there first, but

128

he died, and I lived. I am like the second son, Jacob, beloved of his mother, and of Jehovah."

The sun in July rose high and the bark peeled from the beechwood trees. The stillness of deep summer invaded Panther Hill, save for the clacking of beechbark falling to the pavement, the swish and crunch of auto tires grinding down the bark, trailing eddies of pulverized bits behind.

"Jezebel. You know the story of the painted woman? That's the way to treat a whore even if she is a queen. The Biblical way. Leave her head on a pike and her blood on the wall.

"But I bet you don't know the story of Maachah. She was a queen who worshipped a false idol. Her son Asa removed her from being queen, and tore down her idol, and burned it. That's all he did to her. He should have killed her, shouldn't he? But he gave way to foolish pity."

Duncan sighed and subsided. He took a nip from his glass. "Can you name the books of the Bible in order? No? What do they teach you in school nowadays? I can still do it. Listen." And he trotted through the thirty-nine books of the Old Testament. ". . . Zephaniah, Haggai, Zechariah, Malachi." The effort left him drooping. He did not go on to the New.

The high sun seemed to stun the cicadas, and the pitch of their drone grew fainter. Tree leaves shook in dry rasps at sudden leaps of squirrel.

"Read me from Grandfather's Bible," Duncan asked. I fetched the great Geneva edition from the Big House library and carried it up to my father's room. "The part about God's rules," he asked. "What were the rules that went with the promised land?"

I searched, read bits of Genesis, found commentary from Calvin and Knox that seemed to answer my father's need. When God gave Canaan to the Israelites, "He commanded the whole inhabitants of that country to be destroyed . . . that a city declining to idolatry should fall in the edge of the sword. . . . To the carnal man this may appear a rigorous and severe judgment, yea, it may rather seem to be pronounced in a rage than in wisdom. . . . But in such cases will God that all creatures stoop, cover their faces, and desist from reasoning, when commandment is given to execute his judgment."

Duncan nodded. "Let their houses and temples be destroyed," he said. He reached for the glass, swigged a full shot, coughed and gasped. Regaining composure, he raised the glass with a stiff forearm, as a signal to me for more. I poured from the silver flask. He beamed a great smile at me, and with a toasting gesture repeated, "Let their houses and temples be destroyed."

"He is very unwell, and he is unlikely to get better." Dr. Hunnewell spoke quietly to my mother and Gramma. I had reached my own prognosis several days before. My father's coughing was now a steady sluggish gargle. He no longer sat in his chair. He ate nearly nothing. I knew what we all knew, and what the doctor did not say. Duncan McCalla did not wish to get well.

Then things happened with startling ease. One day my father stopped drinking, apparently lacking the strength to lift a glass. The next he could barely swallow water without gagging. The doctor had an oxygen tent brought in. In this casing, Duncan persisted a few days more. His moments of lucidity were few. I was there for the last such, with my mother and grandmother.

After hours inert, the eyes opened in the pallid, purplish face, and the man raised his fingers as a sign he wished to speak. We peeled back the tent to hear him. He swallowed several times and breathed heavily. Mouth and hands worked silently with the effort of summoning words. He lifted his neck an inch above the pillow and finally spoke:

> "God upon his sapphire throne
> Waits his own anointed son."

The man lay back immediately, his breathing once again shallow and ragged. For a while there was a suggestion of a smile on his lips, before his respiration began a terrible drag, an involuntary suck for life.

"What did he say?" Gramma asked.

130

"From a hymn," Adelaide answered. "Some lines from a hymn."

"A *hymn*, did you say?" Gramma looked at her son. His closed eyes were bare curved lines between bulging lids above and gray pouches beneath. "A hymn? . . . Mercy me."

"Mercy you?" said Adelaide, her eyes upon the man in the plastic tent. "Mercy him."

That night past ten he died, after stertorous sounds and a last wet sigh.

Adelaide rounded the public story into its final form. "Pneumonia," she said sadly. "He was prone to it. Remember when you were little, the time Grampa gave him the new car? He was sick in bed with pneumonia for weeks. His lungs were weakened permanently, I think." Gramma nodded. So the tale would be told at the Lawn, and at the ladies' Mah-Jongg games. I nodded, too.

For the inside story, I had always gone to the Big House. Tea with Martha and Crispin in a sense was seance, a sitting at which I might hear truths screened out by the ordinary membranes of my world. Crispin, speaking to his mother, but trimming nothing for my presence, said how grateful he was that his older cousin had taught him baseball, the only sport he ever managed to play passably. He was miserable with a bat and was afraid of hot grounders after one hopped up and hit him in the teeth, but his judgment was good on fly balls. He had time for them. Duncan had said of him, "for things descended from heaven he was fearless, as distinct from things rising from the earth."

Yes, his dear cousin had made him a passable player, praised him to others, and got him past the problem of derision from playmates. "He told me that out in right field I wouldn't have much to do or to say, except, if necessary, yell 'I got it.' Since my hearing was fine, I was much better off than Dummy Hoy, the old-time deaf mute who used to play for Cincinnati. Duncan said everybody should have a hero, so I made mine Dummy Hoy. I kept quiet, got a lot of walks because I was small, and stole bases." He looked

131

at me. "I'll always be grateful to your father for teaching me baseball.

"Of course Dummy Hoy could go on as Dummy Hoy— I read somewhere that he's still alive in Cincinnati, nearly a hundred years old. But I had to learn how to speak, and to have something to speak about. And there you came in, Mother, dear, with your love of galleries. I roamed through the Carnegie Museum that awful year of operations, with my lower face bandaged and my eyes open. So thank you again, dear Mater. Without painting and sculpture I would have become a pantomine artist, or another back-room securities analyst."

Martha received the compliment indulgently and smiled upon her own Fra Filippo Lippi.

"But poor Duncan," Crispin continued. "He never found his professional passion or his proper trade. And so pneumonia is the end, is it? That's what we're to say? An element of truth: with pneumonia the lungs fill up with fluid, and my poor cousin did die of the inability to draw breath. Alcoholic edema the cause, more precisely."

"Pneumonia," Martha insisted.

"So the doctor said," Crispin went on. "Alcohol is a preservative for dead things and a corrosive for live things. With some it brings on cirrhosis, but with poor Duncan it was pneumonia. He preserved himself prematurely in alcohol."

"What are you saying, dear? You sound a little wound up." Even Martha's love sometimes admitted discomfort with Crispin's candor.

"I am simply saying that my poor dear cousin died by drowning."

"Drowning?"

"Yes, his lungs filled up with fluid and he couldn't breathe anymore."

"You're still being fanciful, my dear."

"I am stating something that we should admit to ourselves. Pneumonia didn't kill my dear cousin. He died of bourbonic plague." Crispin grimaced at his own terrible pun. He put tea to his mouth, but it was too hot and he scalded himself. His face contorted in agony, and his eyes filled with a mois-

132

ture that continued past the pain. He put a forefinger beneath each lower eyelid and reamed off his brimming eyes. "He said I was as fast on the bases as Dummy Hoy. I always loved him for that."

I had hoped to help carry my father's coffin and to shovel earth upon it. I imagined the weight of the body on my shoulder, heard the thud of the dirt thrown on wood. But reality was another deprivation. The casket was bronze, and it rolled easily along with a push from the undertaker's men. When we reached the family mausoleum, the gleaming container was raised by hydraulic jack to a tier with the next designated opening, and the body of Duncan McCalla slid noiselessly in, as to a safe deposit vault.

The chairs that Clellan and Bekka had brought back from China were crawling with worms. They rose from pencilled tunnels in the wood, their green heads and bodies writhing with serpentine meaning. I stood transfixed, the door behind me locked. I yanked on the bellpull for Buddy, but no one came.

I was fixed in hypnotic bondage to hundreds of micro-cobras, rotating in tiny axes. In the dead silence I felt my tuxedo rotting with sweat. I sensed an endless torpid terror of all the acts I could not know, actions I could not foretell, which were here in gruesome mimicry reduced and concentrated.

I suddenly saw their heads, several of them with astonishing individuality, tiny red eyes and forked orange tongues. I was aware that they were aware of me, and I felt a fevered chill. Nothing, I knew, could stop their tunnelling and chewing, and the piling of their minute slime. I was sickened to see that some had moved to the fan-backed chair Aunt Bekka loved, a piece from Singapore with rattan lattice work. They grew longer, lither bodies, moved to more ecstatic weaving and dancing. Lurid, gluttonous, implacable, they framed the chairback like the hair of the Medusa. I stared at my patent leather shoes, lest I lock eyes with them and petrify myself.

133

I reached again for the bellpull, which this time rang a gong. The pull changed into a cobra in my hand, with Buddy's eyes. Which woke me.

One shameful saying of my father's stays with me, one furious summary moment of our conversations before he died. In our talk of baseball and the stock market and friendship and the Bible, there were eruptive moments—just as unexpected as those in my boyhood when my father, fortified by liquor, would corner me in the pantry, clamp a hand on my shoulder, and vow how much he loved Adelaide, getting me to vow, simultaneously, how much I loved my mother. These new moments required my silence, in respect of my father's dying rage. The fiercest of all was one sentence, uttered on the day my father began drinking directly from the silver flask:

"Your mother has been laid, relaid, and parlayed by every man in western Pennsylvania."

How to cope with a statement like that, a sudden pronouncement at peak intensity, by a man with three days' growth of beard and sunken eyes, but a man uncommonly lucid, and in his own fashion, candid, that man my father?

I sorted methodically, far end first, using a Yale education to distribute the pain.

Western Pennsylvania? That was like my father, who considered the region to contain the world. He would never have said, "every man in the Lawn Club," which would have sounded too much like gang rape in a fraternity.

Parlayed? The term came from Duncan's horse-playing days. I could hear him dialing, speaking carefully, quietly, as if to be heard only by the person on the other end. "Hello, Nat? This is Duncan. I'd like Rag-a-bag in the second at Hialeah. To win." My mother heard, too, of course. She did not criticize Duncan in my hearing, but she must have made her view known, because betting on horses stopped when I was in the fifth grade. "Parlayed" contained no suggestion of orgy. Duncan simply chose it as a rhetorical flourish after verbs already strong enough to overwhelm.

"Every man"? Here was a convulsing puzzle. How many,

134

exactly? Who were they? Why, how, had they begun, these affairs? And when, why, had they ended? Would knowing lighten the burden or make it heavier? I only knew that I had to know much more.

"Your mother"? Duncan could have said "my wife." Or simply, less accusingly, "Adelaide." But relationships were at stake as well as individual identities. Duncan's assertion carried a question: how do you feel about your mother betraying your father, and yourself, repeatedly, with other men? Are you the kind of son who is going to put up with that, or not? Show me what kind of a man you are (just as long as you don't tell me what kind of a man I am, for that is not your right).

Weeks of oblique criticism, of Old Testamant rantings, suddenly took shape in this one fearful obloquy. I had the dread sensation that I knew it already. And that the man knew I knew it; and that soon the man would invert the old formula and ask me, by way of revelation and mutual pledge, "We really hate your mother, don't we?"

No defense for her sprang to my mind, no attack; no apology, no critique. Just the terrible question, "Who?" followed by what, when, where, how, why? I readied myself to ask, should the man press me to speak. But he did not corner me that way. He elaborated in the tersest fashion. He gestured grandly for the silver flask. "Lang Delavane," he said, and gulped himself a shot. "Sheppie Cardigan." A second shot on top of it. "Kidder Towne." A third and larger shot made his Adam's apple, under ragged beard, bob with pitiful small swallows.

He sat before me fired with his fury, trembling with weakness, shaking the flask as if to show there's all this left to pour, and much more still to say.

I left the room.

twelve.

MY FATHER'S will added little to my valued McCalla independence, of which I already had my share. The real
inheritance I got from him, I thought, is lack of will. Then
I flushed that notion as unfair to him and to me, for I hadn't
sought, and couldn't use, a militant air of command. I had
received from Duncan McCalla a pathetic fury and a tone
of prophetic accusation. Was it useless? Or could I learn to
employ it as part of life's artifice?

I realized that I had not wept when my father died. I felt
sad now, sad still, but not sad enough. I could not recall
being on my father's knee, or in his lap, or on his shoulders,
and that made my sadness heavier, wishing for the terrible
elevation of true grief.

McCalla independence, whether out of faith, fatigue, or
fear, involved a disinclination to embrace. Those who had
with locked loins conceived me, released me to my safe and
sorry body, my own and lonely envelope. Our Presbyterian
solitude, our culture-of-not-touching, pointed toward happiness in heaven, with suspicion of the tangible joys of earth.
I remember few and formal kisses from my mother, and
none from my father. I would have been mortally embarrassed to give one. As he lay dying, I looked for no new
intimacy. I had not been taught by touch. Far less, by caress. I strained for didactic or intuitive messages. And some
I received.

"Here's something your father left for you. He got up one
night and cleaned out his desk, and tied this old shirt box

136

up with green string. He put your name on it." My mother looked at me as if I knew what it was. I stammered a thanks. She resumed control. "I don't know what's in it. Memorabilia, you might say; or junk, I would guess."

I took the box up to my room on the third floor and snapped the string. My heart was pounding as if I held a love letter, as if in my hands were a wild surmise come true, an emotional legacy from my father, delivered at last.

There he was, popping out from stuffed papers: a silhouette, dated 1908, of a boy in knickerbockers and hunting jacket. A sporting cap with long sloping visor over childish features—Cupid as Sherlock Holmes. With that, a silhouette of a woman with long skirt, Gibson sleeves, backswept hair, wide hat and parasol. Stunningly distinct profiles, black on white, nipped out and pasted up by a boardwalk artist. "How cunning!" the lady with the hat must have said.

I turned my father in the light. Where in those petite black cardboard features was the man who died expressing obloquy for his wife and impotent fury at three men who had been their friends: a ballplayer, a toy manufacturer, an investment advisor?

Beneath the silhouettes lay a photograph: Duncan aged ten, standing outside the Big House in baseball uniform and cap, black socks, baggy knickers, collared shirt, buttoned sweater, hands a few inches apart on a black bat. There was an inadvisable awkwardness in his stance; his eyes squinted at the camera, and his lips, one sensed, were moist with tongue-licked concentration.

Beneath that, stubs of World Series tickets: 1909, 1925, 1927.

Beneath that, piles of letters from Gramma to Duncan at camp, to him at home from their overseas vacations, to him at Yale (autumn and early winter only); and a few letters from Grampa.

Report cards from Panther Hill Public School and the Academy, all C's. A letter from the registrar at Yale stipulating that Duncan McCalla excuse himself from further attendance because of unsatisfactory grades and incomplete courses.

Then a sealed envelope, at the bottom of the box. No marking on the outside. What was this? A note to me? No, the envelope was slightly yellowed. Open it? Why not? The box was marked with my name, so it was my envelope, and the contents, whatever they might be.

I opened it and unfolded a two-page memorandum in faulty typescript. A number of words were typed over without erasure. Two small photographs, bound face to face with one paper clip, fell out of the envelope. The letterhead read "Martin Abendroth, Confidential Inquiries." The memo's contents were telegraphic. Lacking context, I read it three times before it made any sense.

Subject drove McCalla, W. Va. as stated, March 14, 1940.

Local registrar of wills recalls subject's inquiry about that time. Showed her records requested.

Local cemetery has no regular keeper. Too small. Subject could have maybe gone there to study gravestones, as claimed. No restrictions on entry.

Has subject been asked for data from gravestones? Eighteenth century graves are broken falling down. Hard to read. Near impossible. Earliest readable McCalla stone says died 1820; Ebenezer. Next: beloved wife Abigail died 1828. Ect.

Subject not remembered at local lunchroom. Subject not registered by name at Mountain Vue Hotel. Only hotel for twenty miles. Ten rooms. J. Howshall, Prop.

Only two registrants for March 14, 1940: A. M. Feighery, Frederick, Md. Mr. and Mrs. J. D. Bruce, Cleveland.

Proprietor does not ask for information about automobiles. Cannot remember Ohio license plate or any plates.

Proprietor confirms pictures as Mr. and Mrs. Bruce. Probally, he says.

Proprietor doesn't remember details of arrival or departure. Doesn't keep records of that. All rooms are paid for in advance. Room was paid for.

There followed a list of expenses, a line that read "respect-fully submitted," and the penned initials, M.A.

I took hold of the rusty paper clip, lifted an end with my fingernail, and pried rather than slid the clip off the two passport-size photos. They still stuck to each other, face to face. I inserted a thumbnail and tried to tease them apart, but they began to tear. I went down to the empty kitchen and set heat under the kettle. When the water began to boil I held the photos with spaghetti tongs a few inches from the funnel of steam. After half a minute I removed them from the steam and tried again with my thumbnail. I felt resistance still. I put them in the steam again and counted fifteen seconds. Then I took a paring knife, inserted it be-tween the photos, and cut them apart.

The pictures were of a man and a woman. Part of the man's face had come off on the woman's, and the tear left his face with a jagged puzzle-piece of white missing at the jaw line. The photograph had the blurred sepia quality so popular in the thirties. The man was conventionally hand-some by Ivy League standards. He looked three-quarters at the camera with a beguiling semi-smile and a diffidence that drew him closer to anonymity. He parted his hair in the middle.

To the woman's face at the hairline adhered part of the man's jaw.

The photograph of the woman accented a bare neck, eyes demurely focused in the middle distance, not confronting the camera, lips set with pleasant modesty together. Soft-focus idealization made the person appealing, but unindi-vidual.

Nevertheless I recognized the woman.

I had seen the photograph before, in a larger framed ver-sion.

The woman was my mother.

What was going on here? Someone without a secretary, himself a poor typist, had sent my father a report on obscure activities in the tiny West Virginia town named by my forebears for themselves.

139

This someone, it would appear from the letterhead, style of report, and submission of expenses, was a private detective. What was he trying to find out? Why go to courthouse, graveyard, lunchroom, and hotel in nether West Virginia?

Above all, what was my mother's picture doing clipped to the man with his hair parted in the middle?

I resisted the suggestions of the text. I decided to ask some questions myself.

I mentioned McCalla, West Virginia, at the next Sunday dinner. Does anyone we know still live there? No. Has anyone in the family ever visited there? Martha brightened at that. "Yes, indeed. I asked Adelaide once if she would help me trace out the family tree. So she drove down and obtained some names and dates for me. A long time ago; before the war, I think."

"Oh, I don't think I helped very much, Aunt Martha. The earliest McCallas, their graves were of sandstone or something, all wiped out. And the courthouse was a mess. I would have had to spend a week to find anything at all, and I certainly didn't want," laughter like fork clattering to plate, "to spend a week in McCalla, West Virginia. But I got what I could for you in a day." Adelaide took a sip at her wine goblet. "It's a long drive there."

"Yes, dear, and dangerous in winter. It was good of you to risk it," Martha added.

"Why dangerous?" I asked.

"Such narrow mountain roads! They wind around—you never know which way. And slippery—they freeze very fast. Luther comes from around there, so I would drive with *him* to Hot Springs, but I wouldn't care to ordinarily, with just any driver."

Crispin chimed in: "That's where Jim Duffie lost his life." He turned to me. "Your friend Jimmy's father. A fine fellow, but a little too jolly at the wheel, perhaps. He had a Princeton habit of thinking everywhere was his campus. Drank a good bit, always charmingly, but I thought him a trifle too impelled by the Scott Fitzgerald saga. His wife, Natalie, too, by Zelda. Dance, write, paint—anything artistic, she would attack it. But she didn't live long enough, blessedly, to suffer Zelda's terrors. She died of pneumonia when their child was quite small. *Real* pneumonia, before sulfa drugs. A couple of years later Jim skidded off a cliff in West Virginia and that was the end of him."

"What year?" I asked.

My mother sipped carefully from her goblet, eyes lowered in appreciation of the wine.

"Oh, I don't know, you were small, and so was little Jimmy. A good thing his grandmother took him in. If you can't grow up with your parents, then it's a privilege to grow up with a genuine antique. She's on the Board of the Princeton Theological Seminary; for her money rather than her views, I dare say. I wonder if her fellow trustees have ever had a look at her living room and parlors. In nearly every one there's a painting of a Madonna, Renaissance or Baroque, at some cost, I might add. Granny Duffie is quite indifferent to them as investments, small fortune though they represent. She dotes on the Holy Family. There's even a St. Anthony holding the Christ child—not a common subject at all. But nice, don't you think, Mother, to see boy Jesus as bambino in the arms of an Italian uncle?"

"Yes, it is." Martha smiled brightly on her son. "Though I've always thought Victoria Duffie's taste overmixed. She reminds me of those people who won't drink dry vermouth and won't drink sweet. They must have them half-and-half."

"What was Mr. Duffie doing driving in West Virginia?" I asked Crispin.

"Oh, a business trip, I suppose. He travelled a lot for the family wholesale firm. Over a hundred mile radius, or two hundred, maybe."

In the reconstruction of perfidy, for one personally affected, the hunting mind and the storing mind behave as if espoused. The hunter brings down the game, which the companion puts in storage, and urges the predator into the field again.

The next step for me as hunter was to visit the Duffie manse. Easy enough to pick up Jimmy for a squash game. The trick was to set an hour, arrive early, knowing that

Duffie as putterer would have something to finish, then use waiting time to advantage.

"I'll be right down," Duffie called. The maid ushered me to the living room and offered me a neatly refolded copy of the morning *Post-Gazette*. I knew I had several minutes. There were family portraits and photographs in every one of the downstairs rooms, loving, lounging shots, dating to the late nineteenth century and Lewis Carroll whimsy, pre-Raphaelite wistfulness. Etchings and mezzotints of courting scenes dappled the walls: shyness on benches, forwardness on porches; a maid flirting, gloved fingers interlaced, with two strolling swains at once, behind the coachman of a four-in-hand. And, in each room, one statement more. I swept a look at the Madonnas, the Nativities, the St. Anthony and Holy Bambino that Crispin so enjoyed. They looked incongruous with big-legged dark walnut furniture and as-bestos-lined gas fireplaces. The storer stopped me before each, while the hunter urged me on.

The biggest cluster of photographs was in the parlor. I went directly to the Steinway, on which stood in ranged array a dozen portraits in precious metal frames. All Duffies look alike, I thought. Or college boys look similar; time has not yet sorted character from exuberance. There was a wedding picture of James and Natalie coming down the aisle—but so far away from the lens I could read only the nuptial mood. A close-up of father and mother cooing at baby Jimmy, focused not on them but on baby's upturned face. Behind both, however, was an eight-by-ten frame, with a formal three-quarters portrait of the young busi-nessman; a prospering, lightly smiling man who parted his hair in the middle. I turned the frame. On the back, in a neat hand, a notation: "James Douglas Bruce Duffie III, February 11, 1910–March 15, 1940."

"What do you see?" Jimmy stood in the doorway with squash racquet.

"Your family in all their allure."

"Hell, I don't recognize any of them. The only one I know is Granny, in all her majesty. Let's go."

142

So: the passport-size photos that had separated with difficulty, leaving each with part of the other's face, were pictures of my mother and Duffie's father.

They were in an envelope with the notes of a private detective who had checked these photographs with the manager of a small hotel in McCalla, West Virginia.

Were the people in the photos the same people who had registered as Mr. and Mrs. J. D. Bruce from Cleveland?

"Probally."

That laconic reply, however, could have been a way of getting rid of a snooper. Who asked such questions in the town of McCalla? What happened there which warranted investigation, except the sizeable robbery that occurs once a decade, the murder that occurs once a generation? Why investigate, when nothing in McCalla goes amiss?

The report of the private eye was poorly presented, full of lacunae in method and fact, addressed to the apparently troubled sensibilities of a man named Duncan McCalla in Pittsburgh, my father, whose deep disquiet was moving him to pay for information. Martin Abendroth was giving him facts, but not too many; was keeping him guessing; was playing his heart in its tortured fire, rotating the spit at a speed to keep him paying.

Whatever my father thought of the information, it was not enough for me.

I became a lockpicker. Not in the professional sense, of course. I mean that I became one who looks for the keys to desks and drawers that are locked for reasons. I found and opened many; my own family's drawers, secret or confidential; merely personal; mostly banal. My search for a father grew fiercely distorted: a search instead for my father's betrayer.

I began with my mother's desk.

I chose a time when both she and Gramma were out. A nauseous terror seized me, even then, lest a maid discover me in the act. As a child I had seen where she kept her key—in a cubbyhole—for the desk drawers. I slipped my flattened palm in the pigeon-slat, felt with my little finger for the key, swept it out into the cupped palm of my other hand. *Holy Mozart*—Pastor McCracken's stilted profanity hit me as I turned the key in a drawer—*and cuckoo spit*. It worked. Opening it, I felt my heart hammer, my tongue go dry. I sorted through household lists and bills; correspondence of the Junior League and the Presbyterian Orphan Asylum; a drawer of cancelled checks; and, at last, a drawer of personal letters. I learned much of the sentiments and doings of people I knew and did not know, but nothing untoward of the year 1940.

A step on the back stair startled me. The clack, clack of black shoe on brass bolster of rubber mats on wooden stairs. Upward trudged a maid with tired feet, drawn by an image of her bed in the garret, unlacing her shoes, dropping them on the floor, letting her stockinged toes cool on the bedstead of tarnished brass.

I closed and locked all the drawers, returned the key to the cubbyhole, made sure each thing was aligned with brother and sister things as it had been before. I had the foul sense of being a cat burglar who had entered not for jewels, but to rub his privy parts with lingerie.

My grandmother, then? Perhaps Gramma's desk contained some leak of scandal, some further lead?

From Grampa, three or four dozen valentines, dating back from the year of his death, 1949. I lingered over a leather notebook with month by month accounts of wages paid each servant. I tracked the record of Alice B. Cook. She arrived at $70 a month in 1929, was reduced steadily in the Depression to $50 by 1933; did not surpass her original wage until 1943; was raised to $115 a month by 1950 (including Social Security), and to $170 now. After nearly thirty years of service, six days of labor a week for $2000 per annum, plus room and board, in the Year of Our Lord 1958. Was that a just wage? I doubted that Cook complained, though maybe she ought to. As for Gramma, what did she do, I wondered, besides order food, instruct servants, play bridge and Mah-

Jongg, gossip, and go to church? What justified such a life? Yet who could dare call it an unjust life?

Two scraps of paper with notes in Gramma's own hand were tucked in a corner. I unrolled them.

"10,000 times 10,000 equal 100 million." I imagined in my mind's ear McCracken's voice sermonizing. The militant hymn rolled into mind:

> *Ten thousand times ten thousand*
> *In sparkling raiment bright*
> *The army of the ransomed saints*
> *Throngs up the steeps of light*

Who were these saints? Industrialists who knew that time was money, who wasted none, invested all, careened through the perennial gale of creative destruction accumulating with dextrous indirection a sleek and becoming wealth. Add a zero, Rowan said; several zeros, and one was saved. Higher still on the steeps of light were the philanthropists, who gave, with forethought, seemly amounts, laying up for themselves a treasure in heaven, donating with just enough publicity to inspire others, without drawing excessive attention to themselves. No McCalla had risen so high. Their faith had been simpler. The second note helped reveal it:

"Worry is unbelief parading in disguise."

Gramma seldom worried. She was a dogmatized creature of the Reformation, a good sheep of McCracken's flock. Salvation shall be by faith, rather than by works. And who are those elect who are saved? The faithful, who *know* in their hearts that salvation awaits them, and who show the way for others by their undisguised optimism. I returned the two notes to the drawer with the conviction that I had opened the clock of my grandmother's mind and seen its innermost works. A plain mechanism.

There were, of course, two other houses, and more desks. The Big House, with its heavy staffing and sick room busyness, was not a place to try. Clellan's house, however, with Bekka absent would be easy. If any drawer in the compound might allude to something *louche* it should be one of Clellan's. Whereas Crispin saw his uncle as a saint in devotion to Big Rachel, I saw him as Buddy Quick's employer, and that was something else. Still, Clellan was four years dead. I found nothing in his desk. I went to the library and idled through the books. Nothing there either, but giveaways from the Big House, it would appear, a few best-sellers of recent decades, and. And!

An uncleared floor-level drawer contained magazines: *True Detective*, two issues twenty years old; *Esquire*, several issues across the years; *Playboy*, its initial issue. And some yellow sheets torn from an unidentifiable pulp magazine. I flipped through the contents of the drawer, trying to associate a common theme, but could construct none.

Then, as I browsed, a name hit me in the eye. I was stunned to discover in the torn-out articles: "Rowan M. McCalla." I learned nothing about my mother and father by searching in drawers, but I discovered my great-grandfather tied to deeds and deals I could hardly conceive. Here, if I were looking for the male principle in a McCalla, here was a predator and a man of craft. And, just possibly, a colossal fool.

I folded the yellowed pages and stuffed them in my pocket, fearful that the crackling sounds I made would set the house on fire. I dumped the magazines back in the drawer, jammed it shut, and left.

Scholar of the House indeed. Pickpocket, lockpicker, Peeping Tom. I felt a sour shame in my behavior. But the glint in my mirrored eyes told me that I was feeding a demonic appetite which would not yield. So, call it a need. Justify it with abstractions: discovery of the sources of McCalla maleness; search for my father, arraignment against my mother.

What had I learned? That my mother and Duffie's father were associated by clipped photographs in a private detective's report concerning March 14, 1940; and that Duffie senior had crashed over a cliff in West Virginia on March

146

15, 1940. My mind idled on that death: the possible moods of the driver on that day; his skill at the wheel; the weather in that part of the Appalachians; the precise contour of the road. But I was not, I reminded myself, investigating Jimmy's father's sudden end; I was really tracing the slow death of my own father.

As for the couple that registered at the Mountain Vue Hotel: "J. D. Bruce" was a truncation of James Douglas Bruce Duffie III. "Cleveland" was a site for the Duffie business, but an invention as residence. "Mr. and Mrs." was a tawdry fiction. That my mother and a close friend of her husband should go separately under pretext of genealogical research and business travel to an unlikely town in West Virginia did not, as a lawyer-to-be, surprise me. Or so I told myself. It did sicken me that they should record themselves as "Mr. and Mrs." (But how else could they get a hotel room?) I worked myself into cold moral rage, assessed their conduct as despicable (while regarding it as interesting), and wondered about motives.

I could see the widower Duffie, deprived of wife by fatal illness, succumbing to the attraction of a close friend. I tarried on opposing possibilities, for which there was no evidence, that a remorseful Duffie, having betrayed both the memory of his wife and the faith of a friend, had intentionally driven himself off the road; or that a blissful Duffie, in unconscious distraction, had gone sailing into a rural mountain abyss. A marginally careless Duffie in a fatal fractional error was not interesting to me.

As for my mother? This was ugly to confront. My father, fingers tight on his silver flask, harshly summarizing my mother's behavior, had not mentioned Jim Duffie's name. Did that omission cast doubt on the scenes I now visualized? No: it tended instead to prove her involvement with Delavane, Cardigan, and Towne. My father's not mentioning Duffie's name was out of respect for my friendship with Jimmy; but the documentation he left behind certainly did the job and drew the other names along, from assertion to conviction.

So: however acutely bereaved my mother may have felt

on hearing of Jim Duffie's accident, however smitten with guilt and remorse, it did not deter her from other adventures. Whatever the shock of his self-destruction, even if accidental, that blow did not stop Adelaide McCalla, alias Mrs. J. D. Bruce, from other assignations with friends of the family. Alias whomever else, whenever, *inter alia*, and in the language of the private eye, *ect.*

I was two years old when Natalie Duffie died, and not yet four when her husband followed. I could remember nothing of them. Lang Delavane appeared in my life when I was about six, a Yankee castoff, pitching for a second division Pirate team in place of younger war-drafted talent, but still an heroic figure: eyes of sweet lethal blue, sunburned squint lines at their corners, a faint grin on his face as he faced the batter, hurled, snapped his curve down and away. My father called him "Old Sidewinder."

Shep Cardigan's name first arose when my parents were blackballed from the Lawn Club. My father, in drunken jocularity, had called him "Hustler," and Sheppie, on the nominating committee, had taken offense—a manufacturer who cultivated a glazed vacationless charm. How old was I then? Ten or so? And how old when we had become members? Thirteen? What had gone on in between?

As for Kidder Towne: he seemed to be a regular at my parents' Christmas parties ever since my going to St. Luke's. He and Adelaide danced the rhumba to recordings of Xavier Cugat while the party crowd cried "Olé." When had my mother taken up with him? Was she seeing him while my father was dying? Was she seeing him now?

How many men, if any, were unmentioned by name but included in Duncan's terrible epithet—"laid, relaid, and parlayed by every man in western Pennsylvania"?

Was she seeing Kidder Towne now?

I packed the paper evidence back in the shirt box my father had left me. I tied the box securely, put it in my bottom desk drawer, and locked it. I hid the key in the sock drawer of my bureau in a pair of argyles I never wore.

I would have to speak to my mother.

But how speak to her? How raise the subject, and how, once it was raised, ever conclude it?

Adelaide raised it, despite herself. Two weeks after my father was buried, she came to me with a careful smile of concern. "You know you don't have to stay in the house, dear. You can go out and play golf, or even have a date and go to the movies. How come you never have any dates?" She sensed me flinching, and pressed what she imagined as her advantage. "Even Gramma didn't cut out her social activity after she got over Grampa's death. She went back to her Mah-Jongg and her dinner parties. You know, we don't have to wear black armbands and go around telling people to leave us alone."

"I see," I said. I sounded testy to myself, but she still had her smile, and seemed preoccupied with licking her teeth, as if she sensed a speck of lipstick there. "So you're going to go out when you feel like it."

"I certainly am," she said, beaming encouragement at me. Her fingers now reached at her tongue. Was it a fleck of tobacco bothering her from an early morning cigarette?

"And do you feel like it already?"

"Well, not just at this moment, if that's what you're asking."

"I guess I'm asking what you feel about my father's death."

She frowned. "Well, we don't go around keening and wailing like Irish biddies. We don't wear our feelings on our sleeves. We mourn in our hearts."

"I was asking, if you don't mind, what you feel in your heart about my father."

She looked away. She is a beautiful woman, I thought. My mother is beautiful in the same way as Ingrid Bergman, but she spoils it sometimes by fussiness, like now, dabbing at her teeth with her handkerchief. What will she say?

"I'm sorry he died so young. I'm sorry he died so . . . laboriously."

"But what do you feel about *him*, not just about his dying."

149

She looked at me, not quite balefully. "Please have a little respect for my feelings. And tell me about yours."

There she had me for a moment, but an answer tumbled out of me that gave me confidence. "I feel bound to respect his code of honor."

That stopped her, I thought. And it saved me from exploring numb spaces in my mind.

"His code of honor? Is that all you feel about?"

"That's what I feel most about right now. I think my father had an unusual code for this age. He believed in virginity before marriage and faith within marriage, which is a way of defining chastity, I guess." And what is that, and so what? I asked myself. I called on the scholar Harnack to answer before Adelaide found an opening. "And chastity is the essential Christian virtue."

"Well," she smiled with didactic approval, "I certainly am glad you believe in those things. I think you'll make some woman a very good husband, and you'll do your father's memory proud."

I persisted. "Do you believe in those things?"

"Do I believe in those things? What kind of a question is that to ask your mother?"

"I'm asking my father's wife."

She breathed carefully. She laid her forearms with care on the chairarms and her palms on their carved walnut knobs. In the fingers of her right hand was her handkerchief. "I've no time for such questions."

I was torn between wanting to assault her for my father and to protect her as my mother. My brain stopped working. I felt as if my tongue were numb.

But she was still thinking. After a few moments she spoke again, in a reminiscing manner—tenderly, it seemed, about my father, and kindly to me, not as if in answer to a question, but as an amusing insight into someone we both had known. "Duncan once said he had enough virginity for both of us."

I tried not to smile at that. My attack was blunted, but I made another lunge in his behalf. "And chastity? Chastity is different from virginity." It was a weak scholarly stab, which she tolerated well.

"Is it? I don't suppose I know the difference. I am not an educated woman."

I resisted the temptation to define the difference. She wouldn't give a damn. She would listen as a respectful Virginia female until I was done. I kept silent.

She exhaled deeply, once. Then she spoke again, as in a trance, as if disavowing her speech by the vacancy in her eyes. "Duncan was chaste, I am sure. But there is something to be said for ecstasy."

I knew now the answers to questions I hadn't asked, and a little rictus of combat must have stolen over my face. It annoyed her, that unbidden smile.

"It's time you got out of yourself, Randy. Grow up and get out of yourself." Still I didn't answer, and she warmed to the theme. "Fraternity boys I knew, at Wash'n'n Lee, stole a whole freight train and ran off with it, a hundred miles. But all you do is read and play squash."

I tightened up at that, and bit back words. My restraint seemed only to spur her own.

"Why don't you get drunk, Randy boy?" The absurdity of this as maternal advice seemed to seize her with delight. She dropped her handkerchief from the fingers of one hand to the open palm of the other. It fluttered down like a windless parachute. "You know, it might not even hurt to get laid." And she laughed.

"Jezebel," I thought. My father's anger came over me, and I almost puffed out the word, "Jezebel."

A cough on the other side of the curtain made us both look up.

"Excuse me, Mrs. Duncan. It's me, ma'am, it's Cook."

"Yes, Cook, what is it?"

She entered, her pink uniform an incongruity in the dark parlor. Her hands danced and rolled in her apron as if she were drying them over and over. "It's the telephone, Mrs. Duncan. It's Marie. It's over at the Big House. It's Mrs. McCalla Senior. Marie said she didn't wake up from her

151

nap. She went to change her and nothing happened." The hands fought furiously with each other under the apron. "I mean, she says Mrs. McCalla Senior won't wake up and she's afraid she's dead, and Mrs. Desjardins isn't there and nobody's here but you. So Marie wants to talk to you, please, Mrs. Duncan, ma'am."

thirteen.

DUNCAN'S pneumonia, his last desperate snorkeling struggle for breath, had made us all less aware of Big Rachel. She was ninety-nine and we expected her to live forever.

We had been more sensitive, in fact, to Marie's increasing feebleness, for Marie at least could speak, apologizing at defensive length for her inadequacies. Her *rheumatismus:* she was terribly sorry, she could not Madam in bed any more turn over; she was grateful to be able, with the silver spoon of Madam's own *grossmutter,* to feed her still; she would continue to repair Madam's lingerie, and she was in fact even now some wonderful undergarments for the *garderobe* preparing, for the day Madam would feel better again; but it was slow work, she must please be forgiven, because of her fingers—and she held them up, a clump of tiny bamboo shoots with swollen joints, which display looked childish and ancient at the same time. Oh, she was terribly *reumutig,* she said, shaking her head and waving her hands. Martha thought she meant terribly rheumatic and expressed sympathy with her pain. Marie shook her head and tears came to her eyes, which increased Martha's consoling tone and moved her on to her be-bright-and-buck-up-now smile.

Crispin intervened. "I think she said she is terribly *re-morseful,* Mother. *Reumutig,* did you say, Marie? Rueful, regretful?"

Marie nodded, a little smile broke through her tears. Inhaling, she clicked her false teeth.

"It's not the pain in her hands she's complaining about, you see, it's the impediment to her work she's apologizing

153

for. She wants to do everything for Grandmother, but she finds it impossible to do nearly as much as she wishes." Crispin, interpreting, added on his own, "It's an affliction of soul, you might say."

Marie nodded several times. Martha smiled upon her and hired registered nurses to cover late afternoon and the night vigil. For the "easier time," 8 A.M. to 4 P.M., she brought Babs back to the compound.

There I discovered her when I returned with my bachelor's degree and acceptance to Yale Law School. She was someone I knew and did not know, a woman with an acrobat's carriage and a fugitive alertness, part of my childhood and the mystery of myself.

"What do you do up there?" I asked Babs—meaning, on the second floor, in the master suite of the Big House.

"I change her diapers."

I felt a suck in my gut. I had not thought about the problems of greatly advanced age. My elders never discussed it, but assumed that the best care would be provided at home, whatever the cost.

"That's right," Babs said. She was matter-of-fact: "Marie feeds her and I change her, and the bedsheets and all. And I sit and watch her, and I watch Marie sew. She's doing a complete new wardrobe for her, I don't ask for what. I just say how beautiful it is. And it *is*. She can stitch, even with her fingers stiff as clothespins. But so slow. Sometimes I want to say, 'Will you let me help, Marie?' But I know she won't, so I don't say it."

"Well, I'm glad you're back and you're helping. It doesn't sound too hard." I wanted to get beyond the business of diapers, and preserve my ideal of my great-grandmother: a woman of dignity who wore a black velvet choker with a diamond. But my remark made Babs glare at me.

"Just changing McCalla diapers isn't hard. A whole lot of people around here have been cleaning up your family's shit for a long time, and, like your grandmother says, practice makes perfect."

I protested with an apology but she rode over it.

"And that's not all. I'm a second floor and sickroom maid,

and I do stunts at firemen's fairs, and take ballet lessons, and go on dates with friends of Kidder Towne, and friends of Kidder's friends. And same time keep Buddy off the bottle. The whole thing's a high wire, and I've got the kitchen sink on my back. I can't do it all."

I thought she was going to cry, and I wondered what to do, for I had only seen her weep once, while Buddy tried to revive Clellan. But as I watched the luminous moistening of her eyes, I saw fury prevailing over pity of self.

I spoke to her softly, trying to ally with her: "I'm sure you can do it."

"I can't. I'm busting in pieces."

"Not you. You're strong, you always are."

She stared at me. Her nostrils narrowed. "Never," she said. "I never was."

"OK then." I searched for a way through her problem, using lawyer's logic. "Stop doing something. Why not? Pick one thing and quit that. What are you going to stop doing?"

"Nothing. I need the money."

"How much do you need?"

"Anything I can't use, Buddy can use."

"Is Buddy depending on you?" I wondered why and how.

"For some dough. And some company. He had a heart attack last winter. You didn't know? It was right after he lost his job at the Lawn Club. You didn't hear about that, either? Four or five weeks he was looking for work after that, and then one day he got this pain in his back, the right side, and he said it must have been from lifting a ladder, and I said you don't lift anything but bottles, and I didn't think anything was wrong and neither did he, because your heart's on the left side, right? And in *front?* But whammo, suddenly there it was, the pain, and he turned the color of your Aunt Bekka's hair, kind of blue and white. So I got him on the trolley and we went to the hospital. Heart attack. Mild, they said. But watch out. This guy is what? going on fifty-five years of age, and his muscles are only thirty-five years old. Great. But his veins are seventy-five. So watch out; he's gotta watch it."

I was shocked. I said I was sorry, it was terrible. But

anyway, could he work? And what had happened at the Lawn?

"Sure he can work. He likes work. But who wants a tumbler with arthritis and a bad heart? Maybe they'll take him back at the Lawn some day. Part-time, maybe, waiting or something. But not in the locker room. He's finished there, as long as old man Cardigan is around." She told the story: Buddy was shining shoes, doing massage, helping exercise routines, all the stuff he'd picked up and could do. He was popular and everybody liked him. But with some members he had trouble when they treated him too flunkey-like, and the worst was Mr. William Cardigan. Yes, Mr. Shepherd Cardigan's father. He was accustomed to getting his toenails cut at least once a month. So he said.

But, Buddy said, excuse me, that wasn't included in massage, it wasn't part of his duties, he meant.

Well, Mr. Cardigan said, all the other locker room men had always done it for him and so Buddy could do it.

Well, maybe, Buddy said, he wasn't so good at that, and he shouldn't do what he wasn't good at.

He could learn, Old Man Cardigan said.

Excuse me, Buddy said, he didn't really want to learn, it wasn't part of his job to cut toenails, nobody had ever told him he had to cut toenails, and maybe Mr. Cardigan better go to a pediatrician instead.

Podiatrist, Old Man Cardigan corrects him. He has no intention of paying a podiatrist when he can get a simple job done at his own club where he's been a member in good standing for fifty years and it's always been done for him. Always.

Never, says Buddy, has he ever done a thing like that, and there's a limit, and he ain't about to do it.

You damn well are going to do it, says Cardigan, or the manager is going to hear about it.

OK, let him hear, Buddy says.

Cut my toenails, Cardigan says.

Suck a moose, says Buddy. Yes, that's what he actually says. If he hadn't said that maybe he could have got out of it somehow, but shit, Cardigan is the fucking vice chairman of the board of the Lawn Club and going to be the next chairman and he's been insulted, he says, on top of insubordination. So that's how Buddy got fired.

"Well, suck a moose," I said, and I shook my head, taking it all in. "How come he gave Uncle Clellan mouth-to-mouth resuscitation and he wouldn't cut Old Man Cardigan's toenails?" Less a question than an observation.

Babs answered anyway. "He's got pride. And your uncle was his friend." Not employer, notice. Friend.

"Pride's great, but getting fired and a heart attack is rough."

"Sure is. Now he's got no paycheck. He needs medicine that costs plenty, and his liquor costs more. He depends on me coming over and having a couple of drinks with him to slow him up. I make him go to bed so he doesn't go on all night and finish the bottle."

"Come over? Where do you live? I thought you lived with him."

"No. I got a little place for myself. Near my ballet lessons, downtown. It's not too far from the Cork and Bottle. I stop in there for laughs sometimes. They don't mind tears dripping on their piano. What with all the rings and beer slosh on it."

Who is this girl? I wondered. I put the question differently: "The Cork and Bottle? I've heard of it, I guess."

She didn't pick up the lead. She looked away.

"Why not give up the ballet lessons? They must cost. What's the future?"

"Maybe there's a future, maybe no future. Anyway, I got to have them. The ballet is my art." Again I wondered: who is this?

The next thought came slowly and I put it tentatively. "If you're short on time, what are you doing with these friends of Kidder Towne's? Are they a problem?"

"No, they're not bad guys, most of them. They're company anyway, and better than the Cork and Bottle crowd. They come from all over, and they're successful, and . . ." Here she hesitated. "Sometimes I can get a loan from them. That helps out."

157

A red film of alarm formed in my vision. A question rose; I pushed it out of sight. The same energy came back in an aggressive query with a different thrust: "Maybe you should quit this job here. It pays too little, takes up too much time. Concentrate on stuff that pays."

At this her eyes widened, and fright replaced the anger in them. "No." She was suddenly still. "I like it here. I'm glad they asked me to do it." She was quiet an unusually long while. "This has always been home."

I thought; for years, it seemed. "Why don't you move back in, then? Ask Aunt Martha. There are always lots of rooms. One place or another."

"Maybe. Maybe I will."

How long was it since I had been with Big Rachel? Had I done other than stand in the doorway a few times and look in on her these four years since her stroke? Until then she had travelled down and up the walnut stairway on her electric seat once a day at teatime, and on Sundays for supper; and as long as she held court thus, I took no occasion to go upstairs. When she reigned from chambers, so to speak, I had had cause to ascend, but because she was deaf, and blind, and speechless, peeking in the doorway and chatting with Marie was all that my elders expected of me. And all that I had done.

Marie dressed B-Ray each day for whatever audience there might be, and set her hair, and sat her up against pillows in a lace-edged pink bedjacket. She gazed sightless and serenely before her, while I looked soundless in upon her. Once or twice I had thought of sitting down at bedside, but it seemed pointless, and I didn't know how to explain myself to Marie: her territory, really. Her baby.

My father's death changed my mind. I decided on a different kind of visit. I asked Marie if I could be alone with B-Ray. She faded obediently and instantly away, as if she had been hoping for the request. I approached the bed. I saw a wizened, expressionless woman, neck muscles slack with great age, sitting up only by virtue of the pillows behind her, her once regal throat and chin no longer commanding, her mouth not quite lolling, but given to small fluttering breaths poorly coordinated with the shallow arrhythmic labor of her lungs. Faint blue eyes seemed painted, as on archaic Greek statuary, except when they fell under heavy lids. This day Marie had adorned her with pince-nez, which kept its balance and flashed light, reminding me of the day President Roosevelt had died, and I had wept in my bedroom, and wondered why I did so, because all McCallas were Republicans.

Now I stood by the four-poster bed of my great-grandparents, with its dense canopy of white silk. I saw one reason why Marie could no longer cope and needed Babs and shifts of nurses. The bed was almost hip-high; it had a stair-step to climb into it, and required a supple reach to minister to a patient there. I marvelled at the care the family provided its aging women, and its most aged; and criticized myself for imagining the cost.

I reached out and took Big Rachel's left hand in my right and held it like a child's. Unlike a child's, it did not nestle, but bided its time. I spoke to her quietly, unrehearsed, surprised by the resonance and ease of my voice: "I am Randall, son of Duncan and grandson of Andrew, who was your son. We carry on. We McCallas still live around you. We continue on the land your husband Rowan bought. This is the house he built for you, and your bed is the bed you shared with him. I am your great-grandson, Randall McCalla. And I will carry on."

As I spoke, the tiny talon opened slightly and its fingers took one of mine and held it. At the word "Rowan" I imagined that it increased its faint pressure. When I ceased speaking, it relaxed and became again an aimless claw. I placed it on her lap, next to her other hand on the silk coverlet. I turned and left the room, without registering any detail but of the woman and her bed. At the doorway I chided myself for the speech. "Clannish, cabalistic, pompous."

Then I turned, smiled back at the glaucous stare behind the crystal pince-nez, and blew the woman a kiss. That unseen, insouciant gesture was my last to Big Rachel alive.

Three days later Cook appeared in pink uniform and white apron, afluster, to say that Madam had not wakened from her nap.

Marie provided the outfit in which B-Ray went to the mausoleum: white lace undergarments, black velvet evening dress, black velvet choker about her neck, and upon the velvet a diamond. Gramma thought it was a family diamond and hence directed by testament elsewhere, but Martha said that her mother had given that one to Marie as a present on fifty years of service. Gramma, Bekka, and Martha all tried to persuade Marie to keep it herself, but Marie wanted it to go with B-Ray on her choker. There the matter teetered, sensitive and unmastered, until Crispin returned by plane from Florence. He had allotted seven days to obsequies, family councils, and his museum desk, before returning to summer studies and negotiations overseas. Among other matters to clear up was whether the diamond would go to the crypt or not. Crispin adopted the mien of a businessman, and when Marie poured herself out in German, he translated.

"She says there are no grave robbers here in America. She says she came to this land of freedom to get away from grave robbers in Austria, and she never regretted it. She says that my grandmother, her beloved Madam, offered her freedom and she accepted it joyously, and she will be forever grateful in life and after death. She does not stop there, but says a great deal more which I will try to summarize. She says that the McCalla family has always been kind to her and she loves us all because of our kinship to her beloved Madam. We have rarely misunderstood her, but if we do not accede to her wishes on this matter now, we will have wronged her, and she would find it difficult to understand."

Marie listened while Crispin delivered her points, nodding to his voice, its listing cadence, neutral and official. She seemed barely conscious of the syntactical roundness he was giving her thought in English, the diplomatic glosses he might be adding to her heated delivery; but she looked assured, by key words here and there, and by Crispin's earnest tone, that her heart's mind was being conveyed fairly to the family council, reaching, as purely as human agency could carry it through alien tongue, into our mind's heart.

"Because she knows we have always appreciated her devotion to her beloved Madam, the misunderstanding in this case must surely be a practical one. America, of course, is our nation, and she, an ignorant immigrant, is not challenging our knowledge of the customs of our countrymen. Neither is she unaware of the fact that there is thievery about which was not here when she arrived in the days of the Emperor, and of the first President Roosevelt; but still she trusts that her contribution to the eternal beauty and enduring serenity of her beloved Madam will not be refused." Crispin paused, lifted his eyebrows before passing on the next thought. "And the diamond, she says, after all, is hers to give or to flush down the toilet."

Crispin cocked his head as if to hear if Marie wished any of this translation corrected, but she merely nodded, in the same rhythm in which he had been speaking, eager that he pick up the beat again and finish.

"I may have missed something now and then in what Marie has said, and I may have streamlined her reasoning slightly, but there you have it. She concludes emphatically by reminding us that America is not a land of grave robbers, but the land of freedom and opportunity. She hopes that Madam will be allowed to wear the diamond, which was Marie's joy to have received. She has cherished it, but it has never left her bureau drawer. It rightly belongs, she believes, on Madam's velvet choker."

Crispin paused, sighed, and looked at each of us around the seated circle. "I think we might agree," he said, "that the diamond pin would become Marie beautifully, as Grandmother originally intended it to do. Nonetheless, Marie is apparently convinced that its true splendor may be realized only by her being allowed to give it to her mistress. I admit, myself, to a bit of embarrassment at the element of Pharaonic tribute in Marie's intention, *but*, if my opinon were asked"—here he let his gaze dwell on Gramma for a moment—"I would say that we ought immediately to

161

thank Marie for her sublime gesture and for her selfless devotion to the beloved head of our family. And so dispose
of the matter at once."

To that suggestion there was an immediate babble of approval from Martha, Bekka, and Adelaide. I allowed myself
a solo male "Absolutely" to cover Gramma's silence and to
confirm the others.

Marie, who had begun to look hopeful, brightened enormously as Crispin spoke to her in German, and she began
nodding again and uttering "Danke" in cadence with his
sentences. When he concluded, she smiled slightly, said
"Thank you, everyone. Excuse me," and curtsied herself
out of the parlor.

Our council dissolved a few minutes later, with matters
of houses, lands, and servants on its agenda barely scratched
and waiting until after burial. I passed Marie in the hall.
She was seated with her back to the spinet, looking upon
the midday radiance flowing through the stained glass window, the shadows cast by the banisters, listening to the dock-
dock of the grandfather clock in the sunlit center of the dark
hall. On the mahogany bench beside her sat her false teeth,
grinning, and on her sunken lips and cheeks persisted a tiny
purse of a smile.

No one had heard a word from Rachel McCalla for four
years, and she had not heard clear sounds from others for
almost forty. Rowan had died in 1917, and Rachel, of a
generation seldom seen about town without husbands, had
lived little thereafter beyond the life of the compound.
Nonetheless, "a goodly crowd," as Reverend McCracken
noted, was in attendance at the service for her. Old
McCracken was one of the few left who had poured live
words into B-Ray's ear, and he spoke as if he were doing
so once more. "She was the model of a woman, wife, and
mother, and it was her good fortune to be surrounded by
family who grew in her presence, nurtured and bounded
by her love. She was among the first and most faithful of
our radio audience, that now enlarged throng which attends
our services every Sunday though they be without trans-

portation or shut-in with infirmity; and she said to me, rather loudly, I must allow, for control of volume is one of the problems of those afflicted with deafness, that she heard me better over the radio than in the church.

"I am glad that Rachel McCalla kept attuned to the word of God, and I imagine that she did so more closely and faithfully than many of us who harken to the noisy barbaric pleadings of our daily world, and permit them to diminish or shut out the still small voice of calm. Rachel McCalla always heeded that voice. And even in her isolation of silence, as I imagine it, she had a completeness of understanding and of commitment to the role of matriarch of one of the great Scotch-Irish clans of this city, one of the great Presbyterian families of Pittsburgh." (These words shocked me not unpleasantly, and entertained Crispin, who afterward spoke of them as "lurid" and "unlikely.") "And where'er her spirit be transported now, its generous rays, I profoundly believe, will be refracted through the stained glass window she gave in memory of her beloved husband, Rowan, ere these many years ago." ("Tasteless," Crispin said, nearly convulsed with amusement. "Wretched rhetoric. Is he after another window? Damned cheeky.")

B-Ray had little money in her own name. In a will dated twenty years before, she gave half of it to Marie and the other half in fifths to two other maids, since deceased, and to three different entities: to the family mausoleum in enhanced endowment; to the Presbyterian Orphan Asylum for its Christmas parties; and to the church for its altar flowers. So McCracken was not wholly forgotten. And Marie, by any standard known to her, was rich; which would still have meant insecure by the standards of the world around her, were it not for Bekka's taking her in; needing her, indeed, for someone to talk to about her departed mother and brother, and to provide the luxury of custom-made lingerie.

After church, guests flowed like molasses into the Big House: from a dark, slow stream of limousines, a trickle of the aged, somberly dressed. Their number surprised me. They presented a traffic problem getting at Aunt Martha,

163

who was best disposed to receive them. Bekka preferred to stand and fidget rather than "receive" in a formal way. Gramma supervised the maids at the strawberry punch, and made her greetings there. Lolly offered to help. Duffie, hot from golfing, drank punch. All our collateral and distant relatives came, many of them only table names to me; hangers-on clung fast; aged bondholders of the Lawn Club surfaced; radio Presbyterians arrived, and traditional presbyters; up-and-comers appeared, and reverers of matriarchy; the bored with nothing better to attend than funerals; and the aspiring, who wished to brush among families long resident in the urban *polis*.

Their umbrellas overflowed the two blue and white china stands, one from Bekka's house. Their coats burst open the closet doors. They made their way toward Martha who, plumped on a divan, acknowledged each with the crisp brave smile of the bereaved. I helped her settle; backed off a standing gaggle of bankers who temporarily obscured sight of her; set a pattern so that all might make their way around the tables and highbacked chairs and across the parquet floor, chattering with death-inspired amicability, until they could be paired, for this was Martha's preference, one on each side of her on the settee: mated or mismatched, it didn't matter, for she could hold several conversations at a time, and, like a chessmaster, anticipate moves and counters. She rose in antic pleasure to the challenge. Without signals arranged beforehand, she conveyed to me by glances when to introduce the nextcomers, that she might bend her beaming farewell smile upon the thensitters, so sorry that they must go, yet confident that in the formulaic chatter, amidst the twitter of edicts, recollections, wistful gossip, chuckles, and acknowledgments, all had been heard, and the right thing said on behalf of her mother and the McCalla family. Could anyone doubt whence emanated the style of her brilliant son Crispin, just now on the phone to Italy, poor thing?

That night I read again the ripped-out pulpy yellow magazine fragment I had lifted from Clellan's library drawer.

164

Knowledge is power, is it not? There I learned that my forebears had dealt with Andrew Carnegie. I felt powerful in a way I knew was artificial and suspect. But if in the shape and shade of those dealings another knowledge was to be had, of the mystery of McCallas declining, that negative knowledge would give me defensive power. I determined to go after it, and to learn all I could of a truth I imagined priceless.

Should we sell the entire compound, all buildings and lands, to whoever had the grandest conception and the biggest wallet? Or each lot separately to the highest bidder? Factors of time and money, their unpredictable emotional vectors, drew out the discussion, requiring all of Crispin's skill as mediator. Martha was for a bloc sale. Her intuition was that finding individual buyers would be difficult; her own, as the biggest house, with the most elaborate details, might find a perfect buyer quickly; but, quite possibly, in the Year of Our Lord 1958, might never find one at all. And she wanted to move to a small house in Sewickeley, swiftly. She knew just the one, near Crispin,, coming on the market soon.

Gramma, however, was for individual sales. She wanted to realize a price for her house that her deceased husband, A. C., would think appropriate. She was in no hurry about moving to the Fox Hollow apartments, the most feasible alternative for her. As for Bekka, she loved her house and didn't want to leave it. Thirty years without her husband and four years without her brother, however, made her ready to move at a price worthy of the house and the loving care she'd given it, a price she imagined more likely offered by an individual buyer. If they had to move to Fox Hollow, it would nonetheless be a lot easier if she and her sister-in-law moved at the same time and set up nearby apartments; which factor could favor sale en bloc.

All of this Crispin teased out with suppositions and suggestions, treating all he heard with dignity, even when Gramma posed anxious, unanswerable questions on how to move mantelpieces and chandeliers. Privately, between discussions, he fumed to Martha about getting back to Florence: "But I can't appear to favor your view, dear Mother, or that will queer the outcome. Patience, patience."

I was included, not at my mother's suggestion, but at Martha's. "After all, he's the man of the compound now, isn't he?" Adelaide's mouth drew tight, but she opened it to answer, reasonably enough, yes he was. So like her I attended the discussions, not as a property holder, but a potentially displaced person.

I daydreamed through the dandelion fields and loblolly mire of these estate discussions. A peculiar scene came back to me from the day of the funeral, demanding replay and revision. I had been helping Babs move furniture after the reception. We put away the folding chairs, restored hidden objects, and nudged the piano back in its place, from which it had been moved to set up the table for strawberry punch. The last car was long gone, the elders dispersed, the maids to other duties, when we finished. We both exhaled at once, and turned to each other, smiling. Babs suddenly put her hands on my shoulders and rested her forehead lightly on my shirt pocket. She set her hips square to mine and pulled close. I felt a sweet shot of light go through me, and drew back.

She looked at me quizzically. Then she said, "Prude."

What was that she had said?

"Proust," perhaps? Some arcane reference I could parry back? No, not from Babs.

"Prune," was it? Like Cook used to say, tickling me as a little boy, doubling me up on the floor, a defenseless jelly of ganglia—"You're a prune," paroxysms of boy-laughter; "you're fulla prunes," soprano shrieks I couldn't control.

No. I had heard it right.

I sighted one last piece of furniture out of place, a standing Tiffany lamp. The colored glass panes of its leaded shade were in the same tones as the window of the family mausoleum—martyrs' red, prophets' blue, the green of the saints, and sinners' yellow—the colors as well of my boyhood Sunday school pamphlets. I slid the lamp back to its place behind B-Ray's armchair, and in the dusk of the living room I pulled the chain to light it. I looked around for Babs. She was gone.

I had first heard about Dinerstein years before, when he had sought to buy the empty lot. The family was indisposed to conceive of a strange house or houses in their midst, and the main consequence of his offer was a Sunday supper conversation on how to pronounce his name.

Bekka began it by referring to him as "Dynersteen."

Martha gently corrected her. "Dinnersteen."

Amid general headshaking at the table, Crispin had said that if pronounced the German way the first "i" would sound faintly like an "E" and the "ei" combination would sound like an "I."

Duncan almost snarled: "This guy is an American. He lives right here in Pittsburgh, on Panther Hill. So he should pronounce his name the American way: *Dynerstyne.*"

"I don't care what he calls himself," Adelaide said. "I pronounce his name 'M-O-N-E-Y.' "

B-Ray had picked up her ear trumpet at this rapid contretemps, wondering what principled anger deserved her attention now.

As it happened, I was able to arbitrate with authority. "I knew his son at the academy before I went to St. Luke's. He called it 'Dinnerstyne.' "

We declined his offer and soon forgot how to pronounce his name. Now he appeared on the scene again. Crispin had made inquiries of trusted realtors who advised that it would indeed be difficult to sell the three houses separately. Estimates ranged up to two or three years, with prices said to be "soft" and uncertain. Once the word was out, Mr. Dinerstein expressed himself as interested in the entire thing, half a city block, or the "whole kit and caboodle," as Gramma called it.

"You're interested then," Crispin asked, "aren't you, Auntie dear, in how much boodle we kin can get for the whole kit?"

"Well, yes, I suppose so."

"Good then. I will ask Mr. Dinerstein directly about it, using the range that I derived from the realtors to judge what he says, and pushing him as far as I can toward the upper end of it."

The next discussion proceeded from Dinerstein's offer, which was "interesting" in Martha's view, Bekka agreeing, but "stingy" in Gramma's view. Dinerstein's plans to develop the property, should they sell it, became a prominent concern.

CRISPIN: What would be built there?

DINERSTEIN: Oh, some small houses and maybe a big building.

CRISPIN: What kind of building?

DINERSTEIN: Well, Congregation Magen David is looking for a new place, has been a long time.

CRISPIN: A synagogue? My relatives will want to know if this area is zoned for that.

DINERSTEIN: I have had my associates look into the zoning and there is no problem.

CRISPIN: Precisely how many little houses, then?

DINERSTEIN: Oh, six or eight, and one for the rabbi. Maximum ten. Maybe less. Probably less.

CRISPIN: Ten? Small houses, small lots. Does the zoning law not have a minimum? We have to think of our neighbors and their values.

DINERSTEIN: Depends on size of synagogue. Can't say. You're asking me impossible things. I'm asking you, here's the point, does the McCalla family want to sell?

CRISPIN: I can't answer that absolutely. It depends on the price. My mother and my aunts think they can sell individually to people who will give them a good price and cherish their houses.

DINERSTEIN: Believe me, Mr. Desjardins, they're not going to get buyers. Not for all those houses. People want different features nowadays. Modern type. With conveniences. People don't have a lot of servants nowadays. You want to sell this place to a school, OK, maybe they convert buildings like that and use them, make a playground. But you got any schools asking you? And what if you did, your

168

neighbors, what do they think about noisy kids five days a week? Your family, you should think about it. I'm offering you a temple, a House of God.

CRISPIN: We respect your House of God, but your price seems to me about twenty percent too low.

DINERSTEIN: Well, think about it. It's nice talking. Give my respects.

That account drew from everybody appreciation of Crispin's bargaining tactics. But Gramma and Bekka both said, "Wouldn't a school be better than a *synagogue?*"

"Possibly," Crispin replied. "But do you know a school that wants three elaborate turn-of-the-century dwellings and a playground?"

They did not.

They were willing, it seemed, to sell to Dinerstein (whom they now began to call "Mr.") at the right price, without mentioning his project. Gramma balked, saying that her late husband A. C. would dislike such an idea. When Mr. Dinerstein came up by ten percent she ceased objecting. But her mien continued to protest. Finally a compromise was reached. If, through private realtors, they could not dispose of the houses separately at higher prices in six months, they would sell to Mr. Dinerstein together. The developer agreed, and asked Crispin "to tell the ladies of his family how he enjoyed doing business with the Mc-Callas, one of the finest families in Pittsburgh."

That, of course, Crispin did, with a comical remark about Dinerstein and McCracken, their interfaith agreement on the eminence of the McCallas. He took the next plane for New York to make his trans-Atlantic connections, which would get him to Florence just in time for an auction. He was looking at a *Sepulchrum Christi*, reputedly by Perugino. He wanted to inspect it again, very closely, before bidding.

fourteen.

RAIN FELL after the funeral, through the family councils, and Crispin's departure. Between the throws of rain, thick spells of mist arose and hung over humid evenings. The women prepared for the Jersey shore. Longing for sunshine and sea-breeze, they put mourning behind, spoke briskly to maids. The day they left it poured. Clouds, low over Panther Hill, rolled down into Fox Hollow like a smoker's exhalation. After the last limousine slid past the tigers at our gate, the torrent subsided, ceased. Copper beech trees, heavy with water, drooped on the smaller willows, and soggy linden on blossomless dogwood. Rhododendron sagged.

"Tomorrow I have a surprise for you." Babs passed me a small yellowed envelope with the McCalla family crest on it, and slid back into her duties, following up details of departures from three houses. Careful capitals spelled Randall McCalla. I opened the envelope, thinking she must have found it in a neglected drawer somewhere (she, too, delving in family drawers?). I read her hand on the heavy stock invitation card inside:

Tomorrow evening
9:30 P.M.
at the Big House
champagne
spinet music
acrobatics
by the Barbara Quick Company
admission: by card only

I tucked the card in a trouser pocket and felt myself smiling: A circus after a summer of funerals.

I went to my room, reread it, and found myself pacing back and forth from the west window, facing garage and Bekka's house, to the north window facing the Big House. I turned over in my mind my status, sadly circumstantial, a little empty, but more than a trifle exhilarating, as "the man of the compound."

Bekka was gone to Atlantic City, which she still believed a chic resort, as in the nineteen-thirties. She stayed at the Marlborough Blenheim, where Martha accompanied her for a week before proceeding to Italy, and Crispin in Vallambrosa. Luther drove them both. Gramma was chauffeured again to Cape May, where she rented as she had with A. C., newlywed at the turn of the century, oblivious now to the town's post-Victorian desuetude. She never went to beach or boardwalk, but played penny stakes with a summer set of Mah-Jongg sharks. Together they raveled the loose ends of their club lives and genealogies.

My mother as usual drove herself to Rumson. She would stay at the country club only a week this year, before proceeding to Cape Cod, where she had never been before. She was going up there "for a change," she said, long-faced at the Sunday supper table, as if the memories in Rumson of past happiness with my father would be too much to bear. Someone, however—a bridge partner perhaps—had whispered to Gramma implications about Kidder Towne being a regular in Hyannisport, which had given that innocent routine mind something new and raw to think about. "Why, the *idea . . .*" Gramma said. Her range of exclamation was limited and depended on tone for its meaning. She left for New Jersey with her tone uncertain and brow lined.

My mother invited me, pro forma, to join her in Rumson as usual. I declined. We exchanged forced smiles and formulas of regret. I accepted the role of housewatcher along with Cook, for whom it was a vacation to have none or few to feed. I took breakfast with her, got a sandwich for lunch, tried not to bother her for dinner. Sodini's Delicatessen was easier on the spirit than sitting at the head of the dining room table, before crocheted doilies and silver pheasant centerpieces, waited on by Cook in her strict anomalous pink.

Babs was charged to watch over Bekka's and the Big House. She was given keys, and a list of caretaking duties. With chauffeurs and maids at the coast or on vacation, no one else remained in the compound but Elise, who caught up on seamstress work and reading Sir Walter Scott. She smiled more when Luther was away.

This August, then, the population of the compound was four. In a short time it would be none. In one week, family councils and side-parleys had determined the shape of a new era, after the compound was sold:

Marie to replace Bekka's second maid, who was to be discharged, so that Bekka would continue to have a cook and one maid, plus Marie as seamstress-companion.

Martha to take her cook and a maid eventually to Sewickeley (letting one maid go).

Gramma to keep Cook and a maid (letting one maid go).

All three chauffeurs to be retained and summoned by telephone upon need.

A significant increase in pay for Luther, who would have to move out of the garage, and rent his own home; and because Elise would have no seamstress work to do, for which the retained maids would be counted on instead.

Gardening service discontinued; there would be no grounds to keep, except such little in Sewickeley as Martha might contract for.

Black Rachel to be released. The age of the electric washer and dryer was at last to be recognized, and ironing would be added to the duties of the maids in the apartments, for a small increase in pay.

Net: ten people retained to serve three septuagenarian women, while five people were discharged and gardening ended. Three of the five were with the fewest years of service, but we all felt a little pang about Elise, and a much larger one about Black Rachel. Elise was still "with the family" through Luther, but there was no place for Black Rachel. "I seed it comin'," she said, and made no complaint. She declined offers to try to place her with the Lawn Club or with various friends of the family who had large laundry problems. "I seed I got to do something else for while," she said, and accepted a cash bonus as severance. Martha, who considered herself a democrat, invited Black Rachel to tea in the Big House, but Rachel declined, saying she had too much wash to finish, thank you. So Martha instead pronounced McCalla gratitude and farewell benedictions from the iron-rung landing of the Big House laundry yard, while Black Rachel nodded below, lingerie in hand, clothespins in her mouth.

My mother's future was uncertain, though guessable. Mine, through law school and inheritance, had structure and support, which allowed me with covert intensity to "go after Rowan," as I put it to myself: find the flaw in the major figure of the McCalla dynasty.

For Babs, no clear decision was reached. As Martha said, "She has been with the family a long time, since infancy in fact. And she was wonderfully useful when we called her back to help with Mother. But she is really just short-term help; and with Mother gone, what is there for her to do?" The women clucked assent. No cut-off date was declared for Babs. "Let her stay as long as she likes," Bekka said. The implied terminus was the day of demolition. "D-Day," I thought, a bit grimly, and wondered who, if anyone, would spell out the decision to Babs.

So this was death: a need for many decisions, a flurry of logistics, wills revealed, promises kept or not kept, disappointments, rearrangements, continuings-despite. I was surprised how much more seemed to happen after B-Ray's death than after my father's, and I felt him once more slighted. But there is a difference between the end of a life and the close of an era. The most important event for me, in any case, was one of which the compound had no knowledge: my conversation with my mother. Sometimes the picture came back to me, her knuckles white on the chairarms. Truth makes the muscles tighten, the blood race. Truth was my vital potion, my aphrodisiac. I wanted more. I

173

sensed that the truth about Rowan McCalla and Andrew Carnegie, if I could find it, would make me fully blooded as a hunting man.

Departures had left me temporarily the Master of the McCalla Compound. But it stirred me more to think of myself as historian of the clan, searcher for secrets, detective and seer; an avenger with a shaman's power.

"Is this the Barbara Quick Company? In its entirety?" I smiled. There was only she, in leotards. With the big cameo she had worn at Buddy's birthday party.

"Yes, and you're all the company there is to see the Company." She was smiling, too. She swept her hand, palm up, toward a card table at the foot of the stairs. One folding chair, one glass, a bottle of champagne. I sat down, wondering. The bottle read "Mumm's Extra Dry, 1949." She plucked and ripped off the foil, uncoiled the wire about the cork, and, resting the bottle's bottom against her diaphragm, began slowly thumbing the cork free the way her father did, guardian palm on top. "You folks don't drink enough champagne around here. There's lots. It piles up in the cellar."

"Thanks for siphoning off some of the glut."

"Never mind thanks. Just enjoy." The cork came out, an archangelic pop, with a luciferous coil of fume. Standing, she poured. Again I noted Buddy's casual hand in her curling the last drop free of the bottle's lip.

I drank, raised my eyebrows in appreciation; lifted my glass to her, drank again. I poured it full and offered her the glass.

She took an indifferent sip, shook her head, and seated herself at the keyboard. The first spinet to cross the Allegheny Mountains, Aunt Martha liked to say. I had not heard it struck since, in my early teens, I stopped routinely tapping a few notes in passing. She played "The Daring Young Man on the Flying Trapeze." The sound struck me as incredibly poignant, Scarlatti to the ear and Charlie Chaplin to the heart. I nodded my head as she cantered along, and I swung out my glass in an acrobat's arc. Her fingers ran on in the

174

lilt of the song, and I hummed and waved my champagne. I felt as if I were over a darkened pit with only a spotlight to catch me, swinging on the coursing bars of time, sailing above the desperate whoopee of the Great Depression.

When she finished, I applauded.

With a half look she nodded from the bench. As I drank, she moved into the theme song from *La Strada*. She's been practicing, I thought. We had just gone to see the movie, she and Duffie and I.

"Anthony Quinn reminds me of Buddy, busting chains with his chest," I had said. A half-thought remark; but her comeback was serious.

"Who does *she* remind you of?"

"What's-her-name? The waif?" Duffie answered before anything occurred to me. "She reminds me of you."

Babs appeared so gratified that I curbed my usual critical testing of Duffie's moves, and Duff, feeling that he had scored with Babs, for once did not overplay his hand. So we had walked home in silence, locked in our temporary cinema identities, and our imaginings of each other.

I drank. To the sound of the spinet I heard cornet accompanying, from the film. I felt a sting of tears remembering the strong man's impotent brawn, the gamine's unread heart. Babs finished and swung around for approval. I shook my head, signifying it was beyond words, raised both glass and bottle to her, and refilled my drink.

She took a deep breath, straightened her back, and set into "Crazy Rhythm." Did she know that it was one of my parents' songs, one of the few cues that set them to reminiscing about dances at the Lawn and parties at friends' houses before I was born? On the spinet it sounded bizarre. She rose immediately when she finished, slipped on gleaming black pumps, and set off down the parquet hallway in a tap-dance routine built to the song.

Crazy rhythm here's the doorway
I'll go my way you go your way
Crazy rhythm from now on we're through
They say that when a highbrow

Meets a lowbrow
Walking along Broadway
Soon the highbrow, he has no brow
Ain't it a shame.
And you're to blame;
What's the use of prohibition?
You produce the same condition;
Crazy rhythm, I've gone crazy too.
Clackety-clack, stomp, stomp, scuff, scuff, bam!
Applause!

I saw a girl sliding on her knees into a chair, knocking out a baby tooth, holding it in a bloody puddle in her hand while Madison scuttered and scritched on the floor after her, struggling to lick her palm.

Now she put a finger to her lips, kicked off the shoes, and without a pause for breath flipped a cartwheel forward and one reverse in front of me; then ran up the several steps to the first landing. There she did a split and threw out her arms to the crowd. I stood, applauding.

And that took practice too, I thought. She raised a finger as if to signal "time"; she touched the statue of Mercury at winged heel, on winged hat, and under chin, and solicited "time" from him as well. Hermes, I thought, deity of commerce, invention, cunning, and theft. The true divinity of McCalla compound. She disappeared with light leaps up the winding stairs to the second floor.

Next I heard a thin recorded sound of familiar music. The theme song from *La Strada* again, this time played on B-Ray's gramophone. Bemused, bewitched, I drank.

A resonant hum. She appeared standing on B-Ray's electric chair as it wound its way down the banister, one arm extended, circus-style, for applause, which I obediently supplied.

At the stair bottom she stepped off, bowed deeply from the waist, so that her ponytail, flung over her head, nearly touched the floor.

"Brava, brava."

She gestured an invitation to the mechanical seat. I rose

to the gesture, carrying bottle and glass. She shook her head; gently took bottle and glass from my hands, put them on the table, and again indicated the seat. I settled myself in it. She flicked on the switch and as the chair moved upward along the banister she slid lightly onto my lap, smiling into my eyes.

She pointed to Mercury's winged sandals, leaned out to touch his winged ears, waved to him as we passed and rose above him. We turned the slow bend, devotees of Hermes, god of special delivery.

At stairtop she took me by the hand and led me through the doorway into B-Ray's bedroom. I saw that the bedcover was turned back. There was a champagne bottle at bedside and two glasses. My heart was bucking in my chest, trying to break out.

After a pause in which I felt her watching my face, she led me through the room, out onto the open porch over the porte cochere. We stopped at the railing, looking upon the compound in the clear evening air. Above wet hills, the first trick of moon cut between last clouds, threw gleams off the black windows of McCalla houses, the flagpole, the dark disc of the sundial. She turned to me squarely, drew my head down to hers, and kissed me on the lips.

Back to the balcony, hand in hand, barefooted, I see two figures come. Damp beechwood bark crunches under white heels. A single cloud covers the high moon, the glow at its edge bathing in faint light the McCalla kingdom. A wind has risen, rustling leaves on the trees, chasing bark on the asphalt. The two gaze out together upon sleeping houses, nearly empty of servants, wholly empty of masters; upon a garage great with parked cars, and a vacant lot giving way to long grass and weed. They turn toward each other, nude in the summer night. One, slender, tall, bends toward the other, slight, compact; speaks softly in her ear. They clasp under the aged, emerging moon, shining like tarnished silver.

IV.

Love
and Death

1959

fifteen.

"WHAT ARE you doing?" In that resplendent summer, I worked sometimes on papers while Babs sat with me, absent-minded, or stitching oddments for my great-aunts. She had been looking over my shoulder while I read:

> For brains, beauty, and brass, the world has rarely seen the likes of Conning Cassie Chadwick, who parlayed a vivid imagination and a genius for graft into millions of the finest green-paper dollars ever manufactured by a United States mint. As the lusty nineteenth century swooshed pell-mell into the speed-crazy twentieth, green-eyed auburn-haired Cassie, the lush passionate daughter of a poor Canadian section hand, was the queen of her profession.

Pages torn out of a magazine: I was rereading what I had found in Bekka's house, in the baseboard drawer below the glass doors that kept Dickens and Thackeray free of dust.

"Come on," she said.

I shook my head, absorbed in the hypertonic hyphens and the turbulent centuries.

"I want to show you something," she insisted.

"Reading," I grunted. Who had torn and saved this yellowed newspulp? Who stashed it among group shots of testimonial dinners, clippings on the death of Rowan McCalla, photographs of Clellan dancing, and several copies of *True Detective*, taken from a barber shop on Forbes Street, with

pictures of women leering, hiding their faces, lying in pud-
dles of blood?

"Enough reading. Come on outside," Babs said. "I'll see
you in the garden."

"OK. In a minute."

Aunt Bekka subscribed to nothing but *Town and Country*.
She didn't filch magazines from barber shops. In the frag-
mented article about connings, fleccings, and gaffings, I returned to a sentence about Cassie Chadwick, shakily under-
lined: "In Pittsburgh, Rowan McCalla, a multi-millionaire
manufacturer, shelled out $850,000, and was delighted to
do business with her." Clellan's pencil, I supposed.

I read the sentence over, first wide-eyed, then narrow-
eyed. Missing pages left the development and end of the
story unclear, but the grand master of my clan was said to
have been bilked by one whose "total depradations were
estimated at more than $20,000,000." The scale was mag-
nificent—also the cast. "Even as she protested her innocence,
Andrew Carnegie was summoned as a prosecution witness
against her."

Who was Cassie Chadwick? How had she gotten mixed
up with the McCallas? And how did it turn out? There was
something to be learned about my great-grandfather, the
builder of the dynastic compound. Perhaps Rowan could
explain Duncan to me, and from retrieved parts of my father
and great-grandfather I could build a whole self. How vain
this notion seems now. But I was seized by it then.

I tucked the article back in my pocket with some notes
I had made toward research. And went looking for Babs.

We found each other under an apricot moon, and took
each other as found. Mosquitoes drove us closer, dazed and
furious.

Scudding August clouds: dry twitter of leaves in the
beechwood trees.

In B-Ray's bathroom, back upstairs in the Big House,
we found some calamine lotion. With cotton wads we
dabbed each other's bites: on my haunches and shoulder
blades, on her shoulder and flanks. She wriggled away from

my swabbing and grabbed a lipstick. "Stand still." She drew
on me in carmine several signs of the zodiac. "Now you,"
I said. I picked a cinnabar stick, versicolored with age. In
Greek letters I daubed on her buttocks words I learned at
St. Luke's: EROS and AGAPE.

So we passed the summer.

When I came home for Christmas I had Babs on my mind,
and my mother, my great-grandfather, and the law. I found
the law a gross fiction, a contrivance. But experience was
the life of the law, and the law revealer of rules of life.

Family secrets had still greater power. Yet I reared at my
discoveries, like the Remington bronze in Gramma's hallway. I was a horse on its hind legs, in animal fear of the
rattlesnake. I was the cowboy, too, holding onto his hat.

My mother asked for a word with me in the upstairs den.
About property again? Four of the six months of the family
agreement had run out. There was only one low bid for
Bekka's house and no buyers in sight for the other two. All
three households were in a flutter of uncertainty, preparing
for a transition in the spring that could not yet be launched,
but which could not finally be deferred. As a sign that his
bid for the entire compound now looked attractive, Dinerstein's name was being pronounced carefully and precisely.

The shock from my mother was quick and direct. When
we were seated she said, "Kidder Towne loves me, and has
asked me to marry him. I am in love with him and I have
said that after a proper time I will be willing to do so. I
said that one more thing was necessary. I was going to ask
for your permission."

I looked for words and found none. She repeated gently,
to give me time: "So I am asking for your permission."

"If you have his request to marry you, and you want to
marry him, you don't *need* my permission."

"But I'm asking for it just the same. I know Northern
Presbyterians don't do things this way, but this is the way
Southern Presbyterians do it. You're the man of the family

now. By rights, maybe he should ask you, Kidder should. We talked about that, and we decided that I would ask, because I am your mother."

The thought of Kidder asking me was repellent. But I forced myself to think, to talk, to see what could be talked about.

"Well, I think you're right to insist upon a proper time. Isn't it a little soon after my father's death?"

She tightened her lips. "I am not making a mistaken judgment. I love Kidder, I know I love him, and I've known it a long time."

I breathed slowly to the full force of what she said. Did I dare utter my thought? I did.

"I think my father disliked him. Maybe he felt even stronger about it than that. So forgive me for asking: why Kidder Towne? Why him?"

"I asked your father to grant me a divorce. Then we asked him, both together, Kidder and I. Your father said he believed in marriage, not in divorce. He said he had to live his beliefs."

"Why didn't you divorce him, then?"

She squirmed in her chair and answered with eyes averted. "He said I had no grounds for divorce, and that he would contest it."

I tried hard to control an involuntary smile. I imagined clearly the part of the conversation my mother was not repeating: my father saying that he had grounds for divorce, but was not going to pursue them. He didn't believe in divorce.

"Why Kidder Towne?" I asked again, feeling obstinate, my father's surrogate.

"I told you I love him."

"I'm sorry. I still don't quite get it."

"OK." She took a deep breath and straightened her spine, General Randall on horseback, one of Lee's lesser lieutenants. "You don't have to get it. I love him. *I would go through machine-gun fire for him.* But you don't have to understand that. And maybe you can't ever, and won't ever. But I'm

184

asking permission of you anyway. I'm asking permission, do you hear?"

My brain was a dutiful blank. "OK," I said. And then, because that sounded too informal, I added, "Yes, Mother."

She rose from her chair instantly. "Thank you very much." There was no anger or irony in her voice. I stood as she left the room, and I remained standing there awhile, looking at a cedar closet in which I had played as a child. It smelled sweet and sharp inside, and its door, when it closed, went boom.

With the flurry of Christmas and family obligations, half of my week at home was gone before I saw Babs. I wondered why she did not leave some message, or at least expose herself to my sight from a distance. I wanted her to tantalize me a little. Then I began to worry that she might think I was tantalizing her. And then I began to be afraid that Babs' silence meant a change of feeling.

I asked Cook about her. A dangerous thing to do, but less dangerous than asking at the family dinner table.

"Oh, she's sick. Been sick. Doesn't eat."

"Too bad. Since Christmas?"

"Couple of weeks."

So I would have to go see her. I did not know how I would begin. I quaked. I would rather imagine her than see her.

I remembered how, after her performance and the solemn, tender preliminary touching, she had run her tongue in my right ear. My throat made noises of shattered pleading, falling to a faint sob, which I heard across desert leagues and furlongs and Biblical parasangs. I saw Dr. Hunnewell above me with the silver lance, and his instructions to be still and to go ahead, scream; and so I was, and so I did. I did as her body told me. She brought me gently to breaking. All feeling in me was stinging sweet. I inhaled lilies of the valley and odor of wet leaves. I opened my eyes and saw a single firefly, blue-white above her shoulder, now dark, now glowing at a height. I closed my eyes to all but the incan-

185

descence of the mind, which grew brighter and brighter, and burst into darkness with a roar.

I felt a light hand cupping my mouth, from which had flown the freed terror of the body. In sobbing I fled solitude, finding another. Found. "It's all right. I'm here. I'm here," she whispered. "I'm holding you," she said. "I'm holding you."

"Don't look so pale in the face. It's enough I'm white as a sheet. You're supposed to be ruddy, remember? Put the damn tea down and give your ass a chair."

Startled, I did as she commanded. I had brought a tea tray from the Big House, so as not to disturb Cook, or betray the depth of my care to anyone in Gramma's house. I settled it on a chair beside her bed, and sat in the other chair, straightbacked, near the brass footboard.

"Thanks, hey, for the tea and stuff," she said. She poured herself a cup, waving me away as I tilted forward to help. Leaning sideways she spooned herself two heaps of sugar. She slathered marmalade on an English muffin and licked off the long end of an orange rind that overhung its edge. She bit in with a big crunch and sighed.

"Hey, long time no see."

"Right. I've missed you."

"Oh, shit." She took a long suck at her cup of tea, exhaled after it, and clattered the cup back onto the saucer with a little splash.

"I mean it."

"Great," she said. She marmaladed another muffin. "How've you been?"

I told her in a subdued voice about law school—commonplaces about teachers, pressures, routines. I tried not to sound bragging. I thought I was doing well, but wouldn't know until June. Not until the end of the year. No grades at all; then it hinged on exams.

"Tough, I guess," she said.

No, not too tough. I was handling it OK. I was pretty good at it, probably, and I liked it. The competition was good. My classmates were interesting.

"Why didn't you write me some of that?"

I was sorry; yes, I should have, but all my writing had gone into papers and briefs. Maybe I should explain what briefs were.

"I've got some in my bureau."

Yes. I smiled. That kind. Well, these were different. I explained.

She nodded, closed her eyes, laid her head back on the pillow.

When I stopped talking about briefs I said I was sorry she was sick. "What's the matter? Cook didn't say."

Her eyes opened. "Cook doesn't know."

"What the matter is?"

"Right."

"What is the matter?"

She closed her eyes again. "Flu."

"Flu?"

"Just a plain old case of flu. I opened the window and in flew Enza."

"Jesus, that's one of my grandmother's jokes. Don't tell me her jokes."

"I don't tell anything. I hear everything, but I don't tell."

We were quiet for several moments.

"How long have you been sick?"

"A couple of weeks. I'll get over it."

And silent again.

Then she said quietly, "I'm still bleeding."

"From the flu?" Her shifts of direction made me anxious.

Her head snapped forward. "No, from the cunt, goddammit."

I shook my head and raised my hands. "I'm sorry. I never know what to do when you bleed."

"No." She spoke levelly. "I don't suppose you do."

"What would you like me to do?"

"Nothing, thanks. But it's nice of you to ask." She finished her muffin and swilled off the tea remaining in the cup. She did not pour herself another. "Hey," she said. "You want this last muffin?"

"No, thanks. You want me to take the tray off your bed?"

"Yeah, sure, just take it away."

I picked up the tray and stood with it in my hands. I thought about coming back another time. I thought about how to get out of here now. "What'll I say when people ask how you are?"

"They won't ask."

"What'll I say anyway?" I felt my nostrils flare and I pressed my lips shut after the question.

"Tell 'em I opened the dikes and out flowed Enza."

"No, I mean it. How's your flu? When do you expect to get well? What did the doctor say?"

"Tell 'em I had an accident in a dark closet. I ran into a coat hanger."

I felt as if she were slipping a lariat of wire around me. I must stop thinking and talking, must get away from her obscurity. I turned halfway with the tray toward the door. With my head toward her, but my body facing away, I made an effort to speak with sympathy and soothing objectivity. "How soon do you think you'll be well?"

"Soon. Pretty soon." She was looking out the window over the laundry yard. "It was nice of you to come." Her lips were parted a little wider than usual, whether from the need to breathe through them (flu, really?) or through a metaphysical lassitude, I did not know.

"I'll try to see you again before I go back."

"OK, thanks." She kept on looking out the window as I left.

Shortly before I returned to Yale, Crispin caught me alone after Sunday supper. For one who ordinarily found pleasure, despite his impediment, in speaking with uncommon directness, his message was peculiarly oblique. For the first time—was it because of my father's death?—Crispin addressed me as his "nephew." Always before he had behaved with a disarming immediacy which I had cherished, and if anything formal was required, referred to me as "young cousin." Were these heavy preliminaries about Yale as a seat of learning and about my progress in law going to become routine? No, luckily, Crispin seemed at last to reach his intended theme and warm to it.

"Mother, incidentally, saw you taking tea yesterday to the garage and upon inquiring of Elise learned it was for Barbara. Mother was upset, of course, to learn that Barbara was ill, and has sent over a box of chocolates. But I might add, and this is a bit difficult for me to say, she was additionally distressed in some degree that you had not sought her permission to take the silver service out of the house."

I fumed inside and fought for things to say, but my felt surprise and foolishness at being found out made me voiceless.

"Of course, she wasn't worried about the silver," Crispin said with a smile, "and she understands that you should care for our servants in the way that is traditional in our family. But . . . I see the perplexity on your face, and I have another point which is more tenuous still. It may be unwelcome to you, in which case, please forgive me in advance. . . . But if in your demeanor there is just a shade more than loyalty to the household and its welfare, I am daring to caution you about it. You need not comment." He patted his pockets as if looking for a pipe.

"Let me approach this from another and more theoretical angle." Crispin, who rarely shifted position once he settled in a chair, now recrossed his knees. "I can think of examples from the Victorian world of great men making fools of themselves. Gladstone, for instance, walking the streets of London, picking up what he might have called 'fallen women' and taking them home to tea. No nefarious purpose, mind you. Nothing but the highest motives, as befitted Her Majesty's Prime Minister. He wanted to rescue and reclaim, and I suppose we must admire that, without knowing or inquiring into all the ulterior workings of the mind that accompany 'uplift' of any sort.

"You're not taking this amiss? Good. I have one more thought. There was this fellow, they still talk about him at Cambridge, a diarist and photographer, poet of sorts, who recorded wonderful pictures and dialogues of Victorian working women. A great anthropologist before the day of anthropology, you might say. . . . *Munby*, that was his name. Then the poor fellow married the chambermaid next door. Never happy. Great mistake. She was a woman of dignity, indeed, but imagine what a small portion of his life she could truly share, and he of hers, once they got beyond their fantasies of each other. He imagined, you might say, the song of a swift, but had to live with the soot of a chimney sweep.

"Oh, I imagine this is a fanciful and unwelcome essay, my boy. And coming from your unmarried uncle, it may sound to you like so much ignorant rubbish. Nevertheless I should like to think of myself as a romantic, of sorts, and I should be terribly glad if you accorded me such a role, despite the thoughts prevailing from me in this conversation." He paused, and with voice half a tone below its usual tenor, proceeded: "You may take all this either as unbelievable staidness on my part, or just possibly as a useful reminder that we are not so far from the Victorian age even now. Indeed, I am convinced that in some ways we cannot escape it. And that is just as well. Without the past for gravity we would have no orbit. Sputniks astray on tangents, lost in space.

"Oh, I do have a main point. And here it is. My advice about serving girls is, uplift them, or study them, or sleep with them. But for goodness sake, you needn't marry one!" And Crispin at that broke into laughter, doubling up in his chair. The sight of him bouncing on the upholstery made me smile.

Crispin relaxed. "Did I ever tell you how that Perugino business turned out last summer? The *Sepulchrum Christi* at auction, for which I had to return? A forgery, I discovered. The most brilliant fake I've seen in years. Lolly sensed it, just from a photograph. She's working for me, you know. Now there's a girl for you: Laura Contini. Excellent young woman."

I wrote from Yale Law School to the County Clerk of Allegheny County to see if there was any Pittsburgh writ surviving on Cassie Chadwick. My purpose, of course, was to learn if the record would reveal something of her McCalla connection, but I kept that to myself. The answer came back that no records survived from that long ago. I next wrote to Cuyahoga County, Ohio, daring to hope, because that was probably the trial site, that a transcript of the proceedings might be found. Nothing survived there except two indictments, but they were not uninteresting. They charged the defendant, Cassie L. Chadwick, on or about March 14 and April 12, 1904, with forging notes for $250,000 and $500,000 purportedly signed by Andrew Carnegie, and then with passing the forged notes as if they were valid. On these two indictments, the county clerk averred, said Cassie Chadwick was never brought to trial; the prosecutor had entered *nolle prosequi* and discontinued his action.

The fragments of the torn article in Clellan's library sorted only partly, and not clearly, with the surviving court records. I would have to see what I could find in the newspapers of the time that might answer my questions. What had Andrew Carnegie, Cassie Chadwick, and Rowan McCalla to do with each other? Still looking for what I called the McCalla male principle, and torn, regarding the elders, between the sentiments of an acolyte and those of an iconoclast, I needed to know: what was my great-grandfather like?

I imagined Rowan Megowan McCalla from a volume published early in the century by the Chamber of Commerce, praising Pittsburgh's famous men, achievers of great projects for the betterment of American industry and society. They made the city hum. They made a lot of money. They gave some of it to good causes. Each of these Pittsburgh leaders, large, small, or medium, got a page of stiff prose in the book opposite a steel-plate etching of himself in starched collar, wearing some or all of the incidental haberdashery of wealth: cravat with diamond stickpin, vest with pocket watch, chain looped across belly.

When I was a boy, Rowan's picture had looked heroic. The ferocity in his eyes bit into the artist's plate, and the plate bit paper, and the paper hit me forcibly three generations later. The lordly, semi-balding brow, the prominent cheekbones, the sternness from temple to jaw, the moustache obscuring the mouth, all seemed to speak of life lived in creative fury, soul tested in crucible of steel, decisions implacably taken; of mercy as a possible corollary of justice, but of a justice so exacting that it had no smile for folly.

In a book of Crispin's that lay on a living room table in the Big House was Michelangelo's God at creation. In the spirit of the Sistine Chapel, I had thought of my great-grandfather as God without a beard, a powerful original male whose eyes bulged with concentration, whose wrath was suggested by the hints of supple musculature beneath his robes, whose power flowed from a forefinger extended, or would not flow, if he chose to close it in a fist. Thunderbolts! Awakening of the human frame and mind!

But, now.

But now I noticed the paunch. The baldness. The dated attire. Instead of a deity I saw a patriarch, a mortal man.

It appeared that God could be fooled.

If Rowan Megowan McCalla gave $850,000 to Cassie Chadwick, then he surely was not God.

sixteen.

WHEN I came home for a week of spring vacation, I said I had legal research to do. There were no questions asked. The boy was obviously working like a dog, in the finest tradition of McCalla males.

Of course I was actually working on a family scandal half a century old. I amused myself with visions of presenting the findings someday to a Sunday dinner, in a style combining Crispinesque languor and legal tenacity. I loved burrowing in old newspapers, connecting trails of evidence, cornering facts in dispute. I rose each day humming, breakfasted in haste, and tooled Uncle Clellan's Pierce-Arrow out of the garage, down to the Carnegie Library.

The journals and gazettes were ochred with age. Edges disintegrated, despite my caressing care. Timber to pulp to paper to dust. Particles in the air made me sneeze. I drank often at the water fountain, mouth dry with historical pursuit and overheated library air. I urinated frequently. Each time I washed my hands carefully, grinding out soap particles from the dispenser, rubbing them into palms and wrists like Luther after a grease job, wiping thoroughly on the semi-absorptive brown paper towels. The only substance less absorptive was at the toilet: jam-tight box dispensers allowed plucking only one transparent, waxy tissue at a time. Interoffice memo: "Why is the toilet paper at the Carnegie Library in 1959 manufactured for greater durability than Pittsburgh newspapers at the turn of the century?"

I riffed backward and forward through turn-of-the-century dailies, to feel the shape of the story. After a few days I shuffled my notes into chronological order.

First: a picture of Cassie Chadwick on Euclid Avenue in Cleveland, where she was formerly seen almost daily in a "high red-wheeled cart behind a dashing Arabian horse." But the photograph was from a distance, and had printed poorly. I could not make out her features.

A lengthy interview with the Cleveland banker who blew the situation open: a dignified person in "utter despair" over a series of tortured and complex transactions. His social standing, reputation for probity, and credit rating were all in jeopardy. But even that was better than bearing the horrible uncertainties that had arisen from his transactions with Cassie. He yelped to the newshounds, who broadcast his cries by the wire of Associated Press, to every city that would be interested in a scandal involving Andrew Carnegie. Which was all cities, without exception.

Would I discover my own forebear in these pages, also "making a clean breast of it"? Would Rowan McCalla, like this Clevelander, fouled in a sow's mire, seek to be washed in the blood of the Lamb? Having found my mother in adultery, I wondered what I would find my great-grandfather in. My sublime prurience, my thirst for knowledge, my power hunger, my whatever, fed on what I found. The newspapers of December 1904 were filled with speculation about the million and a quarter of Cleveland money borrowed by Cassie. She fled from hotel to hotel in New York City and fainted when two secret service men located her. Arrested, she said she was unable to rise from her bed.

" 'In that case,' replied the marshal, 'I shall be obliged to remain here and keep you under surveillance.' "

"The name of Andrew Carnegie was mentioned several times and the sound of the name each time caused Mrs. Chadwick to smile."

Mrs. Chadwick was relying on her son, who had promised to pay her obligations. She was alleged to have been previously convicted under another name. She was quoted: "I have made absolutely no statement about this Madame de Vere."

194

John D. Rockefeller's name entered the case: "Mr. Rockefeller is to assume a large part of Mrs. Chadwick's indebtedness in order to save from embarrassment the pastor of the Cleveland church, the Rev. Charles A. Eaton, through whom Mrs. Chadwick was introduced to some of the men from whom she succeeded in borrowing large sums of money on the strength of the allegedly valuable securities."

A "private wire" from New York to the *Pittsburgh Gazette* described Cassie Chadwick being taken from her room to the marshal's office. Three times she "collapsed utterly and the crowd formed so thick about her prostrate body that it was impossible to get her to a place of privacy." The marshal's assistants "fought the mob vigorously, but it was one of the most persistent crowds of morbid persons that was ever attracted by a great criminal case. Women actually scratched at the face of deputy marshals. . . . and there were a dozen or more fist fights in which men participated."

Here at last a description of Cassie: "a large woman of majestic figure," about one hundred sixty-five pounds, with snow-white hair, save at the roots, where it was almost brown. In spite of lines of recent suffering there was "a touch of youth about the face." Her mouth was her most distinguishing feature: strong and firm with rather thin lips, and even white teeth. Her chin was "of strong character." She wore a brown dress, a long brown raincoat, with a splendid brown fur boa about her neck. When she entered the courtroom, she threw back her brown veil, "as though she wished people to see her face."

Then the first Pittsburgh echo to the big noise in Cleveland. Three unnamed Pittsburgh men, it was said, had been duped for $850,000 in a separate swindle. But it was closing time at the Carnegie Library.

Back in my room I reflected on headlines.

MRS. CHADWICK WRECKED A TOWN. (So much for Oberlin, Ohio, including its college.)

MRS. CHADWICK SOLD NO BABIES IN CONSHOCTON. (No time to follow up this story, however luscious it might prove.)

EARLY LIFE OF MRS. CHADWICK. (As told by a nameless

Pittsburgh woman who knew Cassie elsewhere in girlhood. Described as a "Lady Bountiful." Enjoyed giving presents without reckoning the cost. "Somewhere" got the money for a trunkful of dresses and "trumpery." Showed little taste but made a striking appearance.)

CHADWICK FORGERIES WILL TOTAL 20 MILLIONS WHEN ALL UNCOVERED. (Could that have been so? An amount equivalent to four times that much in 1959?)

WOMAN WILL FACE ANDREW CARNEGIE. (A reporter's fantasy, elaborately developed in the subjunctive mood. An exercise in selling newspapers.)

CHADWICK HOME SCENE OF REVEL (Not one, but many revels, it would appear, according to a former maid in the Chadwick household. Her mistress received men in her own private rooms. She was a woman of piercing eye. She had boxes of money and jewels. She watched her maids in the mirror. Her servants were afraid of her. And, as a postscript, a man who formerly supplied provisions for the Chadwick larder commented on their French maids, on their "can-can dances," their "couchee-couchee," et cetera, et cetera.)

BLAMES MRS. CHADWICK NO MORE THAN BANKERS (The Reverend Eaton, heard from at last, takes an even-handed stance. As a man of the cloth, does not wish to ascribe blame. If blame there must be, what might be said of gullibility and greed in the behavior of the bankers? Let him who is without sin cast the first stone at this poor demented scheming woman.)

READING CHADWICK CASE AFFECTS A GIRL'S MIND. (Dateline Cleveland: girl thinks people are gazing at her, believing she is Mrs. Chadwick.)

SUBPOENA SERVED ON MR. CARNEGIE (Purely a formal matter, of course. But testimony may be needed about the validity of the documents upon which Mrs. Chadwick has erected such an edifice of debt.)

THE WAY OF THE TRANSGRESSOR (A lead editorial in the *Pittsburgh Gazette* focusing the social hysteria aroused by the case.)

My brain was a sandstorm of allegations and suppositions.

Heading back home I asked myself: Where did Carnegie stand in this affair? And presuming that Rowan McCalla was one of the unnamed Pittsburghers, where exactly did he stand? I went to my desk to plan the next move.

And found an envelope that took over my thoughts. I opened a note from Babs: "Why not come over for tea tomorrow? 5:30." That's all it said. There was only one answer. "Sure," I scribbled, "thanks." I resealed the envelope with Scotch tape, crossed out my name, wrote "Babs" on it, and left it with Cook.

At the garage next day she met me with a pale expressionless face. After boiling water across the hall in the chauffeur's kitchen, she served in her room, using Luther and Elise's Woolworth china and bags of Red Rose. She let me help myself to sugar. We sat on the two straight chairs, with the paraphernalia of tea in delicate balance on a tray at the edge of the bed.

A loaf of French bread and some sharp cheese: she broke an end chunk off the bread, and I another, and it was still a long loaf. She cut a slab of cheese, and so did I, and a big hunk remained. The teapot jiggled when she cut. She steadied it when I cut.

"Well, how's your research? What are you looking up?"

I told her, hesitantly. About my great-grandfather and Andrew Carnegie. About a relationship between them that was still unclear. Maybe business, maybe friendship. Maybe neither. Maybe just a big problem that sucked them both in. There was this woman . . . I paused, uncertain how to describe Cassie.

"This woman?" She barely smiled, her lips parted.

"She is either an unfortunate illegitimate child or . . . a con artist. She is beautiful in a lusty sort of way; big upswept hairdo like the Gibson girls—they're drawings, you haven't seen them?—and the bosom of an opera singer. And particularly piercing eyes; or so various people say."

"What's the matter with her?"

"Matter? I don't know what the matter is, really. Something's wrong. She doesn't do things straight. She's always somebody else, if you know what I mean. She's a terrific actress, she's captivating, commanding, and when she's cornered she goes to pieces. She has to confront herself and it feels like there's nobody there. She collapses like a parachute hitting ground. Or so it seems."

"What makes her that way?"

"I don't know that." I was feeling a little petulant. "I don't even know if I've described her right. I've got to describe her right before I can get on to what makes her that way."

"How long is that going to take?"

"Are you impatient or something?" I looked sharply at her.

"No." She held the breadloaf in her lap.

"Well, it appears she was either the daughter of a section hand on a Canadian railroad or the bastard daughter of Andrew Carnegie."

"So? Which was she?"

"So either one could explain why she is striving upward in society. Couldn't it?"

"Maybe."

"In any case, she finds people greedy to help her. They want access to what they see as 'style,' and she appears to play on their image of the next highest level of society. Then she intrigues them into huge secret personal loans with big interest."

"What's wrong with that?"

"Nothing maybe. If she was who she said she was. There's a question of identity here, which I haven't solved. She arrives in Cleveland, background unknown, presence formidable. She marries a youngish doctor, a timid, socially respectable type, a jellyfish. He travels; she moves independently of him. She befriends some bankers and a minister. Wrongly or rightly she uses the name of Andrew Carnegie on some notes, a quarter, then a half million dollars, maybe much more. Then she comes right into Pittsburgh, Carnegie's home town. What brass!"

"What do you mean, brass?"

"I mean *brazen*. What fantastic nerve. She gambles on the

fact that everybody trusts Carnegie, or hates him, or both, but nobody doubts him. Imagine the scene: she tells her contact that she's Carnegie's illegitimate daughter—downcast eyes, modest voice, choked sobs of appreciation in response to their sympathy—and the guy is ready to do *anything* for her. They believe her because they've been looking for a flaw in Carnegie's behavior for years. They can't stand the idea of the richest man in America being an idealist who plans to give everything to charity. What's the matter with him? Where is he vulnerable? What is his vice? And why, since he has so much to give away, shouldn't I have some of it?

"Some woman," Babs said.

"Yeah. So Cassie answers two of their needs. One is to discover something secretly wrong with Andrew Carnegie. Everyone knows he didn't marry until his mother died. He was in his mid-fifties. So what did he do for a sex life all that time? As a young man, of course, he must have sowed wild oats. Here's proof of it—this magnificent woman, a hell of a lot bigger physically than Carnegie is, in fact. He's a squirt, a tiny yellow raisin of a man. But that somehow feeds the imagination of Cassie's prey. Little man produces giant fortune and illegitimate daughter of mythic proportions."

Babs tipped the loaf of bread from her lap to her breast, whole end up, as if it were a suckling child. "What's the other need?"

"To be a part not only of the secret, but of the fortune. The poor woman is down on her luck and needs half a million dollars. Of course she could get it from her famous daddy, her secret daddy, but she mustn't bother him, he's so busy, you know. He meets her requests from time to time, as his signature on this document shows. Modest fluttering of document along with entreaties *not to tell a single soul*. The man mutters soothingly that he can be trusted, he only needs to know how he can help. She suggests a way. She's not a woman of affairs; she is in financial difficulty, temporary, but large; she'll be happy to follow the

199

judgment of one who is kind enough to think of helping her in her moment of trouble. Any rate of interest he thinks is fair.

"He then makes a rapid mental calculation of how much Andrew Carnegie can afford for helping out his daughter— say sixty percent of the principal—and an agreement is reached, with profuse expressions of gratitude on Cassie's part, and modest disclaimers on the part of the lender that it matters not at all to him. He is glad to be of service to a lady in distress, and indirectly helpful to a giant of American industry and finance, and a leader in world betterment, who is apparently so consumed in those matters just now that he hasn't yet noticed his daughter's plight.

"So, you could say, the man has the pleasure of being paid handsomely for serving as surrogate father of Carnegie's bastard daughter. Even, you could say, the thrill of *being* Andrew Carnegie, for as long as the note shall last. Anyway, so it looks to me. I'm far from done with the research yet."

Babs stuck the loaf of bread under her armpit. Then she sniffed it, made a comic grimace, and pointed it at me. "How do you know she ain't really his daughter?"

"Well," I flushed. I always felt awkward when Babs was intentionally ungrammatical. A prissy reaction on my part, but it often portended something strange on hers. "I don't know, of course. But it sure seems unlikely."

"Prove she ain't."

"What?"

"Prove she ain't Andrew Carnegie's daughter."

First I sipped some tea. "We learn in law school that it's impossible to prove a negative proposition." Babs didn't respond. I added, "Common sense tells us the same thing. You can't prove there aren't ghosts."

"Common sense?" She waggled the long stick of bread with its torn end at me. "Isn't it common sense that a guy is going to screw around, sixteen to sixty, unless he's a priest or married? And maybe even if he *is* married or a priest? What makes Carnegie the big exception? He didn't get married until, what did you say, fifty-one? God knows how many bastards he's got out there."

200

I wondered what to do with my hands. Some tea in the saucer had been bothering me each time I sipped, and I had to keep it under the cup as I drank, so that drops from the bottom of the cup wouldn't fall on my shirt. Now I emptied the saucer into the cup and drank.

"It's no good, being a bastard." She lowered her tone of voice. "You shouldn't bring bastards into the world. If you bring them in, you've got to take care of them. Specially. Somebody's got to pay. The woman always pays. With her body. With her time on earth. The man *should* pay, equally, whatever he's got. And if he's rich, he should pay a hell of a *lot*." She paused as if this argument were perhaps not clear enough.

"What's on your mind, Babs?" I asked, after a moment. I really didn't want to know, but I felt as if I were party to an exorcism.

She was going to tell me.

"That bleeding last Christmas?"

"Yes."

She tapped the loaf on the edge of the tea tray and the spoon rattled in the saucer. "That was the end of a bastard."

I winced, but not at her language. I felt as if I were hunted, an ignoble flight ending. "You mean you . . ."

"Yeah. I cleaned it out myself."

Sweat popped on my forehead. From the tea, I thought. Tea makes me thirsty and makes me sweat. I need some water, but I mustn't get up now. I poured myself more tea. This time without sugar. Why hadn't I known, or allowed myself to figure it out? Does she think me brutal? Or just cowardly?

"Don't you want sugar?" she said.

"No, thanks." I drank it dark as I thought what to say next. Nothing elegant. "You mean you aborted a child yourself?"

"Right."

I drank again. I thought I had never tasted the leaf before, how bitter it was. I spoke, sounding like a barrister to myself, and feeling my heart pound. "I'm terribly sorry, Babs. That's awfully dangerous." With the back of one hand I wiped my forehead. With the other hand I drank again. It stains your teeth, I thought. "I wish you'd told me. Are you OK now? I mean are you all right, really? I wish you'd told me."

"I'm getting OK. It'll be OK sometime. It's easier to tell you now."

"Good God," I said. "Sweet Jesus Christ." At least I was talking, even if I wasn't saying anything.

Her lips parted and her eyes were focusing on something out the window, far away.

"I would have helped, Babs. I really would have. You know that. You should have told me and let me help. I would have . . ." I stopped and wondered what I would have done. I would have paid for an operation, of course, to make it safe. Jesus, at least I would have done that. But what a trivial damn thing to say. What would I have done, really? "I would have married you."

She blinked but did not shift her gaze from out the window. Her eyes moistened. She blinked once again and opened her eyes fast and wide, as if crossing a wire and concentrating. But the mositure kept flowing and it tipped over her lower lashes and she had to blink several times more, very quickly. Her lower lip trembled slightly. With a great effort, it seemed, she closed it firmly to her upper lip.

"We could have married," I said. "I would have asked you." Sweat rolled down my forehead into the corner of my right eye. I blinked away the salt.

"I wasn't sure . . ." She paused, speaking with almost no lip movement, forming words slowly with teeth and tongue: "I wasn't sure it was yours."

Suddenly I was hungry. I took the knife and cut a chunk of the cheese. The knife snapped through, hit the plate and made the tray shudder. She extended the loaf of bread. I shook my head. "You weren't sure," I said. She shook her head once, slightly. I thought about what she had said and the one shake.

We were both silent a long time.

"I've been thinking about diamonds." she said. "The sky

202

is full of them. I learned it in my astronomy course at night school. Interstellar dust and diamonds. The chances are, with all the stuff that there is out there, that lots of it is diamonds. I read an article about it. You figure by mathematics what the stuff out there is likely to be and it doesn't come out turnips. There's a big chance, a really big chance, that a lot of interstellar dust is diamonds."

"OK," I said. "We should go get it. Get our share," I was gathering voice now. "I mean it's a bigger idea than our ice cream factory."

She gave several wet blinks as I talked. "We could get up a company, sell shares, in Pittsburgh Interstellar Diamonds. Sputnik is up there. Soon we'll have the technology in the U.S.A. Then we'll go private enterprise with it. America always does. Our company," I said grandly, "will be ready with the first space probe and diamond collector, a goddam vacuum thing like the chimney sweep uses, only attached to a huge galactic van like a garbage truck, with a gigantic filter on back. So we can sort the diamonds from the turnips. Right *out there*. You like it?"

She nodded and smiled. Then she put both hands in front of her eyes and sobbed silently, convulsively, working the tears back into her cheeks with the heels of her palms.

"Maybe we'd better call it something simple," I said. "Like Pittsburgh Coal and Diamonds. 'Interstellar' sounds too much ahead of our time. We want people to think we have our feet on the ground, so we have to call it something that appeals to the investor. Coal and diamonds connect, too, right? Diamonds are just very old coal. To make anthracite you wait a while, but for diamonds you have to be really patient. Here on earth.

"Your diamonds out there in the sky," I continued. Her sobs were smaller now. "They must be made by a different process. You're right. I mean it can't be millions of tons of dead rhubarb lying on top of coal for millions of years. So those diamonds in space are generated by a different process than here, and all we've got to do is figure out a different technology to collect them.

"It'll be more fun than mining," I said. She had quieted

herself, and was using her forefingers to wipe her cheeks. "It'll be fun," I repeated. She shook once more, a very little, and I was quiet.

After a while I spoke again. "It'll take some research."

"Research," she said, looking straight at me. "You're a regular research machine. You're researching your great-grandfather, right? A lot of time on him? How about your Great Uncle Clellan? How about *him?*"

I probably looked startled or perplexed, but I began an answer about Clellan in the old days working closely with his father, Rowan, and his brother, A. C. She cut me off.

"You haven't thought much about Clellan, have you? You really should think about him some. All those years unmarried? What was he up to, do you think? Did you ever wonder?"

She took my cup off its saucer and put it on hers; then her saucer on mine; then the two cups on the two saucers on the tray.

"*Lots* of bastards, probably," she said.

In the cleared space on the small tray she dropped the loaf of French bread: clunk.

"What are the chances that one of them is named Barbara?" She followed the question with a stare at me, a ferocity before which my eyes dropped.

"You're so good at possible and probable. Have you figured what are the chances that I'm your *aunt?* No, you haven't?"

She took the tray by one corner and rattled it sideways on the bedspread. "Try figuring this. I can't have your baby because I'm your aunt. That wouldn't be good. It wouldn't be incest, exactly, but it wouldn't be good. I mean not whole-hog incest like I was your mother or something. But it wouldn't look good to Crispin, would it? 'Unsee-meemly inbu-breeding,'" she mimicked. She picked up the loaf again, passed it in front of her nostrils, inhaled, and wrinkled her nose. "And what would Aunt Martha say, not to mention Aunt Bekka, and Gramma, and your own freaking mother. That's right, what would Adelaide say?"

Notions rocketed around my head. Before I could reply,

she spoke again. "So, I'm your aunt, honey. Why do you think Clellan gave me this cameo?" She brought the brooch swiftly out from under her pillow. "He said he wanted it kept in the family. He told me, when I was twelve years old, it had come into the family from a great lady. And I reminded him of her, and he wanted me to keep it. Forever."

I murmured in protest, arguments rising in me like a flock of starlings. But she was done. She slugged the cheese into place next to the tea things, rose, and picked up the tray. "Tea's over, baby. Come again sometime."

Research Clellan? That hadn't occurred to me, but it sure did now. I thought Babs was daft, or at least doing a taffy-pull with the truth. About the cameo, I mean. Sure Clellan gave it to her. We all knew that. The McCalla family had worked up its arguments about it twice before: when he first gave it to her, and when she wore it to Buddy's birthday party. But where had he gotten it, and what did he really say when he gave it to her, and what did he really mean when he said it?

Clellan wasn't alive to tell me. I realized, as I thought about him, that I could bring no words of his to mind. He had seldom spoken, never admonished me, didn't quote Ben Franklin or the Bible. But I bore in mind his kind blue eyes, imperturbable; and his bald crown lurching forward in fits of sudden glee. Even his seizures of laughter were almost silent. He was not the kind of man to leave an historical trail.

I ran into him, however, the next morning, Saturday, my last chance at the Carnegie Library before going back to school. Digging hard, I struck at last the McCalla vein of the matter, deep in the mine. Breathing shallow and thin, I felt suddenly like a miner's canary.

"NOTHING IN IT" IS REPLY OF MCCALLA
Pittsburgh Business Man Denies Truth
of the Cleveland Telegram

R. M. McCalla, A. C. McCalla, and C. C. McCalla,

205

and one other man, not named, were mentioned in a special telegram to the Gazette from Cleveland last evening as composing a syndicate of Pittsburghers alleged to have loaned Mrs. Chadwick $800,000, believing she was a daughter of Andrew Carnegie.

R. M. McCalla, when shown the telegram last evening, said, "There is nothing in it," and declined to discuss the matter at all.

The statement that this amount of money is owing to Pittsburghers from the Cleveland woman has been persistent for three days. One variation is that the amount was $800,000, by reason of a loan of $500,000, which was to be repaid with a bonus of $300,000. Until yesterday, however, no names were mentioned in the alleged Pittsburgh transaction.

So Clellan was in it, too, and A. C., his older brother. Rowan and both his sons.

An accompanying story, datelined New York (Special):

When a reporter went to the Tombs tonight and asked Mrs. Chadwick what business transactions she had ever had, if any, with Rowan M. McCalla of Pittsburgh, Mrs. Chadwick's answer was:

"Have you Mr. McCalla's statement?"

She was told that the reporter had no statement from Mr. McCalla.

"When Mr. McCalla gives out a statement, I shall have something to say about it and not before," was her answer.

Cassie sounded experienced in these matters. I turned the pages of the crumbling papers rapidly, sneezing, wiping my nose, taking notes.

MRS. CHADWICK BOUND HOME
says half a dozen prominent men
offered surety for her
will tell her whole story in due course

(Did the excuse of health cover unwillingness to do so? How could even he dodge a subpoena?)

CLOSELY GUARDED
Evident Fear of Suicide in Chadwick Case . . . Mrs. Chadwick emphatically denies receiving a dollar from Henry Phipps or any other Phipps. "I further wish to say that while I have had money from Pittsburgh people, I have never had a particle of Pittsburgh paper."

CLEVELAND WAITS FOR MONEY QUEEN

MRS. CHADWICK IS MET BY JEERS AND HISSES OF CLEVELAND CROWD

MRS. CHADWICK KEEPS UP BLUFF
"Will repay all honest indebtedness"
"Wrongfully obtained money from no one"

Then at a strange angle, and delayed, came a story from New York featuring Rowan McCalla. I read and reread it.

"At the conference were present Mrs. Chadwick, a prominent Cleveland banker, the attorney for the banker, and Mr. Rowan McCalla. According to the story, McCalla insisted to the banker that Carnegie would come forward to save Mrs. Chadwick if only the arrest could be headed off. Intervention to prevent arrest was only possible if parties who believed themselves injured, such as those present, would have faith in Mr. Carnegie and drop the charges against Mrs. Chadwick.

"McCalla placed his right hand under Mrs. Chadwick's nose, covering up the lower part of her face. Turning to the banker's attorney, he said:

" 'Tell me, sir, what you see.'

" 'I don't see anything but Mrs. Chadwick,' was the attorney's answer. 'What do you see?'

" 'I see Andrew Carnegie,' impressively whispered Carnegie's old-time friend. And McCalla repeated what he had told other lawyers. 'Stop all this talk and we will all get our money.' "

Then the story petered away and my time ran out. Was Carnegie pressure behind the scenes able to muzzle the press? Was there even McCalla influence to the same end? I made up my mind when I got home in June to research the story in Cleveland, where it had broken open; where the warrant for arrest had gone out.

I had to see Babs before I left. To normalize our relationship, I thought. What a stupid phrase. Our relationship could never be normal. It was all fever and chills; and maybe it always had been, since we were children. So why was I going to see her? To try to help, I told myself.

The morning I was leaving I headed for the garage. No note; just a knock on her door. I realized then how formal our romance had been, how respectful of each other's privacy; how carefully staged our meetings; how we'd saved our surprises for intimacy.

"What do you want?" She opened the door, still in a nightgown. Torn at the hem, I noticed. Her hair was uncombed and she plucked damp strands away from her face as if peering from behind a Moroccan beaded curtain.

"I just wanted to say goodbye before I go back to Yale."

"Goodbye then."

"Is that all?"

"Goodbye and good luck."

"Why don't we start over? How about good morning?"

She let the hair slide back over her face, but couldn't hide a faint smile.

"Good morning?" she said, as if it were a question.

I wondered if she were going to ask me in. Apparently not. So whatever I had to say would have to be said just standing there.

"You think I'm crazy, don't you?" she said.

"Good God, no. Why do you think that?"

"Because of the cameo."

"That's *yours*," I said. I was suddenly angry and disoriented. The only thing that seemed to make sense was

208

property. "That's *yours*," I repeated. "Uncle Clellan gave it to you. You can do with it whatever you like."

She was silent for a while, then tipped back enough hair with her right index finger to look at me with one unshaded eye. "And I can think about it whatever I like?"

"Sure," I said, in a soft voice, wondering what was coming.

"Sure," she mimicked me, my reasonable purr. "Sure. Sure." She parted her hair cleanly and threw it back, half over each shoulder. "Well, get this. He took me on his lap and gave it to me. He held me in his arms and cried and said it came from a great lady. He said he never loved anybody like her, except me." She sobbed. "He said he loved me, he loved me." She let the hair fall again, and she wiped her eyes with her hair.

"I'm sorry," I said.

"I wiped away his tears," she said, "with my fingertips. Then I kissed him where his face was still wet."

I stood there, shaking, shamed, uncertain.

"So why," she said, now calm and resolute, "why would he give it to me unless I was his daughter?"

"The cameo?"

"Why anyway?"

"I don't know. I'd like to find out. Maybe I can find out something. When I come home again, I'm going to Cleveland to look for the truth about my family."

"The truth." She laughed. "Why go to Cleveland for the truth? Why did he give it to me unless I was his daughter?"

She raised a hand toward the door. I felt emotionally pushed from the room; I took two steps back, clearing the jamb.

"I want to help you," I said.

"Why *would* he?" Her voice was loud, but strangely toneless. "Unless," she said, elaborately and formally and slowly, "I *were* his daughter." She hooked a bare toe around the edge of the door and flicked it shut in my face.

209

seventeen.

By June everyone had moved out. Nearly everybody, that is. Gramma and Aunt Bekka were established in the Fox Hollow Apartments, and Aunt Martha in Sewickeley. My mother stayed on at Gramma's house with a maid to clean and do makeshift cooking. She spent most of her evenings at Kidder's, coming home by ten, decorously early. They were to be married in Hyannisport in early July, less than four months off. By then nearly a year would have passed since my father's death. Adelaide could say, "It's been a year," and it would be all right. My room was still available to me—these brief vacation days in March, and summertime ahead, until demolition began.

The grounds had all gone to weed. Nearly all, I should say. Luther was doing some hand mowing at Gramma's, while living in the garage and answering calls from Fox Hollow. Bekka's yard, however, was overgrown; Martha's had grown high, she having left first; and the empty lot was wild, having begun to go the summer before.

I had thought over and over about Babs' claim to be Clellan's daughter. A suppressed fact revealed? Of course the slam-bang quality of the revelation made me doubt it. But there was more than one secret in the compound, I was sure. I could make a case for Clellan exercising *droit du seigneur* with Wanda; even a case for Buddy assenting. Wanda's later madness I could see as the conflict of her Polish Catholicism with her submission to a desirous master and designing husband. Her throwing the cleaver at Buddy as the delayed outburst of her felt betrayal, guilt, and lovelessness.

Yes, it could be. And would Clellan take Babs on his knee and tell her so? No, too gentle, my uncle, to bruise her with such a truth. And too silent by smiling habit, to say it even if he had wanted to. But he could have declared a love for her in his own avuncular way: a lonely profession of admiration to a twelve-year-old innocent, by a man whose days were spent in devotion to his octogenarian mother, and Saturday nights in the bordellos of the North Side. Clellan needn't have been the one to say he was her father. Wanda might have done it, out of spite against Buddy, or out of mad meandering.

I needed to talk with Babs. I walked over to the garage and found Luther. "The dog's got ticks," he said. He shook his head slowly from side to side, considering the irreversible. "From that high grass, them weeds." Madison, indeed, scratched himself often, right hind paw to right ear or left to left, tag and chain jingling angrily on his neck. He finished by shaking himself out like a rug, followed with an exclamatory snuffle. I counted a high of one hundred and thirty-four scratches in one anguished series. Madison's coat, once like new copper, looked like old leaves.

"Who bathes him?" I wondered. I feared to put the question out loud, lest someone point toward me. "I have research to do," I told myself.

Luther fed the dog, so why couldn't Babs bathe him? That would give me a reason to talk to her. I would offer to bathe the dog in such a way that it became a joint project. Maybe she'd do most of it. I'd never washed a dog.

"Where is she?"

Luther had been under the car; was wiping his hands. "Babs?" His head turned slowly from side to side. "Throwing knives," he said.

I concentrated on trying to catch one of Luther's pupils behind the grease spots on the lenses of his glasses. "Throwing *knives?* Why? Where?"

His head continued its semi-revolutions. "I dunno why, Mister Randy. Maybe you kin ast her. She's right out there in the laundry yard. You kin hear it." He stopped rotating his head and cocked an ear to the west.

211

I heard a faint "tud" from the laundry yard, then a "tok." Then nothing. Then "tuds" again, several seconds apart. "What's she throwing at?"

Luther's head began moving again, moderately fast. "She's got a *door*." Shake, shake. "She ast kin she have the door from your Aunt Bekka's house, the one between the pantry and the kitchen. And kin I get it off its hinges for her. So I says why, and she just says she needs it for the circus. So I says I need your aunt's permission. And she says she's gonna say OK because it's just an old door and it arready had a big mark on it arready, so I says all that to your Aunt Bekka and she says, 'You mean that door where Wanda threw the cleaver at? Mercy me,' she says. And I says, 'That's right, that's the door.' "

Luther interrupted himself to nod his head up and down. " 'Well,' she says, your aunt, 'nobody's going to want that door, and if that door is all she wants, give her the door.' So I says, 'Yes, Ma'am,' and I unscrewed it off its hinges and I carried it over here like she ast." He was shaking side to side again, slowly. "You can see for yourself, out there back."

I thanked him and went out the car entrance on the compound side and around to the laundry yard. I leaned without speaking on the stone wall and looked down. Her back was to me, right arm raised, elbow and wrist cocked. She stepped forward, brought down the elbow, snapped the wrist, and a metallic flash shot through the air toward a man at the far wall. It struck just above his head. She walked forward, picked up one knife off the floor, and with a quick wriggle pulled out the one she had just thrown. Next she took out two about three inches from his ears, two just wide of his shoulders, two at the elbows, two near his hands at hip level, and one between the knees of his parted legs.

That left one knife sticking out of the man's belly, below where the belt was on his right side, at about where I imagined the appendix was. Babs wrenched it out, added it to the knives she held in her left palm, then fanned them out evenly with points between thumb and forefinger as she walked back to her throwing position.

She looked up. "One miss and one no-stick," she said. "Better than I was doing. But still not good. Come on down."

"I can watch up here."

She turned around and addressed the outlined figure on the door leaning against the far wall. A six foot man, of medium build. He was not drawn in to show musculature, or drawn on to show clothing. He was simply and squarishly outlined with black paint lines, except for five darkened areas: two horizontal ovals high in his head, a large black Valentine shape on the left side of his chest, and two black globes close together, below his belly and between his legs.

Babs threw at him: twelve knives in steady succession. The third and the seventh didn't hold and clattered to the floor. She socked in the rest on the outline and looked up at me. "No misses, two no-sticks. Want to try it?"

"No, thanks. But I'll come down." I went back in the garage, down the dank stairs to the laundry room, past the shelves of Mrs. Stewart's Bluing, and out into the laundry yard. She had gathered up the knives and fanned them in her left hand.

"It pays," she said. "If I can do two acts, it really pays. How many shows can say they've got a high wire artist that's also a knife thrower? But I need practice and I've got to find a partner."

"Yeah, practice makes perfect."

"Right. Perfect is what I've got to be. So when I get a no-stick, I subtract fifty, and when I miss, subtract a hundred. Then I have to work off the minus points." She pointed to the dark places with her right hand. "The heart is big, it's easy, worth fifty. The eyes or the balls are a hundred each. They're smaller. A bulls-eye on any of those works off points. But every miss adds ten more. Get it?"

"Yeah, I think I've got it."

"Want to try?"

"No, thanks, I don't really think I do. Where'd you pick this up?"

She looked up and away, as if at an overhead billboard. "Oh, I started with Salim, the Sword Swallower. It was the thing he did first. But you have to have a partner, he said. And it was hard to get girls to do it. So he developed a solo act. Just swallowing, himself."

"He taught you?"

"Yeah, I asked him. I didn't know any women knife throwers. He said he'd teach me if I let him practice on me. So I did. He liked throwing at me. Said I held real still. He nicked me once." She turned her head left, bent the left elbow out, palm out and up, and sighted over her shoulder. "There. That's how I got that." I saw a little white triangle above her elbow, which I'd never noticed before. Above it, her vaccination scar, white on white.

"Who did you practice on?"

"Plywood, for a long time. Then finally he let me use him." Her face clouded. "We had an argument about it. He only let me once. I said he had to or else, all the times I'd done it like he asked. I went wide so he was OK, but times I wanted to stick it in him. You want to try it? Don't worry, I'll throw wide."

"Well, thanks, but really, no, I don't think I especially want to."

"I mean a foot wide. Not just three inches, like for real."

"Even a foot, I guess I don't really want to."

"Chicken," she said calmly. I stepped to her throwing spot, the redlined T-intersection on the floor of my squash court, marking areas for receipt of service.

"Why do you have to do this?" I asked. I knew it was a non sequitur, and a weak escape from her invitation.

"Money," she said. Tud, between the knees.

"Money, money, money," she repeated. Tud, tud, wide of the hips.

"I want money. I've never had money. It makes you independent." Four tuds at elbows and shoulders.

"I want lots of it. Then I can do what I want." Tud, tud at the ears.

"I can say fuck you, McCallas, Kidder, out-of-towners, bill collectors, fuck you." Tud, right above the top of the skull.

"Perfect," she said. "You see? Perfect. Three-four inches all around. And I would have given you a foot."

214

"With money you could get an education."

"Fuck your education. I got one already." She was yanking the knives out of the door. "I'm *giving* education now." She was addressing the black lines on the door. "Right?" Gently, she took a knife tip and with it tickled the black circles below the belly, between the legs of the outlined figure. "Ain't I educational?"

She turned and looked at me with blank eyes and her lips in an O. I felt my stomach quiver two ways at once. I liked it when she said fuck, and I hated it when she said ain't. Now she was saying both with a knife in her hand.

I needed courage to speak, and I had just a little. "Look, I've been thinking a lot about what you said in March. About Buddy not being your father? About maybe Clellan being your father. Who told you that? Wanda—your mother?"

Babs gathered the knives and fanned them in her palm. "Wanda is not my mother. My mother was a great lady. My father, Clellan, told me so. He said he got Buddy and Wanda to adopt me." She began throwing again.

I went away.

I spent a couple of days puzzling over the riddle of Babs' parentage. Then I went back to the old newspapers, thinking perhaps that the matter of Cassie Chadwick's heritage would help me. At least it looked like a soluble problem, as old ones do. I began to think that my great-grandfather had been right, and that the great public of 1904, goaded by sensationalist newspapers, had been wrong. A man who understood fire, the wheel, and compound interest would not, without careful calculation, have composed his own two sons and an unnamed fourth person into a Pittsburgh syndicate making a loan of half a million dollars.

If there were compelling reason to believe that Cassie *was* Carnegie's daughter, then the smart thing was for everybody to keep calm, just as Rowan advised them to do. Carnegie would make sure, indirectly and as appropriate, that everyone got his money as promised.

Married at fifty-one, a father finally at sixty-one, Carnegie would be ultra-protective of his legal daughter, a little girl of seven, over such a scandal. Not to mention protective of the feelings of his young wife. And solicitous of his own reputation as financier, statesman, philanthropist, pacifist. Carrying, in the public mind, a reputation for wizardry, discipline, and far-sightedness would not sort well with owning to a bastard.

Could Carnegie have taken the course that Grover Cleveland had followed? Cleveland had acknowledged a natural child in the middle of a presidential campaign, to cope with the insinuations and slanders of his opponents. By telling the truth he won the election.

No, that kind of honesty wouldn't work for Carnegie. Grover Cleveland had been a bachelor when he fathered the child; had married after his public acknowledgment, and later brought to the White House a bride thirty years his junior. America smiled with pride. Carnegie, however, was already married, already the father of a daughter, and his dark secret was still hid. He could not let loose the truth without suffering attacks of ribaldry and ridicule, and the peculiar Victorian scorn reserved for those who appeared to set the lofty moral standards of the day, but were discovered in not living up to them.

What was Carnegie going to *say* about this whole affair? If he said anything, I was sure he would not take Grover Cleveland's route. He would be silent, hoping it would blow over; he would treat the matter as "not worth dignifying with denial"; or he would simply deny the allegations.

Luther drove me down to the library, chewing tobacco as he never did when driving the McCalla women. He looked sideways at me in the front seat beside him. "Mister Randy, excuse me? Have you noticed anything about Babs?"

I caught a glimpse of his restless eyeballs. "No, I don't think so." Which wasn't true. "Have you noticed something, Luther?"

"Well, sir, yes, sir, Mister Randy, I think I have. Course I could be wrong."

"What do you notice, Luther?"

"Well, Mister Randy, don't you sort of see her acting peculiar? Like she was mixed up or something? She isn't usually that way, is she, do you think?"

"The knife-throwing? Does that bother you, Luther? Her practicing her act?"

"No, sir. That don't bother me at all, it really don't."

"Then what is it that she's said or done, Luther?"

Luther shifted his plug from his right cheek to his left. "Well, sir, I was over at your Aunt Martha's house, just checking like I was ast, like I do a couple of times a day. I was in the kitchen and I heard a noise. It scared me, I'll tell you. I was going to call the police. I even had the phone in my hand when I figured what the sound was. *The electric chair*. Now who's using the electric chair? I thought. If your aunt had sent for something she would of called me. And it's too early for the wreckers. Maybe robbers? What would they use that thing for? Nothing, I figured. Everything was all gone arready. Wasn't nothing in the Big House could move except that chair of your great-grandma's. And no robber could move it anyway but up and down. And *that's what it was doing*." His eyes behind his glasses opened wide in entreaty and he swivelled his head to get a glance at me. Then braked suddenly to a halt behind a baker's truck at a traffic light.

"Nudge him a little, Luther." I laughed, and kept the aftersmile on my face as I spoke. "So: there are ghosts in the Big House?"

"Yes, sir, what I'm telling you is spooky. I mean I open the hall door just a crack and I hear it humming up to the top. And then it stops for maybe a minute. Then it goes click, you know, the switch, and it comes humming down again, round the bend and all. But you know I can't see from there. I just wait for someone to get off. But no footsteps. Just click again and back upstairs, same thing all over. Then, you know what?"

"Then what, Luther?"

"Then click, it started, come all the way back down. This time I was ready. I was out there kind of behind the grandfather clock so's I could see who was riding that thing and still I could run away if I had to. And it come back down to the first floor . . ." He turned, his eyes beseeching me not just to listen to this story, but to *understand* it. A blast of a Diesel horn snapped his gaze back to the road. "I just

217

stood there and watched, and who comes around the bend standing on the thing like a dancer or something, but Babs. Can you *believe* it?"

"I guess I can, sure; you say you saw it, Luther."

"Saw it? Sure I did, I was right there. I took a step out like maybe to talk to her. And the queer thing is she looked right through me, like she was an elevator operator in Gimbels or something, and was I going to get on or not because she had to do her job."

"Well, did you?"

"Did I what, Mister Randy?"

"Get on."

"*No*, Mister Randy. I got out. I mean you're not supposed to wake a sleepwalker, right? That's what she looked like. I wasn't going to wake her up. But I listened at the door before I left. She come all the way up, floor by floor again. Then she started coming down again. That's when I got out. I din't want to be there. I might of upset her or something."

"Probably a good idea not to, Luther. You did the right thing, I'm sure."

"So have you noticed anything like that, Mister Randy? In her, in Babs, peculiar-like?"

"No, Luther," I lied. "It sounds peculiar, but I'm sure there's an explanation for it."

"Like sleepwalking? Maybe she was asleep, huh?"

"Maybe she was."

Luther shook his head slowly from side to side. "Up and down," he said. "Up and down."

"EVERY DOLLAR WILL BE PAID," SAYS MRS. CHADWICK
Thankful for Kind Telegrams and Letters,
Some From Unexpected Sources, and
Many Offers of Financial Help
to Meet Obligations

She chatted to reporters "like a schoolgirl." "Although she wept no tears, she pressed a kerchief to her eyes." "Perhaps some day,' she said, 'I can explain all this. When I do my friends will be astounded at what I will have to say.' "

She told New York newsmen how she had fooled them. " 'Why I walked right past you on the arms of two gentlemen who are very important in this city. They took me up to Sherry's and we dined there, and you did not know a thing about it.'

" 'And then Tuesday night when you all thought I had committed suicide, I was entertained at the home of one of your prominent citizens.' "

A reporter asked if that were Andrew Carnegie's lawyer. " 'I am not going to answer questions. No, I cannot say anything about Carnegie, Carnegie, Carnegie. I cannot talk about him, but it will all be published some day, and then you will know.' "

Her manner, as she said this, was "intensely amused. . . . She rolled her words with a queer lisp, but her eyes were searching as she looked into the face of every man who stood before her."

She could not say anything about Carnegie?

Carnegie finally allowed himself to comment about her. " 'Why should I go out of my way to prosecute this woman? Wouldn't you be proud of the fact that your name even when forged on notes, was good for loans of $1,250,000 . . .? It is enough glory for me to think that my name is so good, even when forged.' "

A marvel of patient adroitness. He hadn't time for her. She had not harmed him. She had in fact given dramatic public proof of his credit rating. There was "pride" and "glory" for him in the power of his forged name.

"I really am very proud of this thing. Why should I mix up in a case which has really given me great personal satisfaction? . . . Besides this woman has done me no harm. She has only brought before the public a very advantageous thing, that my credit is A. No. 1."

No pity for Cassie or those who had trusted her, no creak of humility about himself. He was bold and aggressive. He alluded to forgery, never to illegitimacy. He brushed off the whole affair with a telegraphic grin.

What a masterful canny bastard, Carnegie.

A phrase of B-Ray's came back to me, from a Sunday supper long ago, quoting a Scot: "Andra" was a "daft gallant." Yes, you had to be a little crazy to be as confident as Carnegie. You had to be convinced that everything could be turned to your advantage. While proving it again and again, you had to charm the world, so that it would not too greatly resent your success, or plot to entrap your weakness.

My forebears and their unnamed fourth partner were losing face—Sheppie Cardigan's grandfather publicly joked that they had been "Chadwicked"—but they did not lose faith. Rowan M. McCalla was quoted in the newspapers again. He didn't take Carnegie's pride in his credit rating as a disclaimer of Cassie.

"I know that this woman is the daughter of Andrew Carnegie. He has told me so himself. The confession was made to me one day in his office, in confidence. . . . He told me that he had no very strong objections to a few of his trusted friends and associates knowing the story, but he wished to avoid its becoming public, and he therefore enjoined silence. I would not relate the story at this time were it not that Mrs. Chadwick's affairs are undergoing a severe crisis, and a knowledge of the truth may help to clear up matters for everybody concerned."

The "Pittsburgh syndicate" put more money on its hunches. Another paper reported a member of the team in Cleveland trying to buy up loans made by the Wade Park Bank to Mrs. Chadwick. " 'We are just waiting until things cool down a little here in Cleveland. Then we fellows in Pittsburgh are going to step in and quietly collect our money from Andrew Carnegie.' " How much *more* than their first half million did they invest in Cassie, trusting themselves right, the rest of the world wrong, and Carnegie good for the whole thing?

McCalla money, by investing heavily in Cassie's bastardy, implied that Carnegie was prevaricating. That could not go on. A report from New York stated that "Mr. McCalla is credited with asking directly about Mrs. Chadwick's allegations, which Andrew Carnegie denied."

220

Then a paragraph head:

R. M. MCCALLA HAD THE BAREST ACQUAINTANCE
WITH THE STEEL CROESUS
Despite the evident strength of Mr. McCalla's assumptions about a relationship existing between Mr.
Carnegie and Mrs. Chadwick, it has been clearly stated
that Mr. Carnegie met Mr. McCalla only once previously, years ago at a dinner . . .

Carnegie, or an associate, was putting a clear distance
between him and Rowan. I could find no rebuttal. Did Rowan simply go quiet so as not further to affront Carnegie
in public, relying on the truth, privately conceded, to appear
in the form of a bonus on his loan?

Or was Rowan enchanted? I began to picture my great-
grandfather as a young businessman, spellbound at a dinner
with Carnegie, and naming his first son after him. Then
looking, thirty years later, into Cassie's eyes and believing
he saw Carnegie, too. Whether or not they shared chro-
mosomes, they shared charisma, and emanated the spirit of
the age.

I had to speak to Babs. I found her in the garage laundry
pit, measuring line, hanging wash. She kept wooden clothespins in her teeth while I talked. Out of the basket, a garment;
out of her mouth two pins protruding. One corner went on
the line: one pin out of her teeth clipping corner to line;
other corner, other pin. New handful, new mouthful, and
so forth. The sun fell on her fine long uncombed hair.

She didn't look at me, didn't talk, not even to grunt
through the pins, as I wound out my speculations. She
strung up all the clothes and sheets on the line and then
turned to me.

"So your grandfather believed this woman was Carnegie's
daughter."

"It looks that way."

"And she was a great lady."

"Well, she was an extraordinary figure."

"What did Clellan think?"

"Hmm, Clellan? I don't know. He isn't quoted in the

papers. Clellan wasn't much for talking, you know." I laughed.

"And he was just a young man in his twenties."

She was absently wrapping extra clothesline around her wrist evenly, carefully, a double layer up her forearm.

"I think he was in love with her. She was a great lady."

"But she was much older than he was," I said mildly. Babs didn't seem in a mood for contradiction. Her eyes were upon the line she wound about her arm.

"He loved her," Babs said. She looked up at me once smartly, brightly, her round eyes brilliant with discovery. "She was my mother." She tucked the line tight on her arm, picked up the clothesbasket and strode toward the laundry room door.

I was struck dumb. I stood there in the lightly flapping wash until it occurred to me to call out, "No! It was all too long ago!" She couldn't have been out of earshot, but she did not reply.

eighteen.

THAT NIGHT I went to my room thinking of Carnegie's power, Cassie's witchery, and Babs. Carnegie had displaced Knox as the preeminent Scot of history; had driven out predestination with the gospel of progress; had flushed away infant damnation with the vision of a perfectible society led by self-sacrificing stewards of profit.

He had given away $350 million—equivalent then to a third of the entire national debt of the United States.

He created a god in his own image, and society rose up to follow it.

Cassie Chadwick did not join the train. She had her own idea. She imagined her mother in Carnegie's bed. She draped herself in the glamor of illegitimacy, wore a quicksilver gown. He who looked at Cassie could see his shadow, his dream, his queen of the faery isles. By implying magnificent neglect she attracted burning attention. She need not entreat for funds. Lisping hints, intriguing sighs, documents not thrust upon others, but accidentally disclosed, confirm the potential lender in his inwardly grinning surmise: that old daft gallant, Andra Carneggy, has spawned this glorious bastardess. And the exuberant conclusion followed: by lending this woman great monies, one made Carnegie his debtor.

The chosen sharer of the secret may first have felt lucky. Then he came to believe that good fortune was just possibly his due: a reward for good citizenship, for the sustained sobriety upon which the weal and welfare of so many others have so long depended, in Toronto and Buffalo; in Toledo,

223

and Cleveland; in Oberlin, Ohio, and western Pennsylvania. Just keep the sweet little secret; smile on it, nourish it with his clandestine favor, feed it with a substantial loan.

In a world which revered seven-figure wealth enough to coin the term "millionaire," and held a nine-figure fortune like Carnegie's in a paralysis of awe, Rowan McCalla was an eight-figure man. Why should he not be close to Andrew, as one who knew something special? After so many years of imitating Carnegie, why should he not take knowledge that could intimidate the king? In Cassie, Rowan saw young Andrew's covert abandon in the flesh, and in need. Why not befriend this accident of Carnegie's passion?

To have helped Andrew Carnegie; to have loaned monies it was Carnegie's due to give; what a powerful satisfaction. Especially when Carnegie himself would learn it, whispered to him by his lisping daughter in one of her rare and crucial audiences with him in his New York mansion.

Rowan, building always for the future, took his sons into his confidence, A. C. and Clellan. They met her, I imagined. They encountered those eyes, opened so wide and clear that it was impossible not to believe what one heard while gazing into them. Those brilliant eyes. Why had Rowan in New York covered her lower face with his hand? What moved him to hide the oracle of the strange lisp, to rely on the eyes alone, as "Carnegie's eyes"? Whatever his reasons, his sons had already joined him in a strange philanthropy to bastardy, a secret loan at sixty percent interest.

Clellan. If his father was moved by power, what moved him? The newspapers were full of Cassie's French maids, her trysts and alleged orgies. Had she bound Clellan to her carnally as she had Rowan by lust for power? Actually bedded with him in a tangle of monies, imaginations, interlocking obsessions, middle-aged flesh and young?

Even if she had, it was all a long time ago. Babs could not be her daughter. Cleveland, the seat of the trial, would have the fullest record of what happened. There I would search for the proofs that would clear Babs' mind.

In my dream-nights I saw Mercury in a naked blur, speedy and duplicitous. Mercury, the purse-carrier, god of merchants, and father of Hermaphroditus.

Saving Babs. And self-knowledge. "Self-knowledge," I whispered, while shaving. Learning about the McCalla men through whom and against whom I must model my own being.

Talking to myself required adjusting the angle of my razor. I wish now that I had nicked myself, bled, and felt the styptic bite of the inner truth: that in pursuing Cassie historically I resembled Rowan, pursuing her financially. The siren was the same; only the traveller's detour differed. Self-delusion, in its more insidious forms, masquerades as self-knowledge.

Sunrays pierced through pinpricks in the ancient window-shade, bit into the black-warted mirror before me. By such tiny pencils of light I had awakened: my phototropic alarm.

A dog was barking.

Mad.

Strange. Not for a long time had I heard Madison. The setter's peace with the world and his bones had made him quiet.

But now he was declaring something.

Should I shave and breakfast first, or should I investigate?

I decided to shave, and wait for the dog to quit.

Madison continued barking, with pauses for breath. I shaved quickly, curiosity rising just faster than hunger. I stung myself with aftershave lotion, shambled down the brass-tacked back stairs, and saw that Cook was not yet in the kitchen. I skipped out into the seven-thirty sun to learn what Madison had on his mind.

The dog was standing beyond the flagpole by Aunt Bekka's house. When he smelled Randy, he came loping stiff-legged toward me, then turned and ran back. I followed, lightly jogging. The dog repeated the approach-flee pattern three times, bringing me to the north side of the house where the grass grew high on the border of the empty lot. Then Madison ran just in front, turning his head now and then, guiding me around to the east side toward Bekka's sunken laundry yard. The only one with stone steps descending from the outside. The dog was not barking now as he trotted, panting, before me.

I heard another sound. A swan hissing? I shivered in the

225

morning cool. The early sun, my early run, started beads of sweat upon my brow.

No lake, no swans.

A faint animal moan.

A human sob.

I turned the corner.

Over the stone wall I saw something trussed to the railing of the fire escape.

I stopped and blinked, letting my eye penetrate the shadows of poplar and aspen that blocked the low sun from the laundry pit.

Human wrists tied to the fire escape?

No, Jesus, they were ankles.

Where there might be fingers clawing for purchase, there were toes, crawling in the air like caterpillers impaled on skewers.

I felt a lurch in my belly as if in a plummeting elevator. "Jesus *Christ*." I remember saying that, conversationally, to the dog. I broke into a run around the yard. I entered the stone stairway, yelling as I skipped down the stairs. Skidded on wet leaves, hit my tail on the bottom step, felt a hot shock up my spine. Nausea. My head now on a level with the person upside-down, whose eyes were closed. I got up, one hand on my coccyx; cried *"Shit."*

The dog danced around the dangling figure, whimpering and licking its face. I went over and kicked the dog away. I bent and raised the head of the suspended twisting body and it sucked air, hissed, and cried. At least she was alive.

I sprinted back to the garage, full strides on wet grass, holding my throbbing tail. I whacked my shoulder on the door jamb at the place left open for the dog to come and go. Inside I scrambled for a knife. Found one in the second drawer. Dashed back, lungs gulping in spikes of air, eyes bulging and tearing against the early morning cold.

Slower down the slick leaf-matted stairs.

"It's OK," I cried. "I've got a knife."

Slowly I brought up her head and back. I had not used the tool, but already there were cuts above each temple near the scalp, which had streamed blood into her hair, and now oozed it down her cheeks. She groaned and closed her eyes. She gasped and gagged as I held her. I let her back down a little. Then raised her an inch at a time, until her neck and head lay across my right arm. I held her to ease her trembling breaths for a full minute before I moved again, sustaining her upper body weight while rope and railing still anchored her bound feet.

"Put both arms around my neck and hold on." She slowly did as I told her. I fixed my left arm as a lengthwise brace under her, and freed my right hand to saw at the rope. I cut it through nearly to the iron, laid the knife across step rungs, grasped her legs just above the ankles and tugged her against the rope. She cried at each yank. The third one freed her, and I had her whole weight in my arms. She was shivering and crying. I walked backward to the opposite wall, bent my knees, leaned against the concrete, and allowed my feet slowly to slide outward on the leaves, so that I wound up sitting with her limp in my arms and the leaf-wet seeping through the seat of my khaki trousers to my aching bottom.

She writhed and heaved; turned her face away from me and retched into the leaves. She turned back and panted in my arms with eyes closed.

"I'm here. I'm here," I said. "It's OK. I've got ahold of you. I'm holding you."

She sobbed, writhed, pushed at me, turned away, and retched again.

After a while she lay still in my arms. She opened her eyes. They were darkly bloodshot, with spangles and splotches of red in each.

"Jesus Pete." I said. "Are you OK?"

She nodded.

"Really? All right?"

She nodded twice.

"Thank God. You scared hell out of me."

"No doctor." She gagged from the effort of speaking.

"OK. No doctor. But somebody's got to fix you up. First you rest. I'll carry you back to the garage. Then let me fix up those cuts."

She neither spoke nor moved. Madison brooded over her face a moment, then began licking the blood off it. She held still while he lapped her clean. I noticed the depth of leaves at the point over which she had been suspended, a pile mixed with the setter's ordure. I inhaled the odor of leaf-rot and dog turd, her sweat of fear and exertion, her sour mouth. "We'll go when you're ready," I said. "I'll carry you back to the garage."

I was glad that chauffeurs rise only shortly before masters. Luther never expected to be called before nine. The garage was quiet. She asked to be let down outside to walk in, but her ankles hurt. She would have crumpled if I had not been holding her. I carried her up the narrow dark wood stairs to her room, laid her on her bed, rinsed a washcloth, and began sponging her face free of blood, dog saliva, her own salt.

"How long were you there?"

There was a long pause.

"Don't know."

I paused, sponged, kept the pace of inquiry slow.

"Too long, probably?"

"Since sunup."

I went to her basin and rinsed the washrag, came back, resumed the cleaning, face, neck, arms, hands.

"Why the crazy shit did you do it?"

"Lay off." Her voice was thin.

"You scared me."

"I didn't ask for help."

"And without the dog you wouldn't have gotten any. Good old Mad." I looked over at the setter, head between paws in the doorway, eyelids half over his eyes.

She said nothing. She let me minister to her. She did not look at me.

"I've got to get you some Mercurochrome or something for those cuts, back at the house."

"No doctoring," she said. "Thanks for the nursing, but I don't want any doctoring."

"Why not?"

228

"The cuts will heal. I'll keep inside till they've gone. I'll comb my hair over them. I'll have flu for a few days." The burst of sentences exhausted her.

"OK. If you don't want any breakfast, I mean if maybe you'll feel like lunch, I could bring you some."

"Skip it."

"OK. Could I come for tea?"

"Help yourself."

I came back in the afternoon. She was standing. She wore bobby sox to cover the rope burns on her ankles. She had combed her hair partly forward and peered out from under bangs like a cover girl on an adolescents' magazine. Eyes still spangled with blood. She made tea. Then sat on the bed against a pillow, head back.

After we drank a little I asked again. "Why in crazy hell did you do that?"

"Because it smelled so godawful down there."

"*Because?* Because it smelled so godawful you did it?"

She took an Oreo cookie, snapped it in half, piled the two halves together, and crunched down on it, a multilayered chocolate and vanilla sandwich. "Sure. All those rotting leaves. Nobody's cleaned it out since last summer. Madison's shit piles. They made it even better. Every time he went out he must have gone there. Nobody noticed it until me. His idea of keeping the grounds clean."

"You did it *because* it was shitty there?"

"No better place. We talked about this once, long ago. Just think back."

I thought. "I don't remember."

"Keep thinking."

I thought way back and touched something.

"So you were trying to be a goddam Japanese saint?"

"Not really. Just testing out her act. It's a lot tougher than the high wire."

I thought some more.

"How long were you down there?"

"I don't know. Since sunup, I told you. I tied my ankles together while I was sitting on the fire escape, and then I knotted them to the railing. I got up and sat on the railing, let myself over, and grappled myself head downward as slow as I could with my feet tucked around the rail. Then I let go. I'd measured so I wouldn't strike bottom. My hands would hit the leaf pile, and I could push off."

"Ingenious. Pretty goddam ingenious." I tried to control the irony in my voice, to make myself sound admiring with just a whiff of mockery. But she wasn't listening to my tone.

"The Japanese tied one hand behind your back but they left the right arm free. If you wanted to recant all you did was raise it, and they pulled you out."

"Yeah, I remember."

"Well, I had both hands free. I couldn't tie one behind my back and still let myself down the way I wanted. But once I was down there and the blood went to my head, I kept pushing off with both hands. I *had* to. Headache, felt like my brain was going to bust. So I'd stiffarm downward, arch my back, and raise my head as far as I could."

"Good God. You still could have killed yourself."

She took her time before answering that.

"I cut my temples. Like the Japanese. So the blood pressure could drain off the brain." I didn't say anything.

She remembered more and spoke again. "My arms kept doing things. I didn't tell them to. They just kept reaching out, pushing off the floor, making me arch my back and raise my head."

I felt a little sick at my stomach. "How about some ice cream?"

"OK," she said. Her eyes were round, vacant, faroff. I went to get the quart I'd seen in Cook's icebox: Isaly's butter crunch.

I left for Cleveland a week later. Every day before that I stopped in on Babs. We talked in a desultory way. I brought ice cream each time, the only concession she would allow to being treated. We talked about the dog, what a good dog he was; and Buddy, what a great guy he was; and even the Cork and Bottle, how down there nobody cared where anybody came from, they were just looking for somebody.

230

Once she let me take the talk back to the Japanese saint, the one they had hung upside down for two weeks. She didn't say much. "Do you suppose"—the question was not really to me—"that one morning is enough to purify me?"

"Sure as hell *ought* to be," I said. I was on the verge of adding that three hours finished Christ, but I held my tongue. Not because I always refrained from stupid remarks, but because I was afraid of touching Babs off in some unpredictable direction.

Before I left I called Duffie and Lolly. Jimmy was at Rolling Rock, golfing, and both times I tried, was out on the course. I left word when I'd be back from my trip. I reached Lolly. She was in the midst of preparations for the Third Century Gala at the Lawn the following Saturday night. Even in her flurry I could feel her energy of listening when I told her that Babs was acting strangely. She was not well. Watch her, please watch her, I said, while I was gone. There was this research I had to do. I'd done all I could for Babs before going. She didn't want any attention, just to be left alone. But I was really a little afraid to leave her this way. Babs wouldn't like me telling anybody anything, but she, Lolly, would understand and would know how to handle Babs. Just so things wouldn't get any worse, all right? Could she possible just call, or stop by to see Babs, not letting on that I had called her, but just checking, sort of?

Lolly said she certainly would. And she would see me at the dance on Saturday.

Westward, the road to Cleveland, past mill towns, railroad towns, high school football towns; K of C, Jaycee towns, where the Optimists, the Rotarians, the Lions welcomed you. Then nights in the YMCA, days in the public library. What kind of obsession was this, you may ask. A growing-up obsession is the answer. Trying to prove myself smarter than my great-grandfather, the smartest McCalla anybody every heard of. Trying to catch him in his greatest error; reveal to him, through Cassie, his very innermost flaw. Trying also to pin down Clellan and Cassie, or peel them

231

so far apart that Babs had to stop imagining things. This research was for Babs, too, I told myself. Maybe mainly for her.

I drove myself through low-budget negative microfilm, white on black, tracking and tracing, backtracking and highlighting the story of a driven woman, of plutocratic libidos, of an hysterical city. Cassie's trial by public opinion preceded her trial by jury:

HOWLING MOBS GREET PRISONER
MRS. CHADWICK FACES AWFUL ORDEAL ON HER ARRIVAL IN HER HOME CITY
Men, Women and Children Sweep Police Lines Away to Get Sight of Her
Waives Preliminary Arraignment and is Committed to Jail
FORTITUDE GIVES WAY

Cassie's self-control "failed at the critical moment." She shrank from the crowd at the station, and "wept in the railroad car. 'I can't do it. I can't do it.'" When she finally shuffled out on the arms of marshals, with her son and her nurse preceding her and shielding her from photographers, she wore a long brown automobile coat with a huge turned-up fur collar, a veil over her face, and a large hat.

At the prison there awaited a "howling, hooting, yelling mob of grown men, acting almost like maniacs." They "threw their hats in the air and yelled like schoolboys at a football game." After passing by the mob, Cassie "swooned away at the cold breath of the jail."

She was bankrupt. She pleaded not guilty. She again denied receiving loans from Henry Phipps of Pittsburgh. When there was nothing else to report, the newspapers speculated about Cleveland bankers and Cassie's French serving-maids.

MRS. CHADWICK'S DEFENSE: PROBABLY INSANITY

If Cassie Chadwick was demented, I wondered, what was Rowan McCalla and his syndicate: my great-uncle Clellan

Cartwright McCalla; my grandfather Andrew Carnegie McCalla, named after a man whom his father had once met at a dinner party; and the unnamed fourth?

None would have called them insane for an industrial investment of $500,000 with the expectation of receiving $800,000 in short-term return. But what would you call people who invested in Cassie Chadwick?

In early March 1905, Carnegie spoke up again. The "iron-master," questioned on still other documents that had come to light, laughed at a five-million-dollar note and a "trust agreement." The trust letter, he said, was illiterate, and he had "not signed a note in 30 years."

The United States attorney indicated that Carnegie would not be called to the witness stand unless the defense sought to prove that any Chadwick papers bearing the magnate's name were genuine, in which case he would testify to the contrary.

The prosecution also let it be known that they would go to great lengths to prevent Cassie's discharge on a warrant of insanity. "If necessary some of the best known alienists in the world will be called upon . . . to examine Mrs. Chadwick and report as to her mental condition."

As the day of the trial approached, Cassie made herself available to the press again, protesting innocence, seeking sympathy, flaunting her vulnerability. "The craning of necks and contortions of bodies to get a glimpse of me, a poor woman, you've no idea how it affects me."

Reporter: "Did you ever use the name of Andrew Carnegie in floating your Pittsburgh loans?"

Mrs. Chadwick: "I never obtained one single dollar from . . . any . . . Pittsburgh man by the use of Andrew Carnegie's name to influence the deal; I never told [any such man] that I was Mr. Carnegie's daughter, either."

I reflected, not for the first time, that either Cassie Chadwick was lying or that reporters quoting my great-grandfather were lying. Or both. Between the press and the accused, who was the grosser fabricator, the more pernicious illusionist? I could not stop to determine, but kept plowing ahead, leaving the sorting to later.

Without informing Cassie, but with journalists present, six long-time employees of the Ohio State Penitentiary were brought in to see the defendant. The *Cleveland Press* reporter noted, in sequence, Cassie's puzzled look, her suddenly flaming cheeks, and then her pallor.

Employee: "How do you do, Mrs. DeVere?"

Cassie (to marshal): "I don't want to see any ladies."

Employees scrutinize her further and leave.

The press scramble after the visitors, one of whom is willing to talk extensively:

"Know her? I should think I do know her. After the experience I had with that woman, I can never forget her. She looks handsomer now, a little fuller in the face, and her hair is puffed up in front. Then she wore it combed severely down close to her forehead. But she has not changed greatly. I identified the lisp if nothing else. *And she knew us, too.*"

"She violated with impunity every rule and regulation of the prison, and by the very strength of her will assumed the office of assistant matron."

"She would not wear prison clothes. She had a room of her own, and in it kept six trunks filled with dresses. . . . [She] had her meals served in her rooms. She would say, 'You cannot keep me here.' And she was right. They pardoned her. We were glad to see her go. She kept the institution in an uproar by telling the fortunes of the women prisoners. They believed in her power, were afraid of her, and would do whatever she told them to do. I WILL SWEAR ON A STACK OF BIBLES THAT I KNEW HER!'"

The prosecution did not require Carnegie's sworn disavowal of the documents with his name, and spared the eminent man tribulation on the witness stand. By using jail-keepers to identify Cassie as already convicted of forgery in Toledo under the name of Lydia DeVere, they discredited her without injury to Andrew's dignity. The great need not appear in court.

The tactics of the prosecution and Carnegie's counsel thrust the defending lawyers onto boggy ground. Throughout the trial, they resorted to diversions of attention and plays upon sympathy. A woman had been dragged into the mire. Men guilty of poor judgment or worse had not been tried. The government colluded with the plutocrats. In his summary, counsel for the defense pictured the district attorney as having "feasted with Carnegie on viands in which had been dissolved the choicest pearls, and upon nightingale's tongues, and I suppose when he finished, cried, 'Help us, Andy, or we sink!' . . ."

"Don't think that because the district attorney threw a *quire of paper* at us, we are guilty."

The district attorney replied in kind. Summing up, he called Cassie an "arch enchantress . . . a duchess of diamonds, and a grand duchess of criminality, singing her sweet siren song of gold."

The jury deliberated for five hours. The result was immediately announced in the presence of the prisoner.

MRS. CASSIE L. CHADWICK IS FOUND GUILTY
Complete Collapse of Woman Follows
Succeeded by Such a Display of
Frenzied Grief as Federal
Building Has Never Seen
SOBBING, STRUGGLING, SCREAMING, AND WILDLY
PROTESTING HER INNOCENCE, SHE IS LED OUT

The spectators following the "swaying, tottering, broken woman" coldly proclaimed she was acting. Her moan of anguish rose to a piercing scream. "I am not guilty. It is all a lie. I am not guilty."

There was more, of course. I could not get enough of it. The sentencing: two years on each of four counts, one year on each of two more. Several counts unproven. Total, ten years. Proceedings followed in bankruptcy court. Dr. Chadwick hit the news again: churchgoer, teetotaler, non-smoker, non-chewer of tobacco; young-looking, with a "weak and nervous voice." Eleven days after the jury verdict he announced that he would display his wife's former possessions in New York and Cleveland. To enliven the show, he would give two organ recitals a day, for $100 per week.

I missed Cassie and wondered why. I still wonder. She was, I suppose, an example of hysterical passion in my family's past, just as my father, in the present, had stood for obstinate chastity. Neither of them were happy. Both, in fact, destroyed themselves: Cassie with a suicidally expanding series of projected personae, Duncan by colluding in the slow strangulation of his own ego. Cassie and Duncan perhaps stand for the alternative extremes that I might have pursued in my own life—self-indulgent delusion and anchoritic self-denial.

I see that now. But then, I fear, I was gripped by the infatuation of the elder McCallas with Cassie. Their plutocratic libidos were at work, aroused by money and Carnegie's magnetism, and perhaps even, in Clellan's case, by Cassie's projections and personal enticements. I couldn't learn much for certain about that, but I needed to know more, for Babs' sake. I went over my notes, and guided by them, back through the microfilm reels, looking for evidence that would connect Clellan to Cassie, or somehow disconnect them.

By the time I got what I wanted it was early Friday afternoon. I had been gone five days. I had to get back home for the Third Century Gala. But first a call to Babs. I realized that I had never talked with her by phone before. We had always talked face to face, or sent notes. There was no phone in the garage anyway. I had to try her through Gramma's kitchen, and hope somebody could find her. I called collect and asked Cook. She hadn't seen Babs in a couple of days, but she'd go look. I will say of Alice B. Cook that she was fat and slow and timid, but she loved a culinary challenge or a mystery. Off she went. I hung on, it seemed like five minutes, maybe ten.

Then a voice came on. So faint and toneless it could have been a trans-Atlantic call.

236

"Babs? Babs, is that you? Can you talk?"

"Of course I can talk. What have you got to say?"

"I mean is Cook right there in the kitchen?"

"No. She went upstairs."

"Listen, I've found out. About Clellan and Cassie. What I was looking for."

She didn't say anything, just listened, a blank on the other end of the long line.

I told her how the whole thing came out, the evidence and the verdict, the sentence and the reaction. If she were not going to say anything, I was going to fill her in, fully, so no mistakes would be made, no misimpressions retained. Then I said, listen to this.

And I read her from a description of Cassie at trial, of a journalist's fascination with her gestures and dress. During interview she laughed almost hysterically. She "clasped and unclasped her hands continually. Her only ring was the 'great white gold band' of her wedding to young Dr. Chadwick. She wore a flowered silk waist, a brown tailor-made skirt and coat, and a hat to match."

Still no response.

"Now get this," I said, excited by my discovery, angry with her passivity. "At her throat was a large cameo semi-profile head with five diamonds, one each at the throat and ear and in her hair, with two diamonds for eyes."

I let the silence settle.

She finally answered, as if coming up from undersea, shaking her head, eyes and ears, clear of water. "My father gave it to her. And after she went away, he gave it to me."

"No, he didn't." I tried to make my voice gentle, although I felt triumphant. "If it's the same cameo as the one you've got, *Cassie* probably gave it to *Clellan*. She had to go off to jail, owing millions. All she had was jewels and furs. I bet she gave it to him as a token repayment of the eight hundred thousand she owed the McCallas."

Her voice was suddenly bright and brittle as glass. "He loved her. He told me. She was a great lady."

"No," I said. "She was a great impostor. She was no lady. She was convicted of fraud and forgery. She had already been convicted once fifteen years before. And she got caught again. She was a genius, maybe, but no lady. She was a crook."

"Don't talk like that about my mother." The glass was flying apart.

I had her now. A way open to the truth. The truth to make her free.

"She couldn't be your mother. Not any way at all. I called the courthouse in Cleveland and the penitentiary long-distance. I double-checked it. She died in prison in 1907." I let it sink in. "She died twenty-seven years before you were born." Maybe I overdid it. "She couldn't even be your *grand*mother."

I heard slight sounds on the other end of the phone. Sobs at the liberating recognition of truth? I hoped so. But maybe the sound of shattered glass brushed into a dustpan.

"Listen, Babs. The cameo may be the same one. That's OK. It doesn't matter. He gave it to you. Clellan gave it to you and it's yours. He gave it to you because he loved you, and . . ." Now I was suddenly sobbing, and I couldn't talk and I was thinking, "and I love you, too." But I couldn't say it. Or didn't anyway.

She had found her voice. It came in sharp over my weakening sobs. "So he *lied* to me. Your uncle lied to me and gave me jewels and took advantage of me. He lied to me in his own house and pretended he loved me, and I was only a little girl. He made love to me in his house and I was only a little girl." She stopped to gather breath and then yelled at me in final rage: "*And now it should be my house!*"

"Babs!"

But she had slammed down the phone. I called back. Cook answered after eight rings. I hung up and dialed Lolly instead. She was out.

238

nineteen.

I TRIED again once, on a road stop, to reach Lolly about Babs. But this was the night of the Third Century Gala, the social climax of the city's bicentennial year. I could not get her by phone. I kept on driving.

I thought of Babs and the last summer together. We usually reached for each other in the dark, or moonglow, or starshine. The one time we made love with a light on—the dim bulb beneath the fringed pink shade of the standing lamp in the far corner of B-Ray's bedroom—that one time we wore Hallowe'en masks. Afterward she called me "Master Randy." Only then, and never again. She said it several times in a tender tone that still makes my mind sink and my heart rise. I held her as if she were my own true self.

Why now, face to face, were we strangers? Why unified by mask, divided by countenance?

The thought of Lolly eased my mind. She could help Babs. She knew how to handle the embarrassed, the derelict, the wounded. Once, caught by her in a pretense, Duffie had protested, "Lolly, you see right through me." She narrowed her gray eyes: "No, I can't see through people, but I try to see into them." Then, as if she had said something indiscreet, she shifted the subject to the civic celebrations, her job for the last two years.

My only sight of Lolly for months had been in Adelaide's copy of *Town and Country*. "Pittsburgh: A Man's Town," the cover read, above a picture of Major General Richard K. Mellon, United States Army Reserve, in a double-breasted blue suit, one arm resting on a marble mantelpiece.

Among fashion pictures of "wives of executives and philanthropists" and "leaders of the younger set," there she posed: against a vertical abstract in Crispin's museum, profile right, eyes steady, eyebrows slightly arched, gloved hands resting on her stomach, holding a large bag with a horizontal pattern. "Laura Contini seems undisturbed by abstract art, possibly because she is studying philosophy. Her cocoa-colored slim dress in a linen-like silk is bowed at neck and waistline and worn with a navy cashmere cardigan trimmed in the color of the dress. Lord and Taylor; I. Magnin; Gucci bag."

They didn't mention where she was studying. Duquesne wasn't fashionable. They didn't mention that she was a graduate student. Females of the "younger set" did charities and sports. And they didn't mention that she was concentrating on the Thomistic system. Whatever might that be? How could the daughter of Mrs. Contini of Hill and Hollow Road and Mr. Contini of Rome and Nice have fallen in love with St. Thomas Aquinas?

I changed to black tie. I mounted Clellan's Pierce-Arrow and rode it up toward the Lawn, easing it like a lathered steed over the last jumps. Glimmer on the river; glow behind the hilltops. Lights of city and industry rising, sunlight fading.

Tonight Lolly's Third Century Gala; tomorrow the problems of Barbara Quick. What will she do when the buildings come down? When McCalla compound is rubble and weed; with bulldozer tracks, mudfrozen, like fossilized signs of the dinosaurs?

The Third Century Gala was more select than the Bicentennial Ball the previous Thanksgiving, a giant political blast. This was a private salvo, an occasion for self-congratulation among the movers and doers of the city, particularly those who could claim lineage. Membership in the Lawn gained one an invitation. There was only one other list: the key committee members, the major donors, the figureheads, and the pivotal people of the Bicentennial. They would together celebrate in oligarchic joy the achievements

240

of the last two hundred years, especially the last seven months; then disperse for the summer—to longer weekends, steady golf, disciplined suntans.

Lolly was easy to see, hard to find alone. She gossiped in bright clumps of rainbowed women and tuxedoed men; she laughed on the arms of elder males whose committee assignments she had fulfilled, while the credit went to them; she tilted and whirled with her dancing partners. Fewer asked her than wished to, but many asked just the same, daring to dance with this lame one, whose eyes held to their faces, her head and shoulders dipped to the beat in unique patterns owed to the one dance she'd refused.

"I've found you." I cut in just in time for one of Lester Lanin's breaks. "You've found me," she smiled. We walked to the glass-walled porch. I lifted two champagnes from a waiter's tray and we sat at a quiet end in the semi-dark. In the valleys, on the riversides below, lids lifted from kettles of industry. Sparks rose in the night sky. "Aurora borealis," I said. "Hmm?" she asked, as abstracted as I.

"Or 'australis,'" I said. "I should like to see the southern lights. Solar particles lighting up tropical skies at night."

"Either, yes, north or south. For me, too. And down or up. Lights descending on our cities, or lights arising from them. Either, either."

We sat silently awhile. I said it certainly was a good party and what a lot of work she must have given it. She thanked me. She reached for the champagne she had put on the windowsill and took a sip.

"I tried a couple of times to call you," I said.

"I saw Babs as you asked before you left. She is in a bad way. Maybe very sick indeed." Lolly's eyes were focused far off, but her voice was close.

"When did you see her?"

"Tuesday. Three days ago. I couldn't reach her by phone so I drove over after work and before dinner. She was just sitting in her room."

"Just sitting?"

"It's all right to sit, of course. And even to 'just sit.' But she was just sitting with the shades down. She didn't answer me until I was outside her door, though I called her more than once on the stairs. I thought perhaps she was sleeping. No, she answered in a faint voice. She was just sitting. All the time I was there she seemed weak as a gassed canary."

"Not like Babs."

"No. I never really saw her expression clearly though we sat just a few feet away from each other. She hadn't raised the shades. Something told me I shouldn't suggest it."

"What did she talk about?"

"We didn't talk about anything much. I made most of the conversation. She interrupted me once. She said, 'My eyes are bloodshot,' and I thought she was explaining why she kept the shades down, and I said I was sorry to hear it, was there anything I could do for her or get for her."

"Was there? Anything?"

"She said no. She said, 'I've got bloodshot eyes and a big headache. I've got a hungover hangover.' Then she laughed—one sudden laugh. It startled me a little. It was the only time she laughed while I was there."

"She said she had a hangover?"

"Yes. Has she been drinking a lot? Do you know, Randy?"

"I don't know. Maybe. But I don't think that's what's bothering her."

"What is it then? I couldn't get a clue. I offered to send her anything she needed. I offered to come back soon after the Gala. She said she didn't need anything, thanks, in a kind of toneless voice. The only moment I felt she was there, aside from the laugh, was when I left. She said, 'Goodbye, Lolly.' It was the first time she used my name. I had the strange feeling that I had just arrived, and I must stay. But of course I had to go."

"Of course you did." Then I told her what I had come upon, what Madison had led me to, the week before. I probably should have told her sooner. I sketched it swiftly, urgently, as the band's break-time ran out. I told her what had happened since: every time I tried to put a platform of fact underneath Babs, she had invented a flight of fantasy stairs.

Lolly listened. Her eyes widened and filled with tears.

She broke in once: "Babs must not be alone." When I finished, she said again, "She must have someone with her. All the time. See her tomorrow morning. Call me about her."

Lanin struck up his band.

I nodded to Lolly's order and groped for a way of summarizing about Babs. "It's hard to become a saint, medieval Japanese style." I heard false toughness, superficial gallantry, in my remark, and was trying for something more true when a hand came down on my shoulder. A smiling middle-aged man peered over me at Lolly, asking for the dance. "Certainly, Sheppie," she said.

I shook his extended hand and forced a smile in response to his bonhomie. "Good to see you, Mr. Cardigan."

As she drew past my chair, Lolly spoke in a low tone. "Sainthood, maybe. Perdition, more likely." She flung her short hair with a toss of the head, smiled brilliantly at Cardigan, linked her arm with his, and gave a laughing cry: "Teach me how to dance!"

Three penguins piddling at the South Pole. Black tuxedo backs faced me. I waited while they stood up against the wall, unzipping, sighing, jiggling, zipping. The middle one turned around. Duffie, still fiddling with his trousers. "Hey, babe," he smiled foolishly, extending his right hand. With his left he struggled with his fly. "I'll wait for you."

I shook his hand and squeezed between two fat men studying cracks in the white tile walls. "I called you," I said over my shoulder. "Twice. You were on the course. How's your game?"

"Terrific and terrible. Depends on the day."

"I wanted your help. I still need it."

"Straightening out your long irons?"

"No." I pressed the plunger and zipped up. Cool water glided down the age-cracked porcelain and upon the pink aromatic cake in the drain. I made way for the next man. Duffie was examining the shave lotions and hair cremes at the sink, shaking each, watching bubbles and viscous glide. "You're smashed," I said, without accusation.

"Yeah, but not really shit-faced."

"Can you think?"

"Always."

"Let's talk."

"Where?"

"Down here. Over there."

The Lawn kept a bartender in the locker room for those men who needed stag retreat from dances. Duffie ordered a bourbon on the rocks, I a bourbon and ginger ale. We settled at the furthest table from the bar.

"I was calling you about Babs."

Duffie coughed on his drink. "Easy, babe," I said. The coughing continued, Duffie holding onto his glass, rattling cubes, spilling a sip at each convulsion. I stood up and whacked him across the shoulder blades. He subsided. Then thumbed his glasses back up his nose and stared at his left thumbnail. "What about Babs?" he asked.

"I don't think she's well. I think she's very unhappy."

"I know," Duffie said. "It's all my fault."

"Your fault? How is it your fault?"

"I'm glad you're back in town. I wanted to talk with you and tell you about this."

"About what?"

Duffie rattled the ice against the side of his glass. "I got out of control, I guess. Control is the key. I've got it in my woods, I've got it in my irons. I've even got it on the green. Very few guys my age can putt the way I can. I've got control."

"Yeah, sure you do, but what's that got to do with Babs?"

"If you don't know, don't press me, babe. It's too confusing." He drank, a gulp. "In fact, it hurts."

"What is this? What hurts?"

"What day did you call me?"

"Let's see. Last Sunday, I think."

"And when did you talk with Babs?"

"Oh, briefly, same day, last Sunday. Longer, before that. I was calling about all that."

"Have you talked with her since?"

"No, I just got back, Duff. I just drove in, dammit, from fucking Cleveland, Ohio."

"How did your research go? Still that project about your great-grandfather?"

"Yeah, still, and it went well, and I'm getting the whole thing straight. Which I'm not getting in this conversation. Do you need another drink, or do I need to take the remains of that one away from you?"

"I need another. So do you."

I got two more, and slid the bourbon on the rocks across to Duffie, who sniffed it and sipped with languor. "Crazy damn scandal, huh? In your family, I mean."

I inhaled deeply, exhaled, then drank. If Jimmy wouldn't talk until he heard about the project, then Jimmy would hear about the project. He was the one who knew the most about it, anyway. So I summarized how the Cleveland research bore out the prosecutor's case against Cassie as a previously convicted forger. My forebears were colossally duped, I said, stressing the money part of it. Maybe not for $800,000, as the first reports said, although that was what they expected to get repaid. The loan was for $500,000, sixty percent interest, payable anytime within ten years. If Cassie's testimony in bankruptcy proceedings was truthful and precise, she had actually received only $225,000 of that. Even so, what would be the equivalent of that smallest sum today, 1959, in buying power? A whole million probably? You know what that is? Equivalent of the annual wages of five hundred housemaids, that's what. I happen to know.

"That's real socko," said Duffie. He drank steadily, letting his glasses slip. "Real socko. She really socked it to 'em. Really stashed it in the sock."

"Sure is. Sure was. On top of that they went around buying up other people's loans to Cassie. How much? Double, ten times their own investment? A thousand housemaids, five thousand?"

"Socko, babe, super socko."

"Annual wages of five thousand housemaids. For one hysterical strumpet high on imagination. At the acme of Rowan McCalla's success he gets Chadwicked. Dramatically taken. Not only hugely, but publicly. Beginning of the great descent. Some sympathize, some don't. Even those who sympathize notch his reputation down one, two, three pegs. Not so smart as we thought, they say, not so reliable. They put their money elsewhere. Even worse—Rowan had brought his own two sons into it. They're smeared with it, too. Promising young businessmen in their twenties, thirties? Revealed as complete gulls? Careers go flat."

The door opened. Down floated lavender music by Lanin, to move the imaginations of those who deny they are rich.

"A real downsock, babe. Sorry for you all, old buddy."

"Tell me now, Jimmy. What happened between you and Babs?"

"Too embarrassing, babe, even to tell an old buddy. I'm still a virgin. Only you know that. Nobody else knows that. Nobody suspects. It's a secret. Don't tell."

"I won't tell, Duff."

"Are you a virgin, old buddy? Still a virgin?"

"Secret, Duff. It's a secret. I'm not allowed to tell."

"OK, so you're not. Which of those broads upstairs did you get? Or was it some horn-rimmed bimbo at the Yale Law School? I bet she was horn-rimmed. Not saying? Don't pull gentlemen-don't-tell on me, old buddy."

"I'm not doing that, Duff. I'm pulling brothers on you. Brothers confide and hush. And you're about to confide in me because I've just confided in you about how dumb my family is, and I've bought you two drinks and I'm about to get you and me another. So make up your mind how you're going to tell it while I go back to the bar."

When I set down the new drinks, Duffie tapped his glass a few times with his left little finger, and spoke. He had invited Babs over on an impulse, Wednesday it was, just Wednesday. Well, not exactly an impulse. He'd been thinking about it a long time. In the novels of Colette, young men find older women to initiate them, and he had decided it was time for his own initiation. He believed that time was marching on. Yes, he was breezing through Harvard, aiming to get his Ph.D. in three years. Everything was breaking just right. He had teachers sucking up to him, trying to get him to write his dissertation with them, teach in their courses. Very gratifying, but too much pressure. And no outlet, you see? It was time to stop being a virgin. Did his old buddy understand about outlet?

I nodded.

But he couldn't find an older woman to initiate him. Where do you find an older woman who is neither uxorious nor repulsive? He had tried. That is, he had ventured on some exploratory conversations, and found in one case that the woman licked her lips too readily, and in the other his own mouth went dry as he talked. Just talking around the subject. So he had suspended both negotiations. Not long before he'd come back home.

Then the idea occurred to him—well, perhaps it had been there for some time—about Babs. She might be understood in this context. She was, he meant this as a compliment, evidently a worldly woman. In addition she was young and attractive. It did not alter old friendship with her to say that she looked lavishly interesting, with those breasts too big for ballet, but still a compact figure; and that acrobatic carriage, straightbacked and flat-bellied; and those great moist round eyes; and that slightly open mouth. Furthermore there was her long hair. He fell for long hair. Even when she wound it up and tucked it in a tight coil on top of her head, it excited him. He wanted to unwind it, get lost in it.

Please understand, Duff said, his tender respect for Babs. He had picked her out, with all reverence, as his chosen priestess of love, and he would offer himself, in all humility, as her novice. He made up his mind. It was not easy. But Granny was at Hyannisport and so really it would not be hard. Theirs was a big house. He just thought Babs might fancy the setting, since, if you'll excuse me, all the McCalla places are about to be demolished.

I found myself drinking fast and Duffie not now drinking at all. I reached over and poured some of Duffie's bourbon into my own glass.

She accepted, over the phone. For dinner. Duffie gave the maids the night off. He cooked it himself, as graduate students learned to do at Harvard, and turned out quite a

247

fine boeuf bourgignon, if he did say so himself. They had a good enough time, though he did almost all of the talking. In Cambridge one learns that, too, if necessary. She was extraordinarily quiet. But there was an Alice-in-Wonderland quality about it which made her all the more desirable to him. He remarked on that, in fact, for his initial after-dinner compliment, as he began his approach. They each had a snifter of Courvoisier and were sitting on the big red settee in the billiard room.

He had grown more and more expansive. She was such a good listener, he told her. He loved her demure quality, her shoulders back and head high. He noticed she was wearing her hair a new way, long across her forehead, near her eyes. Her slightly averted face suggested a woman pondering a grand commitment. He ventured to make his thoughts quite express. His heart was beating wildly, and he told her so. He wished, unworthy as he was, to make himself her apprentice in love. Whatever he lacked in skill he would more than repay in passionate gratitude.

Then she spoke; and, as he said, until then she hadn't spoken much at all. His heart was racing with hope. Given her stillness he had expected eloquent brevity. So he was surprised how long and disjointed she was. He couldn't remember it exactly, because it was so disconnected—all about diamonds in the sky, and being Clellan McCalla's daughter—get that? Your Great Uncle Clellan's daughter? And his house being *her* house? Whatever; it sounded like no.

Yet he had gone too far just to take a first negative. So he persisted. He tried to embrace her on the couch. She shrugged him off. He said—maybe this was his big mistake—that he could make her life comfortable after the McCalla compound was gone. She turned on him, blazing. He did remember this, it was interesting: she said, "What's the difference between you and Kidder Towne and a dozen other guys?"

He had got up to think that one over and paced the room. She'd got up at the same time and gone over to the fireplace. There was no fire, of course, in June. But she was shivering

248

all over. Shaking. He thought it might be from restraining her hidden passion for him. So he approached her standing by the fireplace.

Duffie stopped.

I asked, "And what happened?"

Duffie took off his spectacles with his left hand to examine them for smudges. He mumbled as he drank with his right hand. I couldn't hear the burble of voice in the clink of ice.

"What?" I asked. "She needed you?"

"No, babe. She kneed me. Right in the groin."

Duffie's eyes were closing. Mine, I'm sure, were wide open. We sat in silence, drinking.

"Tired of the women, eh?" A hearty voice went by, booming at us. From within the toilet we soon heard a relieved sigh. He roared out at us from the ceramic echo chamber. "Bachelor privilege, right, eh? Good thing, too, bar down here, place to escape. Hah!" He came out, still struggling with his trousers, stopped; bent at the knees to close his fly in one fell zip, bottom to top. "Hah, that's better." He straightened, walked over, and clapped me on the shoulder. "Your mother and I got here late. Wondered where you were. Good dinner party. Could have stayed. But had to show. Great to see you. You, too, Jimmy. How's it going, huh?"

"Just fine, Mr. Towne."

"Randy, boy, dance with your mother, right? Do you both a world of good."

"Sure, Kidder. I'll catch her upstairs."

"Now's a good time. She's over in the corner with some women. Near the big trophy case. I need a drinko, right?"

I said as I rose, "I'll call you tomorrow, Duff."

For once my mother did not criticize my dancing. I held her stiffly, but moved her nimbly through the crowd to the Lanin bounce. The ballroom floor sprang under our feet, its eager creaking covered by music and crowd chatter.

"How are you coming to Hyannisport for the wedding?" she asked.

"Drive, I guess, if it's still OK to use Uncle Clellan's car."

"Oh, it's such a long drive. Don't you want to take the train or fly? I'll pay for it."

"Thanks, Mother. But I like driving. Thanks anyway."

"There won't be many there. We're just having a few. Intimate friends, and relatives we care for. I'm so glad you're going to come."

"I'm glad, too, Mother."

"Somebody has to remember a camera. Somebody has got to take pictures."

"I'm sorry I don't have a camera, Mother. I don't know how to take pictures. But Kidder can find somebody to do it."

"Oh, Randy, I'm so excited. I never knew it could be like this. I wake up in the morning wondering what he's thinking, and I think of him during the day wondering what he's doing."

"And you spend evenings with him."

"Yes, and I love to hear about his day. Everybody he saw, everything he did. But you wouldn't understand."

"I might when I grow up, Mother."

"Oh, you're a tease. I like a tease. My father was a tease. You're like my father. Very bright and a tease. And a little bit fickle? Aren't you? A little bit fickle?"

"Maybe, Mother. Sure, if you think so."

Shep Cardigan cut in. "I like your taste in women, Randy. You dance with the best." He whirled Adelaide away. She leaned back in his arms and gave him her Virginia radiance.

Home. Time to go home.

Bourbon and champagne: liquid lead and nitrogen in my veins. I could not navigate cleanly. I moved slowly among crowds that seemed swift and nimble. I tried to identify myself by my thoughts. But they were mere impulses. The great reality was the crowd, celebrating the coming Third Century of Pittsburgh, iron and steel capital of the world. Celebrating Industrial Man. Past midnight by far, past logic further, people hailed each other with "Two hundred and one!" "Three hundred years!" and "On to the Fourth Cen-

250

tury!" Boys, girls, men, women; foolish, elegant, inebriate, disciplined. They were the signs to each other of their privileged status. They were the ordained favorites who even now, in festivity, behaved like the elect. Wretched infants elsewhere on earth might be predestined to damnation; but these, the chosen and saved, could behave like children together, innocent, worthy, charming, redeemed.

I stood at the top of the stair, at band level, on the edge of the dancing concourse. Saw Duffie dancing with Lolly. How could he hold more than I? Emotionally deprived, Duffie was. Take narrow emotions, prime them with liquor, and you may get one evening of stamina. But across a lifetime, I would prevail.

Across a lifetime, I assured myself, looking at a blurry world of debutantes, ex-debs, their mothers and grandmothers, their swains and sires, and those who longed for them, locked in a summer world of Lanin music, purple-yellow at one A.M.

"Mister Randy!"

Buddy was carrying a tray of champagne glasses, all full. He explained that he had part-time work with the club again.

To test my reflexes I chose the glass diagonally furthest from myself on the tray presented to me. I lifted it gently over the heads of others; and, having once sipped and thus proved myself, returned Buddy's greeting.

"How the fuck are you, Bud?"

"Oh, ho! Enjoying the par-tee, Mister Randy? Be my guest. Take two. One for a ladyfriend. If you can't find a ladyfriend, finish them both." He chuckled and swiveled his head, as if to look away from me while I did what he suggested, and to cow anyone who would criticize two-fisted drinking.

I tossed down one glass. Looked at the other. Sipped.

"Hey, you got a minute?" Buddy said.

I nodded.

"Slip back here with me?"

We faded behind a folding screen. Busboy trays stood seven high with dishes, and napkins tumbled on the floor.

251

A ketchup bottle rolled against a pantry door, uphill when the door was opened, downhill when it shut.

"I'd just like your advice," Buddy said, the wide silver tray lightly in his hand, his arc of fingers holding the champagne steady.

"Shoot, Bud."

The overhead light shone through Buddy's thinning white hair. His black eyebrows worked as he spoke. "It's like this. Mr. Towne, Kidder Towne, you know? He used to come to me for massage? He comes up tonight and says, 'Buddy, you got a great little girl there.' And I says, 'You mean my Babs? You mean my daughter?' And he says, 'Yes,' and he's smiling. And I didn't say anything; and he says, 'I think I can help her along.' And I says, 'That's nice, and how do you think so?' And he says, 'She knows how to give a fella a good time, you know? No tricks, no games; she knows what's work and what's play.' And he gives me a wink.

"So I says, 'Oh?' And he says, 'I can see she goes a long ways. She's made some friends of mine happy, and they're choosy guys. So I'm going to see to it that she's happy.' "

The kitchen doors swung open and shut, rolling the ketchup bottle, and waiters shuffled by in waves of dishwashing noise and whiffs of steam.

"I didn't say nothing. But I'm asking you, Mister Randy, because I know that you know where things are at, what I'm asking is, what should I have said?"

I had a little champagne in my glass, and I tossed it off. I squared my shoulders and wondered if I'd lost my keys. No, the right-hand trouser pocket, as usual. I knotted my thigh muscles. I could feel the keys there. Did I have my wallet? I inhaled deeply. Yes, the right-hand breast pocket, as usual.

"What should you have said, Buddy? Damned if I know. But what he said sounds rotten to me."

Buddy stood there patient, his arched palm and broad tuxedoed shoulder holding steady champagne slowly bubbling, his eyebrows working as he listened. "Rotten?" he asked.

"Fuck it, Buddy, happy or no-happy, I'd tell him to stick

it." But Buddy wasn't going to say that to Kidder Towne, and neither, probably, was I. What should be said?

"Tell Babs to stay away from those guys, Buddy. Tell her to stay clear of Kidder and all those guys." I put my empty glass up on his tray and picked out a full one. For what was on my mind I found it hard to look Buddy in the face. I feared embarrassment or disbelief or ridicule. But I was able to bring myself to say it, with my eyes sweeping the dance floor in a lordly rove. "Tell her I love her, Buddy."

Buddy hadn't seen me cry since I was a boy and was not going to now. Glass in hand, I slid past him with a nod, across the dance floor, through the tables of breakfasters, gorging for the last hour of revelry. I headed for the front door shouldering younger stags on the way, and bumped into someone older, tall. I stood back and apologized to a rangy gray-haired man with a cleft chin, amused squint wrinkles around his baby blue eyes. I passed on, remembering that Lang Delavane was prospering in the insurance business: the first former professional athlete ever elected to the Lawn.

Out in the dark June morning, I switched on the ignition in Clellan's car, listened to the antique rumble of motor, moved into gear, tooled the several blocks home undeterred by the red light, unchallenged by traffic. I called on my father's ghost, but he did not answer.

I coursed past the tigers into the driveway, stopped, shoved back the doors of the garage, and clutch-nudged the Pierce-Arrow into its dark stable, creeping the last several feet by sense and habit, guided by spirits of chauffeurs past.

I shut the doors.

I walked around to the west side of the garage and looked up, leaning against the belly-high wall around the garage laundry pit. There was a light on in the second floor room north of the service line on the brick wall, house-side, of the unique court on which had been held the first international laundry yard squash racquet tournament.

She's OK, I thought.

I turned back toward Gramma's house.

At the mulch pile on the east side of the garage, I stopped,

253

unzipped, and passed water, listening with satisfaction to its trickle in the leaves. Finished. I waved at the garage, a goodnight and blessing to Babs. Then I picked my way around toward Gramma's front door, wide footed, my right hand in pants pocket, to assure myself of the doorkey. Twice my shoes crunched upon the first summer fall of beechbark.

Awake. Head aching. Tongue dry and swollen from breathing through open mouth. Too early to rise. Low sun through pinpricks in the windowshades. The blinds as Gramma calls them. The windowblinds.

Barking. Rise to piss. Relief. Flush. Look at the face in the mirror. Older than I was accustomed to, but something in it still of the baby after sleep. Happy Anniversary. Happy Third Century.

Must call Lolly. Then Duff, too. That would be the devil, sifting out Jimmy Duffie's foray into manhood. Bright fellow as dumb bastard. Anyway, Babs was mine. She hadn't told Duffie that, I was sure. But she'd shown him, with a fast knee to the gonads. Serves him right.

What was it I said to Buddy last night? What had Buddy said to me? What had Kidder said to Buddy? Sit down, sort it out. Get moving on the day. The dog was barking.

Rowan looked up at me from the desk in the shaded room. Who are you, the picture asked of me. Who are *you*, I asked of the picture. Enough. I turned the picture over on its face. My head throbbed. Madison was barking.

I went to the windowblind that faced east, tugged at the crocheted ring at the end of its cord, let it rise slowly. I narrowed my eyes against the low light. A cloudy morning, with shafts of sun.

Barking? I opened my eyes wider. I reached for the curved brass handles on the slightly open window, put a forefinger under each, and pressed upward until the window was wide open. The sound was not far away. Probably not as far as Bekka's house. Closer than that. I looked for the dog but couldn't see him.

I dressed swiftly, casually. Khaki pants, blue buttondown shirt, tennis shoes. I drank two glasses of water. I moved out and down the back stairs, hand on the bentwood pole railing to guide my rocking brain. Cook not up yet. Nothing to eat yet. I would find Madison. What was eating that dog?

Luther told it many times afterward, head shaking as if he doubted what he said. But the words settled after a while, and came out near the same every time.

"I din't know what it was when I first heard it. There was the dog barking. I knew the dog's bark and I din't know what it was I heard. Nothing like it since I left West Virginia. Not even in West Virginia maybe. It was painful-like. It minded me of a dog I once saw, leg broke in a wolf-trap. But it was angry-like, too, minded me of a wolf going hungry. But it started sobbing sort-of, too, like no dog or wolf. So I got up to go see.

"I'll never forgit them sounds. And then the dog starting in again, too, so I knew there was two of them. I come out the garage door and heard it around the corner at the laundry pit. There was the dog, he couldn't git down there. He had his paws on the wall looking down and barking and whimpering.

"And down there was him and her, him holding her and howling with his head against her chest, and her in her white party dress and her jewel pin Mr. Clellan gave her. And she was just hangin' there from the fire escape with her head rolled back and the rope around her neck. Funny thing, the sun come out full for a minute, and where I stood I could see the diamonds on her cammy-o."

V.

Carnegie's Bastards

1961

twenty.

RIGHT AFTER it happened, I couldn't think, except that it was my fault, a lot of it anyway, and I had to cope. Coping was the only way to control the guilt. Where was she to be buried, for instance?

Suicide is a sin, right? Buddy asked a priest about it, someone he called "Wanda's priest," who had married them and had baptized their daughter, Barbara. Buddy reported the answer with a shamed face, taking care to get the words straight: "No suicide may be buried in sacred ground." He didn't like it at all. Neither did we, the McCallas. Suddenly I heard in my kin and felt in my own blood the thrill of the Wars of the Reformation. "Why the idea!" Gramma said, and she raised her eyebrows so high the lower lids showed pink. Bekka said it was cruel. Martha said it was "heartless doctrine." She turned to her son who said of course it was heartless doctrine, but what could you expect of a Polish peasant? Crispin admired the art of the Church of Rome and the manners of the Church of England, but had little use for the rest of the Holy Catholic Church. He suggested we ask Lolly's help. She found us an obliging young canonical lawyer—Irish, as it happened. He looked at the problem differently and said yes instead of no.

By that time we had decided to hell with them. She would be buried on McCalla land instead of in the Catholic cemetery. Not, of course, in the compound, even had the laws allowed. What didn't belong to Dinerstein, he had conveyed to Congregation Magen David. And not in the mausoleum Rowan had built for his parents; where tiered marble compartments stored our dead from floor to ceiling. No, that was for bloodline McCallas, and McCallas by marriage bond. For Babs we chose a place on the plot of grass around our family tomb. Next to the mausoleum of a famous music-hall singer of the turn of the century, whose industrialist lover and whose lover's socialite wife are interred one residence further beyond. A vivacious alley, ours, in the city of the dead.

Denying Babs' body to the Roman Catholic Church satisfied us Presbyterians. Lolly was a good sport about it. Her fine ironic eyebrows enjoyed the vehemence of our claim to Babs, which contained little logic, less theology, much battle fever for the spiritual sovereignty of the individual believer, or unbeliever. We were politicians of the spirit, true heritors of John Knox. We won, and none cared but we.

She died on a cloudy day; was buried on a sunny one. Bekka and Martha attended, which pleased me. Gramma was not moved to be there, but sent flowers. Crispin had already left for Italy. Adelaide excused herself. Wedding preparations, she said. In her name and Kidder's she sent an enormous floral spray and a waterfall of tiny ferns that tumbled the length of the casket; delicate little green things whose name I never learned. I wanted to climb on the box face down and rest my head in them.

Duffie cried more than anyone. He had forgotten to bring a handkerchief. He kept putting his index finger on the bridge of his nose, running it under the rim of his glasses and along the cheekbone to wipe away the tears. First one hand, then the other. He sniffled a lot. He felt terrible about what he believed was his role in her end.

Lolly wore the dress I'd first seen photographed in *Town and Country*. She was the least formally attired of the women, and the least somberly of us all. I knew she had chosen her dress with care, and with tenderness for Babs' spirit, and I was glad.

I wish I could say that a lot of others attended, but it wasn't so. Three or four, I supposed, were regulars from the Cork and Bottle. They looked hungover or naturally

260

squint-eyed; handsome and dilapidated. Several were Buddy's friends from the carnival, Navy, and various pantries. I recognized them from his fiftieth birthday party.

Costelloe came, God bless him. He wore what looked like a nineteenth-century frock coat and kept it buttoned, though it was a warm June day, to hide his tennis clothes. Probably he'd postponed a lesson to be there and had another to get back to. He was wearing cream-colored linen trousers and brown and white saddle shoes with pink rubber soles. But when did he not?

No high school chums arrived, or dear old friends from grade school days. We were those, Lolly, Duff, and I; and we saw our lives more stark and short than we ever had before.

McCracken's most junior assistant conducted the service. A moment before he began, two women in black raincoats appeared at the edge of the grave. One, dumpy and officious, held the other firmly by the elbow. Then she, the warder, took a step backward, looked at her wristwatch, and gazed around the cemetery with the all-seeing indifference of a tourist. The one by the graveside stood still, looking at the coffin. The sun was behind her head. She did not move or change expression. A black babushka tied in all but one lock of hair at her temple, dark brown touched with gray. Her face was gaunt, heavy-lidded as a Byzantine madonna. Her immobility and the sunlight behind her made her seem to be a carving: a somber beauty of slivered almond and smoky walnut, dark rings beneath her eyes, cheekbones struck by bare-knuckled Time.

Wanda.

Buddy moved to her side. With no attempt to speak to her or touch her, he stood at attention with the mother of their dead child. The nurse looked at him with contempt; then turned her back on both and watched a cortege of Cadillacs slide by toward a ceremony on lower ground.

In the middle of the service arrived a boy and girl who turned out to be from the astronomy course. How they heard at night school about Babs' death I don't know, but they appeared in earnest and chose to think of me as next

261

of kin. They lingered afterward to talk of Cepheus and Cassiopeia.

The image of her hanging there haunted my days. I never dreamed about it. But a mint julep, or chives in a cup of vichyssoise, and suddenly I remembered; and trembled.

"Cut her down!" I yelled at Luther.

She was wearing the Gibson girl dress with long sleeves she'd gotten out of a family trunk for Buddy's birthday party. Under it, white leotards. The only skin showing was her hands, her face, her neck.

I had jumped in over the wall and there was no way out. The cellar door was locked from the inside. When Luther appeared at the wall I screamed at him, "Cut her down! Get a knife! Cut the rope!"

Her toes dangled a foot from the floor of the laundry pit. I took her in my arms and held her up, to ease the pull of the terrible knot on her neck. Her head sagged on my shoulder. I felt her shaking helplessly. I realized it was me sobbing. I heard Madison barking.

Luther appeared on the fire escape with a knife. I screamed at him again. He sawed away at the rope on the railing.

The rope dropped and her head fell back. I saw eyes of stone.

Luther unlocked the cellar door from inside and appeared there, head shaking as if watching tennis volleys at net. I yelled obscenities at him, regretting my unfairness. "Get Dr. Hunnewell!"

When he went I laid her down and tried to get the rope loose from her neck. To let her breathe. To let the blood flow again.

I tore my fingernails. The cord was so tight around her neck I couldn't get under it. Her flesh was cold. Her neck was dark.

Luther returned, Madison with him. He said the doctor was coming. And a police car from the precinct. I think I thanked him. I asked him to wait for them at the tiger gate and show them down.

262

She lay there stiff as a doll.

Another woman looked at me. At the breastbone, upon the white dress, was pinned Clellan's cameo. Stonesharp woman with shellwhite features, high-piled, wind-tossed, time-arrested hair. She appeared to have turned from profile to three-quarters view, to gaze at me with eyes of diamond. One at her throat, one for her ear, one in the hair at her forehead, two forever hypnotic eyes. Five diamonds: a constellation.

Madison came over to the body and sniffed its crotch and armpits. Then he licked her face for a long time, slowly and definitely.

I went to a corner of the laundry yard and put my forehead against the angle and rested my palms on the rough concrete of the two converging walls. I heard car doors, then voices. When they came down, and started talking and asking things, my voice answered them. A policeman took notes. Hunnewell slipped a scalpel under the rope, sawed it through, and pulled it away. Her neck beneath was bluebrown, the same shade as the background of the cameo. From the nicks of his scalpel started up little drops of blood. They welled up purple and coagulated, round as beads.

We walked away, talking and shaking our heads. Hunnewell offered to call the mortician. I thanked him and the policeman. I thanked Luther again.

I went back to Gramma's house and headed for the dining room. Mother was there having breakfast. She asked what all the cars and fuss were about. I told her.

My left ankle hurt from jumping into the laundry pit. I went to see Hunnewell the next day and learned I'd cracked a bone.

Her "effects." That's what my mother called them. I tried to keep Adelaide out of the picture, but she insisted on being helpful, gathering Babs' clothes and belongings for Buddy and making the room neat for his coming. The job was simple. All of her clothes, including those for ballet and carnival, and everything else she owned could have fit in her one huge leather suitcase, a handsome old one with a strap

263

around it. My mother sniffed a little and said it had probably come from Clellan and really belonged to the family. A good thing she let the point rest there, or we would have fought. She put the suitcase at the foot of the bed and lined up everything in neat piles beside it.

Did she really expect Buddy to arrive prepared to choose? To make decisions about those piles?

He came in, dazed, respectful. He looked at his daughter's clothes and turned away and wept. He rubbed under his eyes with his knuckles and apologized. I beamed a silent thought at my mother, savagely and repeatedly. It would have been kinder to fill the suitcase and give it to him closed.

There were two issues of *Playboy* and an astronomy textbook on the bed. Buddy fingered the magazines and left them. He picked up the book and put it in a brown shopping bag he'd brought. He selected a picture of her as a teenager on a tightrope, and a picture of her as a little girl doing a handstand on his own hands overhead, palms back and flat. "That's all," he said. "I guess I don't need the clothes or any other stuff."

"The Junior League, then?" my mother asked. "May we give the clothes and costume jewelry to the Thrift Shop?"

"Sure, that's fine, Mrs. McCalla."

"Very well. Now there are these two particular items of jewelry." She used the last word with a little arc in her tone.

One was in a little white box with a pencilled message on it: "Return to Randy." That was the only writing she had left of any kind.

"Is it all right with you, then, that Randy receive this?" My mother was, as they say, punctilious in such matters.

"Sure." Buddy's eyebrows went up. "Of course. She says so."

"I want to be certain that everything is done with your knowledge," my mother said.

"That's nice of you. Thanks."

I took the box and opened it. Inside lay the string necklace with the silver three-cent piece, dated 1854, Rowan's year of birth. They both looked at me for comment. I did not trust myself to speak.

"So," Mother said, resuming official momentum, "that leaves the cameo. The undertaker returned it. Lucky that someone, the police or a mortician's underling, hadn't made off with it already."

It lay on the bed, starry eyes blinking, with auxiliary glitter at throat, in the ear, in her hair. Gorgon of the iron age, Medusa of the coal mines.

"Well, Mr. Clellan give that to Babs," Buddy said. "I already said it was too much for her when he only promised it. She was just twelve when he finally gave it. Still I always said it was too much. Maybe we should give it back now to your family." His eye continued to rest on it.

"It's worth a certain amount of money," Mother said. "You should have it."

"I'll sell it for you," I said. "I bet I can get two thousand for it. I mean, if that's what you'd like me to do."

"That's OK with me," Buddy said, and his eye left the display on the bed, and he looked in his bag, as if he wanted to go.

My mother flung me a sharply curious stare, but I avoided most of it.

"You should have the suitcase to carry things in," my mother said. She took Buddy's paper bag from him and opened the suitcase, set the pictures and the textbook in different internal flaps, filled the major space with tissue paper, snapped and buckled it up, and handed it back to him.

There, her smile said, that's that. Buddy thanked us and left carrying the handle of the giant suitcase with two fingers of his left hand.

Adelaide walked briskly home, a step ahead of me, field marshal and queen of domestic dispatch.

She was commander indeed, in all but two details.

The mortician had called our house, unable to reach Buddy anywhere, to ask what the family of the departed wished her to be dressed in. Mother was out, so I took the call. I was brief. "Let her rest with what she wore when she died." There was a disappointed, even disapproving, silence on the other end of the line. I spoke an order into that void: "Bury her in what she's got on."

So it was done. Somehow it did not occur to Buddy or Mother to ask about it.

To the other matter I gave more thought. Roberts Jewelers appraised the cameo for me at five hundred, belittling the size of the diamonds while acknowledging the craftsmanship of the stone carving. I didn't sell it. I had saved two thousand dollars for a new car. I wrote a check to Buddy for that amount. I told Mother and I told him that I had sold the antique cameo for that price. Everybody appeared pleased.

No loss to me. We dined one Saturday at Aunt Bekka's just before the garage came down. Nobody knew I'd been saving for a new car, so I raised the subject of Clellan's old one, drawing on all the presumptive rights of one who had been using it off and on for five years. I declared a sentimental as well as a practical interest in it. That touched the ladies at table—Bekka, Martha, and Adelaide—and they enjoyed determining in my hearing why I should have it. Because, they decided, I had made the Yale *Law Review*, and deserved recognition for my hard work. "Early to bed and early to rise, makes a man healthy, wealthy, and wise." Quoting Ben Franklin at me as they had in my boyhood, they smiled with the kindliness of careful benefactors.

That's how I came to spend my last two years in New Haven driving what Duffie called my "Pierce Fucking-Arrow." Because of the car and its aged elegance, I acquired something of a reputation as a blade and a dandy. That partially offset the fearful seriousness with which I was working, and my own view of myself as a turkey, a grind.

The cameo? I held on to it, debating with myself what to do with it. Of all the options, my inner mind knew from the start which I would choose.

When the wrecking balls had levelled all the houses but Gramma's, I asked about the schedule for the remainder of the work. The foreman, as it happened, was Ned Ruark—surly still, as he had been in Sunday school. I had time to go to Hyannisport, see my mother wedded, and return. Gramma's house was down when I got back. Cook had gone

266

to Panther Hollow Apartments, Luther and Elise to a rental house within call. Only the garage remained—the simplest demolition for last.

I camped there overnight in Luther's apartment, wrapped in a fringed flannel lap robe, one of the accoutrements of Clellan's car. I stretched it out on the floor, wishing Madison were with me. For a pillow, I opened an abandoned telephone book at "K." The plumbing was all gone. I pissed out the window and retired. Though the night was warm, I slept well.

I rose and drove to Sodini's Delicatessen; breakfasted there; and shaved in the men's room. In the mirror I saw the Pittsburgh names I had absorbed overnight; printer's ink on flesh. Tribes of every kind, the luckless and the fortunate, souls lost and found, in alphabetical order smeared on my cheeks and temples, smudged upon my brow. I shaved and laved them away, feeling at one with them all.

When I got back to the garage, the wrecking had begun. The walls were partway down. I parked outside the tiger gate, sat on the hood of my car, watching beechbark peel off the trees, tangle itself in telephone wires, tumble to the shaded summer street. I rose and prowled the levelled compound, its dirt-filled foundations, its weedy lots, its memories for me. I reviewed my life and Babs', and what I knew of the generations that preceded us.

When the bulldozer got in position for levelling, I readied myself. I faced the machine. It took a rhinoceros rush at a pile of bricks and shattered boards, and rammed the rubble down into the cement grave that had been the laundry yard. I watched it charge two, three, four times. Then I reached into my pocket, grasped the dark talisman. Withdrew it.

Standing on the west side of the pit as the bulldozer charged from the east, I went slowly into a windup, in the most complex throwing motion known to man. I kicked high with my left foot, reached back deep with my extended right arm, cast my left arm before me, rocked my weight toward my left foot and, as it planted, brought my right arm, elbow, wrist, and hand with its fastball grip up and over my shoulder. Down and across my body, all my weight behind the flow, I snapped through with elbow, wrist, and hand. Fingers let fly the cameo. It whined through the clear morning air and hit the giant blade just after the machine dumped a wave of debris; struck the steel square center, shattered, flew, fell into the laundry pit with the dusty clutter.

The driver stopped and looked at me strangely. Ned himself. I smiled and gave him the finger. He replied in kind without the smile, then backed and resumed his bulling and dumping. I watched several more loads go in on top, burying the palmful of wrought gold, carved stone, and diamonds. Then I slid into my Pierce-Arrow, bags and books in the back, and got it moving down the street. I still heard in my mind's ear the crack and clang of my pitch against its target, and I shivered with a terrible relief.

My legal address and domicile were now in New Haven, Connecticut.

twenty-one.

NOT ALL was clear at once, nor would all be ever clear. My habit, in any case, had become to ask. Everyone survived, except Babs. There were people to learn from, about her; about the problems she inherited, bore, and raised; and about me.

Madison disappeared. He couldn't have told me much, but I would have liked him on the front seat in the Pierce-Arrow, reading road maps, so to speak. Have conversations with him across the Pennsylvania Turnpike, eastward through its tunnels and hours of bordering farmlands. But we couldn't find him.

In the confusion after Babs died, each of us assumed somebody else was feeding him. Then the dog simply wasn't there anymore. Luther and I searched and called. No sign. I beat my way through the high grass in the empty lot, fearing to stumble upon him in a clump of wilderness chosen to rest his ancient bones. He was fourteen years old; ninety-eight dog years by the formula I'd learned as a child. Ready to lay down his head in the great sleep? I imagined burying him in the family plot, not far from Babs, and began to fashion defenses against accusations of breach of taste, or breach of law. But we never found him. Irish setters are cunning fellows, Martha always said. We let ourselves think that canny old Madison had read the signs of the end of an era, and had chosen, like the McCalla elders, to make a new life for himself. Somewhere.

So on the turnpike I was left with my thoughts, and they were not easy. I kept seeing my fingers tugging at the rope.

269

Then Dr. Hunnewell slashing at it with his scalpel, shaking his head at the enormous torsion upon her throat. Looking up he said, "She must have jumped headfirst."

I could not avoid imagining the whole thing. I sweated as she calculated the length of rope, like the acrobat she was. I swallowed as she slipped it on. Then I saw her seated lightly on the railing edge, stockinged toes poised on the outermost bar of the fire escape landing. Her hand touches the cameo at her breastbone. Her fingers adjust her thick hempen necklace. She takes a last, deep breath and springs out into the darkness, under the sickle moon, head first, hands out for the mysterious waters below. For a moment I see the white arc of her bridal plunge. I admire her as I always admired her. Then she is gone.

Kidder gave me a lot of attention at the wedding reception. We had already worn ourselves out talking about squash—how this winter he was going to thrash me, how I was going to trounce him, et cetera. He approached me man-to-man off the court as well as on. From his trombone throat came out surprisingly delicate sounds, with breathy little interrogative blasts: "Well, I was sorry about your friend Babs Quick, eh? Life got too much for her, uh? Too bad. She went out sometimes with a couple of friends of ours from out of town. Gave 'em a good time, yeah. No sign of depression or anything, huh? No, of course not. You never know, do you, hah?" And he gave me a hearty consoling grin as if to conclude: with all the misery around us, it's required of us naturally optimistic ones to keep things upbeat.

He was wrong about a lot of things and always would be, but I couldn't hate him for the words he'd just spoken. I had grown weary of detesting him and found it a bit of a relief to smile back faintly, and nod like a man of the world, while I drank his champagne. We had both contributed to Babs' death. Maybe we had both contributed to her life. I toasted Kidder and my mother, and drew compliments from the guests for whatever it was I said.

I saw Duffie up at the Cape, amid the Pittsburgh colony at Hyannisport. For years he had amused me with stories derisive of the Kennedys, but now that one of them was going to run for president, Duffie had grown boring. All he could talk of was Babs and his ineradicable guilt. I listened to his laments about his untimely lust until I could barely stand it. I wanted to break out with the truth about myself and Babs, but I knew that Duff was less capable of listening to me than I was to him. He appeared to need his guilt. He flourished with it, as upon an inverse and compelling proof of his manliness. Why should I take that away from him? I had my manhood from her in another way, and my struggle was to feel no unreal guilt, no defeating weakness.

A terrible fear of intimacy came over me, nonetheless, and I couldn't dispel it. I heard a voice telling me, "Never again, never again." I did not understand the voice, but I strove against it. The struggle produced a quivering at the back of my skull, a trembling of the lower cerebellum, as if its folds were crawling with tension. I thought that passersby would see my palsy, but the pedestrian world marched on. The tremors, invisible, were inside my head.

I realized that I had not written Babs, and had not gone to see her, because I was afraid of her. I was afraid, wasn't I, that she would run her bicycle over my foot? I had feared, hadn't I, that her knife would miss the magic envelope around me and nip instead my feeling flesh? My recognized fear played back into my guilt and my loss. The three chased and accelerated each other in the cycle house of the mind until I was pedalling topspeed, sideways on the bank of sanity, to keep from falling.

One long conversation with Crispin and Lolly helped, just before returning to law school.

"Oh, the cheap thrill of death," Crispin said.

I was enraged at him for the remark, but gratified, too, for some other way to think about Babs. "She had no business doing that," he continued. "She was young and far from consumed. If she was disappointed, who isn't? If she

271

had made errors, done wrongs, there was still plenty of time to do right. If she had sinned, there was time to repent, and the source of grace is inexhaustible."

I had never heard Crispin so close to Lolly in his language. He could quote Pascal and Santayana, but usually did so to support his coolest skepticism. This was another Crispin—orthodox, aroused by facing suicide to a crypto-Catholic blush; new and astonishing to me, like the uncle who had wept at my father's death.

"Why do herself in?" he persisted. "Complete despair, I suppose, and a certain horrid vengefulness upon herself and the world. I am sympathetic to the despair. But I reject the element of vindictive retort, whatever it is all about. Too cruel to the family, her way of dying."

"Are you saying she was trying to punish us?" I asked.

I felt in part she was, and I wanted it confirmed as a way of getting some leverage for my own resentment.

"In a way." Crispin, getting his agitation under control, did not want to pursue that angle. "But, you know," he said, his eyes sliding toward the ceiling, "she was perhaps the last real Presbyterian among us. And the fiercest. Because she saw no trace about herself of visible election, and felt no sign of the visitation of grace, she considered herself condemned. So to fit in with divine purpose, she did away with herself entirely. Feeling predestined to damnation, she throws herself right into the cosmic maw." He sniffed with appreciation at the fit of his own insight. "Her church wouldn't take her for burial, and she knew it. But our church took her body, having, I fear, much earlier taken her soul."

"But surely that's fanciful," Lolly protested. "I found a priest willing to bury her. And none of us knows our own fate, far less that of others, on the Day of Judgment."

"Of course you're right," he answered with a slight, weary smile. "I don't believe in Calvin's elect or Knox's damned. I don't even think Randall does, and he's the only one of us who has studied the matter."

At this I merely nodded.

Crispin went on. "I am simply saying that we may need ideas with which we can hold this tragedy at bay. I am offering the notion that Barbara Quick is the victim of bad Protestant theology from the sixteenth century and impossible social teleology from the twentieth."

I could not help but think of Crispin's own savage skepticism and his upward Anglophile escapism, as he continued: "She was caught between an overly cruel notion of the divine and an excessively optimistic view of American opportunity. She got both from us McCallas: the merciless God and the impossible ambitions.

"Both, mind you, are misunderstandings. We are partly responsible for them, but not fully. And whatever we are responsible for, we did not kill her. She killed herself."

He and Lolly both looked to me as if for corroboration. I was closer to her than they; how close they did not know. I had spoken little. Now I could hardly breathe, let alone speak. But something was owed them in reply, and something to Babs in obsequy.

"She grew chives on her windowsill," I said. "And she liked to chew mint. She picked sprigs of it from the mint patch and sucked them like candy." I knew my eyes were stark with tears and my voice was fearfully soft. I felt myself trapped in the hush of the others, as I visualized the only other thing I knew how to say. "I wish," I began, aware of the vanity of the thought to come, and its inane weakness after Crispin's discourse. But I said it anyway: "I wish she were still alive."

If I really loved Babs I would just let her go. Yet keep certain memories triumphant. That's one argument.

The opposite is: really loving Babs means reassembling her in my mind, to keep her always, as close to the truth of her as I can get. That's the way I'm taking.

Was she really Clellan's daughter, as she claimed? She certainly wasn't Cassie's daughter, as in her deepening trouble she had suggested. But the possibility that Clellan sired her was there.

I could not recall a time *before* Buddy had been butler to Clellan and Bekka. Several years preceding Wanda's madness, had she seduced the master of the house, or he her?

273

Did this account for the estrangement of Buddy and Wanda, and her later alienation from herself? Or, even less palatable but still possible—had Buddy, as procurer for Clellan, actively served up or passively made available his own wife, for whatever sorry reason?

Last summer, the summer of 1960, I caught Buddy for a couple of drinks and ventured into the borders of the question with him. I talked about becoming one of the editors of the law review, and he seemed proud of me. He joked about his arthritis, and said it only affected his bones, thank God. The best parts were not made of bone anyway.

"Is that the way my Uncle Clellan felt, too?" I asked, grinning what I supposed was a salacious grin. Bud's eyebrows danced. He said yes, indeed, it sure was.

"But Crispin says Clellan was a saint. He was devoted to his mother."

"Well, about saints I don't know. But if somebody is only devoted to his mother, where's he gonna get a piece of ass?"

"I see your point."

"Now, there's nothing wrong with that, right? Minding your mother real nice, and heading over to the cathouse on Saturday night?" Buddy liked this conversation.

"No, I suppose not."

He sang in a small voice his favorite song:

> *Don't throw stones at your mother;*
> *Remember how she tucked you in bed;*
> *Don't throw stones at your mother;*
> *Throw rocks at your father instead.*

I joined in on the last line. Then I asked him, "Did you ever go along? On Saturday night?"

"Did I *go along*? A nice boy like me? Hee, hee! I *introduced* him. And your Uncle Clellan he made friends easily. Everybody liked him. He was generous with the ladies. He gave them presents, jewels and all. He was what you might call a prime customer."

"It sounds like fun. What did Wanda think of all this?"

"Oh? Wanda? She didn't like it too much."

"Did she ever make you stop, or did she get involved in some way?"

He seemed to draw a blank on the question. "I dunno." He thought a bit. "Say, would you like me to getcha date?"

"No, no, that's not why I was asking."

"That's OK. Because I can, you know. Just say the word, and I can getcha date. Real nice one."

"No, thanks, really, Buddy. That's not what I meant."

"Because I've been a little worried about you, ya know? I know you and Babs were a little sweet on each other. Maybe not everybody could see that, but I could see it. And I worried you took it pretty hard. You still look kind of pale. A good date will fix you up. Take it from me."

"Sure. Maybe it would," I said. "Sometime maybe."

I had a mental image of Buddy when I first saw him, balancing a table knife on his chin in Clellan's dining room, halfway behind the screen to the pantry. Then I saw the girl Babs, her sprig of mint poking between the screen's partitions.

"You're right, I miss her badly. And you're nice to want to cheer me up. But you must miss her terribly, your own daughter."

"Yeah. I get sad sometimes. But it's fate, you know? You gotta be philosophical, like you say. I remember, she was only maybe fourteen, fifteen, and she went up to Salim the Sword Swallower. Teach me how to swallow your sword, she says. *Just like that!* I told her to stay away from Salim. But she didn't pay me no mind. She got real mixed up with him. She got real mixed up, period. And I couldn't do nothing about it; you neither, nobody."

I nodded, and we drank, and finally I said I had to go. He looked sorry, but he smiled a big smile as if there were a new understanding between us, and he said twice more just to let him know when I wanted a date. He'd fix me up. Real good.

I had a hard time finding Black Rachel. But it was worth the search, reaching her in a tiny flat on a side street where the trolley used to take me to the orthodontist. She wasn't doing laundry anymore. After McCalla laundry, she said, she didn't like strangers' laundry. So she'd gone back into the massage business. I teased her. Strangers' laundry she didn't like, but strangers' bodies she did?

"Sure. They innerrest me. They all different, each one. A good day I work on five–six people. Now what you come to talk about?"

I had forgotten how direct she was. Best to meet her straight on. "I wanted to talk about my family and the people who worked for them. The compound is gone now, and some of the family are dead, and even Babs. But I think it's good to remember people, and places, and the things people did."

"Yes, it's good. Yes it is. What you want to remember?"

"I want to remember everything you can remember. Why not start with when you came to the McCallas?"

So she did, slowly at first. She described herself as half Indian, half Negro, which explained both her straight nose and her black skin. A dancer as a girl; but not much money in that, and they said she was just too big. So she just stayed on with the troupe and helped. She massaged the dancers. Artist's hands, they said. When the troupe disbanded, she earned a living with honest massage.

There were a couple of men in her life, and she married the worst. He brought her to Pittsburgh, and she bore a daughter and raised her and threw him out. Pittsburgh was afraid of massage then, except a few folks. Less afraid now, but still some. Anyway, she took in laundry. Then she did one McCalla house. Then she did them all, nothing but McCalla laundry. Monday, Tuesday, Big House; Wednesday and half of Thursday, Aunt Bekka's; half of Thursday and Friday, Gramma's. By hand, all of it. Reason she stayed, they loved her work. Never done so fine before. So she knew all our cellars and all our laundry yards and some more. Yes, a little bit more.

"More?"

"Yes, the folks. Can't do the laundry without getting to know the folks."

"What did you think of my Uncle Clellan?"

She liked plain questions. "He was the nicest one. He didn't ack like an *employer*. He showed his respeck for me. He complimented me nice about the collars I did, and not too much starch. And the kerchiefs I wore to work round my head."

"Did he like Wanda, too?"

"Wanda? I don't know. I guess so. She was a pretty one. But she didn't like herself too much, so it was hard for others, you know?"

"Did he like Babs?"

"Sure he did, you *know*. She was a apple in his eye. that little one."

"Really?"

"Sure, she come along with Buddy and Wanda and brighten up that place."

"Came along *with* them?"

"Sure, she was three or four maybe when they came. Bright as a button. Make *him* bright, Mister Clellan. Had no children of his own, you realize. *You* realize, of course!" She looked at me and laughed at herself. "No children his own, and this little one she shine up the house, she did. He let her set in his lap in the living room, while he drink whiskey from his big glass." She laughed.

"He had the shakes, you know? God's mercy, he had the shakes, otherwise he would of drunk himself to death. He shake so he spill half a drink, every time." Laughed. "That little girl, that Babs, I saw her once, she sitting in his lap, holding his glass for him in her two little hands. God's mercy!"

I laughed, too. The McCallas wore stiff collars and high-button shoes. We needed other people to starch our collars, shine our shoes, put bibs on us when we ate.

I asked her, "Why did Buddy and Babs move over to the garage?"

She answered more deliberately. "That was after Wanda went looey. After she threw the cleaver at Buddy. They put her away. Your Aunt Bekka never like Buddy all that much, and she never like Babs all that much either. But your Uncle Clellan wouldn't have anybody else butler. So they compromise, him and her. Buddy and Babs moves to the garage, and he stays butler, and your aunt gets a new maid to live in."

"So that's the story." I drew a breath. "Babs once told me that Buddy and you were lovers."

"Hah!" She laughed. "Sure enough! He had his eye on me a *long* time. He had a rover-eye, and everybody could see it. It got Wanda jealous. It help make Wanda throw the cleaver, that wander-eye of his. But they wasn't anything going on then, not between us they wasn't."

"No?"

"Only later. *Later,*" she emphasized. "You remember when Buddy left the place? He got fired, that's what he did. Why, you want to know? And that little girl, Babs, Luther's wife, Elise, had to bring her up, which neither one didn't like. Lasted years, that way. Garage was an orphan asylum. But it's not a bad place to be a orphan, like a park with three big houses in it.

"I near got fired, too, when they found out. I guess your Aunt Bekka said that was *enough* of Buddy and me, too. But your Aunt Martha said there was no laundress like me. So I stayed. That's why. 'Cause of my laundry. Oh, he was fun, that Buddy. Even though he had a rover-eye."

I wanted the story to go on.

"He join the war, even though it was near over. He join the second war, pretend he was young, same way he join the first war, pretend he was old. They made him a coach, what you call it? Yeah, physical education man, in the army. So we won the war and he came out, and he come *back,* too, after a couple years. They hire him again, as long as, he tell me, no monkeyshines with Black Rachel, ooh-eee!" She breathed out and laughed.

"You know everything about the compound, Rachel, seems like."

"I know a little and a lot maybe. But only God knows everything. And He ain't tellin'."

"I wish I knew what made Babs kill herself."

"Oh she done herself in, poor girl. She pull the temple down on herself, poor thing. Sometimes I think she got that cleaver in her head."

"The cleaver? That Wanda threw at Buddy?"

"Like it hit the little girl, instead of the pantry door. She was standing in the kitchen, quiet, while we try hush her mommy. Then she goes to get her daddy. He come running, and Wanda see him and throw the cleaver. Right over his shoulder it go and hit the door and the little girl was right behind him."

"So it might have hit her, too?"

"Wanda see she could of kill her own baby and she run to hug her. But Babs, she shrieking now, hide under the kitchen table and Buddy does an armtwist on Wanda. They take her away and lock her up, poor looey thing."

"God knows what that did to Babs."

"Hm?"

"I mean, who can say what that did to Babs? She was a little girl, just growing up."

"God knows, honey."

"Well, if God knows, why didn't He do something about it? Why does He have to let Babs throw herself into the laundry yard with a rope around her neck?"

She looked at me easily and mildly. "God ain't our kind of folks, honey."

I thought about that.

"Oooh-eee!" she said. "Now you had your bedtime story. How you like a backrub from Black Rachel?"

I hesitated. She grinned and said, "Bodies is different kind of laundry, rub-a-dub-dub." So I said yes.

I disrobed behind a screen while she put a mat and sheets on a table; the same table, I realized, that she had eaten off of, just before I came.

"You can take them underpants off," she said when I came out. "I'll hide my eyes. For good massage you just want a towel on you. On your back first." I felt that I blushed deeply, and I lay down on the table with hot ears. But she didn't notice, or was used to embarrassment and McCallas. She just went to work telling me this was petissage, and this was fleurissage, and these were Swedish strokes with the edge of her palm, and so forth. She knew what she was doing, and I knew it and trusted her. I relaxed.

She said she cupped the oil in her palm and slid it on,

always keeping at least one hand on the person, whatever else. "It connects, you see? That is what massage is all about. You got to connect the person up. They is all disconnected with running around and making a buck, and making a big success, and making theirself beautiful, and you're supposed put them together again. Do that, you got to *stay connected* to them."

When I lay on my belly, she turned down the towel and worked on my bare buttocks in a way that opened my eyes. Then she worked on my back, to the nape of my neck, and my scalp, and I closed my eyes. She controlled the whole switchboard of my spine.

When she finished she said, "Sleepy?" I grunted. "Uh-huh. Really good, Rachel. Really sleepy."

"You sleep some, then." She draped the towel lengthwise on me and sat down in a rocker nearby.

Feeling the oil settle in my skin, I imagined the whorls of her big white thumbtips, sweet pools encircling me, drawing me down. Drifting, listening to her light monologue and the chair creaking in the darkness, I asked her. "Where did you and Buddy make love?"

She chuckled softly. "All over," she said. "Everyplace. But mostly in your great-granny's bedroom. When Marie and her was out for the day. I had to change the sheets, sure enough. But Buddy said he like it dangerous. So we did it in your Big Rachel's bed."

After a silence she added, "One time Babs come in. We quit for a while. Then we went back at it. Another time, Elise come in. That's what got him fired."

I murmured and Black Rachel chuckled and I began coasting on a long slide toward sleep. I imagined Kid Ory's trombone playing, soft as a lullaby, "Down Among the Sheltering Palms."

twenty-two.

Now I know something of McCalla compound and me, of our improbable history, light and shadow of my destiny. The wash is in the sun. I know enough to go on.

None too soon, my boy. I can see Crispin's smile.

(Right again, my avuncular cousin, dear pundit and psychopomp.)

At the same time I can see Bab's gleam of appreciative disdain. Late as usual, she says.

(Yes, my darling. Too late for you. Forgive me. But thank you, my mint, my chive, my apricot; my danger-loving walker of wires. My lover and my danger. Thank you for your gift to me: the hope of escaping from history in love.)

The time came when I tried my findings on Crispin. Sprang it on him, I almost said. But I wasn't trying to trap anybody, just ensnare the truth. Given the wintry rectitude of our widowed presbyters and a formidable loyalty to their version of the past, Crispin was the only one I imagined caring to understand the question of Rowan, A. C., Clellan, and their relationship to Cassie Chadwick.

I made a date with him for dinner and told him the story with no arbitrary screenings out, no rootless speculation—just what the court records and newspapers said. He listened with fascination, laughing, face twitching, puffing, and pursing. He was a wonderful audience, and my love for him grew with the respect he showed for my inquiry. He treated it not as the obsessive detour from life that I myself feared it was, but as a scholarly puzzle addressed in a craftsmanlike way.

281

He allowed himself a few personal outbursts. "Two hundred twenty-five thousand dollars, did you say? As a confessed minimum? Quite a lot out of my inheritance! Grandfather, I am displeased! Equal to a million today, wouldn't you say? Think of what we might be enjoying, each with our share of that. And well invested, of course, it would be massively more. Instead the old boys conveyed it to this impostor!" He banged his head against the booth, rubbed it ruefully, and laughed.

I said that it may have been several times as much, if they had actually bought up others' bad debts as reported.

"Oh, worse, worse!" Crispin grinned. "But just lament the minimum! In fact, my lad, family investing has been less than apt since Grandfather died in 1917. We can't spend what we don't have, and we don't have what has been badly used; and we certainly can't avail of what's been frittered away on tarts.

"My old age, Randy!" He slapped his glass down. "A million dollars now becomes what in twenty-five years? Well invested, with present inflation, easily three to five million by 1986. Enough for me to retire on." He gave a wolfish grin. "Half yours, of course.

"You and I are the first to realize how little is actually left, and we're the last to enjoy it. The way our dear ladies dip into capital! They simply don't ask, they spend; then let the trust officers carry out those grand phrases in the wills about the 'style-to-which-she-is-accustomed.' Strictly non-Presbyterian, I should say.

"But," he hunched forward on the table, "I'm in danger of forgetting whom to be incensed with. Not the present McCalla ladies. Is it this genius of a strumpet, or should it be the three gentlemen of our family who doted on her?

"And being incensed is not really the point, right? The money is of less moment to you, if I'm not mistaken, than the truth? Ah, then, the truth! . . ."

I did not, of course, expect Crispin to possess the truth, but to seek it with me. He would add his knowledge and judgment, and we would sort everything together. Which he did most willingly. He reminded me that the scandal had occurred a decade before he was born. He agreed with me that the women, if presented the matter, even obliquely, would be embarrassed at best, and surely disbelieving. Their brothers and husbands probably hadn't told them the facts. Such was Victorian business style, not to mention McCalla habit.

Nevertheless, the matter had broken open in public. Inevitably became the subject of gossip. And must have required some sort of coordinated male stance within the family. Crispin reached back into memory, particularly about the exclusion of the McCalla compound from the privileged zoning code for the homes of Hill and Hollow Road. In his boyhood he had picked up the distinct impression that old Cardigan and other prime movers had agreed to let Rowan McCalla participate in the Association with his compound; then had turned around and cut his acres out. The matter still rankled with McCalla women, because of the affront to their men.

"But what was the cause?" Crispin mused. "Simple geography?—not enough. Few people would have wanted to cross Rowan McCalla during his rise. But what if he were not on the rise? What if he had deeply embarrassed himself and his sons by connection with a fraud? Made them laughing-stocks at best, suspect of venality? Add venery." He laughed. "I am not supposing they did worse than be duped. But those who heard them putting out half a million to get back eight hundred thousand from a convicted forger could imagine anything they wished. When you add that this Cassie was theatrically voluptuous, I shiver for our three dear forebears. I am sure that people did imagine anything they wished. Dear me, how embarrassing!" He giggled.

"I think we can assume that the McCallas were excluded from the Hill and Hollow Association after the scandal broke, and because it broke. And that although geography was given as the excuse, the family sensed the real reason."

Old Cardigan kept us out of Hill and Hollow, I thought, and his grandson once blackballed my father from the Lawn. But Crispin was rolling on.

"I do remember distinctly the tone in which the family

283

considered Carnegie. I was more than a little impressed by their—what shall I call it?—condescension."

My face must have expressed surprise.

"Yes, odd as it sounds. They spoke as if Grandfather had done Carnegie a favor and not had it returned. It's coming back to me now. I remember A. C., your grandfather, talking at Sunday supper. You remember how little he usually spoke, and how terse he was? There was a big discussion, which I wasn't listening to, when he broke in and used a word I hadn't heard before. It silenced the whole table, and I didn't dare ask right then what it meant. But I remember what he said because he used the word twice in one sentence, and loudly for him, and it shut the subject down with the kind of definitive obloquy innate to his style."

I couldn't bear it. I had to play straight man. "What did he say?"

"He said: 'Carnegie was a bastard about his bastard.' "

We went to work on that remembered exclamation as if it were pure gold. One clear sentence was all Crispin's boyhood yielded, but we made it the foundation of a theory of McCalla family behavior.

Whatever the courts had determined, and however close that might have been to objective truth, the McCallas had seen it differently. Cassie Chadwick was Andrew Carnegie's natural child. Rowan McCalla had generously come to her rescue at a prudent rate of interest in order to assist an unfortunate woman. He was moved by admiration and surrogate responsibility for the man after whom he had named his first-born son.

But Carnegie did not behave as the McCallas thought he should have. He cruelly disowned his daughter out of wedlock in order to preserve his reputation and to protect his lawful family. In so doing he allowed others unjustly to prosecute and condemn an innocent woman, at the same time permitting her to fall victim to public hysteria and acrimony. And, not merely incidental: he repudiated his debts. In these matters Carnegie perhaps was not legally obliged. As a man of principle, however, Rowan had incurred debts to save Carnegie's name. The way things turned out, McCalla honor survived. Carnegie's honor vanished.

Whatever the rest of the world might have thought, the McCalla family believed that Rowan had done right for Carnegie, yet had been wronged by him. That he had done right by Cassie, but the woman had been framed. The end result was jail and a lonely death for Mrs. Chadwick, and unjust ridicule for the Messrs. McCalla, not to mention such shunning and whispered malignities as the McCalla women might have suffered at the time.

"Good God," I said, when we had it worked out, "what a beautiful mess!"

"Lovely. Absolutely lovely," chortled Crispin. His taste for irony and connoisseurship of foolishness were wonderfully excited.

"What other family could manage it?" I exclaimed, laughing.

"None! I'll bet a million on it!" said Crispin, roaring at the folly of his blood relations.

"You haven't got the million!" I shouted, and we guffawed and cackled and doubled up, and made such unseemly screams that the waiter came. We ordered another round of drinks and once again went through the high points of McCalla madness, Rowan's reputation, and the dissipated fortune, as if we ourselves had invented sanity and her sweet little sister, humor.

The first year after Babs died I bore down again on the law. A lancelike stab would sometimes hit me in my right ear. I could not follow lines of black letters, but had to rise and follow my feet, or heed my thoughts, until the pain subsided. The doctors at the health center, using lights and tubes and electroencephalograms, could find nothing wrong. They passed me on to a psychiatrist who mixed patience rather nicely with its opposite. He searched for a while in such phenomena of my mind as I deigned to scatter on his table. He found nothing to remark on. "You're fundamentally OK," he said. "Med students are hypochondriacs. Engineers don't know their ass from their elbow, psychically

285

speaking. The arts and sciences bunch are all out of their heads. But law students know which end is up. You strike me as sensible. I don't know what's bothering you. But I suspect that if you give it time, it will go away."

Thus dismissed, I carried on. I knew what was wrong, of course, But I wasn't going to tell him. I longed for Babs. And I didn't want the pain to go away, because it was much of what I had left of her.

I remembered the first night. After dressing she kneeled in the moonlight and tied my shoes. I almost stopped her. But any embarrassment for her or childish feeling in myself gave way in the eye of surprise. She touched a kingly tenderness in me.

Being with her: stealthy, sudden, supernal. Our ways well chosen. We were monarchs of the compound, but we kept times sober, places chaste. There were four buildings, many rooms, and after dark, endless opportunities. But something drew us to a main room for trysting: the Big House, Big Rachel's room.

We understood that each had the right of invitation to the other, and each the right to decline. We wrote each other notes for the only time in our lives, and slipped them under bedroom doors. "Tomorrow? At nine?" was all that needed reply. I keep hers still, the several that those late summer days allowed. Some read simply, "Yes." Even the longer ones are usually cryptic. Two I remember. One was a question: "When do we meet at the ice cream factory?" I wrote back something fanciful about luxurious curds and concupiscent whey, but she didn't get it or didn't much like it. Not every exchange was perfect.

A later one of hers surprised me with its tone. I think she debated for a while about playing on paper, and then decided to try it. "Hey, Muck Allah!" it read. "Put on your mask and come to the mosque. Tonight at nine." I rummaged in Gramma's attic and managed to find an old black mask once worn for Hallowe'ens. When we met, she had one, too. That night? She taught me new kisses, new places.

When time came to go off to law school—it was, after all, my first year—I grew preoccupied. She made no bones about feeling abruptly left and easily forgotten. I talked at rancorous length about fierce competition, need to succeed, et cetera. I suppose my father was on my mind. For me, fear of failure meant fear of any performance less than excellent. When I stopped she said a few things. Deliberate and implacable, she was.

"You have a horny thumb and a smooth palm. Your eyes are starry blue. And you're a fool."

I smiled a little at that recital, perhaps a lightly forced smile, and with the tip of my left index finger I rubbed the calloused joint of my right thumb. The squash player's lever.

"You've got a big ambition and a big education," she said, "and you're going to get more of them both. When you've got somewhere, and you will get somewhere, just remember me. That's all. Just *remember*." It was afternoon. She was chewing gum. I remember the flaring and pursing of her lips while she was listening to me, the tongue tucking the gum away as she spoke. She stopped, flipped the wad again, and said, "Mark my words." The phrase from my grandmother's generation has ever since for me had the flavor of Black Jack Chewing Gum.

That night she marked my body with kisses. Bruises that kept me away from the Lawn Club swimming pool. And I marked hers. She wore a scarf at her neck all of Labor Day weekend.

Then the family came home. I said goodbye one morning soon after. I made a bad job of it, I think. She smoothed things along by cursing the family in fluent even tones. "You guys are so tightass you can't pass shit. You're always nibbling the olive off the pit with your little McCalla teeth. All of you. Nothing comes out of your mouths but mincemeat. Go to Yale, McCalla. Go fuck yourself."

She was wearing my three-cent piece around her neck. As I headed away, she took off the necklace and in casual circles whirled it around her finger by its string. Her mouth was slightly open, and there was amusement in her eyes.

If the baby she destroyed was mine, she was pregnant then, that moment.

Since Babs died and the compound came down, I seldom return to Pittsburgh. I've learned to enjoy Hyannisport with

287

my mother and Kidder, but in my native city I can't get the hang of their marriage, their superficial parentage of me. Of the eldest generation, Martha is the gladdest to see me, and I her. Her extra bedroom is always available. I can stay here without my mother growing jealous. Perhaps she finds herself younger, fancies herself freer, without me around. Fine for both of us.

So here I am, scribbling at Martha's escritoire, waiting for my Peace Corps assignment. Not enough room for my elbow. The antique trembles with my wrist and fingers, and the penmanship shakes.

I have my passport. I showed it to Duffie in Hyannisport and he flipped to the picture. "You look too ill to travel." I cracked with laughter. Old joke from an old friend: why did I cherish it so immoderately? Because I don't know where I'll be sent?

I've asked for Southeast Asia. I saw Kennedy on TV about Laos. I like pictures of the Plain of Jars, and of tribal peoples. They seem far away, ancient, simple, much in need of care. I know that's naive. But I long for something antipodal to Carnegie, Rowan, and Cassie. My family thinks that when I'm done with the Peace Corps, I'll come home to lawyering in Pittsburgh. I'm not sure.

Duffie is critical, says I'm a fool. As a Tocqueville scholar he thinks on a trans-Atlantic axis, North Atlantic only. Why, he asked, do I want to go to some godforsaken place run by bordello cowboys who play the saxophone badly? He has mixed up Sukarno and Sihanouk and misunderstood both. Never mind. Duffie can't help patronizing me. He has always beaten me academically, and has adopted a Harvard style. What he knows of intimacy he learned from his grandmother. I wait until he's done lording it.

He suddenly changes the subject and the pitch. "When you go back to Pittsburgh, will you put some flowers on Babs' grave for me?" I say I certainly will. He pulls a ten dollar bill from his wallet and passes it over. He had already drawn the bar check over to his side of the table. He's paying, which means there may be things I have to do.

"Of course I've forgiven myself for that evening when I

288

was so awkward with her. But still. I mean, she took her own life three days later. It makes me shudder."

"I know. But not your fault, Duff. Her mother went mad, remember."

"Of course. Insanity is genetic, right?"

"No. Dispositions, maybe. Inherited tendencies accentuated by environment, et cetera."

"That's it. And I was a key part of her environment in those last several days. Unforgivable of me."

"Rot, Duff. Who do you want forgiveness from? You certainly have it from me. And you say you've forgiven yourself."

"True. Thanks. True enough. But I don't know how I'm going to get Babs to forgive me."

"That wasn't really in her style, was it? Wouldn't it be more like her to say, 'Skip it, Duffie, you're a horse's ass'?"

"Yes, probably. True enough."

"You're thinking about something that strikes you as more true? What is it?"

Duffie pondered. "Different plane. Level of compelling ethic and aesthetic perhaps. Have you ever contemplated celibacy?"

"Some. Quite a bit once. But no longer."

"Well, think about it some more. There's a commanding logic to it in this modern world. Control of population. Husbanding of creative energy. Sublimation of instinct. And so forth."

I weighed whether to speak or not. I went ahead. "I've seen an example, Duff, close up. And I didn't like it. I believe my father was a celibate for much of his married life. A bad example, perhaps, because unwilling, or circumstantially excluded. Something of the sort. The main thing is, not for me."

Duffie came back swiftly: "Yes, a poor example. Those are not the reasons for which one commits to celibacy."

He hid his own reasons. I didn't try to knock him off his perch. But I disliked what I felt to be self-denial moved by self-doubt, and self-satisfaction fed by self-denial. I imagined Babs present, ridiculing him. "Do you imagine you're man

289

enough to drive any woman to suicide? Shape up, Duffie.
Stop fucking off. Learn to look a woman in the face."

His voice interrupted me.

"Remember the flowers, won't you."

As she aged, Aunt Martha liked small dinner parties best.
"In honor of your graduation from law school," she said on
the phone. That embarrassed and pleased me. The other
two guests were Crispin and Lolly: balanced seating, and
perfect for playing bridge. My father had insisted that bridge
was next to golf in insuring worldly success, but I hated
that card game. There would be no bridge in Laos, I
thought. No golf either. I hoped that Martha would tire
after a rubber or two and go to bed, leaving us to talk.

Dinner was vichyssoise; broiled lamb chops with clarified
vegetables; and creme caramel. Any available in Laos? I
wondered. At the end there came an incongruous plate.
"Savories!" Lolly exclaimed. "So long since I've tasted savories!" How weird, I thought, to conclude such a meal
with anchovies on toast. Aunt Martha's taste was tied to
her idea of Philadelphia, as Philadelphia's was tied to its
notion of London. This was Pittsburgh, and strange things
happen in translation.

Lolly was serving as a docent, and Crispin's employee.
We spent an hour on gallery tales. She told of leading a
tour of quattrocento pieces that she had not studied, because
two docents were having morning sickness and the chief
curator was grossly indisposed following a banquet. Crispin
roared with appreciation at disorder in his own shop. His
feral, vulnerable laugh set us all on a happy edge, including
himself. He told of trying to persuade his board to buy a
Turner, when the oil, steel, and aluminum stocks in the
museum's portfolio were all temporarily down.

"I said it was the first time in a hundred years such a
painting had been offered, and it might be the last chance
for the next hundred. So they choked down their sherry
and agreed. I know that two of them will never forgive me
for taking them by surprise. We sold shares in South African
diamond mining, their pet. But we got the Turner, and

good comment in the arts press." On this note of her son's success, Aunt Martha rose, beaming, and said goodnight, leaving us with the liqueurs.

"Speaking of diamonds, Crispin, do you happen to know the history of the cameo that Uncle Clellan gave to Babs? That fascinating piece with the diamond eyes?"

"Fascinating? I should have called it grotesque. Lurid, perhaps, if I remember the one. No, my lad, I don't know its source. But dear Uncle Clellan, he was *always* giving away jewels. A turn-of-the-century custom that went with our *fin-de-siècle* fortune. A peculiar bit of McCalla madness: Clellan showered kisses on his mother and jewels on other men's women. Both undesigningly, I should say.

"He was the least selfish man I think I've ever known. A capacity for devotion is rare in the species, especially in modern Presbyterian bourgeois. Accumulation is more the order of our day. But not in dear old Clellan. He was devoted to an ideal of womanhood and to a gentlemanly standard that were quite lovely, in my view, and are now altogether gone."

Well, I thought, moved by what I'd learned from Buddy's perspective, now was the time.

"You often speak of Uncle Clellan as 'saintly.' But how does that fit with his patronage of some establishments on the far North Side? Yes, I know he was generous. But, if I dare ask, can saintliness coexist with Saturday nights in the brothels?"

Crispin looked up at me, and with a simplicity that surprised me, and a colloquial brevity uncharacteristic of him, answered, "You bet it can."

Lolly asked, "What became of Babs' cameo?"

"Sold," I said, "for Buddy. He deserved it. Old Chinese custom—pay the father for the daughter." Crispin and Lolly looked strangely at me, but I could not hold back. "Didn't Uncle Clellan try to get Babs ready for concubinage with a diamond-studded cameo, given her at puberty? Isn't that what he really intended?"

I had managed to shock Crispin. But he quickly regained balance. "What an interesting notion. Yes, of course one might imagine that, taking the view that you do of Clellan's life outside the McCalla family. But I quite reject that possibility, given his respect of his mother and of the compound as her sacred kingdom. We treated, or we tried, at least, to treat servants as family. For Clellan to harbor such an intention is unthinkable to me, and I do not yet see (he slowed down here as he spoke and eyed me carefully) what leads you to imagine that of him. He was not sinless, nor is spotlessness required of saints. But he was certainly far from depraved, as you intimate. And, lest we grow too involved with language of reprehension, I should want simply to say that I never knew Clellan to use the vulnerability of another to his own advantage."

The last sentence I remember exactly. Although uttered with the express aim of lowering the intensity of discourse, it was formidably strong. After a pause, I spoke in such a way, I hoped, as to disentangle me from my own adversary tone. "Babs used to say that Buddy put her on the high wire and she had to have a balance pole. Once . . ." I blushed. I knew I was blushing; I thought that my cheeks and red ears announced our secret life, but I could not refrain from this admission. "Once she said I was her balance pole."

"Ah, and she fell," Lolly broke in swiftly. "And you naturally felt terrible. So did we all. But it wasn't your fault. You couldn't keep her up there. No one could."

"There must have been a way," I murmured. For two years I had imagined other outcomes. If I had not gone to Cleveland. If Duffie had not made his rash advances. If Lolly had been able to spend more time with Babs. If I had only knocked at her door after the Third Century Ball, instead of pissing in the mulch pile and staggering up to my bed. But these all were too trivial. I was trying to see a "when" in the past, further back, a point of longer leverage; and a "how," a lever itself.

"There may have been a way," Crispin said, and from his eyes now was gone the narrow look of a moment before. He was quiet again, garden creature with jungle knowledge, one of the world's reliable ones. "But we did not see it, and we still do not know it. We can only grieve for her, and

292

regret our own limitations. She is buried with the family. Yet she is alive among us, clearly. Now," a bit tauntingly, "settle your mind, lad, and have another mint—solid or liquid. I must go home."

So he did, leaving Lolly with me.

"What are you thinking about these days?" I asked her, ready to learn something about St. Thomas if I had to.

She looked at me, sipped mint, arched her right eyebrow. "Well, if you must know, Randy dear, I am brooding a bit on metanoia."

I probably lifted both eyebrows.

" 'Transcending mind,' " she translated. "It's very different from paranoia, which everyone talks about. Paranoia means you are beside yourself, or out of your head, and very logical about it."

"And metanoia?"

"Means you realize you can't get where you want to go with reason alone. So you go 'above mind.' But not, I think, like the American transcendentalists or the vagabond mystics popping up these days."

"How then?"

She paused a bit, as if the fingers of her mind were trying the grip on a new golf club. "I think it means meeting despair with repentance and deprivation with humor."

"That sounds good. Good and tough."

"Yes. It means walking straight into life, so to speak."

"As distinct from researching life?"

"Yes, I suppose so. If you 'research life,' even though you tell yourself you are putting things together, something is held apart."

"Researching life is paranoid then?"

"It could be, by such a definition." She smiled. "But that's not a comment on your project about your great-grandfather."

"Oh, that's all over. I've done with that, I think. I'm about to take what I hope you would call a metanoic leap. Across the Pacific."

"I wish you well," she said. She meant it. "In the meantime," she finished her mint with a sip, "how would you like to go on a walk tomorrow?" she asked. A walk? Where did she want to go?

"Why not wait and see?" All right, but I like to know where I'm going.

"You don't need to. Just let me lay out a walk for us."

I think I know my heritage now. Out of Knox, by Carnegie, who put him in the shadows, and Rowan Megowan McCalla, who tried to imitate Carnegie. My great-grandfather was a would-be plutocrat who named his eldest son after the master industrial financier and was suckered by a woman who pretended to be the magnate's bastard daughter. My grandfather grew up in these obsessive shadows and raised a son in turn, an anchorite manque and an accomplished alcoholic: my father. In my mother's world, my father contended briefly for the male ground and yielded it after a short contest to a succession of smooth and rangy men. They possessed social or business or athletic prowess, or all three; hearty men with wide nostrils, who sniffed the pheremones of this uptight preacher's daughter and drew instinctive knowledge that they could get her to bust loose, curse pulpit, kiss cock.

So put, it sounds a bit rude, bizarre, conflicted. But it does not control me. It requires nothing but awareness. My life is mine to live. I cannot escape the facts and fermented guesswork I have gathered, of ambitions mauve and faded, infidelities ochred, sere. But this knowledge does not strike me as oppressively determining. Not knowing isolated me. Inquiring held me apart too long. Now knowing something is enough. My family's sorry history is a condition of my freedom. I feel grateful for this strange liberating knowledge, incomplete as all liberations are.

Yesterday I drove up from Martha's to Hill and Hollow Road and parked on the big circle at the upper end of Lolly's driveway. She wore a simple blue dress in which I had seen her golfing. She smiled and cocked an eyebrow at me to assess my puzzlement. I grinned back. Taunt me, OK, lead me, I'll follow; but I won't wriggle on your hook, I thought. Setting out with her was fun, not knowing where we were headed, knowing she had a plan.

At the street we turned toward the Hollow, to my surprise. It was not a long walk to the end of the road. Seven minutes, maybe; ten at most.

"Why did I jump?" Her question was abrupt, but her voice was level, as ever.

My brain careened, trying to get back on track. "The night of your debut?"

"Yes." She seemed placid. "Babs told me once that you said I jumped because I did not want to dance. I was always grateful to you for putting it that way, though I never told you so. It's true, and it's simple. An answer like that ends discussion. Which of course was what I had to learn to do; not only to end the discussion, but to begin *and* end it."

Yes, I understood.

"The question was on people's minds for a long time after that Christmas, and after the operations. I could see it on their minds. So I learned to open up the subject gaily and then kick it out of reach. 'Using Randy's answer,' is what I said to myself."

"I'm glad it helped. I never knew you felt that way."

"Oh, it's time to tell you. It seems so long ago. And another thing: you were the best of those who danced with me afterward. Not many dared. They thought they would get stuck with me, look silly, trip over me or their own feet. You learned so easily what it took. You even made it fun for me."

"It takes two. Yours was the harder part."

As we talked we reached the end of the road: a bit of grassy cliff beyond the groomed lawns and tree-shaded road. She picked a chair rock, and we settled, our backs against Panther Hill, looking out at the city.

"But I had other reasons for jumping. Impulses. Whatever. Babs' death made me think about them again. Talking with you helps me sort them out, remember where I am, what I've come through."

"Go ahead. Say more. I'd like to know."

295

"Why did I jump?" The moist city hummed and bristled below and beyond us. Clouds shaped up and merged over the mid-afternoon sun. Humid air bore the shuffle of railroad engines, bronchial honks from riverboats. "At worst, I think, out of desire to tempt God. Isn't that rather dreadful?" She did not wait for comment nor, at the moment, did she want it. "Would He do anything, anything at all, to rescue me from the impact of those cobblestones? Anything at all for one who loved Him so?

"Of course it's a mortal sin: make God prove Himself by threatening your own destruction. But God doesn't go in for theatrics. He doesn't need our syllogisms or buy our proofs. Sometimes I think He doesn't even attend our performances. He is somewhere else. We call it 'everywhere.'

"Anyway, the answer to my question was: nothing at all. God would not prevent my jumping, soften the fall, or ease the pain. When I came through all that there was something almost unbearable in another dimension—being *so diminished* in the eyes of others. Not only attempting suicide, but botching it. Who *is* this peculiar girl who has shattered her legs and ruined everybody's evening?"

I made a murmuring sound as she mused on.

"In that state, you're worse off than ever. Satan comes sliding up with that long, smooth tango step of his and says, 'Embarrassment? Why should you endure such cheapening humiliation after all else that you've suffered? You're too good for that. You deserve much better. Give heed to me. Et cetera.'

"For a while I was overwhelmed with temptation to do the job *right*, finish myself off, *for good*. But I realized, I kept thinking, that Jesus had already been through it. He had already resisted that temptation—to dash himself on stone. So a bottle of pills looked ridiculous. And he had already been diminished utterly, before the public, nailed on the tree. So what was a little contempt and aversion going to do to me? Just a slight case of social leprosy? It would cure in time."

"A hard way to get to the base of your faith," I said.

"But better than never getting there."

I thought that her god was better than Hermes, at least; grander, more demanding than the McCalla merchant god; and more forgiving than Mercury, who had much to be forgiven for, and moved too swiftly to absolve anyone.

We sat for a while, looking out at the city. I dared a question. "What were you thinking that made you open a window on a cold night and climb out on the ledge?"

Her answer came back fast. "I went out on the sill because I couldn't stand my father's absence." The curve at her lip reappeared. "And I jumped because I couldn't bear Lester Lanin's music."

She laughed, and I laughed, too.

"Come on," she said, rising from the rock, "let's finish the walk."

She made her way along the hillside, and I followed in wonder. We came abreast of the old viaduct. The access path was overgrown, and the wooden barrier to the crossing was missing half its boards.

"Are you ready?" she asked.

"For what?"

"To join Babs."

My stomach flipped. My face must have shown how my stomach felt.

"Not in Valhalla, Randy. I didn't mean that." She was almost giggling; she, the chairman de facto of the Third Century Gala, the parlor metaphysician. "I mean on the list of those who have crossed the aqueduct to the Holy City."

I must still have looked perplexed.

"And returned," she added. "The list of those who have gone and returned. So far there is only one name."

I thought and almost said, "But it's not allowed."

She read my thought. "It used to be forbidden when we were children. But have you thought about it since, as a man? About what you may do, and may not? Of course you may not *wish* to. That's another matter."

She leaned against the wooden barrier and looked back at my frown.

"I haven't done it myself," she continued. "But I've looked

297

it over and thought about it. It's easily wide enough for two side by side, and maybe as many as four. What our parents worried about was our losing concentration, awareness of where we were: doing cartwheels, or something. Just stepping off into space while we munched a piece of long grass. But we won't do that, will we?"

"No," I said, "we won't." I came forward, stepped over some loose boards, and extended my hand to help her across. We stood for a while looking across the unused trestle with its rusted trolley rails and rotting ties. On the other side, a wooded glade, and beyond the glade, lower, nearly out of sight, more houses.

"Don't look down," she said. "Look ahead and around."

"OK." We set out. There was more I wanted to hear. "When you were in the hospital, it was faith that saved you?"

"Yes. And after a while, a new kind of doubt," she answered. "Thomas helped."

"Doubting Thomas?"

"No, silly. That's your saint. Or Duffie's, maybe. The first Protestant materialist. Putting his fingers into Christ's wound."

A wind had come up, moist with anticipation.

"No," she said. "Aquinas, of course. There are uses to systematic theology. One of them is to balance our modern tendency to doubt the cohesive assumption. Reading St. Thomas gave me practice in the counter-tendency: to doubt the erosive assumption. Spiritual calisthenics. It takes patience. Works little by little. Then one finds oneself, one day, overhauled, so to speak. Ready to take time, and men, and the moment as they come, and on your own terms."

We reached the other side. Plain woods, with the same size and variety of flora as on the other side, our side.

"Shall we look," I said, "for the buried Vessel of the Senate?"

"It would be nice to bring it back to Duffie. If we could find it. Where would she have buried it?"

"Maybe we should just buy him a tin of Maxwell House Coffee and tell him we've been here."

We agreed on that, and felt conspiratorial: adventurers, restorers, hardies.

Rain printed on us in random droplets. We headed back. The wind gusted, brought factory smells, hung them before us, whipped them away. I took the windward side. Lolly took my arm. The sky darkened suddenly, houselights on the dimmer. A steady north wind blew wet against us. She kept close to me, laying her head slightly sideways, not quite on my shoulder, but in the lee my own head provided. One step tipped her slightly away from me, the next step closer. I concentrated on my right leg, as a brace against her left-ward lurch. Where her two hands circled my right elbow, I pressed my arm to my side and her hands with it. I felt privileged, enlightened. A giver of security.

I dreamed last night that I stood on the roof of the Pierce-Arrow by the sundial, before crowds of children in the empty lot of the compound, children of all the servants, grandchildren even. Babs and Duff and Lolly urged me to talk, but every surge of my will to speak was preceded by the applause of the crowd, and the lightspeed of their understanding made me laugh with them. Cook appeared in a tall white chef's hat, waving it and crying, *"La toque blanche, la toque blanche!"* and I floated up to consciousness, bubbles of trusting laughter trailing after me.

I know enough about myself now, and reality, to see this as a dream of self-forgiveness. Cook is still underpaid; Buddy arthritic and half-employed. And Babs irretrievably gone. There is no undoing what is wrought in time. Society leagues with destiny in the strange forms we take as givens, structures of money and honor and shame, hot channels of love and hate, fear and awe, through which we pour our emotions. As if we were the only ones to live, and these the only ways.

I forgive myself for being a McCalla. That's all I can be, so let me make what I can of it. I forgive myself for not loving my father enough. He is gone, absent even from my dreams. But I carry him in tender regard. I forgive myself for letting my mother get away with—well, complicity in the extinction of my father. If she loved too much, too care-lessly, she was at least herself; and for all her betrayals of my father, she bore him a decent respect. She never hurt him in public. Usually tried not to in private; until his saintly patience and agonistic rantings provoked her beyond control.

I forgive my forebears, of the third and fourth generation, for all their foolishness discovered and unrecoverable, and all the sins they have visited on me. I say this fully expecting, despite myself, to visit my own flaws three or four gener-ations beyond me, and hoping that they will find it possible to forgive me in turn. Rest easy, Rowan, A. C., Clellan.

You too, Cassie. Rest easy. We are all Carnegie's bastards. Not you alone, but all of us who meld money and com-petition and philanthropy with predestination and perfec-tionism in the peculiar bourgeois formula pursued by Prot-estants of all faiths. Yours was the gamiest style of the lot, the chanciest mode of redistributing social assets, the most selfish of the charities. How would we know ourselves were it not for you, a bastard by choice? Others of us can trace our genealogies, but we are culturally misbegotten, lacking energy to shape and save ourselves, ignorant of the nobler ways to be lost.

Rest easy, Randy, the dream tells me. The compound releases you. The family laundry is done. Hang it up. Let it dry. Time to go.

Only to Babs can I not say, rest easy. She is with me still, as when we played hide-and-seek amid Rachel's work, in and out among the sheets, and slips, and embroidered chemises on the staggered poles in the laundry pits. Even now, and maybe always, I see her shadow lurking behind the linen of McCalla women, and the flirting ripple of her flight among the shirts of McCalla men.